If Vivian Dahl's life had a soundtrack, every song would be the Blues. She's pushing thirty, her singing career is going nowhere, and the partying lifestyle is taking its toll. Plus, a mysterious man is stalking her. But when she's abducted from a singing gig, Vivian is surprised to see her stalker become her savior.

Finding herself on the run, Vivian drives across America with Jason, her werewolf rescuer, and learns about the war her biological father's pack is caught in. Now that an opposing werewolf pack has targeted her, Jason will stop at nothing to make sure Vivian's song isn't cut short.

Werewolf Sings the Blues

OTHER BOOKS BY JENNIFER HARLOW

Werewolf Sings the Blues

A Midnight Magic Mystery

Jennifer Harlow

MIDNIGHT INK
WOODBURY, MINNESOTA

FIRST EDITION
First Printing, 2014

Book design and format by Donna Burch-Brown
Cover design by Ellen Lawson
Cover illustration: Mary Ann Lasher-Dodge
Editing by Connie Hill

Midnight Ink, an imprint of Llewellyn Worldwide Ltd.

This is a work of fiction. Names, characters, places, and incidents are either the product of the author's imagination or are used fictitiously, and any resemblance to actual persons living or dead, business establishments, events, or locales is entirely coincidental.

Library of Congress Cataloging-in-Publication Data
Harlow, Jennifer, 1983–
  Werewolf sings the blues : a midnight magic mystery / Jennifer Harlow.
— First Edition.
     pages cm. — (A Midnight Magic mystery ; #2)
  ISBN 978-0-7387-3612-9
1. Werewolves—Fiction. 2. Paranormal fiction. I. Title.
  PS3608.A7443W44   2014

  813'.6—dc23   2013027486

Midnight Ink
Llewellyn Worldwide Ltd.
2143 Wooddale Drive
Woodbury, MN 55125-2989
www.midnightinkbooks.com

Printed in the United States of America

DEDICATION

For Sandy Lu

AUTHOR'S NOTE

The events in this book take place seven years before the events in *Mind Over Monsters* and eight years before *What's A Witch To Do?*

PART I

THE ROAD

ONE

Oh, I am not feeling good.

Ugh. Waking with a dirty litter box in your mouth, throbbing head, nausea, and just general shit feeling does not bode well for the rest of the day. Seriously, let me at least have a cup of coffee before you begin your misery, world. Of course, this is a misery of your own making Viv, but damn it, still. Oh, that fourth shot last night was a terrible idea. I knew it then, and I am paying for it now. I groan aloud. Karma, baby. Karma. The bitch. The ringing phone in my kitchenette doesn't help the situation. Each shrill tone ratchets up the agony to Iron Maiden status. The machine picks up.

"Vivian, it's your mother." I groan again, and not from the physical pain this time. "It's six o'clock our time, three yours. Your sister just informed me you haven't even called her to wish her a Happy Birthday. I *know* for a fact you didn't send her a present, but really? Not even a call? Beyond the pale, Vivian. Selfish even for you. Call your sister." She hangs up.

Hangover and guilt trip, and I've only been up a minute. Ugh, times ten.

I manage to unglue my eyes. Another shit idea on my part. On days like this, I wish I lived in Seattle not happy, bubbly sunny Cali-fucking-fornia. I flip over, not only to avoid the perky sunshine. Alone. I slept alone. Thank God. The end of last night is kind of a haze. Okay, mostly a blank thanks to that fourth damn tequila shot. I knew better, I did, but that cute Ensign from Port Hueneme was just tipping so well. How could I not give in when he insisted I matched him shot for shot? Made an extra hundred from him alone if I recall. Not too shabby. Almost makes the pain worth it.

Get your flat ass out of bed, Dahl. Yes, ma'am. I toss my covers off and pad the ten feet to the only room with a door in my studio apartment, the bathroom. Halfway there I realize I'm as naked as a jaybird. I don't recall stripping last night, but my clothes are strewn around the beige carpet. Wonderful, I'm becoming a blackout drunk. Mom will be so proud. I turn on the shower and even the sound of the falling water is excruciating. The hot water does help clear my head. An overrated state of being if you ask me. I am a shitty sister. Really shitty. Jessie's birthday completely slipped my mind. Thankfully this is the first time that's happened. She'll forgive me. I'll buy her something tomorrow. There isn't time today. I overslept and now only have two hours to pick up my dress, get a manicure, return here to do hair and makeup which will take an hour, then drive to the hotel, pray I can find parking in downtown Ventura on a Saturday evening, and arrive for sound check on time. Damn, I'm exhausted just thinking about it all. I'm so not going to make it through this day. At least not without help.

After the shower I brush my teeth, pop some Excedrin, and gulp down an entire glass of water before putting on my pink tracksuit and shoving my wet hair under a brown-brimmed beanie. I can spare a second for self-improvement. New Year's resolution to keep and all. I yank yesterday's word of the day from my calendar. Yesterday was "encomium," compliment. Today is "egregious," outstandingly bad. Yeah, today's going to suck big hairy donkey balls. Even my calendar says so. Whatever. Sunglasses, purse, flip flops, ready to rock.

I live in a not-so-nice part of Oxnard, which is mostly known for its gang turf wars and being four blocks from the beach. No matter how many times the super paints the side of the brick building, the next morning the gang tags have returned. After two years I still don't know whose territory I'm in. My car, a twelve-year-old Bonneville, is parked unevenly across two spots. I grimace. I was kind of hoping not to have found it here. I drove drunk last night. *Damn it.* There goes another broken promise to God. I sigh. I really suck. The car appears intact so at least I didn't kill anyone. No time to dwell on what a piece of crap I am. Gotta pay the bills and need my dress to do it.

As I trudge to my car, I notice a blonde man sitting in a black Mustang watching my every step. Huh. I know his face but can't place him, which is becoming a real problem lately. Damn hooch. When he realizes I'm studying him right on back, he turns away. Probably a cop keeping an eye on the building. If I had to guess, at least a third of my fellow tenants are dealers or gang bangers. There have been raids at least three times since I've lived here. Whatever. As long as he's not here to arrest me. I just look away from the man and get in my car.

My tension and misery increase exponentially as I drive to the strip-mall. It's all of five miles away, but with weekend SoCal traffic, it'll take forty minutes round trip. There goes my manicure. Instead of banging my head against the steering wheel, which is my first instinct, I retrieve my cell to call my guitarist/band co-manager/fellow bartender/connection, Cyr. Clicks straight to voicemail, so I leave a message. "Hey, it's Viv. On my way to get ready for the gig. I'm wearing the red dress, so tell the others to wear the red ties. And listen, I hate to ask, but I need you to bring me a little pick-me-up for tonight. I don't think I can make it to midnight without. You are a fellow doll and man among men. See you at five. Bye."

Now to counteract my bad karma with just a little good. I dial Jessica's cell so there's no chance of getting Mom or Barry. My beautiful baby sister answers on the second ring, laughing at something. "Hello?" she chuckles.

"Hey, Jess, it's Viv. Happy Birthday, darlin'."

"Thank you! Oh my God, I'm so glad you called," Jessie chirps.

"Sorry I didn't earlier. It's wedding season, I have gigs coming out of my ears," I lie.

"It's okay. You're calling now."

"Is that Vivian?" I hear Mom ask in the background over loud giggling.

"Yeah, Mom. Hey, hang on," she says to me. I hear the phone jostling as Jessie moves toward Mom. "Sorry. Tiffany and Chrissie are here. You know how loud they can be."

"I remember the sleepovers, yes. Is Barry taking you all out to dinner?"

"Yeah, Rainforest Café. We may go into Disney afterward. You know how much I love the Haunted Mansion."

"I do. When I worked there, every time I'd leave for work you'd beg me to sneak you into the park. You're a bit old for Disney now, don't you think?"

"Twenty-two is not old. Not like thirty," she says playfully.

"Hey," I warn, mock seriously, "I am *not* thirty." Not for a little over a week anyway. I spin the wheel to change lanes. "So, are you enjoying your summer vacation from dental school or does Barry have you cleaning teeth in his office?"

"The latter. I'm learning so much more in the office than in school. Dad's a great teacher."

"I still can't believe you *chose* to become a dentist."

"Well, not all of us can be glamorous singers performing for Tom Cruise."

"Right." Note to self, stop embellishing so much. I'll be singing for Prince Charles next.

"Jessie, love, time to go!" Barry, my stepfather calls in the distance.

"Sorry, we're already running late. Call you tomorrow?" Jessica asks.

"Of course. I love you to death. Have a spectacular birthday. Get plastered and flirt with lots of cute boys. That's an order."

She giggles. "Do my best."

"Say hey to Mom and Barry for me. Love you. Bye." I hang up.

They'll make sure she has a blast. I think Mom mentioned last month during our obligatory quarterly call she picked out a new bedroom set for Jessie's new apartment. I got a twenty in a card for my birthday. I'm shocked she remembered at all. As always, when I sense the green-eyed monster is about to devour me, I stop the train of thought, take a deep breath, and fill my mind with happy thoughts. Me onstage receiving a Grammy. Working the room at Clive Davis' party. Being in the studio with Etta James and B. B. King, laying down tracks on our new album. Mine and Hugh Jackman's children scampering around our Aspen estate and making snowmen. I just can't conjure the images up like I used to. Age has made the divide between dreams and pipe dreams paper thin.

With the aid of daredevil maneuvering a minute later, I pull into the parking lot and step out into the broiling SoCal summer day. My first bit of luck today, no line at the cleaners. I retrieve my dress, then pop next door to buy a salad. Unless I sneak food at the wedding tonight, this is my only chance to eat before midnight. When I step out of the deli, I get the strange sensation that there are eyes upon me. I glance left. You have got to be fucking kidding me. That cop from my building stands about twenty yards away near the Starbucks with his cell phone pressed to his ear. He isn't looking at me now, but it had to be him who set off my internal warning bells which are now louder than seventeen rock concerts combined.

I know I've seen him before today, I just have no idea where. He is damn distinctive. Ridiculously muscular with bowling ball biceps, shoulders from the Pacific to Atlantic, thick torso under a black t-shirt, and long muscular legs the size of sequoias. Probably a body builder. My observer has to be over six feet as the male shoppers who pass are mostly a head shorter than him. His blonde hair, natural I think, is slicked back and almost long enough to be put in a ponytail if needed. He glances back at me again, giving me a snapshot of his face. Not bad looking. Okay, he's damn fine. Like I need fresh panties fine. Slavic features with sharp cheekbones and nose, thin lips, and even from this far, his eyes are startling, like pale blue ice. Glacial, which is exactly how I feel now with them trained on me again. Stone fucking cold.

I look straight ahead and scurry to the safety of my car. More than twice on the drive home I check the rearview for his Mustang but don't see it. Maybe it was just a coincidence. Hell, maybe it wasn't even the same man. Hot, blonde dudes with killer cheekbones are a dime a dozen in Southern California. Still. I return to my building and dash to my apartment, turning every lock, wedging the safety bar against the door, and checking that the pipe in the window track is in place. As close to Fort Knox as I can get. Time to forget all else and start my pre-gig ritual.

I think Nina will help get me in the right mindset for tonight. I leaf through my vinyl collection until I locate Nina Simone's *I Put a Spell on You*. With tender loving care, I remove my treasure from its jacket and set it on the player. Nina's deep, dusky voice fills my studio apartment, and I immediately begin feeling pretty damn good. I have to save my voice for tonight so I only lip sync along to the title track and her iconic hit "Feeling Good" as I begin my beauty ritual. Too bad I can't perform these tunes tonight. No, everyone just wants pop and eighties music. I don't sound terrible when I sing those, but certainly don't shine like when I'm belting Billie Holliday or Mr. Ray Charles. A girl's gotta eat though.

On the topic of food … after I'm done blow-drying my hair but before I start curling, I shove the salad in my mouth. I really do need to eat more. I used to fill a B-cup but now don't even need a bra. Plus being able to count my ribs isn't terribly sexy, and you can't get anywhere in the music business without being sexy.

Since time is of the essence, I do a quick hair and makeup shellacking before slipping on my red dress and checking out the final product in my full-length mirror. Damn, I hate being a ginger. Bright orange hair, pale skin, freckles across my nose, arms, and back that makeup barely covers. This genetic mutation and a kickass record collection are the only contributions my real father bestowed upon me before abandoning me when I was one. My long lips and thin frame are the only traits inherited from Mom besides terrible taste in men.

Tonight the freckles are hidden and my long hair appears full and glossy with the fake magnolia clipped over my ear. My blue eyes seem larger than normal, thanks to Miss Maybelline. People have told me I resemble Julia Roberts. We do have the same nose, minus the gold stud in mine, and large lips but my jaw is longer and cheekbones less pronounced. The red satin halter dress' full skirt hides my now boyish hips. The problem is it doesn't hide my tattoos. Chinese symbol for harmony just below the crook of my right arm. Huge cleft note in the upper center of my back with the lyrics of "It's a new dawn" written above. At least the caged mockingbird singing on my lower back, apparently considered a tramp stamp, is masked. Younger couples like tonight's tend not to care about the ink, but I still attempt to be professional when I can. I slip on my white faux-fur half jacket and gold strappy heels, grab my purse, and head to the door.

I'm extra vigilant, checking every corner and window as I walk through the open hallway and down the stairs to my car. No Mustang in sight. Still. Before I climb into my car, I glance in the backseat just in case. I take my Urban Legends seriously. Empty. Okay, I must still be high from the joint I smoked yesterday before work because I'm only this paranoid on pot. "Dumbass." I'm late enough without my overactive imagination setting up a roadblock. I do keep an eye out for the Mustang as I cruise up the I-10 toward Ventura. I may be dumb, but I ain't a fucking moron.

The Dolan-Velasquez wedding is being held at a swank resort on the beach, and the happy couple should just be walking down the aisle on said beach as I reach the concrete parking garage. The multi-deck parking lot is almost full but I find a slot on the third level. "I'm sorry I'm late," I call as I rush into the hotel ballroom. "Crazy day."

This ballroom is exquisite with about two dozen tables adorned with freesias and daisies. Waiters light the candles in the centerpieces. The other hired help, Vivian and the Dolls, are setting up on the white bandstand. My Dolls are already here, checking equipment and tuning their instruments. We're not really a band so much as a musical collective. Jaime plays both classical piano and keyboard with synthesizers. Muriel is on drums, and tonight has removed her five piercings and covered her green hair with a red fedora. Parker tunes his bass guitar. He's the youngest of us at twenty. Cyr has tied back his long dreadlocks and his skin looks almost coal black when he's dressed in a white shirt. We are a motley crew. I'm more jazz/R&B, Cyr reggae, Parker classical, Muriel alternative, and Jaime pop. We only work weddings together, though Cyr and I both bartend at the same nightclub, and jam sometimes after work. He's the closest thing to a best friend I have. And he has *awesome* drugs.

"You're always late," Muriel says.

"I know. I'm sorry. I'm a selfish bitch. Already got the memo."

Cyr leaps down the three feet from the stage like a cat and meets me halfway across the room. "We have about twenty minutes," he chides.

"Don't worry, it's all good," I say as we walk.

"You memorize the song list?"

"Of course." I set down my purse behind the bandstand. "Did you bring my ... stuff?"

"You're really gonna do the gig high?" he whispers low.

"Rather I do it asleep? Come on. I have a killer hangover, and I barely ate. I'll only do half a bump each time. I swear."

He apprises me with disapproval. The man's a part-time drug dealer, he should be encouraging, not judging. "It's coming out of your paycheck."

"Of course."

My friend reaches inside his bag, pulling out a tiny zip-lock filled with my magic powder. I only do coke a few times a month when I'm dragging. Working nights in a bar while getting the odd singing gig and still going on auditions a few times a week is taking it out of me, especially in the last year. I stuff the coke in my coat pocket before slipping the jacket off. I'll take it right before the guests arrive. "Thank you, dearie."

"I was actually glad you called earlier," Cyr says. "I tried your cell a few times, even the house phone. I was worried after last night."

"Yeah, I did get a bit sloshed. I can't believe you let me drive home like that."

"You were hammered?" he asks, thick brow raised.

"Yeah. I had four shots of tequila on an empty stomach." Not to mention the joint before work.

He sighs. "Okay, makes sense now."

"What makes sense?"

"That guy. The blonde guy in the parking lot. You don't remember?"

"Last night's kind of a blur. What happened? What'd I do now?" I ask with trepidation. The answer can run from leap up on a bar and sing a capella to making out with a drag queen. She was an amazing kisser though.

"Well, you asked Jeff to leave early because you said you weren't feeling good. I said I'd walk you to your car after I poured a couple orders, but when I got back, you were gone. I found you over by your car, and this big blonde cat was grabbing for you. You shoved him away, and I shouted for him to fuck off. He ran off, you got in your car, and drove off. He must have known you were plastered and was trying to take your keys away."

"Had you ever seen him before?"

"Yeah. I noticed him watching you a few times when I came up to your level last night to relieve Juan. He was the one I pointed out, remember?"

That strikes a chord. A flash from last night reverberates through my mind. Okay, I remember Blondie now. In between mixing drinks and flirting with the generous seaman, I was aware that this man never left the bar and barely acknowledged the various women and men who tried to pick him up. He was in Juan's section, and we were crazy busy, so I didn't pay him that much attention. I think Juan did mention Blondie kept ogling me, so I turned and blew him a kiss before Juan and I started giggling.

"Tall, muscular, weird blue eyes, looked like a Russian hit man?" I ask Cyr.

"That's him."

A knot ropes around my stomach. Great, I have a stalker. Just what I need. "You ever seen him before last night?"

"No. You?"

"I don't think so." I pause. "He *attacked* me?"

"Not really. I mean, at first you two were just talking. Then his arm moved toward you, you shoved him, I yelled, he ran off. I think he was trying to stop you from driving drunk, dumbass."

That sure as hell doesn't explain why he was following me today. I'm about to tell Cyr this, when Muriel says, "Are you two gonna yap all night or are we gonna practice?"

She's right. This isn't a *now* problem, if it even is a problem. I'm surrounded by people. I'm safe. The show must go on and all that shit. We climb onstage and Cyr picks up his Gibson guitar. "Let's warm up with Human League's 'Don't You Want Me,'" Cyr says.

"Righty-O," I reply. I step in front of the mic with a long, not helpful, sigh. I remember when this used to be exhilarating. Fun. The only place I wanted to be. Now it's a grind. Same songs, same venues. And I never thought it possible but I'm sick of Etta James's "At Last." Every damn wedding it's on the set list. As if it's legally required for every first dance. It used to be one of my favorite songs, and I can sing the hell out of it, which is why we usually get hired, but now I grimace whenever the instrumental begins playing. This is not how I envisioned my career would end up. I've been singing professionally since sixteen when I started hitting every karaoke contest in the Orlando area, and here I am thirteen years later pretty much doing the exact same thing. Barry's right. I've made no forward progress. I fucking *hate* it when he's right.

Cyr and I do collaborate well when we duet, even with this pop crap. While the rest of me is as Caucasian as a watercress sandwich, my singing voice sure ain't. I'm a bass, so I'm better suited for R&B, which is a blessing and curse. A blessing because it's the music I love, and a curse because A&R departments won't take a chance on a white girl with soul. The few meetings I've had with the bigwigs, I've tried to convince them that just because something hasn't been done before doesn't mean it won't be popular. Since they only care about the bottom line, this truth fell on deaf ears. All they've wanted for years is scantily clad teens lip-syncing bubblegum tunes. Diana Krall and Eva Cassidy were aberrations.

After we finish the first song, we try out Beyoncé's new song "Crazy in Love," which more and more people keep requesting. Last year it was Kylie Minogue. At least Beyoncé is closer to my wheelhouse. When we're done with Miss Knowles, I have just enough time to fluff my hair, freshen my makeup, and discreetly snort the magical dust from my fingernail before slipping the baggie back into my coat pocket. Despite what the movies and after-school specials claim, cocaine doesn't kill on contact. It doesn't even hurt to snort unless you do too much. All it really does is make you feel like you've drunk an entire pot of coffee minus the calories and stomach issues. There's no immediate effect, but after a minute, right when I jump back onstage, my heart picks up speed. As the first of the guests begin filtering in, my arms begin to tingle and warm. The drip starts another minute later, irritating my throat, but nothing too bad. I can sing through it. I've done it before.

The first half hour of the gig is easy. People find their seats and chat about the ceremony, paying us no mind. I phone in, "Don't You

Forget About Me," "Girls Just Want to Have Fun," and "Maneater." Our not-so-adoring audience barely glances at us. Always nice to be appreciated.

The coke starts wearing off when the wedding planner Gracie, Cyr's sister, gives us the signal that the bride and groom are about to make their grand entrance. "May I present," I say, "for the first time ever, Mr. and Mrs. Christopher Dolan!" Cue Stevie Wonder's "Isn't She Lovely," another song I can sing in my sleep. If I ever get married again, and have a ceremony not at the Vegas Chapel of Love like last time, I'd go for "The Hunter Gets Captured by the Game." I've sung at almost a hundred weddings and no one's ever chosen it.

The Dolans are a good-looking couple. Young, probably just out of college. Her dress is beautiful, sleek, with swirling crystals sewn on the bodice. The one thing I really regret about my wedding, besides the fact it ever happened, was I never got to wear the dress and veil. The whole debacle was just an impulsive, idiotic mistake. Louie and I had been together for about six months in New Orleans when we decided to move to L.A. On the way, when we passed through Vegas, we figured what the hell? I got married in a black sheath dress with a long string of fake pearls. He didn't even put on a tie. The ceremony lasted about as long as the marriage. The Dolans seem like good kids, though. I can't see him, after three months of marriage, punching her in the eye, then seconds later her smacking him in the head with a lamp. I filed for divorce the next day.

Vivian and the Dolls perform a few more songs as the guests eat, but we take a short break for the speeches and cake cutting before our marathon set. I grab my purse and head to the bathroom as the others go out to smoke. The one vice I managed to avoid. Touchups and hairspray are needed STAT, along with ... shit. I left my coat. Just have to be extra sneaky when I get back out there. As I add blush, my cell rings. I get it out and check the display. Jeff, from the club. Probably wants me to cover for someone tonight. I'd ignore it, but I need the money. Ugh, I'm turning into a vampire, only staying up at night. I guess the sun *is* overrated.

"Hey Jeff. What's up?"

"I, uh, just want to give you a heads up, Viv. I just had a Federal Marshal in here looking for you."

"A what?"

"I don't know. I think they track fugitives or something."

Huh. I certainly hope I don't fall into that category. "What the hell do they want with me?"

"Don't know. He wouldn't tell me anything except he'd been trying to track you down, and that you weren't in any trouble. I gave him your new cell number and told him you were singing at a hotel on the beach tonight."

"Well, what was his name? What did he look like?"

"Kind of tall and thin with brown hair." So not the blonde. "Said his name was Donovan. Gave me his number."

"Wait a sec." I find a pen and rip off a paper towel. Jeff gives me the number. "703 area code? That's not around here."

"I think it's D.C. Any ideas what this is about?" Jeff asks.

"My ex is probably in trouble again. I had a bounty hunter come around about three years ago looking for him." The man went from saxophone player to drug addict and trafficker in the five years we've been divorced. Probably also why Blondie's tailing me. At least I hope so. "I'll call him tomorrow. Thanks for letting me know. Bye." I end the call with a sigh. Just what I fucking need. They're wasting their time though. I haven't spoken to Louie in years, and if he showed up on my doorstep, I'd call the cops regardless. No use dwelling on it now. Wedding guests to entertain. Gotta keep singing for my supper.

Okay, the situation's not completely off my radar. I move through the lobby back to the reception, scanning for bogies. Sure enough I spot my blonde shadow attempting to remain inconspicuous at the hotel bar, playing with his glass with his head down. Tonight he sports a leather jacket and ball cap but with that bod, inconspicuous is impossible. I'd go confront him, but there's no time. I rush back into the ballroom. The couple are cutting the cake as I enter. A minute to spare. I imbibe in some nose candy seconds before the others return. We get back in place onstage for the main event.

I call the couple center stage for the first dance. As Etta's immortal words spill from my mouth, I watch the couple with the odd smile. The newlyweds only have eyes for each other as he leads her around the dance floor. Ah, to be that in love. A million beautiful experiences ahead of them starting now. So full of hope. Lucky bastards.

Next tradition is my least favorite part of the night: the father/daughter dance. "Butterfly Kisses" by Bob Carlisle tonight. I sing this one almost as often as "At Last." Mr. Velasquez's pride shines on his round face as he takes his baby girl into his arms. I make it a point never to watch this pairing swing around on the dance floor. Even after the hundred odd times I've witnessed this ritual, it still stings to high hell. My biological father abandoned my mom and me when I was a year old. Never sent so much as a card after. Mom married Barry when I was four, but my workaholic stepfather never had much time for me, even before Jessie was born. And the moment she came into the world, I went from being an afterthought to a ghost in his eyes. Mom wasn't much better. Her husband comes first, Jessie second, and I'm about fifth behind keeping fit. Michelle went from living with her parents and working as a dental hygienist to the wife of a wealthy dentist. She drank the country club Kool-Aid and has done everything to ensure it continues flowing, including backing up every negative thought or action her husband inflicted upon me. If I ever get married again, this dance is one ritual I'm happy to skip.

Tonight isn't so painful as I have a six-foot-two distraction to keep my mind occupied. My stalker has now added wedding crasher to his list of crimes. I pretend not to see him wander in or move toward the bar. He orders a drink, then strolls to the back of the room, I think in an attempt to blend in again. Massive fail, Blondie. Even if he is a crazy stalker he won't attempt anything while I'm up here. As always the one place I feel even close to secure is onstage.

I keep track of him through our set just in case. He meanders from empty tables to the bar to the corner. Whenever someone starts glancing at the comely stranger, he moves on. Around song five, Cyr spots him too because once or twice my friend glances at me, then the mystery man. I quickly shrug and keep on keeping on. That is until Blondie drops all pretense and flat out stares with sniper-like precision at me when I perform Ray Charles's "You Don't Know Me." I do my best to pretend not to notice, but he just sits there, strong jaw almost slack with those ice eyes locked on me as if I was the only person in the room. In the damn state even.

No one's ever gazed at me with such intensity before. If aliens landed in this ballroom I don't think he'd notice. I'd be flattered, and I'd be lying if there isn't a butterfly or two fluttering in my stomach, but since the man doing it is more or less *stalking* me, it's still fucking unnerving. I even forget the lyrics for a second. My mouth opens but no noise leaves. That hasn't happened in years. I shut my eyes to center myself. The bastard's throwing me off my game. The butterflies turn back into wormy caterpillars. Not acceptable. When I open my eyes again, I zero in on his with the same precision. Blondie does a tiny double take, almost leaping back in his chair, surprised at being caught, I think. I narrow my eyes to get the point across. Yeah, that's right, asshole. I see you. My stalker immediately glances away and even rises from the chair. A grin crosses my face as he quickly walks out of the ballroom. Always stand up to a bully. Learned that one early on.

Blondie doesn't resurface as the set continues. Everyone appears to have fun, I don't hit any sour notes, and no one seems to mind when I sneak in Clarence Carter's "Slip Away." When it's time for the last dance, "(I've Had) The Time of My Life," the coke's worn off and I'm ready to go home. Another shower, slipping underneath my covers, and zoning out in front of the television sounds like heaven now. I used to do everything in my power not to be home before midnight, now I look forward to it. The magic of midnight has worn off for this broad.

I finish the tune, and we take our bows to scattered applause. Time for the bride and groom to retire for the honeymoon. Thank God. As the guests blow bubbles over the departing couple, the

Dolls and I start packing up. Instruments, microphones, amps, it takes for-goddam-ever, but since I was late and didn't help setup I kind of owe them. And I'd never hear the end to the bitching if I don't.

About half an hour later, Vivian and the Dolls walk out of the ballroom into the hallway together. No sign of Blondie. Maybe he found someone else to creep out. We're halfway down the hall when two men come through the door to the parking garage, striding quickly toward us. They're an odd couple, one short and squat with acne scars dotting his wide face and the other tall and lean with dark brown hair and eyes. Both are dressed in dark jeans, dress shirts, and sports coats. I catch a glimpse of a gun holster on the tall one. He seems the more confident of the two, moving with purpose where the short one glances around the hall as if Jack the Ripper had a thing for acne scars. Those drunken bridesmaids may still be around and can be pretty forceful with the men folk. He is right to worry.

"Excuse me," the tall one says when they reach us. "Are you Vivian Dahl?"

"Yeah. You the U.S. Marshals looking for me?" The men exchange a confused glance. "I'm psychic."

"You are?" the short one asks.

Damn. Guess the Marshals don't give IQ tests before hiring. "She's kidding," the other says. That one's gaze returns to me before flashing his star. "Yes, I'm Deputy U.S. Marshal Donovan, this is Deputy Cooper." His attention moves to my band, who are not even trying to hide their fear. Muriel's practically shaking. "May we speak in private, please, Miss Dahl?"

"Um, I guess." I look to the others. "You guys go on ahead."

"You sure?" Cyr asks.

Hell no. "Yeah, go on. See you later."

Cyr, who I am sure is happy to have an excuse to get away from the fuzz, nods and ushers the others toward the parking garage. I can feel the baggie of coke burning a hole in my pocket. I stop myself from thrusting my hand in there, instead flashing the men my prettiest smile, which Donovan returns. "So, just out of professional curiosity Miss Dahl, how did you know who we were?" Donovan asks.

"What? Don't believe in psychics?" I ask with a coy smirk. When in doubt, flirt.

"Oh, I believe in them. I just know you're not one of them," he says with a matching smile. "Although I am sure you have many other hidden talents." His grin slowly drops. "So, how did you know?"

"My boss called, told me you stopped by the club. I was going to phone you tomorrow, I swear." I fold my arms across my chest. "So, what'd he do now?"

"He?" Cooper asks.

"Louie. My ex. That's why you're here, right? He escape from prison or something?"

"Actually, no," Donovan says. "We're actually here about your father."

"What? Barry?" I chuckle.

"Frank Dahl. Francis John Dahl. He is your father, correct?"

Just that name makes my throat close up. "Um, yeah," I force out.

"Has he tried to make contact with you lately?" Donovan asks.

"Not since I was a baby. Wh—what's he done?"

Cooper removes a piece of paper from his coat. "What about this man?"

He hands me the paper. It's the driver's license photo of the blonde man. Even on paper he's menacing with a deep scowl and glare for anyone who gazes at him. Oh, shit. My throat seizes again, this time from nerves. "Miss Dahl?" Donovan asks.

"I—I've seen him. A few times. He was at the club last night, and I've seen him three times since."

The men exchange a quick, gleeful expression complete with matching grins, but only for a flash. When their gazes return to me, they're serious again. "When was the last time?" Donovan asks.

"About an hour ago," I say, voice trembling a little. Okay, now I'm scared. Shit scared. It's as if I've been hit with a Taser, every muscle is locked from the unnatural event that just occurred.

"He's probably still in the hotel," Cooper says.

"Oh, he's still here," an exhilarated Donovan says. "Probably clocked us the moment we walked in." Then the man closes his eyes and tilts his nose up. "I think I can smell him."

"Shit," Cooper says, glancing around.

"Calm down. We knew this would probably happen."

"What's happening?" I ask. "What the hell is going on?"

The men finally remember I exist. "You need to come with us," Donovan says.

"Wh—" Before I can ask another question, Donovan clamps down on my arm hard enough to bruise and yanks me toward the parking garage. "Ow, asshole! You're hurting me!"

The Marshal ignores my protests, instead whipping out a cell phone and dialing. I glance back at Cooper, who grasps a gun in his hand. A gun. A motherfucking gun. My eyes bug out. What the hell is going on? "Yeah, sir. We got her," Donovan says into his cell. He listens for a second. "He's here too, just like you said."

"Who is he? Where the hell are you taking me?" I ask.

"Shut up, bitch," Donovan snaps.

The ferocity and rage in which he spews those words dials the warning bells inside my head up to eleven. This isn't right. *They* aren't right. Every one of my sharply honed survival instincts is telling me to flee. "Let me go," I say as I try to jerk my arm away.

His grip tightens. "We'll take care of him here," Donovan continues to the person on the phone. "No other choice. If what you say is true, there's no way in hell he'll let us leave with her."

"I said, let me the fuck go!" I shout as I'm dragged through the parking garage door. I glance around for help. Not a soul in sight.

Donovan squeezes me again so tight pain radiates down my bones like a shockwave. "I have to go, sir." We cease walking, and Donovan puts away his cell.

"Listen, I know my rights. I've done nothing wr—"

Oh, fuck.

Donovan slips out his gun, shoving it right into my side. Strangely, the moment that hard muzzle begins to bruise my rib, calm washes through me as I become acutely aware of everything. The warm night air. The faint sound of tires and voices in the parking garage twenty yards away. The distance to the door and the approximate time it would take me to run there. Not faster than a bullet. Also scrolling through my head are the lessons from years of cardio kickboxing. Eyes, nose, groin, solar plexus, knees, feet are the sweet spots. The problem is only Jackie Chan can subdue two men with guns, and that's only in the movies. Plus he never wears heels. Fear begins to creep in, but I slice it dead with a samurai sword. *Keep calm and carry on, Dahl.*

"Here are the rules," Donovan begins. "Scream, I shoot you. Try to escape, I shoot you. Bring attention to us, I shoot them. Don't follow my exact instructions … you get the idea. Follow those instructions, you'll probably survive the night. Now put your hands behind your back. Cooper, get the cuffs off my belt. The ones on the left. The others are silver."

Silver?

Donovan snatches my purse from my shoulder as I force myself to do as he says. Cooper slaps the cuffs on. "What's the plan, sir?" Cooper asks.

"We get to the garage, you flank right and hide. He'll follow me because I have the girl. You see him, you don't hesitate. Brain stem and heart. You really as good as he said?"

"Yes, sir."

"You're gonna need to be. Just make sure to empty the clip in him. Last thing we want is that fucker getting up again. Once it's done, disappear. I'll handle the rest."

"Yes, sir."

"Good." He looks at me, calm as can be for someone who just ordered an execution. "Now, Miss Dahl, all you have to do is remember the rules and look pretty. Can you handle that?"

I glare at him. "Yes."

"Good girl. Let's go."

Once again he jerks me forward on the open sidewalk. There is no way in hell I'm getting in his car, I know that. They can shoot me dead, but I'm not getting in that fucking car to be tortured and raped in a field somewhere. I watch *Dateline,* I know how this shit rolls. No, I'll wait until Cooper leaves, then make my move. There have to be people in the parking lot. Strike, run, scream. that's gonna have to do. Oh fuck, please let it do.

"Sir, do you smell that?" Cooper whispers behind me when we're ten feet from the garage.

Donovan sticks his nose up like a dog and sniffs. "Yep. Sweat and ectoplasm," he whispers back.

Ectoplasm? Isn't that the gooey stuff from *Ghostbusters*? These guys are fucking nuts.

"He couldn't have changed that fast, and not with people around," Cooper whispers. "It's coming from inside the lot."

Donovan sniffs again. "You're right."

"What do we do now?"

"Just shadow me to the car from a good distance. It's still two against one, and he won't do anything to put her in harm's way. Just stay low, quiet and out of sight." Donovan switches sides so the gun is in his right hand and me on his left. At least now the gun isn't trained on me, it's pointed out at whoever's out there.

We enter through a concrete arch into the parking garage. I hear cars starting, up a level, I think. People. The exit is on the opposite side of the garage with an attendant in the booth, maybe thirty-five yards around the corner. That's my end zone. Cooper crouches and sprints to our right—the way I need to go, damn it—as Donovan keeps us moving straight ahead toward the up ramp. There are a lot of cars, one in almost every space, and Donovan's eyes scan for the enemy as his nose twitches. I don't smell a damn thing. We continue walking and the twitching increases, as does his apprehension. The creases in his brow are as deep as the San Andreas Fault. That nervousness is transferred to me like a virus, making breathing difficult.

25

I force myself to calm down and pay attention. Strike, run, scream. *Strike, run, scream.*

I glance behind and spot Cooper poking his head from around a concrete pylon. Fuck. Donovan stops our death march, and releases my arm. *Not yet, Dahl.* Not removing his eyes from the cars directly in front of him, an SUV and the back of the Camry, Donovan slowly lowers my purse while keeping the gun trained toward the SUV. He grabs me again, positioning me in front of him as a human shield, holding the cuffs to guide me. My heart beats so fast and strong it pounds in my ears like a Gene Krupa drum solo. We stop just at the edge of the SUV. Blondie must be hiding between the cars. Not sure how I should feel about that. Fear. All I'm capable of right now. Fuck. Donovan raises his gun barrel up beside his face, waits a never-ending second, then shoves me forward with him moving half a second behind. My body becomes locked, waiting for the inevitable shot to penetrate.

Nothing. There's nobody between the cars, just a slime-covered black jacket on the ground. I smell something now, salty and earthy. I have a split second to process this as Donovan draws his gun at the jacket.

"Vivian, down!"

I'm so hyper-alert I'm on the ground before my brain can catch up just as a gunshot rings out. For a moment I think I've been shot but feel no pain. Shock? No, I feel the grip of my cuffs vanish. When I glance back at Donovan, he's gone, but where he was standing the glass of the SUV has shattered. I see a flash of the Marshal moving back the way we came. More shots from both left and right reverberate through the night. I'm pinned. Fu—

There's rapid fire, four quick shots from my left. On the fourth shot, movement by the Corolla to my left draws my attention. The blonde maneuvers next to me between the cars, in his right hand a smoking gun and the left ... Holy fuck, I've gone crazy. His left hand is a paw, a dog's paw with tan fur up to the elbow and sharp, really fucking sharp claws. I snap my head up to gape at his impassive face. I hear a click as the freak ejects the clip from his gun.

Almost too fast to register, he places the gun in his closed left armpit to hold it, reaches back into his belt, pulls out another clip, inserts it into the gun, and presses the slide back with his paw. "You're going to roll over the hood of the Corolla and the other two cars until you reach the end of the row to stay out of the line of fire," he says, eerily calm as he does the gun trick. "I'll draw their attention and keep them here as long as possible. Move fast, don't look back. My Mustang's right across from your car. Turn around." I do. Fur and hot skin brushes my hands as it moves to my cuffs. One yank, and as if made of breadsticks, the tiny chain breaks. I'm free. I pivot around again as he returns his attention toward Donovan's direction. Blondie peeks around the corner. "Keys and cell phone are in my back pocket. Get them." I obey. "Get in, keep low. There's another gun under the seat. If I'm not there in five minutes, drive off. Do not go home, do not go to a friend's house. Push redial on my cell and tell them what happened. They'll give you further instructions."

"Who ... the fuck are you?"

"Your father sent me. Now go."

"My fa—"

"Go!" He moves from between the cars into the danger zone, and I pounce into action as ordered. I throw my body on the Corolla's hood and roll as the gunfire begins anew. I land between two more cars and take a breath before launching myself over the BMW, then the Volkswagen bug. That's the last one. I stand up and notice the blonde's gone. He said don't look back. I take off around the corner and up to the second level as the gunfire ceases.

This is not happening. This isn't happening. I pump my legs as fast as I can. Running in heels is no easy feat. I have to pay attention to each stride and my footing, otherwise I'll break my damn ankles. I'm just about to round the next corner when I hear a man roar in fury. Out of the corner of my eye, I spy movement and turn back down the ramp. As if hit by the Incredible Hulk, Donovan flies backward fifty feet like a ragdoll into the windshield of a car. The entire car jerks and smashes into the back wall from the force, glass and metal twisting. Holy shit. Wha...

Keep going, Viv.

One level to go. I sprint around the corner just as a car drives toward me. Thank God. "Help me! Please help me!" I shriek as I wave my arms. But the driver wants no part of this. He swerves to avoid me and guns it down the ramp. I begin trembling and have to stop running for a second to stare at the asshole. He didn't stop. For fuck's sake, what is the world coming to?

Just keep going. *Keep going.*

I run.

My Bonneville comes into view along with Blondie's Mustang. Yeah, no way in hell am I getting in that thing. I make for my car but realize I don't have my keys. My bag's on the first level. Shit! I'm gonna have to—

A gunshot slams the air, this one very damn close. My front tire explodes, and I stop mid-stride.

"Freeze, bitch." Crap. I turn around to find Cooper near the stairwell thirty feet away, training his pistol on me. "Don't you—"

In the stairwell, something behind gets Cooper's attention because, gun first, he spins around. The man doesn't even make it all the way around before the back of his head explodes as a single shot booms around me. Cooper's head jerks back as bits of skull and brain splash out. Motherfu ... I'm too shocked and horrified to scream. I can't even move as I hear pounding footsteps up the stairwell. A second later the blonde steps out, gun trained on Cooper's lifeless body. The man bends down, checking Cooper's pulse with his paw. *Paw.* It's really a paw. Cooper must still be alive because the blonde puts two into his head and two more into his heart. I feel nothing, not even revulsion.

The blonde's eyes cock up and look into mine. "He's dead."

"Oh."

Blondie shoves the empty gun into his pants and flops the corpse over to retrieve Cooper's wallet. Just as the blonde finishes desecrating the corpse, my stalker tilts his head to the left like a dog and springs into the standing position. "The police are coming. We have to go." He bridges the thirty-foot gap between us with a few strides, but I can't move. I can't take my eyes off that body. "Vivian?"

That paw touches my arm. I'm snapped back to reality, or this new version of it. Gasping, I jerk my head up to see his face. It's expressionless except for the eyes. A tinge of concern attempts to break through the ice. "Vivian Frances Dahl, daughter to Frank and Michelle, I am here to protect you and deliver you to safety.

No harm will come to you, I swear on my life, but we must leave now. Please get in the car. Now."

Okay, not a fucking clue why, but I believe him. No other option really. I nod, and he nods back. My fate's sealed one way or another. Blondie takes the keys and cell from my hand, which practically has to be pried open I've been holding them so tight. He unlocks the Mustang, and I follow him in. "Get the gun under the seat," he says cranking the ignition. As I do, he maneuvers out of the parking spot. Glock 9mm. "If I ask, hand it to me right away and get down. Open your window." My hand trembles so bad I can barely press the button to lower it. He drives normally, using the paw to turn the wheel. With the other, he hands me the first gun. "There's a spare clip in the glove box. Reload this. Do you know how to shoot?"

"Um, yes. Kind of."

Down the ramp there's a small group of people, including a security guard, standing around the demolished car and Donovan. Bleeding, but not dead. Shit. He glances from the woman fussing over him to our car. Donovan says something and points at us. The guard's mouth flops open, and he fumbles for his walkie talkie. Double shit. Blondie guns the engine, and I'm thrown back into my seat like we're reentering gravity. We zoom past the bystanders and around the corner. Driving like a maniac he maneuvers us down to the gate. The attendant steps out of her booth, waving for us to stop. Yeah, right. I spot flashing lights and hear sirens to our left as the police approach. Without hesitation, Blondie smashes through the wooden gate. Tires squeal and the back of the car fishtails as he cuts a sharp right turn. Blondie gains control with a few quick wheel jerks, but I grip the door and dash for dear life.

"Put on your seat belt," Blondie orders, still calm.

Oh. Right.

Though my arms tremble as if I have advanced Parkinson's, I manage to buckle the belt, though it takes three attempts. "W-What the *fuck* is going on? Who the hell are you? Who the hell were they?"

"Shit," Blondie says as he glances in the rearview mirror.

I snap my head around and count three sets of flashing police lights dangerously weaving between the four lanes gaining on us. Holy fuck I'm in a real-life car chase. It's a hell of a lot more frightening than the movies make it seem. I doubt Bruce Willis would feel like puking, like I do. "How well do you know this area?" Blondie asks.

"P-Pretty well."

"The highway?"

"Um … t-two rights, then a left at the second light."

We careen around the first right, back wheels sliding, narrowly missing an SUV. The entire time Blondie's as calm as the corpse he just created in the parking lot. He yanks on the wheel to make the second right. "Those men were trying to abduct you," he says, emotionless.

"Y-Yeah. Got that part. Why? Why were you following me?"

"I told you. Your father sent me," he says, gunning through a red light as my back slaps against the seat again.

"*Why*? I haven't seen or heard from him in twenty-eight years. The fucker abandoned me and never looked back."

"Is that what you were told?"

"Told? It's the goddamn truth! I wouldn't know the man if I met him on the street. Whatever is going on with him has nothing to do with me."

"I'm afraid it does. Hold on."

The maniac runs another red light as we turn left onto the freeway ramp. The Mercedes inches from us skids to a stop just in time, but not the Camry behind that. It smashes into the Mercedes. *Oh, please let them be okay.* On the bright side they're blocking the exit so the cops can't follow.

"With what I'm about to tell you, you must keep an open mind," Blondie says as he revs the car up to 100 mph. "Is that possible?"

"I-I guess." I *am* staring at a man with a paw after all.

"Twenty-eight years ago, your father was visiting another Marine named Dave Campbell at his cabin near Liberty Lake in Maryland for the weekend. While on that trip, your father was attacked and Campbell was killed by a rogue werewolf."

"A werewolf?" And I have officially entered Crazytown, population this asshole.

"Yes," he says, serious as syphilis. "The Eastern Pack had been tracking the rogue and quickly heard of your father's attack. His new situation was explained, and he was brought back to the compound before he injured himself or others. He remained for three months until he had control of his beast and could return to you and your mother. But when he did, your mother . . . turned him away. She wanted no part of him or the pack. He returned to Adolphus and later became Alpha to the pack."

"No, he met some chick and ran off," I state adamantly. "He didn't become a fucking werewolf because *they do not exist!*"

The man shoves his paw in my face. Damn those claws are sharp. "We exist." He pulls the paw away and glances at the rearview again. "Shit." I spin around and see a helicopter gaining on us. "Is that a field to your right?"

"Yeah," I say after a glance. Like a NASCAR master, he maneuvers past the other cars to the right, taking the first exit. The moment the exit ends near an onion field, the sweet earthy smell invading the car, he switches the headlights off. I can't see a thing. "What the hell are you doing?"

"I have excellent night vision."

"Because you're a werewolf," I say with a scoff.

"As were the men I just rescued you from."

"The U.S. Marshal Service employs werewolves?"

"They were Marshals?" he asks.

"Well, the one guy Donovan, the one you didn't … you know, he had a badge. They said they were looking for you and my fa— Frank Dahl."

"No. They were there for you."

"Say's you."

"Did *I* pull a gun on you?" he asks with a hard glare. "Did I handcuff you? Threaten your life?"

"You've been following me. You attacked me last night," I counter.

"I did not lay a hand on you. You were drunk. I was attempting to take your keys away."

"You've been stalking me."

"I was *watching* you in case something like this occurred."

"So you knew they were going to do this and instead of warning me you just stalked me until I was in mortal danger? What the hell kind of plan was that?"

"I was under strict orders not to engage with you unless absolutely necessary. We knew there was a possibility this could happen, not a certainty." He pauses. "And if it did happen, I was under orders to, if possible, capture the rogue and interrogate him as to the location of Seth Conlon."

I wait a few seconds, but when he doesn't elaborate, I prompt, "*Who is?*"

"Four years ago, after a fifty-six-year reign, Robert Conlon died in his sleep at one hundred twenty-four years old. He had one son, one daughter, three grandsons, and one granddaughter of age. The son was too old and disinterested nonetheless, two grandsons proved themselves to be Betas, which left only two other options: Seth and Tate. As is our custom, before he'd name his successor, the Alphas fought as wolves under the full moon. Seth was bigger, more aggressive. He won. When Bobby passed, Seth was our new Alpha. And for a year we put up with his stupidity. His cruelty. Seth's first order was that your father, I, and several others who could challenge him, be more or less exiled from the pack. Only on full moons were we able to enter the compound, and even then we could not run free with the others. He imprisoned us. He embezzled pack funds as well. The last straw was when he attempted to force some of the younger women to submit carnally."

"Jesus Christ."

"Your father reluctantly agreed to be the one to challenge Seth. He'd been close to Bobby, and was father to his great-grandson Matthew. He—"

"Wait," I cut in. "Stop. I have a brother?"

The man's quiet again. From what little I can see of his face from the glow of the dashboard, he remains expressionless. "Your father married Jenny Conlon, Bobby's granddaughter, soon after the divorce from your mother. Matthew was almost a year old by then."

I scoff. "Fast worker. Ditched one family, instantly got himself another. Sounds like a great guy," I say with a sneer.

"Your father is the finest man I have ever met," he says menacingly. "Please do not say a word against him in my presence."

"Yeah, because abandoning me without a second thought, then dragging me into this bullshit is such a wonderful thing to do. Humanitarian of the year, him."

"Your father loves you. I would not be here otherwise. There is a war back home. People I love have died. Others are in mortal danger. Your father didn't want this life for you. He didn't want it touching yours. So, though it broke his heart, he stayed away. Only a few even know of your existence. He didn't want you to meet a similar fate as ..." The right side of his face twitches.

"As?"

More silence, before, "Your father bested Seth. He won the challenge. Seth was forced to leave the pack, made rogue, told if he remained in our territory, we'd execute him. Through the years we heard reports he was in Canada, in New Mexico, then in the past year, that he was recruiting other rogues. We couldn't pin down his exact location, though I spent countless hours hunting him. Then, three months ago, a D.C. detective and his wife were attacked in the Shenandoah State Park. She died, he lived to kill the wolf, but he was turned. The detective reported that the wolf targeted him first, dragging him out of the tent, biting then licking the wound. It only attacked the wife when she began shooting at it. Price had a knife on him and began stabbing when it set upon his wife, then bashed the wolf's brains in with a rock. It bled to death before it could heal. Price was lucky. We soon discovered the wolf was one of the men alleged to be associating with Seth. Since then we've also seen a significant uptick in maulings, some where the victim died and others where a person reported a bite then vanished or moved away, maintaining minimal contact with friends and family. Pennsylvania, Delaware, New Jersey, Virginia. He's amassing an army around us. We just put the pieces together too late." He pauses. "Then Jenny went missing. And Matthew."

"Oh, God." I don't think I want to hear anymore.

"We first realized something was wrong Thursday. Jenny was supposed to be at a day spa, but when it began growing dark we tried her cell phone with no answer. The spa said they had never heard of her. I was just about to go searching when the first phone call came in. Tate Blue, then soon after Omar in Delaware, Ralph in Pittsburgh, and Jenny's father R.J. in North Carolina. All very close to your father and physically strong men, all shot or set upon by wolves. R.J. and Ralph didn't make it. And in the middle of all the confusion Linda, Matthew's wife, phoned too. Your brother hadn't returned home from his photo studio and wasn't answering his phone either.

"When I went to retrieve her and the twins to bring them to the compound, I made it all of three miles before I was shot at and run off the bridge. I split open my head and almost drowned in the bay. By the time Adam found me stumbling on the side of the road and got me patched up, the calls had stopped, but there was no sign of Matt or Jenny. Until morning. The same SUV that ran me down drove right up to our gate and dumped their bodies. They'd been … beaten, had their throats slit. Jenny was strangled too. Possibly … violated."

"Holy fuck."

"There was a note in Matt's pocket. Said, 'You took mine, now I take all of yours. With interest. S.C.' Following his pattern, striking at everyone close to your father, it was logical he'd attempt to abduct you, possibly even infect you or use you to force your father's hand to step down. You'd be easier to handle than two strong, experienced werewolves like Matt and Jenny. Your father and I agreed I should come watch you. Took the first flight out. I'm actually surprised it took them so long to find you."

This is totally, off the wall, batshit *crazy*. This isn't happening. It can't be. I'm having a horrible acid flashback or something. I've heard that can happen. I'm hallucinating the paw. Those Marshals back there thought I was involved with whatever this asshole was and were taking me in to interview me when Blondie went all Chuck Norris on them. Now I'm an accessory to murder. This psycho beside me executed Cooper without hesitation, and now he's spouting crazy talk. I'll just explain to the cops what happened. This was all a horrible mistake, and that this freak kidnapped me. I mean *werewolf wars*? This guy is certifiable. And a murderer. Oh fuck, I think the shock's worn off. It just hit me that I'm in a car with a man who emptied a gun into another human being without an ounce of emotion. He's a sociopath. He's probably driving me to another field to behead me and wear my skin like Versace.

"Stop the car," I say.

"The police are still nearby. I can't—"

I pick up the gun from my lap, pointing it right at his head. "I said stop the fucking car!"

He glances at me with that emotionless expression. "Please lower your gun. You're not going to—"

I move the muzzle to the right and fire, shattering his window. Damn that's loud. That high pitch ringing in my ears is almost deafening. Does the job though. Blondie's large frame jerks and slams on the breaks. "Jesus!"

"Get out of the car," I say over the ringing.

"Vivian, I'm trying to save your life. Don't—"

"Get out!" I shriek.

"Don't make me do thi—"

"I said get the fuck ou—"

With one fast movement, Blondie slaps the gun to the side while reaching across to me. Before I can react, he's got me by the back of the neck and squeezing like a boa constrictor on steroids. Lights out. Hope the vultures and coyotes enjoy their feast.

TWO

Huh. I'm alive. This is a surprise.

Once again the light from a window stings my eyes as I open them. Maybe this is heaven. Nope, my neck and ankles wouldn't be torturing me if I was in heaven. And Nina Simone isn't around to greet me. When my eyes focus, I check my surroundings. Backseat of a car. I get a few not terribly enjoyable flashbacks from my misspent youth as I lay back here. Of course the snoring blonde in the driver's seat is new. His seat is pushed all the way back and reclined so his head is inches above my feet. Asleep. Good.

I do a quick mental diagnostic of myself for damage. Besides my aching neck from sleeping at a strange angle, I have a headache, though nothing like yesterday's. My whole body's stiff, my arm sore from where the Marshal grabbed me, and I think I have rope burns where the straps of my shoes dug into flesh when I was fleeing. Otherwise I'm intact. Even have my panties on too. Considering all the hell rained down on me last night, I'm in good shape. I intend to keep it that way. Time to get the fuck out of here.

The Mustang is a fabulous car, no question, except when you've been kidnapped and your assailant is in the front seat and you're stuck in the back. Then you really wish they'd made it a four-door. The lever to move the passenger seat is right by my hand, but will make noise, not to mention when its down the seat blocks the door handle. Hard way it is. Careful and quiet. Slowly I unstrap my heels, removing them as I'll move better without them on. I swish my toes and ankles in circles to restart the nerves. Oh, that's bliss. Order restored, and never ungluing my eyes from Blondie, I gradually sit up. His snores continue. So far not awful.

Now the tricky part. Moving about an inch a second, I creep toward the front, never taking my eyes off my comely kidnapper. I'm crouched halfway to the front when he snorts. I freeze, hell I don't even blink as he turns on his side away from me. I don't draw breath for five seconds until he resumes snoring. I breathe a literal silent sigh of relief. Keep on keeping on, Viv.

I clasp onto the passenger head rest, bunch up my skirt, and very very *very* carefully move my right foot into the passenger seat. Ted Bundy continues snoring. Then the left foot. Good thing I'm flexible. Okay, almost there. Using the headrest to brace myself and flexing my back in an arch, I shift my left foot to the floor and lower myself onto the seat. Still snoring. Hallelujah. I reach for the handle and open the door with the same care. Jesus Christ, it worked. I'm free. My bare right foot touches hot dirt outside. I—

Shit!

A hand clamps around my left wrist, and my gaze jerks toward its owner. Blondie is staring at me with his usual cheer. "No."

Fuck it. As quick as I can, I lower my head and bite down on that hand hard enough I taste blood. He releases me, and I leap out into … oh, double fuck!

Nothing. As I survey all 360 degrees of my surroundings, I find nothing. Nothing around to the horizon but dry brush and flat sandy soil. A freaking real tumbleweed rolls by. We're in the desert. Might as well be on fucking Mars. I just can't catch a damn break. "Help!" I scream at the top of my lungs. "Help me!"

Blondie climbs out of the Mustang. "We're ten miles from the nearest town. No one can hear you, Vivian."

My gaze zips back to my captor. "Take me home," I say through gritted teeth.

"I'm afraid that's not possible."

I move around the car to face him, spitting out his blood on the way. "Take me home right now, goddamn it, or I'll…"

"What? Bite me again? Shoot at me?" He meets my eyes. Damn, he's like a robot. I can't find an emotion anywhere on his face. It's unnatural. "The sooner you accept this new situation you find yourself in, the easier this will be for us both. I am on your side, Vivian." He starts toward the trunk of the car. "All I want to do is escort you safely back to Maryland where we can all protect you until the danger's passed."

"You want to escort me to my father. Who is king of the werewolves. I'm sorry, did you forget to take your pills or something? Are the aliens telling you to do this, Blondie?"

He opens the trunk. "My name is Jason."

"I like Blondie better," I say with a sneer.

"I don't." My kidnapper extracts a duffel bag and shuts the trunk. "It's understandable that you require proof. I would have produced it last night had you given me the opportunity before you aimed a gun at me." He unzips the bag, rooting around in it before pulling out a stack of papers. "Here. Your father said I should bring them. As usual, he was correct." He tosses me the bundle. Letters. I recognize the flowery handwriting on the front. Mom's. Even has her name and address in the corner. Michelle Dahl, then later Mrs. Barry Anderson. "She promised to send photos and letters once a year. You read through them. Take your time. I have to take care of some business in private. Please do remember, though, I am faster than you so don't run or I'll be forced to handcuff you in the car."

Where the hell would he go? "Fine," I say, although the word sticks in my throat.

He nods and returns to searching in his duffel. The ground is burning my feet to a crisp, so I return to the passenger side and sit. These could be forgeries. Part of an elaborate con. Why I'd be at the center of one, I haven't a clue. I still want to read them. I open the first envelope on the pile. If they are forgeries they're damned good ones. I even remember the stationery with "MDA" monogrammed on the top of the later ones. Photos too. Me in front of my grand-parent's ranch house when I was about three. First grade, second, all my school photos through high school. That perm at fifteen was such a bad idea. The letters are short at first, just giving the broad strokes of my life. My first sentence. Potty training issues. Asking him to send more money. Later she starts bitching about what a nightmare I'd become. The drinking. My failing grades. The arrest for drug possession and a fake license. In one, when I was sixteen, she even begs him to take me off her hands. Nice, Mom. They stop at my eighteenth birthday, obligation fulfilled. I graduated from high school, and the next day moved to New York City with my band. Lasted a year before I moved to Austin, then New Orleans, then La-La land. Wonder if Frank knew about those too.

There are three loose photos between the letters as well. The first one I've seen. My father making funny faces as he holds infant me. The rest, no. Frank, a pretty woman with dark hair, and two boys opening presents under a Christmas tree. The dark-haired boy resembles the woman with similar hair and eyes, and looks to be about six or seven, but the familiar blonde is older, early teens maybe. I'd recognize that scowl anywhere. He stands apart from the trio, staring and back as straight as a razor, almost as if he's afraid to be near them. In the third, I'm onstage at this club in Santa Monica where I used to sing. Frank was close to take this one. Front row. I was right, I didn't know my own father when I met him on the street.

My head swims. Only one word sticks enough for me to focus on it. *Lies.* My entire life is based on lies. Mom lied to me. I thought he didn't care. Hell, even though it wasn't rational, a part of me had believed *I* ran him off somehow. That I wasn't lovable enough for him to stick around. That he saw something in me as an infant and decided I wasn't worth his trouble. That he was right to leave. I'm gonna kill Mom. It's a damn good thing she's three thousand miles away because if she was in front of me right now I really would murder her. Both of them.

Jason hangs by the back of the car checking the one, two, three wow, four guns laying on the trunk as I get up. "I need your cell phone," I say.

"Why?"

"I need to call my mom."

He sets down the revolver. "Not a good idea. If those men were Marshals, they may have contacted her already. May even have someone watching her."

Shit. "Could my family be in danger too?"

"Unlikely, but possible."

"Then give me the fucking phone," I say, rounding the car toward him. I hold my hand out, and he glares at it as if it's just slapped him. "It's not like I can tell her where I am because *I* don't even know." He continues to glare, which earns an eye roll. "Please?" That works. He reaches into his pocket and hands me the cell. "Thank you."

I return to my seat inside and dial. There's no answer on the house phone, so I try her cell. "Hello?" Mom asks.

"Mom, it's Viv."

"Vivian! Hold on, I'm at the club." Far away, she says, "Paula, if they call us for a court, tell them I'll be back in five minutes." I'm being hunted and she's playing tennis. Fair. I hear her walking, then in a low whisper, "What the hell have you gotten yourself into now?"

"Excuse me?"

"We had a call this morning from a Federal Marshal saying you were involved in a shoot-out last night. What did you do?"

My mouth drops open. "Yeah, I'm fine Mom. Thanks for asking," I snap. "And glad to know my kidnapping and possible death didn't keep you from your doubles match with Paula."

She's silent. "Are you … alright?"

"Considering last night I was almost murdered, then abducted, and oh, I just found out my father is a fucking werewolf, I'm doing pretty damn lousy. Thanks for finally asking. "

More silence, then, "Your father's a what?"

My rage boils up ten degrees more. I'm hotter than the damn desert air. "Don't play dumb. Not now," I warn roughly. "I really do not have the patience or time for it. I am staring at letters and photos sent from you to Frank where, quite a few times, you scribbled the word *werewolf*. And I am with a man who had a paw for a hand last night. For *once* … I am begging you … I need to know the truth. Okay? My life depends on it. *Please*," I say, voice cracking. Shit, I think I'm about to cry. I force the desire away. Emotions have no place in my life right now.

She doesn't speak for a few seconds, then, "It was both our decisions not to tell you. For your protection. It was for the best. For all of us."

Kaboom.

It's real good I'm sitting because I doubt my legs could support me in this moment as the bottom drops out of my world, sending me into freefall. This is reality. This *is* happening. It's true, it's all true. My father's a werewolf. My mother lied to me all my life, and I'm being hunted by homicidal supernatural beings who've already slaughtered the stepmother and half brother I never knew I had. No calm this time, only literal gut-wrenching fear and panic. The wind is knocked out of me, and I have to force more air in. "Vivian?" Mom asks. "How did you find out? What's happening?"

Keep it together, Viv. Falling apart now accomplishes nothing. Not a damn thing. Like the tears, I will keep the fear far enough away so I can speak. "Last night two men, possibly the Federal Marshals who called you, tried to kidnap me. Apparently they were working for another werewolf who wants to kill Frank. There's a war going on or something, I don't know all the details. They've already killed Frank's wife and son, I was just next on the list."

"Oh, my God," Mom says. "I knew this would happen. I knew it! I told him. We'd probably both be dead if I'd agreed to go with him. And I was right."

I don't have the energy for the long fight we need to have. Eventually. "Whatever. Mom, are you and Barry still going to Sandals in a week? I think you should, um, take Jessie with you and start the vacation early, alright?"

"Why? They won't come after *us*, will they? I haven't been in contact with Frank for years."

"Mom, neither had I. They already called you, they know you exist. Better safe than sorry."

"I don't ... Barry knows nothing about Frank. He won't agree."

"Make him. Lie. You're good at that. Just get gone. And if anyone calls about me, *anyone*, say you haven't heard from me. Just keep your cell with you. I'll phone when it's safe to go home." If I'm not dead.

"I can't believe this is happening," she says. "Barry's going to flip. It's going to cost so much to change the reservations. And your poor sister. Her internship. And I was supposed to help out at the cancer fundraiser. This is a nightmare."

Yeah, they get to fly to a tropical island for a few days, and I get to drive across country with Mr. Congeniality while being chased by homicidal werewolves. My heart's breaking for them. "Just do it, Mom. I have to go. I'll call when I can. Bye." I hang up before I lose my shit. I really want to punch something right now. Standard after a call from Mom. It's worse today. A hell of a lot worse. Because today her words not only harm, they completely change the course of my life.

This is real. It's all real. Good thing I am nothing if not adaptable, even to this.

After a few breaths to calm myself, I put my shoes on, and get out of the car.

Hello.

My shittier-by-the-second life momentarily dissolves as I drink in the sight of my road-trip buddy. Without his shirt on. He must spend every spare moment at the gym. His pecs are bigger than my boobs, he has a perfect six-pack, and the rest of him might as well be chiseled in marble. I don't think there's an ounce of fat on him, and his skin's the color of milk mixed with honey. *Yummy.* I collect myself before he looks up and catches me. Eye candy fix achieved. "Here's your phone back," I say as I walk over. "I believe you."

He takes the cell. "Thank you."

"And I'm sorry for shooting at you. And biting you. I was wrong, and when I'm wrong, I own it. From here on, I won't fight you. I'll…do my best to trust you." I hold out my hand for him to shake.

He does. Wow does he run hot. It's like touching a skillet. "Thank you."

I pull my hand away. "So, what now? What's the plan, Blondie?"

"Jason." He puts on a gray v-neck t-shirt. Damn. "We return to the compound as fast as possible. All pack members are assembling there. We're about forty miles from the Arizona border now. We'll fly out of Phoenix and be in Maryland by the afternoon."

"Except my purse with my ID is sitting in a Ventura parking lot or in police lock-up. I can't get on a plane, train, or even a bus without one since September eleventh. So unless Frank has a private jet, looks like we're driving."

"That'll take days."

"About three if memory serves. We'll take shifts behind the wheel."

"Sounds fair."

"Okay then. First things first though." I smirk. "You're taking me shopping, Blondie."

———

Even in the middle of a desert a gal expects to find a damn Target. This is America after all. We have more strip-malls than trees. Not today though. We've been driving for over half an hour and nothing. Not even a damn Wal-Mart. My chauffeur doesn't say a word as the miles pass, and his face remains unreadable. I wonder if he has any other expression. I did see another look last night when he was listening to me singing, happiness mixed with awe. Wonder how to get that to resurface. He's making me uncomfortable just staring out at the road, thin lips set in a straight line. He's so still I can barely tell he's breathing. Maybe it's a werewolf thing.

Whatever it is, it's driving me nuts. The stillness, the silence, I can't take it another fucking second. I might begin to *think*. Can't have that. "We live in a country besieged by strip malls, but there's never one around when you need one, huh?"

"We'll stay on the interstate. There's bound to be one sometime."

That's it. That's all he says for two damn minutes before the silence gets to me again. This is going to be the road trip from hell, I can tell already. "So, Blondie—"

"Jason," he corrects.

"Why'd you draw the short straw?" I ask, ignoring him. "Piss off the old man or something?"

"I don't know what you mean," he says, glancing at me.

"Princess guard duty. I can't imagine there were a whole bunch of your people jumping at the chance to sit in a car for days on end watching me pick up dry cleaning. Especially when there are people back home who are actually in danger. Not that I'm not grateful you're here. Vultures would probably be picking at my corpse right now if you weren't." A stab of fear clenches inside my stomach, even sending its army of bile up my throat, as I realize this is a hundred percent true. The man beside me saved my life last night. Most guys don't even put the toilet seat down for me. "Thank you."

He glances at me again, and for a split second I see a glimmer of that previous happiness cracking through those chilled eyes, but if it was there, it vanishes as quickly as it came. "I was just following orders."

"Do you always follow orders? Even ones that can get you killed? For a stranger no less?"

"Yes. I trust your father with my life. Whatever he instructs me to do, I do. Without question. I know everything he does or says has a purpose. For the good of the pack."

"So, you're a foot soldier?"

"I'm your father's Beta. Second in command," he clarifies. "He gives an order, I carry it out."

"You're his enforcer," I say.

"I'm his Beta," he says with an edge of bite.

I can absolutely see this guy beating and killing people. Hell, I've seen just that. "Call it what you will, I am not judging. As I said, you saved my life. You get a free pass from me for-fucking-ever vis-à-vis questionable behavior. And based on last night, I'm sure whoever you, you know, *betaed*, they probably deserved it." I shrug. "Some people just do." Blondie stares at me with two actual clear emotions. Confusion and apprehension this time judging from the narrowed eyes. "What?"

His gaze whips back to the road. "N-Nothing."

"What? You don't share the sentiment?"

"No. I ... do. I'm just surprised *you* do."

"Well, I am full of surprises, Blondie. One of my many considerable charms," I say with a seductive smile.

He doesn't smile back, just stares straight ahead with his mask on. "I'm sure."

We drive in silence for thirty seconds until it gnaws at me again. "You never answered my question."

"Which was?"

"If you're his second-in-command, and it's the middle of a crisis, why'd he send you for little old me?"

"You're his daughter. You're family. And I'm the one best equipped to protect you."

"Once again. Why?"

"That's a question for your father," he says in an almost menacing tone.

Civilization rolls into view, saving him from further interrogation. He's keeping something from me, that much I know. I'll wrench it out of him. It is three thousand miles to Maryland after all. Project.

We pull into the Target parking lot, which is surprisingly busy for a Sunday morning. Even the Linens 'N Things is bustling. All the families in the lot stare as we walk toward the store. Guess they don't see many redheads in cocktail dresses and fake fur or musclebound blondes in this neck of the world. At least the handcuffs are gone. He had a spare key in the duffel bag. My wrists are red and raw, which can't help matters. Inconspicuous, we ain't.

Since I'm not footing the bill, and I need one of everything, I go a little crazy shopping. Enough clothes for a month, toiletries, munchies, and soda to feed us for a week, magazines and CDs to keep me occupied as Blondie has proven himself a lousy conversationalist, pillow and blanket for napping, and a huge suitcase. Basically, anything I saw that I wanted, I threw in the cart. All he contributed was a first-aid kit, a thousand Slim Jims and protein bars, a map, and Gatorade. He doesn't say a word as I keep adding items. A whole new wardrobe. Thank you, Daddy Dearest.

After the teenager rings up a few items, I take them—khaki shorts, cerulean t-shirt, flip flops, hairbrush, and deodorant—into the restroom to clean up while he pays. It's no wonder Blondie was immune to my flirting, I'm a mess. Makeup smeared or gone, hair a rat's nest, dress so wrinkled it could double as an accordion. I do my best to reassemble myself, changing my clothes and brushing my hair. Have to do. Blondie waits beside the restroom door when I step out. My improvements go unnoticed as he never unglues those eyes from the man with a headset who keeps glancing over. "What?" I ask.

"Let's get out of here," Jason says. He looks back at the man as we hurry toward the exit.

"What? What is it? Who is that guy?"

"Manager. My card was rejected. Had to use the pack business one. Then that man came over."

"Forget to pay your bill there, Blondie? Don't be embarrassed. My cards are always being rejected." We walk out of the store into the scorching day. "You should at least pay the—oh, fuck."

We stop dead when we spot the police cruiser beside our Mustang with an officer reading the license plate into his radio. Guess someone got the plate last night as we made our getaway. "Now we know why your card was flagged," I offer.

"Shit," Jason says.

"Yeah, we have about a minute before they get word you just tried your card inside. We have to get out of here."

"My weapons are in there. My clothes."

"Forget them. Come on." I tug on his shirt. He snaps out of his fog and follows me away from the police, blending in with the happy families. We need new wheels. Lucky for us I've known some colorful characters through the years, including a car thief. He dated one of my roommates in New Orleans. Always liked the guy. Today more than ever. I push the shopping cart toward the back of the lot.

"Where are you going?" Jason asks.

"Employees have to park far from the store. If we're lucky, we'll boost one of theirs. It'll be hours before they report it." We have a winner. "Here. This one," I say with a grin.

A Honda Civic, one of the most nondescript, widely bought models around. There are two in this row alone. It's white as well, the most popular car color. It'll do the job. My smile drops at the sound of a police siren. I glance back at the Mustang and spot an officer walking into Target as another cruiser pulls up beside the Mustang. Shit. I reach under the back wheel of the Civic. Nothing.

"What are you doing now?"

The front right wheel. Nothing. Front left … yes! I yank off the magnetic key box with a triumphant grin. Thank you, Bubba. The corners of Blondie's mouth twitch in what I think is his version of a smile. I unlock the car. "Hurry!" We quickly toss all our bags into the backseat and climb in the front. Jason starts the car and pulls out, away from the swarm of police.

"Marshal Donovan's been a busy boy," I say.

"All my guns. All my ammo. Clothes. Emergency cash."

"Speaking of cash, the card that went through at Target, they'll probably pull the number. If you use it again, they'll track us with it."

His scowl deepens along with the creases in his forehead. "We need money."

I think for a second. "ATMs. We find another shopping center, hit all the ATMs in the stores, get the limit from each. Use cash for everything. Untraceable. We need to change the license plates on this car anyway."

"We do?"

"Yeah. We find the exact same model and color, then switch their plates for this one. That way if someone runs them, the car doesn't come up stolen. No one ever notices their plates are different."

He glances over at me, confusion overtaking his face again. "How do you know all this?"

"How do you not, Blondie?" I ask with a proud smirk.

He doesn't answer. He just returns his attention to the road. Think I offended him. This time we don't have far to go for another strip mall or another white Civic, only about a mile. I wait anxiously in the car, scanning the highway for police, as Blondie hits the stores with an ATM sign in the window, all four of them. He returns after the second, a hardware store, with my requested screwdriver. He continues on our funds run as I take care of our other problem. My heart pounds as I remove the license plates from the cars. The few times people pass by, my throat closes up as I pretend to tie my flip flops. If they don't believe my pantomime they don't say a word or stop walking. Thank God for modern apathy. Blondie returns as I screw in the back plate on our new car. "We need to hurry," he says.

I give it two more twists. "Done." Like a gentleman, he holds out his hand to help me stand. "How much you get?"

"Thousand."

Should be more than enough—*shit*. Sirens. My protector and I exchange a glance before rushing into the car. I barely get the door closed before he pulls out. As he drives out of the lot, I start rooting around in the bags in the back for the maps. "Drive about five above. Do the limit or below, it's suspicious. Above five, risk a ticket." Oh, my sunglasses. I retrieve them and the map book before plopping back down in my co-pilot chair. "We can't take I-40 anymore," I say as I open the book to California. "They know we're using it. Plus you have to stop at the California border to check for vegetation if memory serves. We have to assume if they have the Mustang's description out, they have ours out as well. Our best bet … yep," I say, reviewing the map, "is to backtrack to I-15 then take I-70 through Utah, Colorado, so on. Other option is I-80 through Wyoming, Nebraska, etc. 80 is farther so probably safer, but it'll add half a day. My vote's still for 80 though. *What*?" I snap. He's been glancing at me damn near slack-jawed through my instructions. It's making me self-conscious.

"N-Nothing. Just … surprised."

"By?"

"How good you are at this."

Oh. Huh. A satisfied smile crosses my face. "Well, Blondie," I say, kicking up my feet on the dash, "I may have barely passed high school, but I have a damn Ph.D. in street smarts and survival. Stick with me, handsome." I slip on my cat's-eye sunglasses and stare at the wide open road. "Might just learn a thing or two."

And I settle into the seat of our stolen car. I may have just committed a felony, I may be on the run from both police and homicidal werewolves, I may be riding shotgun with a killer, but damned if I'm not enjoying myself a little. Just hope this walk on the wild side doesn't end at a cemetery.

THREE

THE ENJOYMENT DOESN'T LAST long. The thrill of our escape wanes within the hour, giving way to boredom. *Massive* boredom. I talk for almost an hour straight when I can't take the five minutes of complete silence a second longer. I tell Blondie about my career, all the places I've lived, and I think he listens. Can't be sure. He doesn't say a word, just nods. I feel like I'm talking to myself, so I shut up after my life story's complete. He doesn't offer one fact about himself in return. Guess sharing and conversation aren't his forte.

After my monologue, I spend my time fiddling with the radio, staring out the window at the desert, or biting my cuticles. Thrilling. I almost wish we'd get into another car chase just to break the monotony. Still Blondie doesn't utter more than ten words in seven hours and most of those were to the drive-through attendant at McDonald's when we buy lunch. The man scarfed down five Big Macs like he was in a competition. I can add "almost only eats meat" to the werewolf file growing larger in my brain. Went through an entire box of Slim Jims too. I pity any cow that crosses his path.

We make it over the Utah border and have to fill up. I leap at the chance to take over driving duty when he suggests it. His eyes have been drooping since Vegas, where he refused my first offer to switch. Control freak. Blondie's snoring by the time we're back on the interstate. Cruise control does my heavy lifting. We haven't passed a single speed trap, but I still only keep it five above. People, even trucks, pass us once or twice with a rude hand gesture, but probable cause trumps rudeness in this case. An hour into my shift, Jason moans in his sleep as if in pain and flips over to face me. His brow is furrowed again, and his face is scrunched up as if he's smelled something foul, but a second later he relaxes. Bad dream.

I take this chance to study his peaceful face. I've tried a few times when he was awake, but he'd notice and turn to glare at me. Don't think he likes to be looked at. No clue why. He's fucking gorgeous, especially asleep. Gone is the off-putting menace and thorniness that he always seems to exude, on purpose or not. His lips are a lot fuller than I thought. Pinker too, like the color you'd paint a room when you found out you were having a girl. He has long blonde lashes too. I'm jealous of that front. Add that to the muscles, thick hair, and cutting cheekbones—he's a babe. I'll bet he's fierce in bed too. As take charge and masculine as he was last night when he was fighting for my life. I do like it a little rough sometimes. And we do have days and days of dull driving all alone together. A quickie or two *would* break the monotony. Not to mention he did save my life and everything. Can't think of a better way to thank him. I smile at the mere thought of those lips on mine, him stretching me apart as I writhe against him. Damn, I'm wet already. It's decided then. Before we reach Maryland, I'm gonna ride that man like a rollercoaster.

The question though is how best to go about seducing him. I wonder what his type is. Flighty and sweet? Damsel in distress? Strong and take charge? Of course he could be gay. Or married. Hell, come to think of it, I don't know a fucking fact about him. Not even his last name. Not that I get the last names of a lot of the men I sleep with, but still. Might help to know these things for the seduction, if not just in general. The more I know the better I'll be able to play him in any given situation. You can't adapt if you don't know the environment.

As I'm culling together an interrogation list, his cell phone rings. All that survived our great escape was what he had on him: wallet, cell phone, and Glock with an extra clip. Blondie stirs and opens his eyes on the third ring.

"Hello?" he croaks before listening to the person on the other end. "Hey, Tate, what's going on? Is everything alright?" He listens. "Thanks. Appreciate it. It's good to hear your voice too. How are things there?" Silence as he listens for a full minute. "No, you, Adam, and whoever can stay at my place as long as you need. Sounds cramped at the main house." More silence. "Yeah, ran into some trouble. No question." He's quiet, then glances at me. "I don't want to talk about it right now." I believe my ears are burning. "Yeah." He listens. "Don't know. Think we're still in Utah on 15 going to 80?" He glances at me, and I nod. "Yeah, probably two days if we don't stop." Silence, then he glances at me again. It could be the setting sun, but I do believe his cheeks are turning as pink as his lips. "That is not going to happen." His mouth sets vice tight. "I'm not you." Quiet. "I'm hanging up now if—" Silence for a few seconds. "That may be required. Thank you for the offer. I have to go. Talk to you later. Bye." He ends the call.

"Your boyfriend okay?" I ask.

"M-My what?"

"Boyfriend. Call sounded a little naughty is all. I mean, no judgment here. I live in Southern California, I know more gay people than straight."

"I'm not gay," Jason says, slipping the phone back in his pocket. "Tate is my friend."

"Oh. My mistake." One question ticked off. "So, what's going on in war-torn Maryland?"

"Lockdown. The majority of the pack who live within a hundred miles have reached the compound. Families are still arriving though. It's chaos. They're having to set up tents outside, RVs on the lawn. Over forty men, women, and children in a house with ten bedrooms."

"How many werewolves does my fa—*Frank* have?"

"We're thirty-two strong, spread from Maine to Florida. The Eastern Pack is responsible for all werewolf activity from the Mississippi River to the Atlantic."

"And only thirty?"

"There's an estimated hundred fifty werewolves in America. Not all are pack because they haven't made themselves known or did not want to join."

"Only a hundred fifty in all of America?"

"We were once much more, thousands even, but the hunters and witch finders brought us close to extinction. Like the true witches, our ancestors fled to the wilds of Russia, Canada, and the United States, and built from there."

"How did you become one? Is it like the movies? Do you have to be bitten?"

"No, my father was a werewolf. You are either born one or the curse can be transmitted through fluid exchange while in wolf form, when there is a higher concentration of the magic and virus. Most who are attacked fail to survive, and those who do often take their own lives after their first change."

"Why?" I ask.

"It is difficult to control the beast, even with years of experience. More often than not they don't know what they've become and fail to take the proper precautions. A loved one often dies."

"Jesus. That's terrible." It is. This werewolf thing sure does sound God-awful. Good thing I only want a one-night stand, not a relationship with one. I pause. "So, your children are werewolves?"

"If I ever have any, yes. The first change occurs during puberty."

No kids. Check. "And the full moon? Silver bullets? It's all true?"

"Yes. With practice some can call their beast at will, no matter the phase of the moon, but during the full moon the magic overtakes us, and the change must come. Silver burns and makes it difficult to heal, so we bleed out. Normally we heal ten times faster than humans, we're immune to most diseases, and we're five times stronger than you. Our senses are more acute as well, along with our reflexes."

"You *are* the Incredible Hulk," I say with a smirk.

"I beg your pardon?"

"Never mind." I drop the smile. "So, what do you do when you're not doing Frank's bidding? Have a job? A girlfriend? Wife? Hobbies?"

"No girlfriend or wife." Double check. Rollercoaster is a go. "My friend Adam and I own a contracting company with a few other wolves. We do home improvement, construction, things like that."

"Hobbies?" I prompt.

"Woodworking. I construct beds, chairs, even a boat once."

"Cool. I love men who work with their hands. It's so … rugged."

He glances at me with confusion. "It's just a hobby."

"One I am sure you excel at."

His eyes narrow. "What makes you say that? There's no basis for that statement."

"Um …" I have no clue what to say. "I don't know. You seem like someone who's good at whatever he sets his mind to. I'll bet when we get to Maryland, I'll be proven right." I glance over at him. His eyes have returned to normal. Guess he buys this. I've got him talking now, don't want to lose the momentum. "Do you have any brothers or sisters or anything?"

Those eyes become pinpoints again, aimed at me. Now what? "Why do you ask? Why are you asking so many questions? Why do you care?"

I do a literal double take at his vehemence. "Whoa. Okay, I'm just trying to get to know you. I'm not trying to steal your identity or anything. Chill. God. Are you always this defensive and paranoid?" I shake my head and stare straight ahead. "Forget I asked."

I don't look over, but out of the corner of my eye, I spy Jason studying me again. I pout as if he's bruised my feelings. He is an odd one. Limited social skills for sure. Good thing I enjoy a challenge from time to time. I pretend to literally shake the negativity off and turn up the radio. He hangs his head a few inches, properly cowed. Works every time. "I'm sorry," he says.

"It's fine," I say, a little short. "Your orders were to protect me, not talk to me, right? You want to remain a grumpy man of mystery, no skin off my nose. Just trying to make the trip more enjoyable. I won't try to bring you into the fun again."

"I didn't … I …" He stops stammering. "I'm sorry. I … don't talk much. Especially about myself."

Oh, my God. He's shy! Huh. I dig it. I've never met anyone as hot as him who was anything but a narcissist. He is so adorable, I could just melt. Must keep this to myself though. I don't want to scare him back into his hole. "Fair enough. We don't have to share intimate details if you're not comfortable yet. I will get it out of you, though." I raise an eyebrow and smile seductively. "I have ways of making you talk, Blondie." Damned if he isn't blushing again. Once again, *so* adorable it makes a basket of puppies look like a basket of rats. "But I am about ten seconds from falling asleep at the wheel, so as co-pilot it's your job to entertain me. Them's the rules."

"How?"

"I don't know." I think for a second. "Tell me about my sperm donor."

"Da—*Frank*?"

"Yeah. What's he like? Get me prepped for the reunion."

"What do you want to know?"

"Uh, how'd you meet him? Start at the beginning," I suggest.

"It was … complicated."

I roll my eyes. "Come on, Blondie. You can do better than that. He's my bio-dad, I kind of have a right to know what he's been up to since he ditched me."

"He didn't ditch you," Jason insists.

"Sure. Whatever." I roll my eyes again. "So, how'd you meet? When he joined your pack?"

"No. He brought me in some years later."

"*He* brought you in?"

"When I was eight. He saved my life," Jason says.

"How? What happened?" Jason doesn't answer. He stares out the window at the brown prairie and rolling hills outside. "Sorry. Too personal, I'm sure. You don't have to answer."

"No," he says, glancing back at me. "You're right. You should know what kind of man he is."

"I'd appreciate it."

Jason's jaw sets, and all the muscles in his face stand at attention. He hasn't even begun the story, and he's already rigid. "My father … was not a good man. Before I was born, he was exiled from his pack in Russia. For the rape of another member. He wasn't arrested, but he emigrated to America, worked as a translator for the government and later as a bodyguard for the vampire Lord of D.C."

"Wait, vampires are real too?"

"Yes. Our kind doesn't mix well with theirs. My father was an exception. He was fond of Peter. Loyal, though *only* to Peter. With everyone else, my mother and myself included, he was brutal. One of my earliest memories is of him beating my mother for making a comment about his haircut. When I was six, I fell asleep to their fighting, and when I woke, she was gone. He claimed she abandoned us, *me,* but I know now he must have killed her."

"Jesus."

"For the next two years, I was basically on my own. Alone. The only times my father paid attention to me was to beat me after a stressful day. I took care of myself. Cooking, cleaning. I didn't go to school, I just stayed in the house watching TV as I was told. No one but him, the odd girlfriend, and colleague ever came over. I'd hide in my room. Then one night, he didn't return home. I thought nothing of it. He'd been angrier, more agitated than normal for days. I know now he was scared."

"Why?" I ask, captivated.

"Bobby Conlon and Lord Peter had no love lost between them, but they tolerated one another for decades until they both wanted to buy a piece of property in D.C. A few days later, one of the pack was found drained of blood—Abigail was seventeen. Then another wolf was murdered in the same manner. In retaliation, some wolves took it upon themselves to slaughter a few vampires, along with their human companions. That brought in the F.R.E.A.K.S."

"The who?"

"The preternatural police. They investigated, then acted as mediator between our two factions. The men finally agreed to a cease fire when it was uncovered my father was responsible. He'd been dating Abigail, and when she refused him sex one night, he beat and raped her. Fearing she'd talk, knowing she was pack, and that there were tensions between the wolves and vampires, he made her death seem like a retribution vampire attack. Then he murdered another wolf for good measure. When the pack was given definitive proof of his actions, they broke into my house looking for him, your father included. They found me in the closet, clutching a butcher knife."

"What'd you do?"

"They'd invaded my territory. I stabbed R.J., slashed at John. They still bring it up. Still haven't forgiven me. Your father was the one who grabbed me as I thrashed around. I bit him, scratched him, cut him, but he just hugged me and whispered it'd all be okay until I ran out of energy."

Nice of him. "What happened to your father?"

"In the spirit of their newfound cooperation, Peter informed the pack where he was hiding. Abigail's father executed him."

"I'm … sorry?" Not sure of the appropriate response here.

"Don't be. If ever someone needed putting down, it was Ivan. I'm just sorry I wasn't the one to do it," Jason says, cold as the Arctic.

He stares out the window again, deep in thought. I give him a few seconds of reflection before asking, "So, what happened next? The pack invited you in with open arms?"

He all but jerks at the sound of my voice. I think he forgot I was here. "What? No. Not exactly. I was wild. Assaulted anyone who got close. I wouldn't eat, wouldn't put on the clothes they gave me. Wouldn't speak. I was afraid to go outside. I thought they were going to kill me. Most gave up even trying, except Maureen Blue, her son Adam, and Dad."

Huh? "Wait. *Dad*?"

Jason glances at me again, I think a little guilty if I'm reading his eyes right, but quickly looks away again. "The others didn't want me there. Sins of the father and all. A constant reminder of Ivan. I've never blamed them for that." He pauses. "But Dad saw something in me. Maybe he wanted to atone for leaving you, I don't know. He convinced Bobby not to ship me off to another pack or foster care. He later told me the moment he looked into my eyes when he was holding me that night, he knew I was to be his in all but blood. Just *knew*, as if God whispered it to him. We werewolves take those instincts seriously," Jason says with another uncomfortable glance my way. "Dad took things slow, just being in the same room as me so I'd get used to his presence. Then talking, bringing me toys, sometimes he'd even bring Matt so I'd get used to him too. It was about a month before I'd let Dad within a foot of me, and another two weeks before I said a word to him. Almost two months to the day I met him, I moved in with him, Jenny, and Matt. They adopted me. Raised me. As I said, I'd be dead if it wasn't for Frank Dahl."

I stare at him slack jawed. "So ... you're my brother?"

"Adopted. I guess. Yes."

Okay, brain overload. I don't know how to feel about this information. I mean, I'm more than glad Jason was rescued from that life. No one deserves a father like that. I'm sure as hell shocked he's turned out as well as he did. It explains a lot too. The social awkwardness. Not wanting to talk about himself. Not to mention I'm hella embarrassed I'm lusting after a relative, but it's not as if he's blood, or even that we were raised together. Still. A little fucked up. But, if I'm honest with myself, what's bubbling most to the surface is ... rage. Pure goddamn rage, hot and powerful enough to fuel a power plant.

And resent. Really fucking resentful. Beside me is my replacement. All the love I should have received went to him. He's the one who got the bedtime stories. The scoldings for bad grades. The chicken soup for flus. The passing of wisdom. The building of confidence only supplied by unconditional love and a sense of true safety. I always figured Frank had been a selfish bastard incapable of those things. You really can't fault someone for something when they just don't have it inside them. It'd be like blaming the deaf for their lack of musical appreciation. But he could. And he did. Just not with me.

This time I'm the source of the uncomfortable silence. "I've upset you," Jason says.

"No," I lie. "I just … that was a horrible story. I am *so* sorry you had to go through all that."

"It worked out for the best."

"Right. I'm glad. For you." Okay, that's all the sharing I can stomach for now. I dial up the radio again and keep my eyes straight ahead. Blondie doesn't take the hint. He stares at me, I think attempting to read my face. I stand the scrutiny for all of thirty seconds. "What?" I snap.

"You lied."

"Excuse me?"

"You lied about what upset you."

"Of course I didn't! I wouldn't wish what happened to you on Osama Bin Laden!"

"I trained myself to recognize subterfuge in others. You just did it again. You lied about lying. So, why did my story upset you?"

Okay, now I'm just getting annoyed. "Why do you care? It's not important. Just leave it alone." He continues staring. Thirty more seconds, then, "*What?*"

"You don't want me as your brother."

"Huh?"

"It's the most logical answer," he says, emotionless. "You reached maximum agitation when I told you that. The muscles in your face tensed and your breathing deepened."

Once again I look at him, literally slack jawed. His face is a mask, but when I meet his eyes, my throat tightens. Oh, shit. I've hurt his feelings. He thinks my anger is directed at him, not Frank. I've learned that there are two reasons people who never show their emotions and act tough do it. One, they're just a bastard and have none. Blondie and I fit into the second. We feel things too deeply. We've had to build a wall, otherwise we'd be nothing but a raw nerve and couldn't function. I think I just exposed that nerve.

It couldn't have been easy being thrown so young into what sounds like such a close-knit group as the pack, especially after what his father did to them. All the looks, all the whispers behind his back. The suspicion. Knowing that, save a few, they didn't really want him there. That he was an interloper. Called family but not fully embraced by them, no matter how hard he tried. I know *exactly* how that is. A sliver of him will always be that eight-year-old starved of love and acceptance. And I just slammed a sledgehammer into that part.

Very quickly, I lean across and peck his cheek. He flinches and his eyes double in size as if I'd just poked a cattle prod into his side. "What—Why did you do that?" he asks, almost horrified.

Good thing I didn't follow my first impulse and kiss him on the lips. "Because you're cute. Because I like you. Because I don't want you to think for a second I don't. As I said before, you saved my life. Anything you do or did is alright by me, Blondie."

His eyes haven't left my face since the kiss, haven't stopped examining me. The man doesn't know the meaning of the phrase face value. Since every word is the truth, he believes me. His tense shoulders drop a millimeter or two. "Then why were you agitated?"

Damn. He is like a fucking dog with a bone. Or I guess a werewolf with one. "Because I'm a selfish bitch, okay? It's all me. It has nothing to do with you. Let's just leave it at that, alright?" He continues staring, and once again thirty seconds is my threshold. "*What*? Don't you know it's not polite to gawk?"

"I don't want to leave it at that."

I roll my eyes. "Why the fuck do you care so much?"

"I want to understand you," he says, as usual emotionless. Jesus Christ, it's like Spock's riding shotgun. "I want to get to know you. You're part of my family. It's normal to—"

"Wait," I cut in. "Just stop right there. Let's get one thing clear right off the bat, gorgeous. I am not your family, okay? My sperm donor might have raised you, even made it legal, but I am not your sister. I have a sister. I grew up with her. We have a shared history. Shared experiences. Shared love. She's the only person on this planet I *really* consider family. You and I, we haven't known each other even twenty-four hours. I didn't know you existed until yesterday. We're strangers. Frank saw to that.

"Now, I like you. I truly do. And I appreciate all you've done for me more than words can cover, but when this whole shebang is over, I will not be popping over for Dahl Family Thanksgiving or Christmas every year. He may be your savior, and you may love him, but all Frank Dahl is to me is the asshole who abandoned me. And sending you, and keeping yearly tabs on me doesn't make up for twenty-eight years of nothing. He *thought* about me? Where was he when I had my appendix out? During my first concert? Every single night across the damn dinner table?"

"It was necessary to protect you," Jason says harshly. "To give you a normal life."

I scoff. "Yeah, a normal life with two narcissists who ignored me except when they decided it was time to criticize me for *everything* I was doing wrong. Not to help me, no, because it reflected badly on *them*. My weight, my clothes, my hair, my grades, my choice in music, when I was a kid none of it was good enough for them, especially my mother. Barry, my stepfather, well he never had much use for me even before Jessie was born. I was literally the redheaded stepchild. I was a weed he couldn't remove from his precious rose garden of a family. He didn't even visit me in the hospital when my appendix burst. Never came to a single performance. Then, when I finally gave up trying to get their approval and started acting out? Forget it. People accepted Lizzie Borden post massacre more than my parents accepted me. They shipped me off to boarding school a hundred miles away with a week's warning.

"And you know what? I actually liked it there. I made friends, I got decent grades, I even had this wonderful music teacher, Miss Tyson, who molded me into a better singer. But no. Barry didn't want to spend any more money on me, so back to Orlando I went, and once again I wasn't good enough. Got into any trouble I could find, didn't give a shit about anything but singing. What was the point, right? Nobody ever gave a damn about me, why should I?

"I barely graduated from high school, left the next day, and never looked back. Hell, maybe I would have been better off with a pack of wolves. But I'll never know, will I, because I wasn't even presented with the option. So, I've never really had a family. I've taken care of myself, and I don't see that changing just because my sperm donor finally decided to look out for me, alright? When this bullshit is over, I'm gone. He doesn't get to be my father *now*. So please don't think of me as your pack or family or whatever. You're just setting yourself up for a big damn disappointment. I don't do long haul. I meant what I said, Blondie. I'm a selfish fucking bitch, because I learned very early on when that hammer drops, in the end all you have is yourself. People will just drag you down."

Oh, thank God. Escape. I maneuver the car onto an off-ramp toward a gas station. I want the fuck out of this car. "So, fair warning Blondie, I like you. I do. But it's every woman for herself. If it's a choice of saving your ass or saving mine, I'll choose me every damn time and not look back." I park beside a gas pump and take off my seat belt before smiling cruelly at my protector. "Glad you got to know me now?" Smile dropping, I open the car door. "Excuse me."

It's hot as hell when I step out. Out of the frying pan into the fucking fire. I feel his eyes on me as I walk into the station. The ladies room is deserted. My first bit of luck ever. I splash cold water on my face and stare at myself in the mirror before sighing. As always, it's Frank's face I see reflected back. No wonder I hate the sight of myself.

FOUR

GUESS WE GOT TO know each other well enough. I return to the car, we get in, and drive in silence save for the radio. Fine by me. I drive us through Salt Lake City, and soon after we merge onto I-80, which will take us across America. Just not tonight. An hour outside the city, my eyes begin gumming up, then growing heavy. I'm running on empty. Blondie reached his limit before the city limits and is snoozing away. Good. I can make an executive decision without his input. We're stopping for the night. I need to sleep in a real bed, take a shower, maybe even swim in a pool. I can't stand another fucking second in this car.

Right over the Wyoming border, I veer off the highway. I pass a few of the chain hotels, instead settling on a brown, dilapidated one-story popular with prostitutes judging from the woman in fishnets and tank top sitting outside in the hallway sucking on a cigarette. I doubt they'll ask for a driver's license or credit card here. Like the hookers they probably charge by the hour. The stopping motion draws Blondie out of his hibernation. His eyes flutter open like dancing butterfly wings, and he glances at our new surroundings and the almost setting sun. "What's going on?"

"We're stopping for the night," I say as I tuck my hair under my hat.

"No. We should keep going," he says.

"Look, I am in no condition to continue driving all night, and neither are you. Plus we could both use a shower. You especially. We stay for the night, recharge our batteries, wake up early, and hit the road. I won't give our real names. Hell, *I* don't even know exactly where we are, how could Donovan?" I remove my seat belt. "I'm staying. If you don't want to, that's up to you." I hand him the car key. "Feel free to drive off and leave my ass here if you so desire. The choice is yours." I grab some cash from the glove compartment before climbing out. There is no way in hell he'll ditch me. My father raised him right.

I pass the growling and barking pit bull staring right at our car, lunging at it too on its chain. I keep my distance, though it ignores me. Must not be a fan of werewolves. "Shut up, Maisie," a man shouts from inside the office. The clerk inside the front office is far more clean cut than I expected to see running a roach motel.

"Good evening, ma'am," he says with a bright smile. "Sorry about my dog. Don't know what's gotten into her."

Werewolves seem to bring out the worst in us bitches. "It's fine. I need a room for the night, please."

He hands me the paper register. "Just you?"

"My husband and I." Mr. and Mrs. Barry Anderson according to the register. I pay cash and as expected he doesn't ask for ID or a credit card. Called it. I do make a hell of an outlaw. When I stroll out of the office with my key, the hooker has vanished but not my bodyguard. Didn't think he would, not for a second. Our room is on the other side, out of sight of the interstate at my request. I move the car closer to the room, and out of sight from passing police, before gathering all the Target bags to consolidate inside. Jason doesn't speak as I hand him the goods or as he trails me to our room. Who's Alpha now?

I step inside the room with a groan. The décor hasn't been updated since the seventies—with orange wallpapered walls and what I think was once brown shag carpet that's no longer shaggy. No visible cockroaches, no blood or other stains on the walls or bed and an ancient television facing the bed with a magic fingers feature. It's no Hilton, but it'll do. I've stayed in far worse but maybe Jason hasn't. He stands with his back to the door, cracks forming not only in his forehead but behind that stony veneer. "What?" I ask as I drop the bags and giant empty suitcase on the mattress.

"There is only one bed," Jason observes.

Oh. Isn't he cute? "Well, you can always sleep on the floor if you're concerned about your virtue," I say with a sly grin before glancing down at the cigarette-burnt carpet. "Though I'd be more worried about getting fleas from the carpet than me taking advantage of you in the middle of the night." He doesn't smile at my quip. There has to be a sense of humor buried deep down in there somewhere. I *will* find it. "I'll try to keep my hands to myself if you do the same, alright?"

Damned if a glimmer of relief doesn't seal those stone cracks. Holy shit, is he scared of me? What does he think, I'm some raging nympho who's gonna roofie him?

"I'm going to walk the perimeter." Jason scoops up the key from the table by the window and walks out, locking the door behind himself. What a strange man.

Whatever. I flip on the television just for the background noise. Three fuzzy channels. I settle on the least snowy, I think the news. I'm halfway through pulling the tags off my new wardrobe when Blondie returns. "Any bogies on the radar?" I ask.

"No."

"See? Nothing to worry about. We're safe. Why don't you go get us some dinner? There was a K-Mart back about a mile. You should pick yourself up some new clothes too."

"If I leave, you leave."

I roll my eyes. I forgot this man is incapable of processing subtlety. "You're gonna make me say this? Okay." I sigh and set down the sundress. "I need some alone time. Once again, nothing against you, I just want, no *need*, like half an hour to myself. You probably do too, especially after our ... whatever. I will be fine. I'll lock and bar the door. You can even leave me the gun. Anyone but you tries to come in, I swear I'll put one between their eyes without hesitation. We each need this. Please."

He stares at me for a few seconds, once again unreadable, before reaching into the back of his pants and removing the gun. "The safety's on, but there's one in the chamber." He sets it on the table. "My cell is (410) 555-8723. I will return in half an hour. Do you have a preference for food?"

"Salad, large fries, strawberry milkshake. Thanks."

He nods and grabs the car keys. The moment the door closes, I let out a long sigh. Damn that man is intense. It's like being beside an unexploded bomb. They say it's defused, but you can never be too sure. I chain the door and wedge a chair against the handle as promised. Half an hour of peace, quiet, and stillness. I flop on the lumpy mattress and stare up at the water-damaged ceiling to clear my head. There's a lot to fucking clear.

If someone came up to me yesterday and told me I'd be in Wyoming running from the law with my long-lost semi-brother, who also happened to be a werewolf, I would have asked for a hit of whatever they were smoking. Jesus, not even twenty-four hours ago I was onstage, now I'm a federal fugitive. A car thief. Accessory to murder. Being hunted by werewolves. Oh, fuck. Panicking again.

I curl into a ball, hugging my knees to my chest. The short breaths soon give way to sobs. *This* is why I wanted him gone. I needed to have an overdue meltdown in peace. Jason doesn't strike me as a man who tolerates weakness or outpourings of emotion. Really, I don't want him to think any less of me than he already does.

I've never been a crier. Only when stressed. This qualifies. I sob until I can't see or breathe right. Images and thoughts fuel my misery. Cooper's brains splattering out. The car chase. Reading those damn letters. Mom's lack of concern about my life. Jason's story. His pain radiating like Chernobyl when he thought I was rejecting him. And my father. My fucking father. He's ruined my life all over again. I can't go home. I'm an accessory to murder. If the werewolves don't get me, the law will. My life is over. It may have been small, and more often than not shitty, but it sure as hell beat this.

Okay, calm down. Calm down, Viv. Deep breaths. I inhale and exhale in rhythm just as Miss Tyson taught me until the sobs become weeps. With the fog of panic huffed and puffed away, I can think again. Maybe it's not as bad as I imagine. I doubt Donovan wanted the Marshal Service to know he was kidnapping innocent singers for his werewolf leader. Who knows if Cooper was even a real Marshal? Maybe I'm not even in their system. These thoughts all but stop the tears. I glance at the rotary phone on the nightstand. A little voice in my head whispers *it's a bad idea*, but as always I ignore it. Even if he doesn't know anything, I just really need to hear a familiar voice. I roll in Cyr's number.

"Hello?" he asks skeptically after the fourth ring.

"It's Viv."

"Holy shit, Viv. What the hell happened? Are you okay? Where are you?"

"I'm fine. Sort of. But it's better if you don't know where I am."

"Were you kidnapped? The police didn't know if you're a hostage or what. They said it was the guy from the club the night before. He hasn't hurt you has he?"

"No. I'm fine, and he didn't kidnap me. Not really. It was those other guys, the Marshals. *They* tried to kidnap me."

"What? No, Viv. The guy you're with is real bad news. He's killed and raped at least three other women. They tracked him to the club, figured he'd been following you for days. They were putting you into protective custody when he killed that other Marshal."

"Cyr, *Donovan* pulled a gun on me. He handcuffed me. He was gonna kill me. *Jason* saved me, okay? You weren't there. Don't believe them."

My friend's quiet for a few seconds. "Is he there? Is he making you say this? Cough if he is."

"Oh, hell. He's not here, okay? I swear on Nina Simone's grave. Don't believe a damn word Donovan says. I just need to know if anyone besides him has contacted you, and what they said. What do they think happened?"

"I told you. The Marshals were taking you into protective custody, the blonde guy ambushed you, beat up one Marshal, killed another and abducted you. The Ventura PD called me in today, asked me all sorts of questions. I told them about the blonde, whose name isn't Jason by the way. It's Gavin McHale. He escaped from custody in Sacramento before his murder trial two months ago. I told them he was watching you all night, but that you said you'd never seen him before."

"So, I'm not in trouble? I'm not a fugitive?"

"Of course not! You've been fucking kidnapped, Viv! By a murderous rapist. If he really isn't there, just run. Go to the police. Call the Marshal. He gave me his card. It's here somewhere..."

"Cyr, listen to me. Listen. The Marshal is real bad news. If he calls you, or anyone asks you about me, don't say a word. And don't tell anyone I've called you, okay? Promise?"

More silence, then, "I promise."

"Thank you. I don't know when I'm gonna be able to come back, okay? Can you pick up my mail for me?"

"Yeah. Sure."

"Thank you. I'll call when I can," I say. "I gotta go."

"Viv—"

I hang up. A tiny wave of relief ripples through me. I'm not a fugitive, I'm a victim. I can return to my life when this is all over. One less worry. I'll just tell them Jason kidnapped me, then let me go. The rest is for him to deal with. I stand and sigh again. There is actually some light at the end of this crazy train tunnel. I just have to survive the werewolves, Blondie, the open road, and a shitty family reunion to reach it. Piece of shit-covered cake.

As I return to my task of organizing my new wardrobe, I attempt to watch TV, but my mind just won't let up. It bothers me that I can believe the werewolf crap more than Jason being a raping serial killer. I just dismissed it without a second thought. I have the feeling he's killed enough times to qualify as a serial, but not that he enjoys the act or performs it without a legit reason. Yet, I don't feel unsafe around him. Quite the opposite. If I had to go through this alone I'd be raped, dead, or if I was lucky enough to get away I'd be curled up catatonic in the fetal position on a bathroom floor. And yet I was a total bitch to him for something Frank did to me. Me and my damn temper. It's true what they say about us redheads, we are a fiery bunch.

I'll think of a way to make it up to him. Maybe not Project Rollercoaster though. Pretty sure that train won't be leaving the track. In his mind I'm his kid sister, and unless he has an incest fantasy, which ewww, I don't see it being successful. Which is a damn bummer. I was looking forward to seducing him, not to mention the end result. Us sweaty, panting, him sliding in and ou—

The knock on the door snaps me out of my mental porno. I glance at the clock. Exactly half an hour. Time sure does fly when you're breaking down. "It's Jason," he says on the other side. I unlock the door before pulling the chair away. The smell of charred meat and grease wafts in, and I salivate a little. I grab the Burger King bag and milkshake from Jason's hands and start chowing down on my fries before the door even closes. I dump everything out, all ten Whoppers and my salad. As I set the table in-between fries, Jason places his K-Mart bags on the bed beside the suitcase before sitting across from me at the table. "Get everything you need?" I ask with a wad of fries in my mouth.

"Yes." He unwraps the first burger, biting it in half.

"Like hamburgers, huh?" I ask, eyeing the pile. "That a were-wolf thing?"

"Our metabolism is faster than yours. We are required to eat twice as many calories as you, and we prefer meat for the protein."

"Good to know." I finish off my fries. "I'm a vegetarian, in case you hadn't guessed. Started out as a diet thing Mom put me on when I was thirteen. Had to lose weight, at least according to her. Just stuck."

"Then you shouldn't do it anymore. You're too thin," he says matter-of-factly.

I don't think he meant it as an insult, but I still scowl. "You're not around women that often, are you?"

"There are women in our pack, and I often work for women as a contractor. Why do you ask?"

I roll my eyes. I'm beginning to think this guy's autistic. Or maybe a robot. "Never mind."

"No. Did I say something wrong?" he asks, genuinely curious.

"Um, yeah. Rule of thumb, unless you're asked, never mention a woman's weight or age. It's rude."

"But you *are* too thin. It's a sign of unhealthy habits or disease. You should be aware of this fact to correct it."

Is this dude for real? "Yeah, but ... just don't okay?"

"Okay."

We eat in silence for a few moments. I hate it. "So, I called a friend of mine. Apparently Donovan—"

"You did what?" he asks, mouth still full.

"Don't worry, I didn't tell him where I was. I'm not a total idiot. Besides, he won't narc. He promised. Don't you want to know what he said? About the police?"

"You mean that I'm an escaped convict named Gavin, and that I've kidnapped you? I know. I have since this morning. We have a contact inside the F.R.E.A.K.S. This Donovan must have switched my photo inside the system into the file of a real fugitive. My real name would trigger a F.R.E.A.K.S. investigation. Neither party wants them involved. There's bodies on both our sides. Agent Price is just feeding the pack information. We're on top of this. You shouldn't make any more calls. It's too dangerous. Don't do it again," he says, catching my eyes. His voice was neutral but those eyes are cutting. On instinct, I lean back farther in my chair.

"I-I won't. Sorry." I stare down at my food, away from his gaze. I think I prefer him commenting on my weight more than attempting to draw blood with his eyes.

"Just don't do it again. Please," he adds as an afterthought.

I nod. Once again, we fall into agonizing silence. After a few seconds, I look up and see his head hanging as he chows on his burger. Crap, did I hurt his feelings again? He notices me glancing up. I smile apologetically. "Not quite the sister you imagined, huh?"

"No."

"What did you think I'd be like?"

"Softer. Fragile. Innocent."

With each of those words my urge to laugh rises, but that last adjective pushes me over the edge. I let out a chuckle. "Oh, man."

"What?"

"Nothing, it's just … those are the exact *wrong* fucking words to describe me. What the hell did Frank tell you? I was a Disney princess or something?" The chuckles die off a few seconds later as he doesn't join in. I don't know, maybe he's incapable of laughter. "So, is my lack of princess status a good or bad thing?"

"I'm sorry?"

"Am I a huge disappointment? Do you wish I was swooning every five seconds?"

His eyes narrow in confusion. "Of course not. That would slow us down."

No guile. No guile whatsoever. Refreshingly cute, yet aggravating. "Right. Didn't think of that." I move my gaze down to the food I shove in my mouth. I cannot get a read on this cat. It's driving me nuts.

"Did I say something wrong again?" he asks.

"No," I say with a reassuring smile. Thank God I'm done eating. I collect my trash, sticking it in the bag. "I think I'll take a swim."

"That's not advisable. You should stay in the room, out of sight."

I rise anyway. "Yeah, that's not happening. If you're worried, you can always join me."

"I didn't buy a swimsuit."

"Then wear your underwear. Or nothing," I suggest with an impish grin. "I'm game if you are."

Yes! Score another blush. And he thought *I'd* be the innocent one. I start rifling through my freshly packed suitcase for my bikini.

"I'll sit nearby and watch you."

As I pull out the bikini, I raise an eyebrow. "Oh, so that's what you're into, Blondie? Think that can be accommodated."

"That's not—I ..." he says, flustered and now red as a stop sign.

I giggle. "You are adorable, you know that? Really." I give him a big smile. "Be out in a minute, handsome."

I close the bathroom door and begin undressing, a thrilling tingle sparking my motor to life. Maybe I should reinstitute Project Rollercoaster. The blushing virgin routine is tantalizing for damn sure. I have cured one or two men of that affliction in my time when I felt like a challenge. Most of the time I go for the cocky, smooth type. Less work. Still ...

I apprize my naked body and grimace. He's right, I am too skinny. I can count my ribs, my stomach's concave, and I've definitely gone down to an A-cup. Not to mention the bruises from last night, the semi-brother factor, and I'm not a hundred percent sure he's into me. Hell, I'm not even sure he *likes* me. Of course that never stopped men before. I'll play it by ear. I put on my tiny yellow polka-dot bikini, emphasis on *tiny*, and check for coverage. Thank God for cardio kickboxing. I may resemble Olive Oyl, if she had toned legs and ass. If this doesn't do it ... *no*. Seriously, what the hell am I thinking? No, it's too complicated, which I avoid like a child does a trip to the doctor. We—

When I open the door, and Jason sets eyes on me, second thoughts about aborting the plan overload my brain. I'd recognize that hunger anywhere, especially those ravenous eyes as his gaze moves down my body. He drinks me in, mouth opening millimeter by millimeter as his gaze moves up. I don't have to be a werewolf to smell his lust from here. Well, one question answered. Fuck it. Rollercoaster's a go.

"Like it?" I ask, caressing the strap of the top. "I always wanted an itsy bitsy, teeny weenie, yellow polka-dot bikini. Just hope it doesn't fall off like in the song."

He tears his eyes off my flesh. "Um, yeah."

I smile to myself and reach back into the bathroom for a towel. "You gonna need a towel too?"

"Um, no."

"Too bad." I turn back to him with a grin. "I'm dying to see if you're a boxers or briefs man." My eyes graze his crotch, which is bulging more than it was before. "Of course I'm sure I'll find out eventually. Ready to guard my body, Blondie?"

As we meander down the hall, I make sure to walk ahead of him and sway my hips a little. I may not have much, but I do know how to use what I do. I don't glance back all the way down the hall, but I'd bet even money his eyes don't leave my swishing ass. If you got it, flaunt it.

The pool is small and missing a few tiles, but the water's clear. We're the only people out here enjoying the desert evening, but in the room right across it sounds like someone's auditioning for a porno. Mood music. As I lay my towel on the lounge chair, Jason keeps glancing at the room. Though the only light comes from the glow of the pool, I can tell he's blushing again. I love it. "Someone's having fun," I say. "Or doing a very good job at faking it." I wink, and his eyes immediately avert down.

I wade into the pool and let out a deep sigh. The water's amazing against my hot skin. There's nothing like a cool pool on a hot summer night. "Holy shit, Blondie, you need to get in here. You don't know what you're missing."

"No, thank you," he says from his seat.

"What if I promise not to look when you undress? Cross my heart?" I say as I physically do it.

"I'm fine."

"Your loss, handsome." I just float on my back for a few seconds, staring up at the stars and moon just peeking out. I never get to see them in California. The moon is especially gorgeous as a wispy cloud passes across it. I don't think I'll ever look at a full moon the same again. "Does it hurt when you change into a werewolf?"

"Yes. Very much so."

"Do you walk on two legs or four?"

"Four. We resemble wolves in every way except size. We're bigger."

"Huh. I always liked wolves. Saw one in a zoo once. I wanted to reach through the bars to pet it *so* bad. I even snuck away from Mom and Barry so I could go and watch it some more. Took them an hour to find me. Or to notice I was even gone, not sure. I begged them for a Siberian Husky after that, but Mom's allergic." I chuckle. "Define irony, huh? A woman allergic to dogs ends up married to a werewolf. She was literally allergic to her husband. Maybe that's why she kicked him to the curb."

"It wouldn't have affected her. He would have been locked up, away from her, in wolf form unless on pack property. It's the law."

I stand up to look at him, brow furrowed. "Why? Are you that dangerous?"

"We're like any other wild animal. Caution is required."

"That must put a damper on the old love life, huh? Most women won't even tolerate hairy backs, let alone fur all over. Not to mention how to even tell her. 'Hey, babe, I'm a mythical creature who wants to eat you at least once a month.' Imagine it'd be a deal breaker for a lot of chicks. Unless you're a player, then you don't really need to tell them."

"A player?"

"You know: wham, bam, thank you ma'am, gotta jam?" He blinks. "One-night stands? Casual sex? Sex, then you never see her again?" Oh, please don't let him be a virgin. Even I have some scruples.

"Oh. I attempted casual sex on one occasion at Tate's urging. I did not enjoy it. It was ... hollow. I did not particularly like her beyond the physical."

"So you're a romantic," I say with approval. "Don't meet many of you anymore. Makes sense, though. Aren't wolves monogamous?"

Even in the dim light I can see him turning away from me. "Yes."

"So, you just haven't found her yet. Don't worry, I'm sure you will." I float flat on my back again. "Doesn't mean you can't have fun in the meantime. Just because you didn't like something once doesn't mean you should give up on it. I hated veggie burgers at first, now I love them. If at first you don't succeed, try, try again and all. That's my motto. Like marriage. I had a crappy first one, doesn't mean I don't want to try it again should the opportunity arise."

"I do not wish to continue with this topic of conversation."

Damn. "Then what do *you* want to talk about, Blondie?" I flip over and start stroking toward him from the far end of the pool. "Come on. Ask me anything." I rest my chin on the edge of the pool and gaze up at him with wide eyes and a sex kitten pout that's brought many a man to his knees. Literally. "I promise to tell the truth even. You must have a million questions for your long-lost little sister. Come on. I'm an open book. Start reading, handsome."

His eyes narrow a little to study me for artifice. This cat really needs to work on his trust issues, and that's coming from *me*. When they return to normal size, he asks, "Why do you hate yourself?"

"Uh…" Okay, not expecting that. I have no idea what to say except, "I-I-I don't hate myself. Why the hell would you think that?"

"I've watched you. You don't take care of your body. You don't eat, you drink too much, you engage in reckless behavior, you … give yourself freely to strangers. In my experience only people who have little regard for their life engage in such activity. Even when you sing, the majority of the time there is no joy in it. I wonder why."

With every fiber of my being I want Donovan to show up and shoot Jason or me or both of us in the fucking head. Don't care which, so long as I do not have to answer that question or be examined by his apathetic eyes. This isn't fun anymore. If I wanted a therapy session, I'd go back to Dr. Cruz. I only lasted three sessions because I felt like shit for days after. But I promised I'd answer. I'm trapped by my own master plan.

"I don't hate myself," I begin. "I don't eat because I have to stay thin. No one signs or hires fat singers. End of story. Blame society for that one. I drink because I work in a bar and the tips are better if I drink with the customers. And I give my body freely to strangers, as you so judgmentally put it, because I enjoy sex. It's fun. It feels good. As for the no joy while I was singing…"

I shake my head. "I've been trying to launch my career for thirteen years and the farthest I've gotten is wedding singer, which is about one step up from hustling karaoke contests, which I still sometimes do when rent is due. I turn thirty in a few days. In show business if you haven't been discovered by then, you have a better chance of winning the lotto *while* being struck by lightning than getting signed. Doesn't help that I can't write a song or dance to save my life. You can only live on hope for so long before real hunger finds you. But, if I give up, then all my sacrifice, all that hard work, will have been for nothing. I'm stuck on a damn treadmill with no stop button." I scoff. "Not that I really want off because all I've ever had was that treadmill. It's all that's kept me going. I have nothing else. No husband, no kids, no college education. If I get off, all that surrounds me is uncertainty, desolation, and the fact I just wasn't good enough."

Jesus Christ, I've never told anyone this. These thoughts have kept me awake so many nights, in the past year especially, but I've never said them out loud for this very reason. My stomach churns as my hands shake in rhythm. Because it's all true. I am well and completely fucked. Hell, I don't even enjoy singing anymore. I haven't for years. And it's not as if I haven't done all I could to make it. I did everything right. I spent over ten thousand dollars on vocal lessons, I learned guitar, I sang in clubs, I went to every audition I could, I charmed the few producers and managers I could get close to, and still nothing. There is *nothing* more I can do. And what do I have to show for it? Fifteen grand in credit card debt, a shitty apartment, and dreading doing the one thing I used to love. I've wasted my youth on a pipe dream just like Mom said. Even if I make it back to California, there's nothing for me there. It's over. There's no hope left in me. The treadmill's broken.

Jason's voice jars me out of Depressionville. I was so deep in there, I momentarily forgot he existed. My gaze whips up to his, which is of course blank. "What?" I ask.

"I think you sing beautifully, especially when you're putting your soul into it. You're … haunting."

I open my mouth to protest, but find myself saying, "Thank you."

I meet his eyes and he immediately looks away, I think he's ashamed for some reason. "Just my opinion. I don't know much about music."

"Still. Never been called haunting before." I swim backwards with a smile. "Kind of like it."

"It's accurate," he says, eyes jutting everywhere but my way.

"Too bad you're not a record producer, huh?" I reach the other side before turning around to swim back. "Got anymore questions for me, Blondie?"

"No."

I hold onto the side again. "Come on. There must be something else."

"No. My questions upset you. That's the last thing I want."

He's got me there. Despite the compliment, I'm close to panic and on the verge of tears again. I thought "Come to Jesus" moments were supposed to make you feel good, full of potential, not like slitting your fucking wrists. That's why I avoid self-reflection at all costs. Not once have I ever found anything I liked. So I do what I always do, distract myself with something handsome. "You're really a great guy, you know that? That's rare, especially in someone as good looking as you."

"It is?" he asks.

I start wading toward the steps. "Yeah. Most drop-dead gorgeous men are total assholes. Arrogant. Selfish." I stroll beside him, slowly bending down to grab my towel. "Especially in bed." I meet his eyes again with a grin. "You're none of those things, are you?"

He looks away. "I can be."

"I very much doubt that, Blondie," I say, toweling myself off. "From what little I know, I don't think you have a selfish bone in your body. Fact you're here with me proves that. Deep down you're just a big old puppy dog, aren't ya? Don't worry. I won't tell a soul." I wrap the towel around myself and wring out my hair. "Enough with the outside exercise, huh? Time for bed."

With a coy glance, I sashay in front of him to our room. When I step into our future love shack, I drop the towel halfway to the bed, and once again bend at the waist to rummage around my suitcase for the toiletry bag. I glance over at Jason, who hangs by the door with his back against it again. Wonder if he's afraid of me or himself. Either way it's a good sign. "I call first shower," I say.

"Fine," he says gruffly.

I retrieve the bag and smirk at the damn near scowling werewolf on my way to the bathroom. I shut the door and let out a quiet sigh. The only problem with a challenge is I have to do all the heavy lifting and have patience, neither of which are my strong suits. I've learned *they* have to make the first move, or they'll get scared away. It is a pain in the ass, but the few times I've bothered it ended up being worth it.

I turn on the shower, count to three, then let out a loud groan. This should do the trick. I pad out of the bathroom and sigh. Jason is by the bed dumping out his K-Mart bags. "Jason, I can't get the knot undone on my top. I tied it funny. Can you ..."

"Um ... okay."

I pivot around and slowly brush my hair to the side. There's only an inch between us, close enough I can enjoy the intense heat radiating from his body onto my bare flesh. Tickles all over. *Every-*

where. I glance back to watch as Jason hesitantly raises his hands to my neck. For some reason they're balled into fists until he forces himself to unknot me. His pinky brushes against my wet, naked skin, sending another wave of tingles through me. Over too soon. He quickly unties the knot and yanks his hands away. My top falls, but I hold it in place with my arm to cover myself. "Thank you," I say as I twirl around. I peek up at him under my eyelashes, forming my best seductive smile.

He's stopped breathing. Stopped blinking even. His hands are fists again, his face his usual mask of nothingness, but there's a trace of turmoil revolving in those eyes. He wants me. *Bad*. I can even smell it oozing from his every pore. I want him too. Every nerve calls to him. Just this, him being so close, those raw eyes on me and only me, I'm literally pulsing for him. Burning for him to be inside me. When it becomes a three-alarm fire, I raise my free hand to touch his stubbled face, to caress it.

Mistake.

The instant I move, the spell is broken. He blinks and the chaos vanishes, replaced with something akin to fright. Jason takes a step back. "You should take your shower now."

Mortification acts like an allergic reaction, squeezing my throat closed. He has got to be fucking kidding. What am I, a crone with warts dotting her body? I'm all but naked and throwing myself at him, and he's rejecting me? For the first time in years I feel … vulnerable. I fucking hate it. "Fine." He takes another step back, probably in case I attempt to touch him again. I don't. I walk to the safety of the bathroom and shut the door. *That* could have gone better.

I step into the shower and let the grime of the past two days slosh off. The stench of failure too. I haven't been rejected so outright like that since puberty. What the hell is his problem? I know he said he wasn't into casual sex, but he's still a man. Sort of. He wants me, any fool can sense that. So it's not me, it's him. I just have to convince him to give in. Take a walk on the wild side. Good thing I'm a licensed tour guide there.

A setback. That was merely a setback. I shouldn't have tried to touch him like that. I knew better. Just couldn't help myself. Not again. He's a tough nut to crack, one swift wallop won't do it. Slowly wearing away at the shell at pressure points will. His resistance *will* crumble. It's already begun to. Poor bastard doesn't stand a chance.

Don't know if it's the shower or pep talk but I feel a hell of a lot better when I shut off the water ten minutes later. Smell better too. I wrap the tiny towel around myself, brush my teeth, grab the toiletry bag, and step out. Time to add some pressure. Blondie is over by the bed folding his new wardrobe while watching *Die Hard* or at least that's what I think it is. The picture's so fuzzy it could be *Friends* for all I know. He stops mid-fold when I open the door, face impassive as usual. "Bathroom's all yours," I say with a sweet smile.

"Uh, thank you," he says, eyes down.

I swish over to the other side of the bed with my smile affixed. My prey continues his chore, glancing up only as I sit across from him. He glances again when I throw up a leg onto the bed and open the lotion bottle. "If you want," I say nonchalantly as I massage lotion onto my leg, "I can finish packing for you while you shower." I catch his eyes, which are glued to my exposed leg. For a split second, he's startled at being caught, mouth gaping over for a millisecond, but

I just grin. "I don't mind. Really. The sooner you shower, the sooner we can ... go to bed." I switch legs. "I don't know about you, but I'm just dying to slide under the sheets. I'm betting the feeling's mutual." Literally.

Jason grunts in affirmation as he diverts those eyes of his back to his clothes. Damn. I lower my leg and start lathering my arms. Still not acknowledging my presence, my shy friend grabs some clothes. "I'll, um, be quick."

"I'll be waiting," I say in a dusky voice as he rushes into the bathroom. He is so freaking adorable I can hardly stand it. Facing two werewolves with guns, cool as hell. Flash him a little leg, he becomes as flustered as a teenage girl around her celebrity heartthrob. He better be careful, the flattery will stretch my already overinflated self-image to the breaking point.

I reach for our suitcase, pulling it closer. What to wear, what to wear. Normally I sleep au natural, but since Blondie's kind of a prude, he'd have a coronary if I was totally nude when he came out. The pajamas I bought are drab, shirts and long pants, but I could probably get away with a white thong and pink tank top. Slutty, yet girl next door. Perfect.

I change, adding white socks and braided pigtails to up the cutesie factor, then start packing as I promised. Should the shit hit the fan, and we need a quick getaway, I don't want to have to go on another shopping spree. There's no way in hell they'll find us but still. Safe, sorry and all that jazz.

Blondie's in the shower awhile, long enough for me to pack and apply a little makeup. I check myself in the mirror and smirk. Damn am I adorable. Close to irresistible. Up the sex kitten routine a tad more and despite this idiotic reluctance of his, I may just get my rollercoaster ride. Oh. Condoms. We didn't buy any. Well, he did say he can't get diseases, and I do have a year left with my IUD. I don't—

Jason's cell phone rings on the table. I glance over to read the display. With that one word my throat closes up.

Dad.

Shit. My first impulse is to toss the cell across the room, smash it into nothing, but my second is much stronger. Overpowering even. I swore to myself if the bastard ever reached out, a letter, a phone call, candygram, I'd never respond. Not even a, "Fuck you." Werewolves trying to kill me kind of blew that plan. I'm going to be stuck in his house for the foreseeable future. Gonna be hard to avoid him. Fuck it. I pick up the cell and accept the call before I can stop myself. "J-Jason's phone."

There's silence on the other end for a drawn-out second, then, "Vivian?"

Holy shit. That single word knocks the wind out of me. That's my father. That's my father on the other end of the phone. His voice. That's what he sounds like. His voice isn't as deep as I imagined. Of course I always thought he'd sound like Harrison Ford for some reason. Don't know why I was always casting Ford as my dad. I did like *Raiders* as a child. Still, it—

"Vivi, are you still there?"

My real father's voice snaps me out of the mental stupor I didn't realize I was in. "Y-Yes, I'm here. Sorry." Why the fuck am I apologizing to him?

"Are-Are you alright? How-How are you doing?" he asks nervously.

"F-Fine. W-We're safe. Stopped for the night to get some rest."

"Good." A pause. "That's good."

More unbearable silence follows. I have no idea what to say. I always thought I'd scream or cuss or cry. Tell him what an asshole he was. How I didn't need him. How I hoped he'd get cancer. Just thinking these things made me upset, angrier than normal even, so I put a stop to them and decided if he did reach out I'd ignore the gesture. Now the moment's arrived, and I just feel … exhausted. Uncomfortable. Awkward. As if I'm stuck in a conversation with a stranger who I have nothing in common with. I just want it to end and walk away. It is an option. "Um … Jason's in the shower right now."

"Oh," Frank says, sounding shocked for some reason. "Is he … how are you two getting along? Any troubles?"

"No. He's … good. Quiet, but seems to be very good at what he does."

"He is. There is no one I trust more with my life. Or yours."

"Oh. Good … to know." Another pause. "So, I'm gonna … I'll tell Jason you called."

"Thank you."

"Well, then … bye."

I'm about to end the call when he says, "Vivi?"

"Yeah?"

"I'm sorry. For … everything."

Silence, then, "Okay. Bye." I hang up before he can utter another word.

I stare down at the phone, not sure what to do next. I just spoke to my father. He's … real. I slump on the bed and keep staring. Shit, I'm really going to meet him. In a matter of days we're going to be face-to-face. He won't be this mythic monster I've created, who I've hung all my hatred on. He is a real man who breathes, sleeps, who kept tabs on me, apparently came to see me sing once, who sent his top man to save my life.

"Are you alright?"

My gaze whips from the damn phone to the bathroom door. I was so deep in thought I didn't hear the shower shut off. Jason's dressed in black sweat pants and white undershirt, his f.r.e.a.k.s. series blonde hair dripping. The shirt clings to his every muscle but my usual lust doesn't rise. I feel nothing. Uncomfortably numb. "What?"

"You're upset again," he says, once again confused.

"I'm…" No idea. "Da—*Frank* called. I'm sorry, I answered it." I hold up the phone. "I know I shouldn't have but…"

"It's fine," Jason says, taking the cell. He stands above me, those blue eyes examining me again. I suddenly feel more than a little naked, probably because I almost am. "Did he say something?"

I know he means did Frank say something to upset me, but I don't want to discuss it. "He just wants you to call him back." I grab the suitcase for something to do. I can't stand him looking at me anymore.

He gets the hint this time. "Okay. I'll, uh, go outside."

"Fine."

Jason hangs his head before walking out. I stop searching for nothing inside the suitcase the moment the door shuts. So much for my seduction scene. Even if he did want to get it on, I sure as hell don't anymore. Nothing kills the mood like having a head full of your father. I quickly remove my thong, exchanging it for pajama pants before turning off the TV.

"… no, it's fine. I think we have enough," Jason says outside. I stop moving. I shouldn't listen, I know this… "Nothing since last night. Anything on the car?" Quiet. "She switched the plates so it shouldn't be a problem unless we're pulled over." Silence. "Actually, very well. She's been clear minded. Helpful. No breakdowns. She is definitely a Dahl." That one brings a smile to my face. I've impressed him. Doubt that's an easy feat. "I won't, sir." Quiet. "Of course not, Dad. She's ... your daughter. I would never take advantage of your trust." *Huh?* "I know it's for both our sakes." Damn, I really want to hear what Frank's saying. "I know," Jason says, dejected. "I will. I love you too, Dad. Bye."

Shit. I rush over to the bed as Jason enters so I don't get caught eavesdropping. "Everything alright?" I ask.

He glances up at me, then back at the floor like a chastised child. "Fine." He moves over to the suitcase across from me. "I'm going to brush my teeth."

"Okay."

Head bowed, he finds the toiletry bag and walks into the bathroom, closing the door. Okay, what the fuck did Frank say to him? From the way he refuses to look at me *yet again*, I'm positive it had to do with me. Taking advantage of me? That's a laugh. If anyone's taking advantage, it's me. Obviously he's attracted to me. But ... *fuck*. I think I'm having a crisis of conscience. It only happens once every blue moon, so I can't be sure. Tiny pit in my stomach? Almost sour taste in my mouth? Tiny voice in my head that began shouting when I stepped out intent on seducing him? All present and annoying.

I'm torturing the guy, aren't I? In his mind, I'm his freaking sister. If he gave in, no doubt he'd end up hating himself. Or me. Especially if Frank, his mythic hero, got wind of it. Now I literally have a bad taste in my mouth. Damn it! God, I hate self-reflection. It's such a downer. Fucking conscience. Fine, you win this time. Hope you're happy. Fucker.

Jason steps out of the bathroom just as I pull the sheets back on the bed to get in. I glance over but that handsome head of his is still hung and mouth set with a scowl. Who's he angry with, me, Frank or himself, I don't know. Probably the latter. He moves over to the suitcase now on the table to replace the toiletry bag as I climb into bed.

With his back to me, he says, "Can you please throw me the other pillow?"

"Why?"

"It would be safer if I slept by the door," he says, positioning the chair so its back is to the table.

"Safer?"

He places the pistol on the side of the table. "I can hear better from here."

"Don't be ridiculous. No one knows we're here. You need sleep. I'll be on my best behavior, I promise."

"I can sleep anywhere. I'll be fine. I'm sleeping here," he says with finality.

Wonderful. As if I wasn't feeling guilty enough as is. I toss him the pillow as he sits. I'm too tired to put up much more of a fight. I flop down onto my pillow and flip my back to him. A second later Jason shuts off the overhead light. Bedtime. Or that's the plan. Hard to put into practice though. I try to get comfortable, shifting around in the bed, but like the pillow the mattress is lumpy from overuse. Not that I could sleep on a cloud right now. With every creak of that chair he's in, my guilt wretches up a notch.

After about two minutes, it's cranked up to eleven. My eyes fly open. "Jason, for God's sake! Just get in the bed!"

"I'm fine here," he insists.

"Right. I also wiggle around like a Mexican Jumping Bean when I'm comfortable. You need sleep. We both do. We're safe here, okay? You're no good to either of us without a clear head. I'm sorry for earlier, alright? I just … it was stupid of me. I'm not going to say another word, and I am not going to touch you, I swear on Nina Simone's grave. I'm sorry I made you uncomfortable. I know I put you in an awkward position. I wasn't thinking. I am now. It will not happen again. So just … get in the fucking bed!"

There are a few tense, silent seconds before the chair creaks again as he rises. I keep my eyes shut as the bed shifts under his considerable bulk and the sound of him setting the gun on the nightstand. We lay back to back for a minute. Jason doesn't get under the covers but that could just be because the man is a walking furnace. His heat radiates against my back. It's not an unpleasant sensation, save for the tension I also sense wafting from him. The man's barely breathing.

"I am sorry, you know," I say. "I shouldn't have fucked with you like I did. It was a shitty thing to do. Are we alright?"

Silence, then, "May I ask you a question?"

"Anything."

"Why did you attempt to seduce me?"

A chuckle escapes. The man does love to go right to the heart of the matter. Cut through the bullshit. I can dig it. "I don't know. Thought it'd be fun. Thought you'd be good in bed. You're hot. I like you. You're saving my life, thought it'd be a good way to start repaying my debt. Pick one."

"You don't owe me a debt," he says. "And even if you did, you should not use your body to repay it. That's beneath you."

"That's not what I…" I groan in frustration. "I wanted to sleep with you because I wanted to sleep with you. It happens. But don't worry, the feeling has passed. Now just relax and go to sleep," I say harshly.

"Fine. Good night."

"Good night," I snap.

Blondie and I simply lay back to back inches away, but it may as well be miles. And once again I've fucked everything up with the one person who's trying to help me. Who I swore I wouldn't hurt. It is a gift. My only one.

FIVE

... THE FUCK?

The sudden spring in the bed jars me out of shallow sleep. Damn it, it took me an hour to push down the guilt enough for sleep to come, now this. The warmth behind me vanishes. Damn. My eyes flutter open, and I flip over. Quick as a cheetah, Jason moves toward the window, gun up and ready. That sight is like a shot of adrenaline to the heart, instantly waking me.

"What—"

"The dog's growling and barking," he says, peeking out of the curtains.

It's faint, but I hear the pit bull too. "So?"

"Did the same with me. It's threatened. Put on your shoes."

"This is rid—"

"Put your shoes on, Vivian," he orders, voice hard.

His tone sends a chill down my spine. I toss off the covers and rush over to him. His eyes never leave the crack in the curtains. "It's probably just—"

His head cocks to the side and eyes close to hear better. "Get the suitcase, cell phone, and car key." After slipping on my flip flops, I pull the suitcase off the table and grab the rest beside it. "Very quickly, I want you to run to the car and get in the driver's seat. Stay low and out of sight. Do not let your presence be known," he says, moving to the door then unlocking it. "Do not turn on the car. If something happens to me, drive and don't stop until Maryland."

"Jason—"

"Go. Now."

He flings open the door and steps out, gun first. He swings it left then right to cover me. Shit. I sprint the twenty feet to the car, pressing the button to unlock it. The adrenaline makes it difficult to keep my hands steady so I fumble with the handle. When I get it open, I toss the suitcase in the backseat then climb into the front. The moment the door shuts Jason retreats back into the room, quietly shutting the door. I slip the key into the ignition and wait.

The seconds drag like hours as I scan left to right. This is insane. We used cash. Fake names. The manager didn't even see Jason. The car's not visible from the highway. We didn't tell anyone the name or location of the motel. There is no way in hell . . .

The sight of Donovan rounding the corner with the manager knocks the damn wind from my lungs. How the fuck . . . ? As the motel manager points down the hall, Donovan's head starts turning my way. I crouch down as instructed. My breath escapes me in loud, short bursts so I cover my mouth to muffle the sound. Oh, please, please, *please* don't let him sense me. Oh, fuck. What do I do? Fuck. Plan. Need a—

The sound of splintering wood and a thud makes me peek up. Donovan enters our dark room, gun up and ready for damage. I jerk upright as a moment later there are two explosions of light and booms from his gun. That's the last I see of the fucker as he moves deeper into the dark. "Shit." Shit. W—

Gunshots right on top of each other reverberate through the otherwise still night from my room. I can't count them all. Four? Five? One punctures our room's window, then the Dodge Ram's front window beside me as well. "Shit." The barrage ceases, only to be replaced by a man's howl and breaking furniture. It's an old-fashioned werewolf brawl. There's a flash of movement inside as a body is tossed onto the bed. There are two more gunshots as I think Jason rolls off out of sight just in time. Bits of feather float up from my pillow that a little over a minute ago I was asleep on. Holy hell. Jason leaps up from the floor and charges like a bull just as another shot erupts. Something. I have to do something. I can't just sit here. What the hell can I do? Leave? I start the car. No. *No.* I wait for him. He—

Oh, thank you God.

Jason backs out of the door, firing another shot inside as Donovan, still cloaked in darkness, returns the fire. His bullet hits the doorframe inches from Jason's head as my protector shoots again. With his arm raised, I notice his white shirt sleeve is saturated with blood. He fires once more before the slide moves back. Out of bullets. Jason ducks right as Donovan fires again. Time to leave. I put my foot on the brake and shift into reverse as Jason zips toward the passenger's side. The millisecond his door shuts, I stomp the gas pedal. Donovan steps into view as I do, pistol pointed right at us. Shit! The bullet cracks both our windshield and back window, once again narrowly missing Jason, who ducked as I did. I slam on the brakes, shift into drive, and spin the wheel to get us the fuck out of here. So much for a restful night.

I have to break cover to see where I'm going. Donovan fires again, I think hitting the bumper, before sprinting after us in the parking lot as he shoots again. I yelp as the rearview mirror explodes, raining plastic and glass over us and the dash. Better it than my head. I jerk the wheel to the right to maneuver us out of the lot with Donovan way too close behind. The man can move, I'll give him that. Jason opens the glove box, retrieving another clip as I gun it down the deserted road toward the highway. He grimaces as he pushes in the clip.

"Are you okay?" I ask, glimpsing at his bloody arm.

"Just keep going," he orders through gritted teeth. Not a problem. Don't think I could let up on the gas pedal even with a crowbar. With another grimace, Jason pivots around to watch out the back window. "Shit."

Checking the side mirror, I see headlights barreling toward us. And gaining. Not good. I punch the gas pedal down to the floor, picking up speed. I make a hard right onto the highway ramp and for a split second lose control, back tires skidding. I brake hard and turn the wheel to gain control again, then punch the gas to get us revving again. We lose another second we don't have as the tires spin in place before the car jerks forward like a rocket. Of course Donovan uses my miscalculations to bridge the gap between us. The Civic is a great car, but its pick-up sucks. Too damn slow. Donovan's five car lengths behind, then three. Two.

When we merge onto the highway, the bastard's right on our bumper. Jason rolls down his window, leaning out of it. Taking quick aim he fires, cracking Donovan's windshield. The Marshal swerves, then Jason aims lower to strike again. There's a spark on the pavement near Donovan's front tire. I'm so immersed in watching this in my side mirror I almost hit the semi-truck in front of us. We'd smash into it if I didn't switch lanes in time. *Pay attention, idiot.*

Donovan mimics my swift move into our lane, right before ramming into us. Jason roars in pain as his bad arm smacks into the side of the window as we crash back and forth. He falls back into his seat, clutching onto his bad arm and wincing.

"Are you—"

Donovan rams us again. Fuck. I lose the grip on the wheel. We twist out of control, left, right, left, almost off the damn road, until I grab the wheel to straighten us out. *No matter what, do not let go of this wheel, Viv.* I keep a vice grip on it as he smashes us again. And again. And again, my companion groaning in agony with each assault. This is bullshit. Another car appears in front of an SUV, and I pass it with Donovan as my shadow. Except he moves into the parallel lane and speeds up. He's beside us. He's going to swerve into us, force us off the road or be close enough to aim. Either way we're screwed.

I hate being right sometimes. He collides against Jason's side. I can barely maintain control as half of our car slides into the grass. Donovan is now a car length ahead as I straighten and return us to the asphalt. He slows to smash us again. Another car appears in his lane. Donovan pumps the brakes to change lanes. He's behind us again, then moves again to our right when its clear. Next time he'll really do it. He'll hit us with the force of all of the car's tons. We'll probably flip over and either die then or he'll walk over to the crash and shoot us in the head. Fuck that.

The world slows to a crawl and all its working parts crystallize in my mind. The distance between the car behind us and Donovan. The angle of his current swerve. The amount of time it'll take for him to smash us. Jason beside me slowly raising his gun in preparation for the onslaught. I relinquish all control to the reptilian section of my brain. Just as Donovan's car completes its move to the right lane, I slam on the brakes. The force slaps us both to the back of our seats but the reptile barely notices. She's too happy that we're stopping. "Jason, tires!" Donovan continues forward for a millisecond before he brakes too. Jason only has that moment to lean out the window again and take aim. Damn good thing his reptile is just as badass as mine.

When he's out, gun ready, I punch the gas again. Our car remains stationary for a second, tires skidding on asphalt, then jerks forward again. The moment it does, Jason fires twice at Donovan's still slowing car. Despite the smoke brimming from the burning rubber, I can tell one of the bullets hits home from the loud pop. Donovan's car lurches to and fro like a drunk as he loses control. I maneuver us past him as the SUV Donovan just passed, who isn't as fast on the brakes as the Marshal, clips his left bumper. Donovan's car does a full one eighty into the SUV, walloping them both off on the side of the road into a cloud of dust. I keep the pedal to the fucking metal until they're out of sight, and I say a silent prayer for the SUV driver. Donovan's on his own.

Jason thumps back into his seat with a groan. I'm too amped up to pay him much attention. I'm focused on the road. *The road.* We can't stay on the highway. Police are probably on their way.

The werewolves know we're using it. Once again, the reptile takes the wheel. Before I realize it, my foot touches the brake again. "What are you doing?" Jason asks through his heavy pants.

I slow enough so we can safely veer left onto the sandy divider. We switch from the eastbound lanes to westbound, back the way we came. "They'll be looking for us on 80. We can't use it anymore. We're ten minutes from the Utah border. It'll take time for the Wyoming cops to coordinate with the Utah state police. We go back to I-15 then I-70 and switch cars when we can." Within seconds, we pass the accident site. Thank God. The SUV driver stands outside his car, talking on his cell phone. I don't see Donovan, but his car remains still. Too bad. I had hoped it flipped or exploded. I'll have to settle for out of commission.

We drive a mile. Two. "You should, uh, slow down," Jason says, or really moans. I glance at the speedometer. Shit, I'm doing ninety. I decelerate to seventy and loosen my grip on the wheel, which proves difficult. My hands may as well be superglued into position. Damn, my fingers are numb and I wiggle them to bring back sensation. Another mile and my breathing normalizes. The hypervigilance fades enough for me to stop scanning the periphery for cops or other dangers. Nothing. Another mile, and I realize I'm not alone in the car. I glance at Jason who is clutching his blood-soaked arm.

Oh, shit.

Now that it has time, my brain processes just how bad a shape he's in. The back of his head has a gash that isn't bleeding anymore but was bad judging from the fact his blonde hair is now red and tacky, along with his neck. His right cheek is swollen as if he has an egg underneath. Of course the biggest concern is his still-bleeding bicep. He moves his hand enough for me to see the wound. The saturated shirt is almost glued to his arm, especially where the bullet entered. Bullet. Which means … "Holy shit, you're shot!"

"Yeah," he whispers.

"Jason, you—"

"Just keep driving," he orders, pressing the wound.

He's right. We need more distance between us and the crash. All I can do is keep my foot on the accelerator, one eye on the road, and the other on him. He removes his hand again, and mutters, "Fuck."

"What?"

After he turns on the light above, he puts pressure on the hole again. I tense as he slams his head a few times on the headrest in frustration. "Silver," he winces through gritted teeth. "Still in there. Won't stop bleeding."

"Jason …"

"Just drive."

I do. He takes a few deep, cringing breaths, then moves his hand again. Blood spews in a steady stream as he removes his shirt from the right side first. When it comes time for the left, he whimpers as he slowly peels the sleeve off. Oh my God, that's fucking disgusting. The wound looks like it's exploded outward, and I can make out the pinkish muscle inside. Stinging bile rises up my throat, but I swallow it down. The car's disgusting enough without adding vomit to the mix. Jason's panting just from the effort of this simple task. "I'm going …" He takes another breath, "… take the wheel. You … tourniquet with shirt. Tight." He tosses the drenched shirt into my lap. "Ready?"

I nod. He leans over, good hand on the wheel and wound right beside my face. More bile rises, but as I wrap the shirt over the grotesque hole, my automatic pilot pushes it down. I make a knot and yank it tight. Jason cries out in pain and releases the wheel. I quickly reclaim it as he falls back into his seat. He closes his eyes and pants.

"J-Jason, that's not going to do much good. You need a doctor."

"No, just … give me a minute to think. Just drive."

God, the pain must be insane. I don't want to even imagine it. Instead, I keep driving. He's been shot before, or at least had more experience with it than me. And he's a werewolf. Super-healing. What might kill me is just a flesh wound to him. *Just keep going. Get out of the damn state. That's your only job, Viv.* Carrying us forward to safety. Don't fuck it up.

When we cross the state border back into Utah, his panting has lessened. It's about ninety minutes to Salt Lake and the interchange. We'll lose about five hours getting to I-70. Definitely need to ditch the car. I'm positive there's exterior damage, not to mention the bullet holes in the windows. The sooner the better. I check the clock. A little past three AM. Shopping centers are out. Hotels will have the best selection. Ten, twenty miles, then I'll pull off, do the exchange, haul ass. I got this. I chuckle. Who'd a thunk I'd be so good in a crisis.

"Okay, Jason, we're—"

I glance right, and my throat closes tighter than a nun's legs at an orgy. Jason's head bobs to the right in time to the movement of the car, eyes shut and jaw open. "Jason?" I touch his face. His skin feels normal to me but not his usual raging inferno. Think this is the werewolf version of clammy. "Jason?" I shout. Nothing. I give his face a slap. He doesn't even stir. I glance at his exposed chest. It doesn't move. Oh God, he's dead. His … no, his chest moves up and down as he takes shallow breaths. Mine comes out in ragged spurts and tears rise to my eyes. Thank God. Thank you, God.

The tears spill out regardless of how hard I'm trying to banish them. Crying won't do any damn good. He needs me strong, thinking clearly, not a pathetic fucking girl. He may not be dead, but he could be dying. I have to do something.

After several deep breaths, my tears haven't ceased but the panic has cleared enough that logic can find its way through the fog. Plan. Need a plan. And what I come up with is … fuck all. All I know about gunshot wounds are if you get one it's go straight to the hospital and pray. I can't bring him there because we're wanted fugitives. Oh, and he's a freaking werewolf. Werewolf. Werewolf …

I check around for the cell phone Jason gave me. Can't find it, not even when I feel around in the back. Just as I turn front again, a minivan has materialized from nowhere. I swerve into the other lane just in time. Not even this rouses Jason. Okay, okay, I have to pull over and tend to him. Stop the bleeding. No choice. I take the next exit a mile down. There's nothing around. No lights or houses, just infinite darkness. I drive down the two-lane road for a half mile before maneuvering down another and pulling to the side. I leap out of the car, the cold desert night adding goosebumps to my goosebumps. I find the cell underneath my seat. First-aid kit too. I collect both and hit redial.

"Jason?" Frank asks on the other end after four rings.

"Frank, it's Viv. Jason, he's … been shot," I say, voice cracking. "He-He-He won't wake up. I don't-I don't know what to do-do." Shit, I can't even talk.

"Vivi, doll face, calm down. Calm down," he orders. "Take a deep breath." I listen to the man. It helps a miniscule bit. "Good girl. Now, where was he shot? Was it silver?"

"The arm, and I-I think he said it was silver. It won't stop bleeding."

"Okay. Are you safe?"

"I-I guess. The police are probably looking for us. I don't think Donovan's dead."

"But you're not in immediate physical danger?"

"No."

"Good. Okay, do you have a sewing kit? First-aid kit?"

"First-aid. W-Why?" Stupid question. I already know the answer but my brain won't accept it.

"If he hasn't started recovering by now, then it was definitely a silver bullet. The only way for him to heal before he bleeds out is for him to turn, at least where the wound is. But the bullet has to come out first or when he shifts it'll cause more internal damage."

"You want me to dig the bullet out of his arm? Are you fucking crazy?"

"Vivi, you *have* to do this. It sounds as if it nicked an artery. He will continue to bleed, and he will die. Doll face, you can do this. I know you can."

I can do this. *I* can do this. I *can* do this. "O-Okay."

With my quaking hands, I switch the phone to speaker before setting it and the first-aid kit on the hood. Inside the kit are the basics: gauze, tape, burn cream, aspirin, and plastic tweezers. My throat snaps shut at the sight of the last one. I can *do* this. It's damn near impossible to slap on the latex gloves as my fingers won't stop twitching. I can't even put gloves on, how the hell am

I supposed to get a damn bullet out? "Frank, my hands are barely working. I can't—"

"You can," he insists, voice hard. "You have to."

I have to. Right. Fuck.

It takes two attempts, but I manage to pick up the tweezers and cell before moving to the driver's door. Jason's still unconscious and the shirt covering the wound grows redder by the second. I set the cell phone on the dash. *I can do this.*

"You have to wake Jason up if you can. The pain will do it, but he may attack on instinct if he's not aware what's occurring right away."

"Right." I quickly get out to retrieve the smelling salts. They work for Victorian ladies, why not a two-hundred-plus werewolf? I snap the packet open under Jason's nose. Damned if he doesn't jerk awake.

"What the—"

"Jason, it's Dad," Frank says over the speaker. Jason's a little out of it so he glances around for the source. "Vivi needs to get that bullet out so you can change."

"Dad..." he says, still searching.

"He's on the phone," I tell him.

"You need to keep incredibly still for her. Vivi, see if you can locate something for him to bite down on."

"Um..." I spot a shell casing on the floor. I grab it and hand it to Jason, who wearily stares at me. "It's good enough for Clint Eastwood."

Despite the pain, Jason quickly smiles then opens his mouth. He actually bites the bullet. Okay... here goes. I untie the tourniquet. Oh, shit. I manage to poke my head out of the car to dry heave. I think I can see bone amid the gore. That is so fucking disgusting.

"Vivi?" Frank asks.

"I'm okay," I pant. I sit up inside the car. "I'm good." I glance at the stoic Jason. "Sorry."

"You can do this," he says through the bullet. "I believe in you."

Those words bring fresh tears to my eyes. "Thank you." He nods.

Just get it the fuck over with. I take another deep breath, snatch the tweezers from the dash, and before I lose what little bravery I ever possessed, I plunge them into his arm. Jason moans in pain. As the blood pours out onto my hands in gushes, and the moans become groans, I move deeper until the tweezers are halfway inside his body. I'm too busy to force the vomit back down my throat but do keep it in my mouth. I hit something. I grab the bullet, yanking it to the surface. The moment it's out, I vault from the car and throw up. Twice. Oh, Jesus. My stomach seizes a third time but nothing comes out. Fuck. At least I didn't puke on Jason.

I take a few seconds to collect myself, panting the freezing night air in and out before I return to the patient. He's taken over, pressing the shirt against the hemorrhaging wound. Not even cloth can soak up all the blood. "Jason? Jason, talk to me!" Frank shouts. Shit. He's fading. Jason's eyelids lower like a slow curtain. He's passing out again.

I give his face a hard slap, leaving my handprint in his own blood. "Wake up!" I shout.

Jason jerks back to consciousness. "Don't do—"

"Jason Sergei Dahl, this is your Alpha speaking," Frank says in a harsh tone. "Listen to me, Beta. You will change, do you hear me? That is an order."

"I don't think I c—" Jason says weakly.

"*An order, son,*" the Alpha snaps, voice steel mixed with diamonds. "You will change, and you will *only* change your injured arm. You will control your beast. You will do this for Vivian, do you hear me? She needs you, son."

"She needs me…" he whispers.

"She needs you healthy, whole, and intact. So no matter how weak you may feel, you will change your arm and only your arm. For Vivian."

"For Vivian…" He nods. His eyes close again as his jaw sets tight. For a second I think he's passed out again. Then his brow furrows as if he's deep in thought. A second after that, his face contorts in pain, though this time he doesn't scream.

"Jason?" I ask.

Holy shit, a thick, mucous gel-like substance sluices from the pores on his arm, mixing with the already present blood. Oh, that is rank. "Get out," he says. "Get away."

"Listen to him, Vivi," Frank says. "Get out of the car."

Don't need to tell me twice. The sickening crack of tendons and bones breaking as tan, slime-colored fur sprouts, rocks my already tender stomach. I grab the cell and spring out of the car, walking toward the trunk and setting the phone on it. Jason's whimpers and groans echo through the night. I wonder which hurts more, a gunshot or changing into a wolf?

"Vivi, are you alright?" Frank asks.

I glance down at myself. I'm splattered with blood like a disgusting Pollack painting. "I-I'm fine." I yank off the gloves with a shudder.

"Listen, he's very weak. On the off chance he goes into full transformation, I want you to lock yourself in the car, alright? Drive away if necessary. You can always come back for him in the morning."

"O-Okay."

"What about you? Are you injured?"

"No. I—I'm fine." I wipe a stray tear. "Relatively."

"Good. Good." He pauses. "I'm proud of you."

Don't know what it is about those words, but they're like a knife into my already tender gut. I can't take any more emotional upheavals tonight. "Okay, um, I'm gonna go now. I need to go. I have to go. We have to get out of here. Bye."

"Vivi—"

"Oh, uh, thank you." I end the call.

Okay. Okay. It's over. The worst is over. I'm alive, Jason's alive, judging from the noise in the car. We just have to keep moving. Keep going. Just not this second. I give myself a minute to calm down, but I can't stop shaking. Large, spastic quakes like an epileptic's. Adrenaline overdose along with the fact it's freezing. Stupid desert. Rubbing my arms helps both problems. Except I can't unglue my eyes from the blood all over me. A clear, icicle chill rocks my body. Clean. I have to get clean. I glance behind into the car. Jason's gone silent, but as far as I can see is still human. He lays on his right side with his eyes closed. Thank God. I don't think I could handle werewolf wrangling right now. Hell, I don't think I can handle speech right now.

The suitcase and water bottles are in the backseat where we left them. I grab a water bottle from the pack on the floor and unzip the suitcase, pulling out a long-sleeve black shirt and slacks. I change my pants first, then pull off the ruined tank top. My arms, upper chest, even my face are caked in sticky, disgusting blood. I pour the water on myself and scrub with the tank top. I think I take more whore's baths than regular ones. God, I'd kill for a bath right now. This will have to …

As I wipe my naked chest, I sense someone's watching me. Either the hills have eyes or … I glance at Jason. His gaze is glued to my exposed breasts. He closes his eyes the moment I catch him. I should care the man's peeking like a pervert, but I feel nothing. Not anger, not titillation. I'm just really fucking cold. I turn my back to him and finish scrubbing.

When I'm as fresh and clean as possible, I return to the backseat, retrieving a water and a shirt for Jason. If I felt filthy he's gotta feel like a landfill. I open his car door. Holy hell. My mouth drops open when I realize what I'm seeing. From the left shoulder down, he's covered in blonde fur still wet from the blood-tinged mucous. His hand is a paw, complete with claws two inches long. The rest of him is normal by comparison, except for all the blood. Damn. His eyes open. He seems so weary, so miserable I snap my jaw shut and regain my senses. *Stop gawking at the freak, Viv.* "How you doing?"

"Fine," he says softly.

"Let's get you cleaned up," I say with a half smile. "Can you sit up for me?" He manages to push himself into the sitting position and pivots his legs outside to face me. I start with the handprint on his cheek. "Sorry about hitting you."

"No need to apologize. It was necessary."

"How are you feeling?" I ask, wiping his prominent collarbone.

"Tired."

I advance down his ripped chest with the cloth. Even bloody it's a damn fine chest. "Well … you've done enough for one night. I'll take it from here." I lean forward to get the back of his neck. I can feel his hot breath against my own neck and know his eyes are upon my face. "Thank you."

"What for?"

I glance over to meet his eyes. "Saving my life. Again."

"Thank you for saving mine."

We just stare into each other's eyes for a second. I do love his eyes. Honest. Penetrating. Fathomless. And like mine, lustful. Fuck it. I lean down, gently pressing my lips to his. Don't know if it's the shock or exhaustion but his don't move under mine. Still nice. Sweet. Haven't had a sweet kiss in years. Forgot I liked them. I break away with a smile. "Think nothing of it, Blondie." He stares at me, dumbstruck. I love having that kind of effect on a man, especially this one. I grab the clean shirt from the dash, handing it to him. "Now get dressed. Pit stop's over."

I move to the backseat to gather more provisions, including my faux fur jacket which I slip on, a soda, pillow and blanket for Jason. As I do, I glance back at my hero. My grin stretches across my whole face as he presses his fingers to his lips, I presume to make sure they're real. That what I did was real. God, is he adorable. And good. Even after all the shit I pulled tonight, that man didn't hesitate. Holy shit, he took a bullet for me tonight. *For me.*

As I stare at him, something comes over me, through me, like nothing I've ever felt before. Gratitude? Respect maybe? Both of those, but something else. Something stronger. It warms me from the inside. A spark, like the moment an orchestra begins playing a masterpiece. It's not lust, though that is certainly there. Whatever it is, it is scary as fuck. But I can't wait to hear the rest.

No time for reflection though. I have thousands of miles for that. I climb into the driver's seat and hand my knight the pillow and blanket. "Here. You ready to rock?"

He stares down at my offering. "I shouldn't sl—"

"I told you, Blondie." I shut my door and grin. "Settle in. I got this." It's three thousand miles to Maryland, we've got a full tank of gas, half a gram of coke in my pocket, it's dark ... and we're not wearing sunglasses. I start the engine.

"Let's hit it."

SIX

OH, CRAP. OH, HELL. I think I snorted too much coke. My heart is about to burst out of my fucking chest, and I'm shaking almost as bad as I was last night. Every nerve ending jangles like a plucked guitar string. Not to mention I'm as horny as a boy in a cheerleader's locker room. I'm blaming absolute, utter exhaustion for my lack of better judgment. At least today's bad judgment. I don't think I've ever been so tired in all my damn life. It started halfway to Salt Lake City as the adrenaline wore off. I downed an entire Mountain Dew in five minutes so I could be at least halfway conscious while I boosted us another car. It worked because the theft went down without a hitch. The hotel parking lot was unguarded and lousy with cars. I chose the first Accord with a key holder, switched the plates, and drove back to the demolished Civic a quarter mile away. I wanted to buy time before the two were linked. I transferred our possessions and my groggy companion, then got the hell out of Dodge.

After that, smooth sailing. It took a little over three hours to drive down to I-70. I got to see a beautiful sunrise and the Acura owner was a jazz fan so I have decent tunes, but boredom quickly drained my reserves regardless. As we crossed the Colorado border, what little energy I had burnt out. Not even fumes remained. I'd had three sodas, two cups of coffee, and still couldn't keep my eyes open. I debated waking Jason but figured he needed sleep more than me. He hasn't woken since the car exchange in Salt Lake. I'm nothing if not stubborn, so I let him sleep and did a bump. Damned if it didn't work. Powdered energy to the rescue. I made it another three hours before my eyelids started their fight again, and a massive wave of depression washed over me. When I stopped for gas just outside of Denver, I did two full lines. Bad idea.

Being hyper-vigilant while driving in a major city? Insane. Every time a car changed lanes, I jerked in fear it was about to hit us. Then, when I spotted a cop, my throat closed to a pinpoint, and my mouth became Death Valley. It passed us, but I couldn't stop trembling for ten minutes. That was an hour ago. My heart hasn't slowed. Mostly because I am convinced, *convinced* that cop radioed ahead, and there's a trap setup here somewhere. I just know it. And yet in spite of my racing heart and superhuman vigilance, my eyes are growing heavy again. Fuckers.

I'm in hell. Absolute hell. I feel like plowing this car into the concrete divider. Seriously. I had to stop myself from doing just that. I know it's the coke—chemical reactions and whatnot—but that knowledge doesn't help keep the depression from swallowing me whole. No matter the cause, I still *feel* it. The exhaustion. The hopelessness. Maybe I should just kill myself. If I died, really who'd care? Mom for about an hour, Barry maybe a minute. Jessica would mourn, but she's resilient. She'd get over it. They'd move on. Really, my death wouldn't impact a single life. Like ten people would attend my funeral. Oh God, that's so fucking sad.

No impact. I've left nothing lasting in my life. No husband, no kids, not even a damn album. It'd be like I never existed. Why the hell is Jason risking his life for a nothing? People *rely* on him. An entire pack. He's essential to other people's lives. People *love* him. He should just leave me. Go back. Let Donovan have me. Instead the man gets shot because of me. He almost died, and it was my fault. If I hadn't called Cyr, Donovan never would have found us.

I've had hours to work out how the Marshal tracked us. We used cash, didn't tell anyone where we were, we were so damn careful. It wasn't until Jason's phone rang, and the display showed the name and number of the caller the pieces, locked into place. When I called Cyr the hotel's name and number must have popped up on his display too. Thinking he was helping, he phoned Donovan with the info.

It was stupid of me to trust Cyr. The man is a drug dealer after all. For all I know Donovan threatened to arrest him unless he sold me out. So I am the reason Jason almost died. My damn fault in every way. As if I didn't have enough to feel guilty about already. Shooting at him, biting him, making him uncomfortable with my lame seduction scheme, suggesting I only wanted to sleep with him for his good deeds, *then* I also get him shot? God, if I were him I'd leave me at a gas station and phone Donovan myself. What really depresses me is I think I would. *I* wouldn't get shot for *him*. I really wouldn't. I'm so not worth any of this. And I'm scared shitless the second he realizes this, it's gas station time. Wouldn't blame him at all.

Just the thought of this hypothetical situation brings me to damn tears. Not that there's even a small part of me that thinks he'll do it. Never. He'll protect me until his dying breath. He's too good. Too good for me, that's for fucking sure. I finally meet a decent, hardworking, adorable man with a chivalrous streak a mile long to boot and he ends up being my adopted brother. And a werewolf, but nobody's perfect. The brother factor bothers me more than the werewolf thing—go figure. I could overlook them both, already have really, but not the fact I'm not fit to polish his fucking gun. I take a long, deep breath and sigh. God, I'm depressed. Stupid drugs. Stupid me. I shake my head to clear it. Stop this. Stop. Distraction. Need a distraction.

I grab the *Best of Gershwin* CD and pop it in. The bluesy trumpet from "Summertime," begins and I feel a bit better, more so when Ella Fitzgerald begins crooning. I love *Porgy and Bess*. One of Gershwin's best. So sad and sexy and strangely sweet. No matter how much Bess fucks up, Porgy always comes after her. Used to think that only happened in fiction. The CD continues with more classics. "They Can't Take That Away From Me," "S'Wonderful," oh! "Someone to Watch Over Me." I love, love, *love* this one. I was merely lip syncing the others, but I can't help myself. I actually sing along with Ella, getting lost in the melody, the words, how fun it is to croon.

I'm transported back to the first time I ever sang this tune, when I was fourteen at my boarding school. Damn, I loved it there. No one ever believed in me before, not like Miss Tyson. I was one of only three soloists and the only freshman. I worked my ass off getting that song literally pitch perfect. Hours doing scales, practicing breathing techniques, even reading a book on Gershwin to really understand what the song meant. It was my life's mission to make hat woman proud of me. It was there, up on that stage with that spotlight on me alone, everyone in the audience applauding, that I'd never felt so happy. My first fix, and sixteen years later I'm still chasing that particular dragon even though my feet are nothing more than bloody stumps now.

When I reach the second chorus, I realize I'm being watched again. I glance toward the source. Jason stares at me with that same intense gaze he had at the wedding when I performed "You Don't Know Me." Dazed. Reverent. Titillated. Yearning. Shit, my cheeks warm in a blush. "Sorry. I didn't mean to wak—"

"Please continue singing. *Please*."

The deep need in his voice is jarring, but I'm flattered more than anything. A command performance. First one ever. Can't disappoint my adoring audience. I oblige with zeal, belting the rest with everything I possess and swelling with pride in time to Jason's soulful, emerging smile. It brings a matching one to mine. God, I've missed this. *This* is what it's all about. Feels like the first time. Better than coke. When the song ends, I turn back to the road and force my cheeks to return to their normal color, failing miserably. There's that damn internal orchestra again, continuing their symphony inside me. I'm tingly all over with every note.

"You're astonishing," Jason says.

"Shut up." I turn down the volume, at least on the radio. That orchestra continues to play the blues away. "I'm good. I only have a range of two octaves and can only hit high notes half the time."

"I think you're spectacular." He pushes himself into the sitting position. "For what it's worth."

It's worth more than I'd care to admit to either of us, Blondie. "How are you feeling?"

"Stiff. Hungry. Thirsty. How long was I out for?"

"Oh, about fifteen hours."

He stares out the window at the grassy plains of east Colorado then glances around the car in confusion. "Where are we? Is this a different car?"

"The answer to A is an hour outside of Denver. I changed our route to throw off Donovan. We're on I-70. And the answer to B is, yes, this is a new car. Upgraded from our bullet ridden, bloody Civic to a cleaner Acura in Salt Lake. You don't remember that?"

"I ... no. Fifteen hours?" he asks in shock.

"Blondie, you'd been up for three days and lost half your blood. If you needed to sleep for double that, I'd let you. I told you, I got this."

The sides of his mouth twitch into a momentary smile. "Thank you." He twists open a water bottle with his human hand and chugs the contents. "I need a toilet and food."

"Think that can be arranged." I glance at his furry arm. "Although you might wanna ..."

He stares at the limb. "Oh."

"Looks like it worked, though. The bullet hole's gone without a trace. The gash in your head and cheek healed too. You're as good as spanking new."

"Yeah," he says, touching his cheek with his paw.

Strange how quick I got used to that paw. Forgot it was even there. "Can I ... touch it?"

"What?"

"Your fur. Can I touch it? I want to see what it feels like. I almost did a few times before, but didn't want to molest you in your sleep," I say with a smile. "I mean, how often do you get a chance to pet a werewolf. So can I?"

"Um, okay. I guess."

I reach across and touch the fur. Holy hell, that's soft. I run my fingers through his thick pelt with a grin. It's so thick my digits almost vanish inside it. "Cool."

"It doesn't bother you?"

"Hell no. I think it's fucking awesome. You're so soft." He's staring at me again, studying me for I think evidence of a lie. Of course he doesn't find any. This werewolf thing is pretty nifty. "What?" I ask, pulling away my hand.

"Most people find it … unnerving."

"Blondie, I've lived in New York City, New Orleans, and Los Angeles. I once did a gig with a guy who surgically inserted horns in his forehead. One of my roommates dated this cat who was covered in tattoos literally from head to toe. Your arm barely cracks the top five."

"Oh."

"So how do you want to do this? Change in here?"

"No. It gets messy. Gas station, I guess."

"Aye aye, Blondie."

We drive in silence for a few seconds as he wiggles around. Must be stiff. The man barely moved in his sleep. As he does, he notices his cell phone under the gearshift and picks it up. "I have five missed calls."

"Yeah, didn't want to overstep my bounds." Again. "I did text Frank this morning that we're alive and well." Oh, good. An exit. "It'll keep."

I pull up to the pumps and walk inside the station to retrieve the key to the bathrooms and twenty bucks unleaded. Jason waits by the bathroom with a blanket covering his arm and blood-stained pants. We exchange the key and smiles. While he's transforming, I do the same back at the car. My hair's frizzy in the braids, I don't have makeup on, and it's way too hot for long sleeves. I change into my blousy, off-the-shoulder peach top sans bra, slap on lip liner and concealer, and brush my hair. Massive improvement. Be better if my hands would stop jittering though.

At least the depression's held at bay for the moment. Maybe I should do a tiny bump just to level out. Taper off. And I'll be witty and charming as I only am on the stuff. Fuck it. I open the glove box where I've been keeping it, but just as I pull out the baggie, I hear Jason's voice. Shit. I stick it back in as he strolls toward the car, now fully human and clean with his phone pressed to his ear. "… no, if he's willing, we could sure use the help. I have four bullets left." Jason tosses his pants from last night into the trash as he passes. I stand up. "I know we have to pass through Kansas. Just don't know how long it'll take us to get to him." He listens. "Limon, Colorado." He listens. I mouth, "What's going on?" and he holds up a finger. "Just set it up. Get directions from I-70. We'll find it." He nods. "You too. Bye, Dad."

"What's up?" I ask after he hangs up.

"We might be making a pit-stop in Kansas. A friend of the pack offered to get us some extra ammo."

"Can we trust this friend?"

"Seth's responsible for his wife's death, so yes. He's been feeding Dad information as well."

"Can't wait to meet him then."

Jason moves over to the driver's side. "You ready to go?"

"As I'll ever be. You sure you're okay to drive?"

"I got this," he says with a half smirk. A joke! I do believe I'm rubbing off on him.

Blondie takes the wheel and after a quick stop at Arby's, away we go. By the time we're back on the highway, two of his five sandwiches are gone. I add the Arby's sauce to the third and hand it to him. "Thank you." He chows down, getting some sauce on the side of his mouth.

"You are such a messy eater." I pull out a napkin. "Here."

I move toward him with the napkin, but he shies away from my touch, intercepting the napkin and snatching it from my hand. "Thank you." He wipes. "You should get some sleep. You look exhausted."

I pull my hand away, trying and failing to hide my hurt. I stare ahead as the chemically induced depression floods back. Fine. Fuck. I grab the pillow and blanket from the backseat and lower my own, turning away from the werewolf. Sleep is impossible with my heart thudding a hundred miles a minute. God, I wish I had a Valium. That usually brings me down. I close my eyes anyway, willing my heart to slow. My concentration is interrupted a minute later by his buzzing cell.

"Hey, Tate," Jason says quietly, followed by silence. "I know. I've been asleep all day. Sorry." Silence. "Fine. I'm fine. Had worse. I'm healed now." He's had worse than last night? Damn. "Yeah, she did." Think they're talking about me now. "I ... agree." Damn it, what's

Tate saying? "I don't want to talk about that." A pause. "Yes." Damn it, why can't I have werewolf hearing too? "Because it's not appropriate. And this is a bad time." A pause. "Somewhere in Colorado on I-70. We had to change our route." Silence. "This really isn't a good time. I'll call you later, okay? Say hello to your mother and Adam. Bye." I assume he hangs up.

"You've had worse than last night?" I ask.

"What? Oh, sorry. Did I wake you?" he asks.

I flip onto my back. "Too amped to sleep." I raise my seat. "So, you've been shot before?"

"Actually shot? Once. Took some birdshot to the leg when Dad and I were chasing a rogue seven years ago. Wasn't silver, though. Been stabbed in the chest once too. That *was* silver. Had to do a full change. Tate had to run down the rogue alone. Got him though. The worst was this time in Maine. Husband and wife. I was trying to round him up with a F.R.E.A.K.S. agent. Didn't know the wife had changed. Came out of nowhere, almost severed my arm. Ripped open my gut too. The change helped, but I was still out of commission for a few days. They got them eventually."

"Jesus Christ, Jason."

"All part of the job. They hurt innocent people. They're a threat to our way of life. Someone has to do it."

"How many people have you … never mind," I say, shaking my head. "You don't have—"

"Including the wolf in Ventura? Eight. Most rogues who step out of line, I just put the fear of God into them. They've usually killed accidently on their first change. We talk to them, help them, and warn them there is no second chance. They usually listen. But some … they either bring too much attention to themselves, threaten to out us to the public, or as Dad calls it, they get 'drunk with power.' They think the rules don't apply to them. Let the wolf take over. They're the eight."

"Does it ever bother you, what you do? Keep you up at night?"

"Not often. It was always necessary. Always. For the pack." He glances over. "It's … hard to explain."

"No, I get it. You're protecting your family. Your people. Hell, even perfect strangers. It's kind of noble. Selfless. I mean, as long as you don't get a perverse thrill out of it. You know, enjoy being sadistic or something. Skin them when they're alive just to hear them scream."

"I don't like killing, if that's what you mean," he says.

"Didn't think you did, Blondie," I say with a smile. He doesn't return it. O-kay. I move my gaze straight ahead again. "*I* couldn't do it. Putting my life on the line for others. Getting shot for a woman I've only known a day."

Fucking depression. The wave of sadness that's been rolling to the surface since the stupid napkin incident crests. A flood of images and regrets ride the wave. His fright when I threw myself at him. His pain when he thought I was ashamed of him because of his God-awful past. The abject terror I felt when I heard those gunshots and had no idea if he was dead or alive. His torture when I dug that bullet out. That chaste kiss I shouldn't have instigated. The awe and pride he had when I sang. No one's ever looked at me like that in my life. Like I was all that mattered in the universe.

"I'm sorry," I say, voice cracking. "I'm so sorry. It was my fault Donovan found us. My fault he shot you. That you almost bled to death. It was Cyr. He tipped off Donovan. It was so stupid of me to call him. I'm so sorry. Please don't hate me. I'm sorry."

Jason's half of the car is quiet, and I'm afraid to glance at him. I feel like I have no skin, and one look from him will cause untold agony. I wipe my stupid tears. God, I'm never doing coke again. This is horrible. I hate *feeling*. It never brings about anything good.

"Please don't cry," Jason says tenderly after a few seconds. "I don't hate you." Another pause. "I could never hate you." I gather my confidence and glance over for confirmation. His usually rigid face has softened with either sadness or pity. "It was a mistake, one I'm sure you'll never make again. And considering the impossible position we've forced you into, I am... damned impressed with how well you're handling this all. You've kept your head when most would have lost theirs. You saved us last night. You saved *me*. Thank you."

Damn it. Those words bring fresh tears. "But—"

"No, buts," he cuts in. "Take the compliment. You deserve it. You've earned it." He pauses. "You did good, Vivian. Better than good. I'm proud of you. I'm *proud* you're in my pack."

I don't know what to say. I want to protest, absolve him, but I'm too choked up by... I don't know what. Whatever that spark was last night ignites again, striking up the orchestra again so their beautiful music is almost deafening, overwhelming so nothing but the beauty they bring to the world remains. I can count on one hand how many times someone's told me they're proud of me and now twice in one day. Where with Frank it made me uncomfortable, when Jason says it, I *feel* it. I believe it. Hell, I think I'm proud of myself too. "Thank you," I whisper, wiping the waning tears.

"No, Vivian," he says, catching my eyes with his, "thank *you*." With a reverent nod, he gazes back at the road.

A quick smile crosses my face along with a blush. I'm getting as bad as him in that department. The urge to lunge across the car and kiss him until our lips bleed damn near overwhelms me. I keep it at bay like a lion tamer with a whip. Impulse control has never been one of my virtues. She's building her strength now, that's for sure. My smile doesn't wane until the buzzing phone breaks the spell, bringing real life back into this car. Thank God.

Jason picks the cell up. "Hey, Dad," he says before a long pause. A huge yawn escapes me. Catharsis is exhausting. "Great. Where and what time?" Another pause. "That sounds fine. Hold on, let me find a pen and paper to write them down." He places the phone on his thigh and glances at me. I'm ahead of him, grabbing the Arby's bag for a napkin as Jason opens the glove box to root around for a pen.

The moment it opens, my baggie of coke falls right beside his hand. *Oh, hell.* Jason stops searching to stare at the baggie. Fuck. Double fuck. I stop breathing, stop blinking in an attempt to become invisible somehow. Just when I've impressed him, made some headway, I go and cock it up again. In that instant, my emotional suit of armor is yanked on. Bring on the lecture. The disapproving looks. The contempt.

But none comes. Jason slowly blinks at the bag before resuming his pen search. When he locates one, he hands it to me. "Dad, I'm putting you on speaker. Read off the directions."

Jason presses a button with his left hand while picking up the baggie and closing the glove box. I can't look at him, I'm so embarrassed. "Can you hear me?" Frank asks.

Jason rolls down his window. "We can." He chucks the baggie out the window. "Go ahead."

I can barely concentrate on the directions I scribble on the napkin, I'm too preoccupied with glancing at Jason. That firm, unreadable mask of his has returned. He keeps his eyes ahead as Frank drones on. God knows he's regretting those words now. I went from Wonder Woman to a coke whore in one fell swoop. "Got it?" Frank asks.

"Yeah," I say.

Jason picks up the phone. "Thanks, Dad. Talk to you later." He hangs up.

We drive in agonizing silence as I stare at my lap with my head hung. As usual, thirty seconds is all I can stand. "Jason, I'm—"

"You will never put that poison into your body again," he says with finality. "*Ever.*" A pause. "You're worth more than that, whether you believe it or not. Treat yourself as such. Promise me. *Promise.*"

"Okay. I promise," I say. And I mean it. I swear on Nina's grave, I will never touch it again.

"Good." He nods, which I take to mean that's the end of the discussion. "We have a little over five hours before we reach Stoker. Try and get some sleep."

"Alright." I hand him the napkin, and he nods again.

I lower the seat, pull up the blanket, and turn on my side away from him with my eyes closed. I lay here fifty shades of miserable for a few minutes. "Jason?" I finally say.

"Yes?"

"Thank you."

A pause, then, "You are welcome, Vivian." Silence. "Sleep."

And the misery parts enough for the exhaustion to roll in. The last thing I remember before I drift off is my knight pulling up my blanket to cover me from the cold. I think I fall asleep with a smile on my face.

SEVEN

THE STOPPING CAR BRINGS me out of sleep. Damn. I blink a few times to clear the blurs away. Movement and the fluorescent lights to my left simultaneously draw my attention. The bar, or I guess it'd be classified as a genuine honky-tonk, judging from the motorcycles and pick-ups in the lot, is nothing like I thought it'd be. Outside two such bikers in leather and denim with beers in their hands engage in conversation under the neon NO EXIT sign. I've played in places just like this when I was desperate for cash. Not many jazz fans among this contingent.

"Where are we?" I ask.

"Stoker, Kansas," Jason answers.

"Kansas? Thrilling," I say, pushing off my blanket.

"We're early."

"Then let's go get a drink and wait for him inside."

"I don't think you should—"

"Appreciate the concern but I've been in more places like this than you have, Blondie. Plus I have to pee. Come on." I wink. "I'll keep you safe."

Before he can protest, I climb out of the car. So this is what it's like to have someone give a shit about your well being. Annoying yet heartwarming at the same time. Must take getting used to. Jason rushes to my side as I'm about to pass the bikers. One puckers his lips at me, and Jason gives him such a glare of utter hatred even I get a chill, followed by a thrill. Heartwarming overtakes my annoyance.

It's early to be going to a bar—things never pick up until ten—so there are a little over a dozen men and scantily clad women either at the bar or playing pool. It's smoky and not only from cigarettes. My attention diverts to a small stage where a man in a John Deere cap butchers Johnny Cash's "Ring of Fire" as his three friends in front hoot and holler. Jason ignores all this. He ushers me to a table in the back corner with a view of the door. Every man who shoots me an appreciative glance receives a glare from my protector. Blondie's the jealous type it appears. I forgive him this when he pulls out my chair for me. "Thank you."

He plops in the chair beside me without a word. The waitress in Daisy Duke shorts and black tank top immediately struts over. "Welcome to No Exit. What can I get y'all?"

God knows I could use some tequila, but for once I listen to the nagging voice in my head. "Two coffee's please," I say. "Cream and sugar."

"You got it," the waitress says before walking away.

"So, what time are we supposed to meet this mystery man?" I ask.

"Ten minutes."

"Good. I need to use the powder room." I rise and Jason does the same. I press him back down by the shoulder. "Think I can handle this alone, Blondie. You hold the fort." I pat his shoulder and move to the bathroom. After I answer nature's call, I do my best to fix myself up, fluffing my hair and pinching my cheeks to bring some life to my face. When I step back out, Jason's eyes are glued to the bathroom door in case I need a rescue. I don't think he blinks until I sit again. I sip my watery coffee with a smile as two women get their groove on onstage singing, "It's Raining Men." Not half bad.

"You ever done karaoke?" I ask Jason.

"No."

"Ever wanted to?"

"No."

"You ever sing along to a song you love when you're alone in the car?"

"No," he says after a sip of his drink.

"Well, now that's just plain wrong."

"Why?" he asks, genuinely inquisitive.

"I don't know. It means you never get swept away in something you love. That you can be silly, even when no one's looking. Music is an expression of the soul. It should touch you." His face has gone stony again. "Not that it doesn't affect you. I know it does, I've seen it."

"You have?"

"Oh, yeah," I say with a smirk. "The only times I've seen anything close to a smile on your face was when I was . . . when there was music playing. Seems like we have the same taste in music. Frank left behind his record collection, you know." I sip my coffee.

"Those damn things practically saved my life. When things got shitty, or I just felt shitty, I'd go hide in my room and listen to Ray or Billie, and my troubles seemed to be carried away with the music. I think I became a singer just to chase that feeling." I start playing with my mug. "Made it my whole life. It was the only thing I could count on. Lost its luster through the years like most highs. You can only chase the metaphorical dragon for so long before exhaustion makes you tumble, and you don't have the energy to get back up. And even if you did, you're miles from where you intended to be." Great, now I'm depressed again. I am really *never* doing coke again. I sip my coffee. "Anyway."

"I like when you sing."

"Huh?" I turn to Jason. I forgot he was here. "Sorry?"

"I like it when *you* sing," he says, staring straight ahead at the door. "Always have. You're right, it makes me smile when you put your soul into every word and melody. You make me ... feel what you're feeling. Your love. Your agony. Your joy. It's like you said, it makes me forget the world. Makes me empty yet full at the same time. You ... *move* me." He hangs his head. "You're good, is all. I like your singing." He chugs his coffee and sets the mug down. "I need to use the restroom. Be back in a second." With his head still downcast, he rises and walks to the bathroom. My slacked jaw doesn't snap shut until he's out of sight.

I move him? I *move* him? I don't think anyone has ever said something so lovely to me before. The sentiment burns the dark clouds away as those words cycle through my head. He really has to stop saying such nice things. I'm beginning to enjoy them a little too much. Might get addicted. Still. I let the sunny sensation he gave me light me up. I move him. Haunt him. I kind of want to pay it forward. I know the way I *really* want to. It took more willpower than I ever thought I possessed not to kiss him when he was saying those wonderful things. It's getting harder and harder to stop myself like I promised us both. He needs to stop being so goddamn irresistible. A girl can only withstand so much. Well, if I can't do the first thing I'm good at, I'll do the second.

I move toward the stage to get the song book. I'm pleasantly surprised to find some classics in here. I quickly decide on an old Sinatra tune, and write the number down.

"What are you doing?"

I pivot around to find Jason behind me, face unreadable again. "Killing time. Go sit."

"You shouldn't—"

"Go sit down, Blondie. Enjoy the show."

I hand my selection to the MC, a man with a ragged, ZZ Top beard. "What's your name, darlin'?"

I glance behind at my glaring companion. "Dagwood."

"Whatever, darlin'," the man says. "Get on up here."

With a grin, I step onto the stage. There are a few catcalls and whistles, and Jason's glower immediately whips toward the men. I barely notice the noise. Nothing I'm not used to. Jason keeps his eyes welded on the men as he slowly makes his way back to our table.

"Got someone new up here tonight," the MC says into the mic. "Mrs. Dagwood. Let's all give her a round of applause."

While most applaud, one man shouts, "Not the only thing I'd like to give her!"

I spy Jason seething in the corner, but I just grin at the man as sweet as honey. "Sorry, I already have herpes." The audience groans and laughs at my joke. Works every time. "This one goes out to my partner in crime there in the corner. He's saved my bacon more than twice. Don't know how I can ever repay you. Hope this is a good start, Blondie."

"I Get a Kick Out of You," written by the fabulous Cole Porter made popular by Ole' Blue Eyes begins playing. Wrong for this audience, perfect for my one and only. I vamp it up, especially on the cocaine lyric, wriggling my hips and shoulders in time to the music with a cutesie smile on my face. Rita Hayworth would be proud. For the first time in awhile, I'm enjoying myself onstage. I forgot how much fun this can be, hamming it up while belting out a song I love. That sunny feeling I had before doubles, especially when by the chorus a matching smile forms on Jason's face, made that much brighter by his awe. This is what it means to light up a room. We're the only two people in the spotlight though. Just us, the music, and whatever the hell is passing between us. Whatever the hell it is, it scares and thrills me more than … No sentence ever uttered, no music ever composed could come close to expressing what this mere exchange does to me. Magic. This must be what magic feels like, as if my soul is playing Carnegie Hall with little practice. It knows it doesn't deserve to be there yet. I have to look away as I feel my throat closing up. I finish the song staring at the bored foursome in front.

"Give it up for Mrs. Dagwood," the MC says to scattered applause. "Nice set of pipes she has on her, huh? Good job."

I nod and step offstage. Damn, I need a drink. Or seven. Shit, no time. A man with a small duffel approaches Jason, who holds out his hand to shake, which the stranger does. Must be our guy.

Thank God, I don't think I could stand a moment alone with Jason after whatever that was. At least not with people around.

I guess the stranger would be considered attractive if he wasn't standing beside my Adonis. He's an inch or two shorter, and though a big man, not as muscular as Jason. Still, his Roman nose, strong jaw, and thick floppy brown hair suit him. The men sit as I stroll over.

"Hello," I say.

"Special Agent Will Price, this is Vivian Dahl," Jason says.

"Nice to meet you," I say as I plop down. "And thanks for helping us."

"Wish I could do more," Price says. With his foot, he pushes the duffel to Jason. Cool. Feels like I'm in a spy movie or something. "Couldn't take much without Dr. Black knowing. There's a box of silver bullets, a Glock 9mm, silver dagger, and can of silver pepper spray."

"Hope we won't have use for them," Jason says. "What else have you got for us?"

"Your Marshal Donovan attributed the shoot-out in Wyoming last night to that Gavin guy. Your real name hasn't been flagged yet. This guy must have someone inside IT or records because not only was your photo swapped for Gavin, but the autopsy on the man from Ventura mentioned nothing about werewolves or even silver bullets. He's covering his tracks."

"Was Cooper really a Marshal?" I ask.

"No. He was identified as James Cooper of Highgarden, Pennsylvania. Former army sniper. They're claiming he just got caught in the crossfire, that he was attempting to save you and Gavin executed him."

140

"Am I still considered his hostage?" I ask.

"I'm sorry, no," Price says. "They found the stolen car from California. Your prints were on the wheel and tags so there's a federal warrant out for you for interstate car theft."

"Jesus Christ," I say almost doubling over in my chair.

"We'll take care of it," Jason says.

I am officially a federal fugitive wanted by the law. My throat closes up. "This is insane," I whisper.

Jason rubs my back, which does help. "It'll be okay."

"You really should let me go to Dr. Black," Price says. "She's a civilian, we can intervene."

"She's pack," he insists, still rubbing. "Under pack law, as offspring of a member, unless she declares herself rogue, she is pack. This is two warring werewolf factions, not your jurisdiction. Under F.R.E.A.K.S. law, unless an unaffiliated human is injured by preternatural means, you cannot intervene."

"He is correct, William," the drop-dead gorgeous man approaching us says with a British accent. *Hello*. My g-spot springs to attention. This man gives Jason a run for the money in the looks department. Flowing brown hair, pale skin, full lips, piercing gray eyes. Yummy. Both werewolves bristle and scowl when he saddles up to our table, Jason especially. The Brit receives the full force of his glare as he sits in the free chair to my right without invitation. "I know you are new to our organization, so I shall enlighten you, Special Agent Price. The exceptions are if no formal declaration of war was made, in which all parties are legally responsible for any murder committed. I doubt Francis Dahl or his aggressor would make such an oversight though. The other exceptions are if the crimes begin drawing attention, i.e., maulings in the press, drained

141

bodies, etc., and violence crossing the species. Werewolf on vampire, vampire on witch—"

"You know all about that last one, don't you, Oliver?" Jason sneers.

The man grins, showing his pearly white teeth. "Jason Volynski, happy to see Alpha Dahl has let you off your leash for a spell. I swear, as the years pass, you grow more and more like your dear, departed father." The grin slowly drops. "Especially in the eyes. You can tell so much about a man's soul, or lack thereof, through the eyes."

I didn't think it possible but Jason's scowl deepens almost to snarling proportions, upper lip twitching. Before he can attack the man, I say, "I'm sorry, um, we haven't been introduced." I hold out my hand. "I'm Vivian. Dahl."

"Oliver Montrose," he says, ungluing his eyes from the men only to use them to fuck me twelve ways from Sunday. "Enchanté." He kisses my hand with his cold lips. I can't help it, a shiver of lust radiates down from that spot.

"Don't look in his eyes," Jason orders. I glance over at him. "He's a vampire."

On instinct, I yank my hand away. Oliver chuckles. "Oh, Mr. Volynski, no need to frighten the poor girl. As if I would ply my considerable charms on your beautiful mate." The word *mate* makes Jason visibly stiffen. "At least not in front of you."

"Did you follow me here?" Price asks.

"But of course. I noticed you wandering out of the armory carrying a bag, and naturally grew suspicious. You have only been with us for a few weeks. For all I knew, you were supplying our flamethrowers to the Taliban. I suppose a wanted serial murderer and his mate is not *as* troubling."

"I am not a serial murderer," Jason growls.

"I apologize, your kill number is under three? No desire to beat Daddy's record?"

"I am nothing like him," Jason snarls.

"Not from what I hear, *гроМаДНЫЙ*." The vampire turns to me. "That is what Lord Peter called his father: his monster. Dear Peter unleashed him when he did not desire to dirty his own hands. Sound familiar, monster?"

The table rattles as Jason shoots up, hands balled into fists. Both Price and I rise as well in case he decides to attack the smug vampire. I grab onto his fist. "Don't," I warn.

"Listen to your mate, *гроМаДНЫЙ*. I am a Federal Agent," he says in sing-song.

"Shut up, asshole," I snap.

"Oh, but you are fiery," Oliver declares gleefully. "I do enjoy that in a woman. If you were brunette and not so emaciated you would be my ideal woman. I shall overlook those flaws in your case, though."

Jason takes a step to lunge, and hell, I'm about to let him when Price body blocks him. "Let's go. Let's get out of here." Though he's still literally seething, Jason listens, following Price toward the door. I glare at the grinning vampire as I round the table for the bag, which I pick up.

"If you ever tire of Alpo boy, you know where to find—"

With my free hand, I lift the mug and toss coffee in his face. "He is ten times the man you have been or ever will be. You're the only one lacking a soul here." That wipes the smile from his face. "How sad for you." With a pitying smile, I stalk out of the bar, shaking my head at this idiocy. At least I wasn't the source of it for once.

Price has Jason by our car, and they're talking when I come out. "...sorry," Jason says. "I shouldn't have put you in this situation."

"The pack all but saved my life. You recommended me for this job. I owe you. Besides, I can handle him. From what the others tell me, deep down he's a coward. Doesn't give a damn about anyone but himself. He'll probably forget all about it in an hour. And if he does say something, I'll lie."

"Still. I'm sorry," Jason says. "And if this doesn't work out, you know you're always welcome in the pack. We'd love to have you."

"We'll see, huh?" Price turns to me. "Good luck to you both." He nods at me, then Jason before walking toward a truck. Nice guy.

"Are you okay?" I ask Jason.

"I'm sorry I lost my temper. I didn't mean to frighten you."

I squeeze his hand again. "You didn't," I assure him. I release his hand. "And besides, you weren't the one who threw a drink in his face."

"You did?"

"Hell yes! That guy was a total asshole! Had to defend your honor somehow. What are mates for?" I ask with a wink. "Now, let's get the hell out of here before I decide to go back in there and add to my list of felonies." I flash him a cute smile before climbing into the car.

Jason gets in a second later. He stares straight ahead as if solving a dilemma and doesn't start the car. "I ... what he said in there ..." He glances over. "I ..."

"Hey," I say, reaching for his hand again. "Don't you dare give that prick a second thought, okay? You are *nothing* like your father."

"How do you know that?" he asks quietly.

"Simple, Blondie. I wouldn't be here if you were. I'd be dead in a ditch somewhere. You are no monster. You are the most selfless man I have ever met. The *best* man I have ever met. Don't you *dare* let anyone make you doubt that, yourself included." I squeeze his hand. "So stop beating my mate up, or I'll be forced to kick your ass. You know I will too. I may not be a werewolf, but I'm vicious and I fight dirty when I need to. I can take ya," I whisper with a sweet grin.

He stares at me, looking for the lie again. All he finds is sincerity. "Thank you."

"No, *thank you.*"

His eyes slowly move to mine. The moment they connect, that same feeling I experienced while I was singing invades my body like a ghost passing through. Exhilarating and frightening and joyous all at once, stronger than anything I've ever experienced before. No spark, no orchestra, just a … churning, a glorious metamorphosis in my soul so strong it literally takes my breath away. I don't know how I know it, but I do. This moment is important. Nothing in this universe will ever be the same. Everything I've been through, everything I'll have to go through, it's all worth it for this moment. The moment when … I know I'm not alone. That I'll never be alone again, not really. That someone good and pure and worthwhile saw the same in me. That this man's hands will catch me if I fall. But that's not what scares me. It's the miraculous realization that I'll do the same for him. And I will. No matter the storm, no matter the sacrifice, I will fight to the bitter end to be the person he believes I am. I can do it. For him.

He must see the change in my eyes, the determination, the desire, but he doesn't like it. Sheer panic flashes through his eyes, and he drops my hand. If that's not ego bruising enough, he recoils up against his door, as far from me as he can get. "We, um, better get going."

"Right. Yeah. Okay," I whisper.

"Halfway there," he says, starting the car.

Yep, so close, yet so far away.

He maneuvers the car out of the lot. Off we go again into the dark night. But this time I'm not scared. I can feel the warm light on the horizon. Been awhile. Hope this time I get something more than sunburn.

EIGHT

"Come on. Everyone knows the words to 'Somewhere Over the Rainbow.'"

"I don't. Sorry."

I playfully narrow my eyes at him. "I'll bet you do know it. I'll bet you know the words to all the songs I've mentioned, but you're lying to get out of singing with me, you sneaky werewolf you."

His mouth twitches into a quick smile. "I really don't know them. I swear."

It is my new life's mission to get that man to give me a genuine, huge, brilliant smile that lasts more than a heartbeat as often as I possibly can. To get him to let his guard down like when I'm singing. I'm beginning to wonder if it's possible. It's almost as if he's reluctant to, even afraid maybe, as if allowing joy inside could crack him in two. I truly, deeply hope his father is not only burning in hell but is Satan's personal bitch for all he's done to his son. I keep my own smile plastered to hide these evil thoughts.

"A likely story, Blondie. I'll get the truth out of you yet. I have ways of making you talk," I say in a terrible Clint Eastwood impression. This gets another brief grin. I do think they're getting longer each time. Oh. In the distance, I see a sign. "Look! Look! Wait for it … wait for it …" We pass under the "Welcome to Ohio," sign attached to a big blue arch. I blow a kiss behind us. "Goodbye, Indiana! You will be missed!"

I turn back around with a grin, but Jason doesn't share my enthusiasm. He's too busy yawning for the fourth time in ten minutes. Once again, I catch the bug. I'm exhausted, but unlike him I managed to catch an hour or two of sleep since leaving Stoker. I offered to drive a few times through the night, even suggested we stop. Nope. Good thing I like my men stubborn. So I've been making him stop for coffee every two hours and am doing my best to keep him entertained. I sang the entire Gershwin CD complete with dazzling jazz hands. I interrogated him within an inch of his life. I was pleasantly surprised, shocked even, that he never hesitated to answer. What a difference forty-eight hours makes.

I learned his best friend Adam, who no matter how many times Jason literally snapped at him when they first met, never stopped trying until he wore Jason down. Then there's Tate, Adam's older brother, who taught Jason to fight whether Jason liked it or not. Maureen, their mother, who has the patience of Job. She taught him to read and was like a mother to him. Jenny, our stepmother, who never took a shine to him nor him to her. Probably intimidated by him. That and she was too busy playing Queen of the Pack to spend much time with her children. Frank sure does have a type. He spent the most time talking about Matt, our little brother.

That was the only time he seemed reluctant to speak. I didn't press, though I was dying to know. I think he sensed that and without further prompting began talking. He started with how frightened they were of each other at first, but Frank kept pushing them together until coexisting became love. It all started a year after he moved in. Some of the boys in the pack were picking on Matt, and Jason heard them. He just walked up, punched the ring leader in the face, and probably would have put the kid in a coma if Frank hadn't intervened. The gesture didn't endear Jason to the pack, save for Matt. He became Jason's little shadow. Big brother didn't mind. He was even the best man at Matt's wedding to Linda and is godfather to the twins, Dustin and Nicole. My niece and nephew. He sounded sweet. Artistic. He loved nothing more than walking around a forest snapping photos or playing with his children.

Though Jason shared these stories in his usual monotone manner, there were moments when the façade cracked, manifested in twitches or clearing his throat. I realized halfway through, when he was deep in a story about Matt's first change, that he hadn't had time to process, to come to terms with the fact his little brother died. Maybe when we reach Maryland, he'll feel safe enough to break down. Mourn. And I'll make sure to be there to help in any way I can.

Jason began yawning around three AM, and by the time we passed through Indianapolis just after dawn his eyes started drooping. I'm not much better. I haven't left the car for more than twenty minutes in over twenty hours. Hell, even the little sleep I got was shallow. I don't know how we'll get through the next eight hours to Maryland. I—

The sound of a gunshot solves our exhaustion problem. We both jerk our gazes back at the source. There are no cars behind us and no further gunshots, just a thumping. Oh, thank God it's just a flat. Upon realizing this, I also realize my hand is in the map holder where I stashed the Glock Price gave us. Jason had a similar reaction. His free hand is on the knife he attached to his belt. We exchanged a relieved sigh. "I better pull over."

"Yeah."

He maneuvers onto the shoulder. Since I've been sitting four hours straight, I take the opportunity to stand. My back actually cracks when I'm fully erect. Much better. At least we broke down in a lovely part of America with full, tall trees and gentle rolling hills. It'd be nicer if the trucks and cars zooming by weren't so damn smelly and loud. I literally choke on exhaust.

Jason's first to the open trunk. The good news is there's a spare tire. The bad is that it's almost as flat as the one we need to replace. Jason stares at the tire as if he can't wrap his mind around what he's seeing, like there's a trunk full of pixies playing banjos. I'm kind of at a loss too. As someone whose car often breaks down, I know the towing company asks for a license and writes the license plate down at the bare minimum. Not advisable with a stolen car. "Thoughts?" Jason asks.

"Um … I don't know. We're dead on our feet. You more than me. We switch the full flat for the flat spare, drive to the nearest town, I drop you at the first roach motel we find, and I go buy us a new tire while you shower and sleep."

"No. No motel."

"Jace, it's still over eight hours to Maryland. I don't know about you, but I don't have eight hours in me. I won't make any calls if you don't, alright? This is the universe's way of telling us to stop." I grab the socket wrench. "We're listening."

I know he's bone deep exhausted because he doesn't say another word in protest. Thank God because I'm too tired to fight back if he did. I hand him the tools as he switches the tires. I give the spare about fifty miles before it's as flat as a pancake. I suppose we could just steal another car. No, it's easier to buy another tire, not to mention I do want to keep my felonies to a minimum. We toss everything back into the trunk when we're done, and I take the keys. My turn as Alpha dog.

It takes two towns and three motels before I locate one that doesn't ask for a credit card. The Midnight Motel, a seedy one story with a communal porch for all rooms letting out onto the parking lot surrounded by strip malls and gas stations on a busy street. If the manager's any indication the rooms are disgusting, greasy, and reek of B.O. At least a room won't eye fuck me. I have to pinch Jason to wake him. Ugh, I was right. I lead him into the disgusting, stuffy room where a cockroach sleeps on the bed. I don't think the window's been opened for a decade, the same amount of time since a maid serviced the room. Still, in my worn-out state, it's the fucking Four Seasons.

"I need a shower," Jason says.

"Yes, you do," I say, opening the window. Of course I'm one to talk. My deodorant wore off five hundred miles ago. "You better get to it. Don't want to pass out in there." When I return to the room with our suitcase and weapons bag, he's already in the bathroom. I leave them on the bed—oh, Lord I think the bedspread has mold sprouting on the fake flowers—then leave again. Tire shopping to do.

I have to endure another round of eye coitus with Walt the manager to get the name and address of the nearest tire store. Pep Boys save the day. Good thing I stole a newer model car otherwise they might not have the right tire in the store. The clerk seems reluctant to sell it without attaching it. Guess I'm the only person ever to buy a tire and not want installation. Doesn't help I pay in cash. We're running low on that as well. We have maybe enough for gas and a fast food stop or two. We'll make it to Maryland by the skin of our teeth.

Walt must have been watching out for me because I'm barely out of the car in the Midnight parking lot before he strolls out. I really have no patience or energy left for his bullshit. He's by my side as I walk to the trunk.

"Got your tire," he says.

"Yep." I roll the new tire to the side and retrieve the tools in the trunk.

Walt pretends to look at the license plate when he's really staring at my ass. "Oh, Utah, huh? You one of those Mormons?"

"Yep," I say, positioning the jack. The only thing Barry ever did for me, taught me to change a tire. Probably because he didn't want to spend money on adding me to his AAA account.

"Sexy and handy. Nice."

The last straw is reached when the asshole touches my bare shoulder. I do what I always do, react. I drop the bar and grab one of his offending fingers, bending it back to get my point across. Walt gasps more in surprise than pain. I stare at him. Hard. "Touch me again. I dare ya." I release his finger. "Fuck off." Shaking my head, I return to work as the perv retreats to the safety of his office. Should have broken it.

When I'm done, I return to the room. I've earned a nap. Jason is asleep in bed facing me with a large strand of wet, golden hair falling on his cheek. Strange how I notice that before I take in his bare chest. Really I take him all in, utterly captivated. I don't know what it is, but he is the sexiest man I've ever laid eyes on. Hands down. Yet he is absolutely not my type. I usually go for the androgynous, lean men. There's nothing feminine about him whatsoever. Still I can't take my eyes off him. Every fiber of my being is screaming at me to crawl into that bed, bring him inside me, and bring us both to ecstasy. I force my eyes closed and take a deep breath. My will power is getting buns of steel with the workout I'm giving it. Shower. *Take a damn shower, Viv.* A cold one.

I never knew I could achieve bliss just by taking a shower. It's glorious. I wash my hair twice, scrub and scrub the dried blood I didn't know I still had on me, and let the scalding water baptize me of my considerable sins. I'd stay in for hours but my eyes keep closing on their own. After toweling off, I change into a large t-Jason's face is scrunched up as if there's manure spread under his nose as he moans. Bad dream. This isn't the first time he's done this. It happened on and off in the car during his marathon sleep yesterday. It passed quickly, though he was never curled up into the fetal position like now. His demons find him even in sleep.

I carefully climb into bed beside him so as not to wake him. He lets out another moan as I turn on my side so our backs face. I still feel him though, that always present heat burning from his body. There's maybe an inch or two separating us. *Ignore it. Sleep.* I squeeze my eyes tight, but with every pained whimper that sweet oblivion grows farther away. Oh, fuck it.

My will power officially gives up. I've never been a big spooner, but I'll make an exception now. I flip over and bridge the miniscule gap between us, curling against his tense body. He moans again. "Shush," I whisper, "it's okay now." He doesn't wake as I move my arm around his waist and up his exposed torso, resting my hand on his powerful heart. "It's okay." I feel his body loosen a little. I cling tighter.

The whimpers cease a minute later. The storm has passed. We can both find peace now. Just as I'm about to drift off, he moves his hand to mine, lacing our fingers together. I finally succumb to the steady rise and fall of his breathing with a smile on my face. No bad dreams for either of us now.

———

A truck's loud horn jolts me out of sweet oblivion, not that I mind. I'm greeted by something equally delicious. It seems in slumber our roles reversed, for the better. Jason's arms embrace me like a seat belt, one around my waist and the other across my chest, securing me tight against his scorching body. In sleep I've locked my arms to his. I'm glued to every contour of him so not even a sheet of paper could get between us. His breath tickles the back of my neck, as does the thumb tracing circles on my exposed collarbone. *This* is a fine way to wake up.

I close my eyes to relish all the sensations, even the feel of his erection pressing against my back. I'm afraid to move, afraid if I do he'll wake up and this will end. But I have to. My left arm is prickling with pins and needles from my weight on it. The pain's clouding everything else. I shift a tad to move onto my back. Jason lets out a moan as I rub against his erection with my butt, exactly what I was trying *not* to do. Honest.

He releases me from his embrace. Damn it. I flip over to face him and sure enough his eyes are open and staring at me. The agony in them startles me. "What?" I ask quietly.

"I … I dreamt you ran away from me, and when I found you my father was eating you. He made me watch," he whispers, voice cracking. "I couldn't save you."

"Oh," I say, stroking his cheek. "I'm here. I'm right here."

He presses his hand against mine, closing his eyes and almost grimacing. He huffs and puffs in an attempt to exorcise the bad memories. It physically hurts me to see him suffering like this, as if my stomach's in a vice, the pressure growing with every second of his torment. "Shush, shush," I whisper, cupping his other cheek. I kiss his forehead. "I'm okay." I kiss him again. "I'm right here. I'm safe. I'm safe."

I caress his sharp cheekbone with my thumb, never dropping my tender smile. Slowly the sides of his mouth move up to match mine. Until our eyes lock. What I see staring back gives me a bigger rush than any gunfight, car chase, or drug combined. It takes a wrecking ball to all my defenses, all my will power, all my resolve. Hunger. Bestial hunger. For me. I've never seen it in a man before this intensely, but I recognize it because my beast roars as loudly.

Neither of us moves, even blinks as this primal electricity vibrates between us. He's waiting for me to make the first move, to give him permission. I don't disappoint. I run my thumb along his dry lower lip. Upper, never breaking eye contact. His lips part, allowing me inside him. His wet tongue rolls against my thumb. Even this makes my g-spot throb. I wet his lips with my thumb before lowering my own onto them. The moment they make contact, he kisses me greedily, tongue pressing between my lips. I open to accept him. Dear God, can this man kiss. His hands are just as demanding, snaking under my shirt to urge me closer to him if possible. A flame passes up my body from my pulsating groin to my fluttering chest, stoked with dynamite by the feel of his manhood brushing against my engorged self with only my pants and his briefs separating us.

He pulls away from the kiss but only for a moment to lift off my shirt before finding my lips again. He starts there, teasing me with kisses and nibbles before trailing his tongue down to my left breast, tasting me. He takes my nipple into his mouth, rolling his tongue around its circumference, destroying me with that mouth. I moan. Then whimper as teeth bear down. The pain is savage. Sweet. Intense. He does it again. Tongue, teeth, tongue, teeth. Moan, whimper, moan, whimper. Soft, hard, soft, hard. I dig my fingernails into his back to steady myself because I'm about to fall off the edge of the universe.

This torment, this barbaric onslaught continues even as he yanks my pants off, then his underwear. He doesn't give me time to see him before he impales me, crashing into my body like a star hurtling to earth. Holy shit! I cry out loud enough to be heard in Maryland. The pleasure, the pain as he reaches the very end of me, my maximum depth, the shock of invasion all but makes my eyes fall back into my head and teeth clench. Then he pulls all the way out again, leaving a god-awful void only to ravage me again. And again, filling me until I'm nothing but lost in my twitches and quivers. In him. He surges into me over and over with the force of a tidal wave. Each stroke reverberates in my belly, strange agonizing pitches used to punish me. I want him to. My legs curl to draw him in deeper and I grab his luscious, muscular ass as he pumps furiously into me as his cock grows larger with each thrust. Shudders accompany each coupling. He's rough as hell, but goddamn does it feel amazing. Pulsing. No love is this act, just frenzied animalistic fucking like it's the last time either of us ever will. Still not good enough. I meet him pound for pound with each violent thrust, causing as much damage as he is to me. I bite and scratch, I'm sure drawing blood as I rake my fingers down his back and to his ass. Mine. *Mine.* The world's ending but I can die happy in this moment when he's inside me, filling me. I'm overfull, stretched to the brink of oblivion.

The tightening, the fire, the agonizing friction, the bliss, the tension, the sheer and utter fucking joy builds with every second, every attack, every pull in my groin until I cannot stand it a moment longer. The world tilts, spins, explodes, and crescendos like the end of a beautiful symphony as I orgasm, which brings him to nirvana too as we come what's left of our brains out. Perfect. Holy shit, that was fucking perfect.

He pulls out, sending my body into a state of shock with his absence like a junkie craving a high. A millisecond gone and I *need* him inside me again. Nothing in this world is right without him inside me. Jason stares at me again, panting as heavily as I am, the hunger replaced with surprise. Shock. At himself, at me, at the situation I haven't a clue. Thought is pretty damn difficult right now. I do know I don't like it. Especially when surprise morphs into horrific fear.

"What?" I ask. "Jason, what is it?"

His eyes search mine, for what I don't have a clue. He must not discover what he wanted because with a grimace his eyes jut down.

Away from me. "I'm sorry." The man leaps out of bed as I watch, mouth agape. I grab the sheet to cover my nakedness. I've never felt so exposed, so confused in my life. What the hell just happened? "I shouldn't have ... I promised ... I ..." he mutters to himself as he picks up his underwear.

"You promised who?" I ask. "Frank?"

He ignores me. Instead of answering, he pulls on his briefs then jeans from earlier. I've done a number on his back, drawing tiny pinpoints of blood down the red welts. My anger clears the confusion. Fury fueling me as usual, I climb out of bed with the sheet wrapped around me. Jesus Christ, I'm already sore. "Hey! I'm talking to you!" I get right in his face, even closing the suitcase on him as he attempts to retrieve a shirt for his escape. "Jason, talk to me! Look at me!" His eyes move momentarily up to mine, revealing nothing, before shooting back down. "I'm not your real sister, Jason. We didn't do anything wrong here. And Frank never has to find out." Jason looks up again, thorny and scornful at the same time. "No matter what you promised Frank—"

"This has nothing to do with him."

"Then what—"

"*Me*," he says, staring down at me with wide eyes. "I promised *me*."

My own eyes narrow in confusion. "I-I don't—"

"Forget it. Just ... forget it," he says, stepping away from me. "This never should have happened. I have to go. I have to get out of this room." He has to get away from *me*. I don't know what else to do but watch in silence as he puts on a black shirt and shoes. "Um, just keep the door locked and don't make any calls. I'll ... be back."

"Jason—"

He grabs the room key and hurries out without another word. I stare at the spot he just inhabited, part of me willing him back into it. What … the *fuck* was that? I'm used to guys rushing out after sex, but—

Out of nowhere, I burst into tears. Hard, wracking sobs I can't control. I crumple to the floor, clutching the sheet for some semblance of comfort. I have no idea why I'm crying or how to stop. It's just so … overwhelming. The desolation. What did I do wrong? I don't know what I did wrong or how to fix it. My eyes. It was fine until he looked into my eyes. He looks into them and doesn't like what he sees. What's the matter with them? *Okay, stop this. Stop.* This is exhaustion at work. Stress. Mortification. *Calm down, Viv.* Calm down. Fuck him. His loss. He doesn't deserve a single tear.

The pep talk doesn't work. Even I know I'm lying.

It was my fault. I should have stopped it. I knew he was conflicted. I knew he doesn't do one-night stands. I must have made this feel cheap and tawdry. Like I make everything feel in my life. I broke my promise. This is my punishment. I'm no good. That must be what he saw as he gazed into my eyes. A selfish bitch. No good. No use to anyone.

I sob until my eyes ache, and my skin is raw from wiping the tears away. The only thing about being bone tired is I have little energy to fuel a long crying jag. Five minutes is all I last. When I'm spent, when I'm empty, I dab my eyes one final time, take a ragged breath, and pick myself up off the floor. I don't feel a hell of a lot better, but at least I'm not a weeping mess anymore. I glance at the clock. Three hours. I only got a little over three hours of sleep. Despite my fatigue, I don't think I could drift off now. Hell, I don't think I want to even look at that bed again. Like him I just want out of this damn hotel room. The scene of the crime. Really, I want to take the car keys and drive off, never to see him again. He'd be better off without me. To my addled brain this seems like a brilliant idea. Go it alone. Maybe return to Kansas, beg the agents to protect me. I pay taxes when I remember to do my returns.

As I'm cleaning him from my body in the bathroom, the more I contemplate this, the better the idea becomes until I've convinced myself it's the best course of action. I'm running. Stick with what you know, right? I return to the room and begin throwing his clothes out of our suitcase before I can talk myself out of this. There's a loud, screaming voice in my head telling me this is idiotic. Just plain wrong. My heart not my head is in the driver's seat though. Its voice carries a megaphone. Overpowering. It's telling me to run. I'm fucking listening. I pull on jeans and a black v-neck shirt before frantically grabbing all my stray items around the room. I toss them into the suitcase, zip it up, slip on my flats, and walk out the door.

The motel's gotten busier in the last few hours with double the cars in the lot and even a line at the gas station across the street. Two clean-cut men in baseball caps walk out of the room next to mine, eyes glued to me. They probably know I was the one screaming. I don't care. I barely give them a second glance. I throw the suitcase in the backseat and slam the door shut. I start moving to the driver's side. I should at least leave a note: "Going rogue. See you never." He'll be fine. He'll steal another car, drive—

"Vivian Frances Dahl?"

"What—"

Fuck. The men in caps are bridging the ten-foot gap between us, the one in front holding a pistol down to the ground but holding it none the less. The second man, a step behind, has his hand on his belt, no doubt reaching for a gun as well. Shock and utter fear squeeze my throat shut, so I can't even draw breath. This is it. They've found me. I die in the parking lot of a flea-bag motel in Ohio. The first man raises his gun. "Drop the key and step away from the car with your hands above your head!" With trembling arms, I do all he orders. "All units move in. A and B. Now! Now!"

Those words ratchet down my fear to a reasonable decibel. Oh, thank God. I've never been so relieved to be under arrest. A flurry of activity occurs all at once it's difficult to focus on one. With the gun still on me, the second man approaches, pulling out his cuffs. At the same time, sirens ring out as two cruisers barrel out of their hiding spots from the side of the motel near the manager's officer and McDonald's on the other side. The officer grabs my wrists and yanks my arms down while reciting Miranda. The handcuffs cut into my flesh as four more officers leap out of their cruisers, guns pointed right at me as I'm patted down. "Do you understand these rights as I've presented them to you?"

"Y-Yes."

Holy shit, this is really happening.

The cop pushes me toward one of the cruisers as the rest siege my room. Jesus Christ my life has changed from horror movie to porn to an episode of *COPS* all in one day. This realization makes me laugh out loud. "What's so funny?" the officer asks.

"Nothing," I chuckle. I'm still laughing as I'm forced into the backseat of a Crown Victoria.

"... officers in need of assistance at Burger King, 18976 Ringrold Road," the radio in front says. "Two officers down, repeat two officers down. Suspect is Gavin McHale, 6'4", blonde hair, approximately two hundred fifty pounds wearing blue jeans and black t-shirt, last seen running fast west on Route 57. He is armed with a knife and police officer's gun and is extremely dangerous. Proceed with caution."

West. The opposite direction from here. Still, a huge wave of relief warms my amped body. He got away. Thank God. Thank you, God. The rest of the officers, having cleared the room, sprint out to their cars, I assume to chase Jason. Poor men don't stand a chance.

"Ambulance en route. Nature of injuries?" the dispatcher asks.

"Um, possible dislocated shoulder on Officer Kopek, and I think I broke a rib. Guy's strong and real fast. He may be high on something."

"Copy."

The officer who slapped the cuffs on me opens the car door. "Where did he go?"

I keep my mouth shut tight. I learned the first time I was arrested to just remain quiet. Don't even ask for a lawyer unless absolutely necessary. The officer glares at me for a few seconds, seething, but when that doesn't work slams the door shut again. Just pissing men off right, left, and center lately. It is my greatest gift.

The officers exchange a few more words outside that I can't hear before my officer rounds the car to get into the driver's seat. "I'm taking you to the station," he says, starting the car. He scowls back at me in the rearview mirror. I mimic Jason's usual expression, blank. "Looks like your boyfriend ran out on you."

"Karma is a bitch."

NINE

SINCE I'VE BEEN ARRESTED three times before—underage drinking, possession, DUI—I know what to expect. Fingerprints, mug shot, strip search, not fun. This station is small with the holding cells actual old school bars just down the hall from the bullpen and interrogation rooms. I'm one of three women in residence, one attempting to sleep off a hangover in between vomiting in the communal toilet and the other tweaking out of her gourd. She spends an hour just scratching at her arms to kill the imaginary bugs. We all ignore one another, lost in our own bullshit.

My bullshit involves eavesdropping on the officers down the hall. I only hear bits and pieces of conversation, but it seems the hotel manager ratted us out. Called in the police with our "suspicious behavior." There was a nationwide bulletin sent by Donovan with the Accord's make, model, and state stolen from. We should have changed the plates again when we left Utah. Or *I* should have. An oversight that probably just cost me my damn life.

Since the car was linked to a federal fugitive, the locals were told to just surveil until Donovan arrived. When Jason took his walk they followed him. But it was when I came out with a suitcase they figured I was leaving, and the officer who held the gun on me decided it'd be smarter to apprehend us before we left the jurisdiction. The whole station heard his boss ream him out for jumping the gun. Good. That bastard signed my death warrant. I hope they bust him down to crossing guard.

So I sit, listen and wait. No rescue this time. No storming the police station. I don't have Agent Price's phone number or Frank's, not that they could do much. Neither could a lawyer. I know because I asked. I can get one when I'm in "Federal custody." I can't see Donovan following that particular protocol. The locals don't even ask me questions. The only contact is when the guard spits on my bologna sandwich. You don't make friends with police when your alleged boyfriend beats up two of their fellow officers. I just eat the apple.

Hours pass, each slower and more painful than the last. Waiting for your execution, knowing it's coming but not being able to stop it, it's downright torture, no question. By hour five my fingernails are down to nubs and not even pacing helps alleviate the stress. I'm as jittery as the tweaker, jerking at every cough and ringing telephone. The guilt weighing me down like a lodestone doesn't help. The "if only's" cycle through my head. If only I hadn't insisted we stop. If only I'd switched the license plates. If only I hadn't seduced him. If only I had begged him to stay. If only I hadn't decided to abandon him. That's the one that haunts me. It's my fault, it's only my fault. I should have stopped it. Gotten out of the bed. Pushed him off me. I just wanted him so badly. I don't blame him at all for abandoning me to the wolves. God knows I was about to do it to him. All for pride. Just to punish him. Guess he wised up, saw me for what I am. No good. At least he got away. I didn't drag him down with me this time.

After my thousandth lap around the cell, the guard who brought me lunch returns with cuffs in hand. "Dahl, back up against the bars with your hands behind you."

Guess my executioner's arrived. About damn time.

After slapping the cuffs on again, the officer leads me down the hall toward the grinning Donovan. Bastard. He looks from me back to the man in a suit he was speaking to before. Donovan signs a piece of paper on the clipboard the suit's holding. "I cannot tell you how much I appreciate all your department's hard work on this," Donovan says.

"Glad to be of help," the suit says. "We still have officers combing the area for McHale. We believe he may have stolen a car from a Wal-Mart parking lot. There's a BOLO out, but he's probably long gone."

"Let's hope not," Donovan says as he hands him the clipboard. "Extradition warrant, signed and sealed."

"Thank you."

The guard removes my cuffs only to push me toward Donovan who pulls his own out. "Hello, Miss Dahl. Always a pleasure." He closes the cuffs so tight I wince. Donovan's all smiles though. "Lieutenant, thank you and please thank the officers who were injured. I hope they make a speedy recovery."

"I will. And if we find McHale, you'll be our first call."

"Appreciate it. Have a nice day."

Donovan tugs on my cuffs to lead me out. I could scream. I could fight. I could tell the police the truth, but there isn't a chance in hell they'd believe me. All I can do is attempt to maintain dignity. Not let the fucker know how shit scared I really am. How I manage to keep my legs from giving out, hell if I know.

"You are a major pain in the ass, you know that, right?" he asks as we step outside into the hot soup of the day. "I have used up every favor, ever inch of clout I had trying to track you and keep this thing under wraps. You also owe me the deposit on the rental car you destroyed."

"Gee, sorry I made it so hard for you to kill me. I'll try and be more considerate next time," I say in a monotone.

He yanks me toward a Lincoln town car where another officer with a clipboard closes the trunk. "All the evidence we recovered from the car and motel is in the trunk, sir. Just need you to sign this chain of custody form."

"Excellent. Someone else from the Marshal's service will be by to retrieve the car," Donovan lies. "Let me just secure the prisoner."

"He's going to kill me," I blurt out. "Help me. Please don't let him take me."

The men glance at one another, the young officer confused but Donovan cool as ice. That is until he breaks into a laugh, the officer joining him a second later. "Oh," Donovan chuckles, "that's a new one. Usually they accuse me of framing them." He shakes his head. "Oh, I needed a laugh." The bastard opens the back door behind the driver's side.

"Please!" I plead to the officer as I'm shoved into the car.

Deaf ears. Donovan unlocks one cuff to thread through the thick plastic door grip, then resecures me to it. He shuts the door before moving to the officer, using all his good old boy charm on the man. Patting his back, cracking jokes as they both laugh. The car thief/serial killer's accomplice doesn't garner a second glance. My stomach clenches as the officer walks away. Donovan waves with that sickening saccharine smirk, which drops as soon as the officer's back is turned, morphing into a hard glare when he pivots my way. I throw one right back at him.

Donovan climbs into the driver's seat. "Nice try."

"Fuck you."

I barely get out the second word before out of nowhere he spins around and backhands my cheek. The force knocks me sideways into the corner. My temple collides with the door, and I taste blood as I bite my lip. The throbbing pain from both is instantaneous.

"That was for Wyoming. I'll give you your *real* punishment for making me look bad in front of my Alpha when we get to the house. I'll let the others have a go too." After a cruel, twisted smile, he revolves back around and starts the car.

God, I wish I had a lamp to smash over his head like the last time a man hit me. Instead, I have to lie here, letting my cheek and mouth pound in time to my racing heartbeat hard enough I worry my eyeball is about to pop out. *Just keep your mouth shut, eyes open, and brain on, Viv.* If I see an opening, I'll take it. Grab for his gun, get him to crash the car, whatever it takes.

Because if I am dying today, by God I'm taking this fucker out with me.

We pull out of the parking lot and start toward my place of demise. In a minute or two the throbbing fades enough so I manage to sit up and watch the town go by. My kidnapper doesn't admire the view. Every thirty seconds Donovan's gaze whips up to the rearview mirror. By the time we reach the interstate, a large smile stretches across his face. When I glance back, I see nothing but cars. I was hoping a tank or a horde of zombies were coming to my aid.

Donovan pulls out his cell phone. "Seth, it's Phil. Yeah, I got her. No problems." He's quiet. "I think I spotted him. He's trailing us as I thought he would." I glance back again. The same cars from before remain, one a white Civic three behind. Jason. All the pain and terror is momentarily replaced with beautiful relief. I actually feel lighter, like I don't have to struggle to breathe. He didn't leave me. Of course he didn't. How could I have ever believed he would?

Donovan's cruel grin brings me back to reality. "Yeah," he says before listening again. "No, I think I'll be safe. He won't risk her getting caught in the crossfire. He'll just follow." More silence. "Really? Well, that makes things a hell of a lot more interesting. The others know?" Quiet. "We know what kind of firepower they're bringing?" Silence. "No, I have the guns they got in Kansas. He might have one on him, I don't know." How the hell does he know we stopped in Kansas? "Four hours without stopping. Everyone will be there by then?" Donovan listens. "Yes, sir. Keep me posted when you receive more information." Silence. "I appreciate your confidence in me, sir. I won't let you down again. Bye." He hangs up and lets out a long sigh. "Why is life never easy?"

"Karma."

"Oh, shut up."

"You know, it's not too late. You can pull this car over. Surrender. Join the good guys."

"Yeah, no thanks," Donovan says.

New tactic. "You're an officer of the law, sworn to protect people, not kill them."

"You know what I've learned from thirteen years on the job? Despite what the movies may want you to believe, the bad guys win. I may slow them down a little but they get right back up and out there doing what they do, and making a shitload more money than I ever will. All I've got to look forward to is a pension my ex gets half of that I can't live on."

"You're doing this for money?"

"There's millions in the pack account. I've been promised fifty grand to start. Plus, once we get the East settled, Seth promised we'd try for the Central. I'd get to be Alpha. The boss. Costs a few people?" He shrugs. "That's the life of a werewolf. I'd tell you to get used to it, but I doubt you'll survive the night." He stares at me in the rearview with a chilling grin. "And from the way things are shaping up, it is gonna be a fun one."

Yeah, the bait always has a ball right before it's slaughtered.

TEN

MORE WAITING. AT LEAST this time I have something prettier to look at than a tweaker. We drive. And drive. And drive some more all along my old friend, I-70. Donovan barely acknowledges my presence the entire ride. He's too busy keeping track of Jason and answering phone calls. From what I piece together, they're constructing a massive trap at someone's house in Pennsylvania, a trap Jason is driving right into. I'm sure he knows this. Still he follows mile after agonizing mile. Him and his stupid honor. They're gonna massacre him.

Part of me is joyous that he's here, that there's a glimmer of hope trailing behind me in an Accord. But the other 90 percent is literally praying he'll wise up. Turn that damn car around and not look back. There's no reason for us both to die. It's just stupid. *Stupid.*

If I could only move, I'd crash the car. Donovan never drives below seventy, and my hands aren't free. I can't kick him because I'm behind him. The cuffs are so tight I don't think breaking my thumbs would even work. For a second I consider flinging the door open, but even that doesn't work. The child lock must be engaged. From every angle, this is hopeless. After an hour, I just give up. I slump against the door, collapsing from exhaustion. The cat naps help, but I seem to jerk awake whenever he takes a phone call. The sun begins to set, and when I wake for the third time only a little orange remains behind us in the west. I don't think we're in Ohio anymore judging from the signs. I sit up and glance at the clock. We're been driving for four hours.

"I have to pee," I say.

"Almost there. Keep being a good girl and maybe I'll give you a lollie."

Ten minutes later, we pull off the interstate onto a two-lane road heavily wooded on both sides. Trees soon give way to a field, then more trees. It's beautiful. Desolate. No one will ever hear me scream. About two miles down, Donovan turns onto a dirt road. We follow it about half a mile before rolling through a wooden covered bridge badly in need of more red paint. I glance back, but the Accord has vanished.

My 10 percent selfishness rears its ugly head. My body locks from fear as I stare at the empty road. He wised up. He's left me. Perhaps that wasn't even him. I keep my eyes glued behind us, waiting with bated breath for the Civic to materialize again. No joy. A quarter mile of nothing but thick trees later, we pull into a small field with a tall, middle-aged man holding a shotgun standing by the road. Donovan slows, and I face front. A farm house. I die in a farm house. Not even a nice one. Like the bridge it's badly in need of paint, the shutters on the second story are literally hanging by a nail. The barn farther down the clearing is in the same sorry state.

If not for all the lights on inside and out, three cars on the lawn, and a man on the porch, also with a shotgun, I'd think the place was abandoned. No such luck.

Donovan rolls down the window to speak to the first guard. "Everyone here?"

"Yeah. No sign of anyone else. We've done two sweeps."

"He probably just got into position now. I figure a minimum of an hour. Keep vigilant anyway."

"Wish our guy was with them, huh?"

"Can't have everything." The guard nods before we continue toward the house. The moment the car shuts off, stinging bile rises up my throat. If it wasn't closed so tight, I'd barf all over the car. This is literally the end of the road for me. No more miles to save me. I die here. It's so . . . final. My breath escapes in short spurts through my nose like a pig. Bacon. I'm bacon.

Donovan exits the car, waves to the burly man on the porch, and opens my door. I'm trembling so bad he has difficulty unlocking my cuffs. They rattle right along with me. Donovan's thin lips purse in annoyance, but he frees me. It feels good to stand, even if my legs are seconds from giving out on me. Donovan must sense this because after re-cuffing me, he holds me by the waist as we walk up the creaky porch.

"Phil," the burly man says.

"Gig," Donovan says back as we walk inside.

The interior is about as pretty as the exterior. Martha Stewart would faint if she saw this place. Just in the foyer, which is just a hall, there's a thick coat of dust on all the mismatched and cracked knickknacks. The varnish on the hardwood floor wore off decades ago and a few planks are missing. On the stairs to my left, a grizzled old man with a scraggly gray beard dressed in overalls sits with a rifle in his lap. The stairs groan as he rises. "You Donovan?" he asks.

"Yes, sir," says Donovan. "We can't thank you enough for the use of your farm."

More creaking to my right draws my attention. A man my age with short brown hair and a goatee comes down the hall with a pistol in his jeans and shotgun slung over his shoulder as if he were strolling down Park Avenue.

"That son of a bitch killed my boy. Heard he put him down like a dog in some parking lot. That true?"

"Yes."

I think they're talking about Cooper. I do see a resemblance in their height and sturdy, squat build.

"He was a good solider until the end, sir. And the man who pulled the trigger is right outside. Your son's death will not go unavenged."

"Appreciate that."

"Is there somewhere out of the way we can keep her? We may need her later."

"Root cellar. Moon cage down there," Cooper answers. "Key's on the peg next to it."

"Thank you," Donovan says, digging out the cuff key. "Mick, she needs to pee. Let her, and then take her to the cellar." Goatee exchanges the shotgun for the key and me. Nice to know my worth. My new jailer eyes me up and down, all but licking his chops. Yeah, after a day in jail I'm a real centerfold. "Mr. Cooper, if you could give me a tour of the house so I can learn the layout? We need to start setting up."

Mick jerks me by the cuffs down the hall as Donovan follows Cooper upstairs. There's a bathroom just after a photo of Cooper Jr. in Army fatigues. I can't look at it. All I see is his brain splattering over that parking lot. That horror is replaced with one in real time, a stinking bathroom with black mold in every cranny. Adding insult to injury, Mick refuses to take his eyes off me. He stands in the doorway, gaze glued to my exposed legs and above. Truth is I have to pee so badly there could be ten men watching and I'd barely care.

"See the carpet matches the drapes," Mick says.

"Yeah, haven't heard that one before."

When it's time to wipe, my jailer says, "I can do that for you if you like."

"Think I can manage, thank you," I say with a hard edge.

I don't like the glint in his brown eyes one iota. Twice I've seen that look, as if I were nothing but a piece of meat. A toy. Inhuman. Both times I came *way* too close to becoming a rape statistic. I think tonight the "third time's a charm" rule will be tested. I hike up my pants and flush the toilet, or at least try to. Bad, groaning pipes.

Nature's call answered, Mick snatches me out of the small room and pushes me into the kitchen. There's another man with dark hair in a ponytail with his back to me, fixing a sandwich. That's five. Five against one. Not even Jason can withstand those odds. He *cannot* come into this house. Which means I have to get out.

My jailer opens the door across from ponytail and shoves me down the rickety wooden stairs. The cold, damp air gives rise to goosebumps instantaneously. Mick switches on the light. I will say this for regular jail, they keep the dust and cobwebs to a minimum. My new cell hasn't been cleaned since the Eisenhower era. There are boxes close to disintegrating. Children's toys like rocking horses are now spider colonies. Racks of rusted canned goods fill an entire wall. If the werewolves don't kill me, the toxic mold will. The floor is actual packed dirt. It's a large grave. My grave.

What really captures my attention sits in the back corner. A cell, rusted like everything else here. It's maybe 9 by 11 feet, small, but up to the ceiling with some bars bent outward in the middle as if whatever was inside desperately attempted to get out. A werewolf judging from the claw marks covering the back wall. Mick retrieves the key for the padlock, undoes the lock and chain holding the doors together, and shoves me in. The reek of mold vanishes, replaced with a strong salty and metallic odor. There are tufts of fur mixed with what resembles dried glue covering the back wall and floor. Ectoplasm. Better than what my first thought was.

I make note that after he relocks the chain, he places the key in his right pocket. "Come here," he says.

"Why?"

He pulls out the handcuff key. "Want those cuffs off?" Since my hands are all but numb from lack of circulation, I step forward. He grabs my hands, jerking me into the bars so hard my chin whacks against them. He's oblivious to this new pain of mine, oblivious to everything but my chest. It's so cold my nipples stand at attention. "Good girl." He unlocks me, caressing my hands and wrists far more than necessary. I keep on a mask of indifference. "Cold down here, huh? If you're nice to me, maybe I'll bring you a jacket. Would you like that?"

I want to spit in his face, bite his nose off, but hold back. I may need him on my good side later. Right now, I just need him gone so I can think. "Thank you," I say when the cuffs fall off. I move back as far as I can against the clawed wall.

Mick literally licks his lips as his eyes devour me one last time. "Be back, babe."

I don't allow myself to relax until I hear the upstairs door shut. I let out the ragged breath I was holding before sliding down the wall into the sitting position and hugging my knees to my chest. I don't know what to do. I'm locked in a fucking cage. Even if I managed to get out of here, there are five werewolves with guns upstairs to sneak past. I don't stand a damn chance.

This is insanity. I'm gonna die here. I don't want to die. I'm not ready. I thought I'd have more time. I want Jason. This is all me. This is all my fault. *I* made him run. *I* insisted we stop. *I* seduced him. Now *I'm* going to get killed. No, I can't fall apart now. *Don't you fall apart, Vivian Frances Dahl.* You need to get the hell out of this cell. You need to get out of this house before he commits suicide for your undeserving ass. *Earn* all he's done and will do for you. Keep your damn promise for once. Be the person he seems to think you are. Who you can be.

Fight.

My eyes rocket open and like the night in the parking lot calm burns away the fog of fear. The world around me becomes crystal clear as all my senses heighten. The smell of werewolf, of Jason still on my skin. The sound of footsteps above my head. The soft warm breeze wafting from the right. My gaze whips in its direction. At first all I notice are boxes piled on top of boxes like steps, then I notice a piece of white lace atop one billowing a little. I follow behind it and spy slats of wood at an angle obstructed by boxes. Cellar door. Exit. Excellent.

The cage. I stand to examine it inch by inch, then testing the more rusted parts for their strength by pulling with all my might. Only one wiggles where I assume a werewolf threw himself against the cage. I *will* have better luck than he did.

At least I have a project to pass the time before my execution. There's a sharp but thin edge keeping the bar in place that I must dislodge. I kick it as I learned to do in cardio kickboxing. Whack. Whack. I get in two five-minute rounds before Mick comes to investigate the noise. Each time he finds me in the corner hugging my knees and rocking back and forth. When he asks what the noise was, I rock harder in response. I can't risk a third visit, not by him. Plus my legs are killing me.

I resort to alternating between shows of brute upper body strength, which I am sorely lacking, and the more precise jiggling of the bar, slowly wearing down its resistance. I don't know how much time passes, hours I think, as above me furniture skids and thuds as men walk to and fro, getting ready to murder my Blondie. I do my utmost to not to think about that. All that matters is getting the bar out. Just get the damn bar free. For Jason. For me. Just get it free.

Little by little it gives way. Whenever my patience is tested, and I'm about to scream in frustration, give up, I call up an image of him. Watching me onstage in awe. In the car in Kansas when something magical passed between us. The expression of sheer happiness as he entered me for the first time. I want more of these moments. *Keep going.*

I think two or three hours pass, it's hard to gauge. My hands, my shoulders, even my legs ache. Almost there though. Two hard kicks and the bar clatters to the floor. Yes! I reach through the bars for it. Part one complete. I wedge the bar inside the chain to pry it loose. Nope. Whacking the padlock fails too. Which leaves riskier option three.

"Hello!" I shout. "Marshal Donovan! I need you! Marshal!"

It takes a full minute of hollering before I hear the door above open. Shit, I'm really gonna do this. I *can* do this. Fear closes up my throat, but I *will* do this. Mick walks through the boxes. *I can do this, I can do this* ... "What?"

"I have to use the bathroom again. It's an emergency. I'm about to crap my pants." The last one isn't a lie, just not literally.

"Go in the corner."

"No, please," I say, rushing to the bars. "I'll do anything. Anything you want, I won't put up a fight. Just please let me use the toilet. I'll be good. Please."

The werewolf scans me up and down. All he sees are my pleading eyes and defeated body language. What he doesn't see is the jagged metal bar riding up my spine tucked into my waistband. If he did he'd never step toward me to undo the padlock and chain. I reach behind as he moves in. "Better make it fast, though. We think your boyfriend—"

Like a bolt of Zeus's lightning, I swing the bar around, smashing it against the side of his head. Hard. I don't know if it's the pain or shock, but Mick cries out as he bangs against the cell from the force. The moment he hits, I swing again. And again. And again. Blood splatters everywhere, on me, on the floor as I bash and bash and bash. I barely notice. Again. Again. He slumps to the floor, blood streaming down his face in three different spots. Breathing as if I climbed Mt. Everest in one shot, I stare down at him for a second. He doesn't move. I think I killed him. Footsteps above distract me from further thought. Fight now, cope later.

I take a step out of my cage. Part thre—

A hand clamps onto my ankle. The next thing I know, I'm toppling to the dirt, ending with a jarring thud onto my stomach and jaw. The pain in my mouth is instantaneous as teeth knock together and on my tongue. Blood fills my mouth. The pain, the copper taste distracts me from what's really important, which I only realize when that same vice on my ankle wrenches me backward on the dirt floor. I glance behind to find a pissed Mick drawing me in with one hand and moving the other from his back with a . . .

Oh, fuck.

I kick with my free foot and bring the bar around, but the gun's already trained on me. Instinct makes me swing away. The rod connects with the gun arm. A shot rings out the moment a searing, white hot line of pain slices across my arm. Somewhere in my brain it registers I've just been shot, but I'm too busy to realize it or that people are shouting and running upstairs before Mick recovers. He whacks my hand holding the bar against the cage. More intense pain rockets through my pinky. I drop my weapon. Before I understand the ramification of this, the psycho backhands my left cheek. I see literal stars and my head smacks against the floor near my bar. I shut my eyes to play dead.

"Bit—"

A loud gunshot from outside cuts short his words. The subsequent explosion, rattling of the house like a tremor hit and all the lights vanishing a half second later startles me even in my fuzzy state. I open my eyes to almost total darkness. More gunshots echo outside. Running footsteps. Shouting. I think someone screams, "Mick, get up here!" Chaos.

Jason.

Though it's dark as hell, using the tiny bit of light from outside I can make out Mick's body rising. *Now.* With one fluid movement, I grasp for the bar, and while sitting up thrust the jagged end into what I hope is his side. It must be because he howls in pain, though it's barely audible, overshadowed by the automatic gunfire upstairs and outside. I pull the rod out again, only to impale him once more. He lets off a shot, and in the light from the muzzle I see I've hit him just under the ribs. The moment we're plunged back into darkness, I sweep his feet from under him and jerk the bar out again. He lands beside me. I hear the gun drop. Roaring like a madwoman, I raise the bar above my head and plunge it square into his chest. Once. Twice. Half a dozen times, one right on top of the other. It feels as if I've floated beside myself, watching in horror as my twin continues this heinous act. In, out. In, out. Mick screams, but she puts an end to that, moving up and stabbing him through the neck. This is much easier to get through, fewer bones, though she hits an artery because blood geysers onto her face. Not even that stops the onslaught. Not even the gurgling as he chokes on his own blood. In, out. In, out. She only stops when that does. The silence calls me back into my wet body.

"Fuck, fuck," I gasp. *No guilt, just get up.*

I grab the gun. My hands are so slippery with blood, and I can't move my pinky, I can barely hold it. Even standing is painful. I push that aside. Part three, get the fuck out. I keep whacking against boxes in the almost nonexistent light, with only a tiny crack of it leading my way to the root cellar door. Not that I really want to go outside at present. Gunshots, screaming, snarling all alternate out there. Not much better above me with hard footfalls and the odd gunshot. *Stick with the plan.* I push boxes out of my way up the root cellar stairs. Get out, just get out. I clear the path but scream in frustration when I reach the top. Another chain and padlock. Please don't let the movies be wrong about this.

I place the gun right against the lock and fire. The second shot works. The lock breaks. Yes! I pull the chain off and push up. No! It barely budges. There's another chain and lock outside. "No, no!" I shriek as I fight against it. "N—"

Shit!

There's a low, threatening growl as something presses back on the doors. I only get a brief glimpse of tan fur before the doors slam shut. I shriek and leap back. I take another step down as claws begin furiously scratching against the wooden doors. Werewolf. Fuck that. Door #2 it is.

I work my way toward the stairs, collecting more bruises from the boxes. With my arm, tongue, and pinky throbbing like they're auditioning for a gig as a heavy metal drummer, I barely notice. Gun and me as ready as we'll ever be, I race up the stairs and wait by the door, listening. No footsteps, no gunshots. Find a door outside, run toward the tree line, stop for nothing.

Go.

I throw open the door and step into the kitchen. Empty. Amazing. Gun leading like in the movies, I check left. Running footsteps make me swing the gun right, finger on the trigger. The second I see movement, I fire. Too wide. The man ducks but keeps his shotgun pointed on me as he continues charging. I'm about to fire again when the man shouts, "Vivi!" and steps into a stream of light. It strikes his orange hair first, giving it a fiery glow, then his face. *My* face.

"Daddy."

I'm so shocked I don't even put up a fight as he pulls me into a tight hug. "Thank God, thank God," he whispers as he strokes my hair. My father's hugging me. My *father* is hugging me. He releases me a second later to examining me. "Are you alright?" he asks, voice breaking.

I give little nods. I can't speak right now. This is my father. He came to save me.

"Doll, how many were in the house?" Frank asks.

"F-Five," I sputter. "I-I-I k-k-killed one. In the basement."

He cups my bloody cheek and smiles. "Good girl."

A literal howl outside ends the macabre family bonding. Frank glances that direction, then pulls a walkie off his belt. "Omar, we're coming out. Car. Now." He replaces it. "We're going now. Don't leave my side for anything. We're headed for the black SUV. Come on."

My father lifts his shotgun and starts back the way he came with me a step behind. No one attacks as we charge down the hall toward the open front door. I have to step over a man in overalls missing most of his head and part of his chest to get outside. Mr. Cooper. I don't feel a damn bit of sympathy for him right now.

Smoke assails my nose when we step onto the porch, into the crisp night. Crackling flames light up the side of the house, I think from an exploded generator. Jesus, I'm in *Die Hard.* Through the thick, acrid cloud, I spot headlights moving closer. Frank dashes off the porch for the SUV as I trail behind. Frank's head whips right, and I follow his gaze. Holy shit. Ten yards away, a huge, light-colored wolf is muzzle deep into a man's chest, chowing down. The corpse's head lolls back and forth, protesting this invasion even in death. "Donovan." The wolf glances up from its feast just as the headlights hit his eyes. Its ice blue eyes. Dear God.

Jason takes a few steps toward us, but Frank points the shotgun at him. "No! Stay!"

The beast bares its bloody, ragged teeth and hair along his spine sticking straight up, but ceases moving. The wolf doesn't take his eyes off me. The SUV slows before us. A bald African American man with a sniper rifle climbs out of the driver's seat and rushes over. "Vivi, get in the car," Frank orders. I listen, rounding the car to the passenger side. "Status?" Frank asks.

"I got the one downfield," the man says in a Boston accent. "Jason another."

"Adam?" Frank asks.

"Chased one into the trees. I heard shouting. Think he got him."

"Take that truck and go confirm. Should be two in the house as well. Five total. If any are alive, secure them, then clean up here as best you can. No bodies, alright? When Jason and Adam change back, hurry back double time."

"Yes, sir," Omar says.

"Thank you." Frank climbs in beside me and shuts the door. "Seat belt, doll."

Right. Safety. Important. It hurts, everything hurts, but I manage to secure it. Frank swings the SUV around, and I get one last glimpse at the carnage. House toppling as it's consumed by fire. Two visible corpses. My lover throws his bloody snout back, howling as we drive away. I feel nothing. Not a thing except tired. So tired.

"It's okay now, Vivi," my father says beside me as the battle-field fades in the mirror. "It's all over. You're safe. I'm here doll. I'm here." He takes my good hand, squeezing it. "We're going home."

I squeeze my father back. Home.

PART II

HOME

ELEVEN

"Jason!"

I jolt awake right as Jason literally rips my throat out. The light stings my eyes, and it takes seconds of blinking to clear them. When I'm capable, I glance around the large bedroom I find myself in. Definitely not the skuzzy motel in Ohio from the dream. Billowy white curtains on the bay windows. Handcrafted wooden furniture that matches the brown suede lounge chairs in the corner. Huge TV. California king bed with what I think are Egyptian cotton sheets. I'm alone too. We were making love, slowly this time. Painfully slowly. He barely moved inside me, maybe a millimeter a second for what felt like hours. Amazing hours. Just as he brought me to the brink, I felt him shifting. He wouldn't release me, wouldn't leave my body as the slime coated him. As the fur sprouted everywhere. As bone shifted. I screamed and screamed and scratched as his claws pierced my skin. As blood flowed from my back, as he ripped me open in more ways than one before delivering the killing blow, jaws clamping on my throat. I touch it now just to make sure I still have one.

Damn, my neck's the one area that doesn't hurt. My legs and arms ache from working the cage for so long. My stomach feels like it's been punched, as does my jaw from the fall. My mouth and tongue are still raw from the bites. My splinted pinky throbs. Broken. The worst is my arm. The bullet grazed but still took a chunk out. Gonna leave a scar. It couldn't be stitched for the five hours it took to drive from Pennsylvania to Adolphus. About a mile from the farm, Frank pulled over to provide basic first-aid. The pills he gave me must have knocked me out because the next thing I knew, we were pulling up to this huge gate, easily twenty feet tall, with floodlights along the top. After passing through that, we continued on the driveway about four hundred feet with RVs and tents setup on the grassy lawn like a shanty town. One or two people came out but most remained asleep. Good thing I wasn't expecting a parade.

The main house wasn't as grand as I imagined. Big, but not a mansion. Two stories with a mix of Colonial and modern architecture. The main house is symmetrical like a rectangle made of white brick, with a gabled roof, paneled door, and maybe two dozen multi-pained windows with shutters. A few more people came out to greet us, barraging Frank with questions at the get go. He handed me off to an African American woman who stitched me up, gave me more pills, and escorted me to the second floor master bedroom. The pleasant narcotic blur returned when I was in the shower. I stumbled to the bed, put on the clothes the woman must have brought, and passed out again. Cue nightmares.

I glance at the clock on the nightstand. I've been asleep in this bed a little over twelve hours. I sure as hell needed it. Still groggy though. And I have to pee like crazy, but there isn't a force on earth than can make me move from this bed right now. Leaving the bed is the first step to leaving the room, and I'm not ready for that. Meeting the family. Seeing Jason. Maybe they'll leave me alo—

"She's awake, Mommy! I heard her!" a little boy shouts outside the door.

A woman, I presume the mother, shushes her son. Shit. As the door slowly swings open, I shut my eyes to feign sleep. There's a rattling of plates and quiet footsteps moving toward me.

"Should we wake her up, Mommy?" a little girl asks.

"No! Be quiet!" Mom whispers.

"She's awake!" the boy whispers. "I heard her yell for Uncle Jason." The bed shifts as someone climbs onto it.

"Dustin get—"

"Are you awake, Aunt Vivian?" the boy practically yells in my ear.

"Dustin!"

Shit. I have to open my eyes now. An Asian woman in white shorts, orange peasant top, and square bangs holds a tray of food. At her hip is her tiny double. The girl's about five and dressed in a yellow sundress. She stares at me, almond eyes stretched to the brink as if I had claws or three heads. I'm sure I look like I've gone ten rounds with Holyfield. Her, I assume, brother has no reluctance. He plops down right beside me with a smile on his cherubic face. He resembles Frank more than the girl, with a long jaw and thick nose. Still more of his mother than father. My brother.

"I am so sorry," the woman, um … *Linda* says, as she sets down the tray.

"It's okay."

"Told you she was awake," Dustin says.

"How are you feeling?" Linda asks.

"Shi—lousy," I say, glancing at the little girl. Whose name is ... *Nicole*! Thank you, brain.

"I brought you some lunch. I'm Linda, by the way. I'm, um, I was, um—"

"I know," I say, saving her. "Nice to meet you. All."

"Are you really Daddy's sister?" Dustin asks.

"Seems so."

"Our Daddy's in heaven with the angels and Grandma," Dustin informs me.

"I know. I'm sorry." The little girl peeks from behind her mother's leg. "And what's your name, little one?"

"That's Nicki," Dustin says. "She's my sister like you're Daddy's sister."

"Nice to meet you, Nicki."

The girl retreats into her mother's leg. "She's shy," Linda says.

"It's okay. I'd be scared of me too."

"Did the bad werewolves do that to you?" Dustin asks.

"Yeah."

"Grandpa and Uncle Jason are gonna murder the bad were-wolves who killed Daddy," Dustin says matter-of-factly.

"Okay," Linda says, voice rising a notch, "let's, um, let your aunt rest. Come on." Linda holds her arms out and Dustin literally hops over me to reach them. She lowers Dustin beside his still uneasy sister before the trio walks to the door. Halfway there, Linda remembers something and turns. "Oh. They brought your suitcase last night. It's over there," she says, gesturing to the corner.

"They? Jason's back?"

"Yeah, early this morning. He and Adam are probably still asleep though. A quick change turnaround takes a lot out of them."

"But he's okay?"

"As far as I know." Linda smiles. "If you need anything else, there's a million people around, just ask. I'll tell Frank you're awake."

"Thank you."

She nods and ushers Nicki out. Dustin gives a little wave, which I return, before he shuts the door. I fall back into the pillow with a sigh. Okay, that wasn't so terrible. I officially have a niece and nephew, not to mention an in-law. *Damn*. Seem nice enough though. She's younger than I imagined. Must have had the kids right out of high school. A widow in her early twenties with two small children. Life is so fucking unfair.

Linda brought me a turkey sandwich, apple, and OJ. I inhale the apple, chug the juice, and since I haven't eaten in over twenty-four hours, I even devour the whole sandwich. Been years since I last ate meat. Desperate times and all. With fuel in my body, I think I may actually be able to get out of bed now. I throw off the covers. Even that hurts, but I keep going. It's gonna be a Vicodin day for sure. Sluggishly, I pad over to my suitcase. Jason's clothes are on top. I attempt to grin but the pain in my cheek and jaw won't let me complete the gesture. Still. Perfect excuse to find him.

I retrieve my own clothes, a bright red sundress and underwear and toiletry bag before going into the bathroom. Fuck. No wonder small children hide from me. Black eye, swollen and bruised cheek, cut and swollen lip. My arms and legs aren't much better. It looks like someone tapped a message in Morse code using bruises. The bandage on my gun wound is saturated through. When I pull it off, I want to hurl. The black stitches and puckered, exposed flesh are raw and weeping blood. I redress it as fast as possible before changing into the red sundress and slapping on half a bottle of foundation to cover the bruises. When I resemble an actual human, I return to the bedroom, grab a white cardigan to hide the rest, and gather Jason's clothes. But as I grasp the door handle, I can't turn the knob. My new friend fear does a jig on the corpse of my nerves again. I really don't want to go out there. I've just traded one House O'Werewolves for another. And Jason's out there. What if he refuses to see me? Yells? But I can't stay in this room forever. Fuck it. I turn the handle.

Dustin and another boy have setup camp in front of my bedroom, Legos carpeting the hallway floor. "Hi, Aunt Vivian," Dustin says. He turns to the freckled kid. "This is my Aunt Vivian. She sings songs."

"Uh, hi kids," I say awkwardly. I haven't been around children in years. I'm rusty.

"We're building a rocket ship to send Rex up to the moon," the other boy says, holding up a green dinosaur.

"Awesome."

"Mommy says we're 'aposed to leave you alone. Why? Are you mean?" Dustin asks.

"I-I don't think so."

"Okay. My other aunt, Park, won't let me have sugar. Will you let me have sugar?"

"It—It's up to your mom, I guess."

"Uncle Jason lets me. Grandma said he wasn't really my uncle, not like Aunt Park and Uncle Russell. She didn't say anything about you. Are you my real aunt?"

"Um, yeah, I guess." How the hell do you explain genetics to a pre-schooler? You don't. "You two, um, get Rex to space. Have fun."

I leave the future engineers of America to their space voyage. They're just the first natives I encounter as I walk down the long hall. The four people smile and nod as we pass one another. Two even stop me to say how happy they are I arrived safely, as if they already know me. Everyone's being so nice. It's fucking weird.

Downstairs is worse. Squealing children dash up and down the hardwood floors with parents or older siblings following. Just as I step into the first-floor hallway, I count almost a dozen people, ages fifteen to seventy, of all ethnicities strolling in or out of rooms. I keep my head down but they still smile and say hello. I just wander in a daze, clutching the folded clothes to my chest for comfort. I don't know exactly what I'm looking for. Jason, sort of. He's not in the dining room, where a dozen people can sit comfortably along the huge table. Right now it's covered with half-full plates and bowls of food laid out like a buffet. Women filter in and out of what I presume is the kitchen, replacing empty bowls with more chips and plates of sandwiches. He's not in the family room, which is setup like a makeshift pre-school where I think a toy box exploded. *The Lion King* plays on the TV but only two children watch it. A pretty teenage girl with blonde hair, cutoff shorts, and yellow halter top wipes Nicki's nose as nearby two male teens, one with sandy hair and the other auburn, pretend to play cards but really scope her out. There's another boy watching in the corner too, though his laptop does a good job of hiding his interest. No Jason. He's also not in what I assume is the parlor. This must be off limits to the kids because I only find adults reading or working on their laptops. I leave without making a sound.

"You look lost," a man says behind me.

I spin around. A man about my height with buggy blue eyes, light brown hair, stocky build, and bright smile strolls toward me from the front door. "I, um …"

"Looking for the laundry?" he asks, glancing at the clothes.

"No, um, I'm looking for Jason. These are his."

"Well, I just left him. He's still asleep." The man holds out his hand for me to shake. "Adam Blue."

"Viv Dahl," I say, shaking it.

"Oh, I know who you are. Heard *a lot* about you." He pulls his hand away. "Glad to see we got you out of that house in one piece."

"Relatively," I say, holding up my broken hand.

Another man steps out of the room with two sliding wooden doors straight across from me. He looks remarkably like Adam, just with brown eyes and maybe an inch or two taller. Must be his brother, Tate. "There you are. Thought I saw you walking up." The brothers just nod at one another. "You okay?"

"Barely even a scratch," Adam says.

"And you must be Vivian," Tate says to me before eye fucking me. That is really getting annoying. "I can see what the fuss is about now."

Adam clears his throat and mercifully Tate's attention returns to his brother. "Sorry," Adam says. "Frog in throat."

"Oh," Tate says. "Viv, go get him a water."

"I—"

"Thanks." Tate throws his arm over his brother's shoulders. "Come on, baby bro. We're in the middle of war counsel. Frank sent me to fetch you."

Before I can tell Tate where to shove his water, he maneuvers Adam back into the room and slides the doors closed. O-kay. As I'm thirsty too, I retrieve water bottles from the dining room before returning to the sliding doors with muffled voices on the other side. I knock.

"Come in," a man says.

Okay, I feel like I've just walked into a scene from *The Godfather*. Frank sits at his desk with a portrait of two wolves running under a yellow moon behind him on the wall. Lots of those types of paintings on the walls around here. I recognize the three other men in the room. Adam on the antique couch in the corner with Omar, the sniper from last night, and Tate in the chairs directly across from Frank. Wonder if Al Pacino's just running late.

"Vivi," Frank says with a smile.

"I was just bringing Adam his water."

"Come in. Sit. We were just discussing last night."

Yeah, sounds like fun. Talking about the worst night of my life. Can't wait.

I slink over to Adam, sitting beside him and across from the giant bay doors that look out onto the shanty town and field. He gives me a reassuring smile as I do. "Thanks for the water," Adam whispers.

"As I was saying," Omar continues, "I salvaged one computer along with two cell phones, including the Marshal's, but as of this afternoon all the pertinent numbers are out of service. And the computer is password protected."

"Have Devin start cracking that password," Frank orders.

"What about the bodies?" Tate asks.

"Threw them in the house as it burned. I smashed out the Marshal's teeth so he couldn't be ID'd."

"And his car?" I ask. The men all glance at me as if they'd never heard a female voice before. "What? I was seen leaving in it by police with a Federal Marshal who will now be missing. If he's ever tied to the house and other bodies, it's a one-way trip to Death-penaltyville for me."

A quick, proud smile passes over Frank's lips. "She's right. The others have no real link to us. A Marshal and federal fugitive going missing will attract a hell of a lot of attention."

"I took off the plates and rolled the town car into a nearby lake," Omar says. "With him burnt and without teeth, it'll probably take weeks to ID him. By then, this should be over. We can ask George Black to delete the warrants for her and Jason."

"This Donovan was supposedly on vacation," Adam adds. "He had a friend altering records. None of his bosses knows what he was up to. He won't be reported missing for a while."

Really doesn't make me feel much better.

"So, we're fairly clean on last night," Tate says, "as long as the princess here doesn't get her ass arrested again."

I'm about to sling some choice words at this asshole, but Frank beats me to it. "Watch your tone, Tate Blue. That is my daughter, your pack member, you are speaking to. Apologize."

Frank stares at the man, mostly neutral but with a hint of menace in those blue eyes. Tate returns the gaze for a second, fighting for dominance but loses and looks away. "I apologize, Vivian, for my disrespect."

"Um, okay. I forgive you."

"Good," Frank says, neutrality returning. "Now, Vivi, I need you to tell us everything that happened when you were alone with Donovan and the others. Everything that was said or done in as much detail as possible."

The men listen, faces impassive, as I recount my living nightmare. There isn't a lot of intel I can give them as I was either asleep or locked in a cage most of the time. They listen as if I were telling them about a trip to Bermuda, like what I went through was just another day. Either they've been through a lot worse or I'm surrounded by sociopaths. I hope the first because I've reached my limit on sociopaths, thank you. Only Adam throws me a few sympathetic smiles.

"I don't know," I conclude, "I just got the impression that they didn't really want *me*. Even in the parking garage, I was incidental. Bait."

"What else struck you as odd?" Frank asks.

"Couple things. I mean, how did they even know it was Jason you sent to California? They came there looking for *him* not me. And Donovan mentioned our pit-stop in Kansas for weapons. Unless that vampire NARC'ed to Seth, the only people who knew we went were you guys. He also knew you were on your way to Pennsylvania. What he was saying at the time didn't make sense, but it does now. I think he even asked how many of you were coming. Add all of that to the bowl, plus Jason said you never advertised my existence, Frank, and I'm thinking there's a rat among the wolves."

"That's ridiculous," Omar says. "We're a pack. We—"

"The same pack that was once under this guy Seth's rule," I point out. "Who's saying there isn't a loyalist or two around?"

"She has a point," Tate says.

"So who knew about it all?" I ask. "Kansas? Me?"

Adam scoffs. "Come on. Who didn't? This pack is worse than any group of teenage girls when it comes to gossip."

"Wonderful," I say. "And here I thought I was a secret. That was the point, right?"

"There is no one who'd betray us like this, sir," Omar insists, talking over me. Protesting too much maybe?

"Okay, enough," Frank says, holding up his hands to stop the chatter. "I need time to think. Omar, you and Tate take Reid on the Costco run. Maureen says we're out of almost everything. Again. Try and make sure your guns stay hidden this time. And I don't want any of this rat business leaving this room until I decide how to proceed."

"Yes, sir," Tate says. He and Omar rise to leave.

"Adam, take over for Sam on perimeter duty if you feel you're up to it."

"I am, sir," Adam says as he stands. Adam shoots me another bright smile before walking out as well.

And I am alone with my father. Swell.

"Did you sleep well?" Frank asks.

"Yeah. Fine. Thanks," I say, glancing everywhere but at him.

"And how do you feel? In any pain?"

"I took some pills."

And cue the excruciating silence. I mean, even if I were operating at full capacity, I still wouldn't know what to say to this man. I study him for a split second. The resemblance really is uncanny. Same long jaw, same blue eyes, same red hair. Hell, we even look the same age. No way in hell would I think this man is in his fifties.

Mid-thirties maybe. Must be a werewolf thing, the lucky bastards. I look away before he catches me.

The thirty-second awkward silence tolerance must be genetic too because after second twenty-nine, Frank says, "Vivi, I—"

"You're sorry," I cut in. "You're sorry you dragged me into this nightmare. You're sorry you left me, that you never called me, that I inherited flat feet from your side of the family. I get it. I just... don't care. I'm too tired and freaked out and overwhelmed to even hear it right now. Thank you for sending Jason to me. Thank you for coming for me last night, okay? I appreciate it. I do. Everything else... just don't expect a Hallmark moment between us. Ever. There is no water under the bridge because the water swallowed that fucker up years ago. Okay?"

"That's... fair."

"Okay," I say, standing, "then I'm gonna try and make myself useful. Let you get back to work. You just became a rat catcher on top of all else."

"It seems I have," he says with a quick smile. "Thank you for all your assistance in this matter. It's appreciated. Good work."

"Always glad to be appreciated." I nod and walk out.

The moment I slide the doors shut, I take a deep breath and let it out. That went a million times better than I thought. Of course I always figured it'd end with me being arrested and him bleeding.

With Jason's clothes in hand, I walk out the front door, stepping into scalding soup. Steamy Maryland felt just like where I grew up in Florida, although I hadn't been back in years. I forgot how much I hate humidity, especially when it's in the high nineties already. The majority of people must be inside as the shanty town to my right is almost deserted. Air conditioning is a gift from the gods, no question. I remember Jason saying he had a house on the property, not sure where though. Thankfully Adam is in the driveway talking to a man standing beside an ATV. The sweaty man with black bushy hair, must be Sam, hands his helmet to Adam as I approach.

"Hey," Adam says with a smile. He does like to smile. "Sam James, Vivian Dahl."

"Hello," I say. "Call me Viv."

"Nice to meet you. See you around," says Sam before walking back to the house.

"We have two guys driving the perimeter at all times as lookouts," Adam explains.

"Smart." I pause. "You aren't, by any chance, driving by Jason's are you?"

"Yeah, but he's probably still asleep."

"Take me anyway? I have some of his clothes, and—"

"Oh, I can take them," Adam offers.

"I'd, uh, rather do it myself."

"Um, I don't know if that's a good idea. You're safer he—"

"*Please.* I need … I can't stay in that house right now. And I need to see him. I need to set eyes on him. The way we left things …" I shake my head to clear my list of bad deeds. "Please?"

I understand his reluctance. I am the siren that almost crashed his best friend's boat after all. Thank God he's such a softie. My pleas break him down. That smile resurfaces as he hands me the helmet. "Hop on."

He is officially my favorite. "Thank you."

I hold onto Adam as we careen down the paved driveway to a gravel offshoot through the trees. It is beautiful here. Thick trees with green leaves exploding from large branches. I forgot how green the East Coast is compared to brown California. The trees grow sparser by the second though, replaced with brush and wild grass, then sand, as dark blue water comes into view. As does a wooden bungalow at the end of the path. It's small with three windows visible, one on the triangular second floor. There are two trucks with planks of wood and tools in the back parked out front. As we stop beside one, I see the trucks have "Top Dog Construction" with a picture of a wolf on the side of the trucks. Their contracting business.

"You know he practically built this place himself," Adam says as I climb off. "I mean, we helped, but …" He shrugs. "The door's open. I'll be back around every fifteen minutes if you want a lift back. Flag me down."

"Okay. Thanks."

He puts the helmet on. "Just … be gentle with him."

"What—"

Adam speeds away before I can finish. What the hell did that mean? Whatever. I walk up to the house and enter through the ornately carved wooden door. The eaves around the roof have the same pretty, wavy pattern with tiny rosebuds sprinkled in. Bet it took him forever to carve those. Worth it, though. They're beautiful. The inside is bigger than I anticipated but still cozy. It's a large open room like my apartment, with a living room and kitchenette attached. The similarities stop there. His furniture is much nicer than mine, most of it carved wood, but mixed with various blue and plaid cushions softening the couches. There are huge bay windows along the back wall looking out onto a deck and water. The snoring werewolf in the loft above me cuts through the calm.

There's a ladder, but when I walk into the kitchen I see him asleep in the bed next to the only other piece of furniture up there, a nightstand. I love this place. If not for the beer cans, dirty plates, clothes strewn around, and sheets on the couch it'd be perfect. Houseguests can be a pain in the ass.

As quietly as I can, I start cleaning up the living room and kitchen. It's the least I can do. The very fucking least. I locate the washer and dryer inside a pantry but no trash can. My search leads me to the only other room besides the bathroom, his workshop. The scent of varnish and sawdust assaults my nose the second I open the door, and I step in regardless. It's almost as large as the house itself with workbench, assembly table, saws, racks, drills, even a sink. He was working on a guitar judging from what's propped up on the workbench. I'll bet he spends all his free time in here. If what I've seen before is his work, he's a master craftsman. I'm impressed. Not surprised, but still impressed.

My clean-up project has a wonderful side effect, I get to poke around in the name of helping. I glean he only reads magazines and books on woodworking. He roots for the Baltimore Ravens. Really it's the photos on the walls that capture my interest. Several group shots taken on the lawn outside the manor portray the pack through the years. I recognize a few faces from the house. They've barely aged. There are also several photos of just the family. One is from when the Dahl boys were teens, on dirt bikes, with Linda off to the side. Beside that is their wedding photo. Linda and Matt stand in front of a tree with their parents on either side. My brother was a good-looking kid with shaggy brown hair and the Dahl jaw and nose. His mother, Jenny, wasn't nearly as good looking as my mother even before the plastic surgery, but she was still pretty. Petite with brown eyes, long brown hair, but thin lips and a hooked nose. Wish I could have met them, well Matt, at least. He looked like a sweet guy, my kid brother.

There are more photos. One of Jason changing a diaper beside Matt as he changes one as well. Jason and Adam sitting in a john-boat holding up fish. Adam and Tate with a short old woman wedged between them. My smile falters a little when I see the one of me onstage singing in this dive bar in New York City when I was nineteen. After a few more of Jason with various men engaged in sports or holding Matt's kids, I spot another of me, this one more recent. Once again I'm onstage in my red silk dress with a magnolia in my hair, holding an old-fashioned silver microphone. It's my publicity still, signed even. Sometimes people write or e-mail my website asking for a photo. Doesn't happen often. I'm ... honored to be on his wall amid family. Among the people he loves.

Though it ain't easy with a broken finger and slashed arm, I continue cleaning, even tackling the bathroom that sorely needed a scrubbing. Manual labor helps keep the doubts and guilt at bay for a while. I finish the bathroom and search for more to do. Nothing. Jason's still in bed, but the snoring has ceased. I'd watch TV but that'd wake him. I sure as hell don't want to go back to that manor with dozens of grinning, well-meaning werewolves. I grab a bottle of beer from the fridge and wander into the soup outside.

Crickets and birds ring out through the stillness. I follow the breeze to the lapping water of the Chesapeake. At the end of the wooden dock, I kick off my flip flops, and lower my still-aching body into a sitting position. The water's refreshing against my feet, helping to chill the rest of me. I can even enjoy the warm press of the sun against my skin. I close my eyes to heighten the sensations. Cool, warm, fresh. Close to heavenly.

What a difference a day makes. Twenty-four hours ago I was being driven to my death. Didn't think I'd live to see this very day. Now I'm at a manor sunbathing and sipping a sudsy beer. I made it. I'm alive. Feels pretty damn good.

An image of blood pouring out of Mick's mouth as I drove the bar into his side over and over breaks the tranquility I was fighting hard to maintain. My eyes open to banish it. Nope. Not going there. No way in hell. I chug my beer. I blink, and for that instant I see him again, lying on that dirt floor. The crickets' song is overshadowed by his gurgling. Choking on his own blood. *Stop it.* Another blink, another horror show. *Stop.* It had to be done. He was going to kill me. Kill Jason. It was self-defense. Him or me.

Still … I took a life. I'm a killer.

He may have had a family. People who loved him. *He'll* never see the sun again. Enjoy a beer. Take another breath. His blood will always be on my hands. And yet, if I'm honest, the guilt weighs about an ounce. I feel worse about feeling next to nothing. Maybe I'm still in shock. I'll be in the grocery store one day, and it'll whack me against the head. I'll have a nervous breakdown in produce. I mean, is this lack of intense guilt normal? Am I just a despicable human being?

I've done a shit ton of things I'm not proud of, that's for damn sure, but in a weird, fucked-up way I'm … kind of proud of this. He was a threat to me, to Jason, and I had the strength to do what had to be done. I didn't enjoy it, don't want to have to ever do it again, but I would if I had to. No question. I pull my feet out of the water and hug my legs against my chest, resting my good cheek on my knees to stare at the tranquil water. I'll ask Jason if this is normal.

Jason. *Now*, the guilt comes? My throat closes up as another memory floods my brain. Me, seconds away from abandoning him in that motel. The man risked his life for me a dozen times over, but the second he bruises my feelings, I cut and run? And even after that, he risked it all over again. Even if he didn't have the others for backup, there isn't a doubt in my mind he'd have stormed that house alone. For me. I owe him my everything. He's…right behind me.

The dock shakes as someone steps onto it. I turn and almost burst into tears at the sight of him standing there, staring at me as if I were a mirage with equal parts astonishment and disbelief. I know because I'm gazing at him the same way. His emotion vanishes behind that mask of his an instant later. The sun almost halos his messy, wild blonde hair as if he's an angel. He is in my estimation. My blonde guardian angel. I slowly rise, but after that I'm not sure what to do. The last time I saw him he was eating Donovan. The time before that he was disgusted. By himself. By me. He—

Oh, fuck it.

I sprint up the dock as fast as I can, throwing my arms around his neck and squeezing until my arms hurt. He doesn't hesitate. His solid arms embrace me back so tight if he hadn't already taken my breath away it'd be forced out now. He's here. He's holding me. I was wrong, *this* is heavenly. In his arms. Heaven on this damned earth.

We cling to one another for a few seconds as if we were life rafts in the choppy ocean. I listen to his strong heartbeat, his breathing, and part of me can't believe he's really here. That he doesn't hate me. "I'm sorry, I'm so sorry," I whisper.

"You have nothing to be sorry about. I shouldn't have left. I shouldn't have let him get you. I should have protected you. He never should have …" he says, voice cracking.

Guilt pierces me down to my very core. I have to tell him. Even if he loathes me forever, I could live with that better than I could with him hating himself. I pull away to meet his eyes. "I … it was me. It's all my fault. I made us stop. I made you run. I was leaving you, and that's why the police took us. I got arrested. I got caught. You, you did *nothing* wrong. Don't you *dare* blame yourself. It was me. It was my stupidity. My selfishness. It was all me. You did everything right. You saved me. And I'm sorry. I am *so* sorry. Just please, *please* don't hate me. I couldn't bear if you hated me. I—"

"I don't hate you," he whispers sadly, "I could never hate you. *Never.*"

"Really?"

"Of course not."

My legs almost give out in relief. I wrap my arms around him again not in case they do fail me, but because I want to hold him again. I just want to touch him, savor his body against mine for as long as he'll allow. He nestles me back, heightening the joy of the moment. "I thought I'd never see you again," I whisper. "I was so scared."

"Me too," he whispers, squeezing tighter. "I almost went inside that house a thousand times." He releases me just enough to see my face. "Did they hurt you? Did they …" he can't finish.

"No. Broken finger, some stitches and bruises, I'm fine. Really. I just, I—" I look down. I don't want to see his face when I confess this. "I killed one of them last night. I stabbed him and I stabbed him until I lost count," I say, voice quaking. "All I could think about was you coming in the house and them killing you. I was so scared, and I killed him."

"Good," Jason says. I gaze up at him with surprise. "He deserved it. You saw what you had to do, and you had the strength to do it. Most wouldn't. And I am *so* proud of you."

Once again those words light me up more than all the lights of Broadway on at once. "Really?"

"Absolutely," he says with utter certainty.

I rest my head over his heart again. "Thank you." Then, when the absurdity of those words penetrates my brain, for the first time in days I chuckle.

"What?" he asks.

"Oh, nothing," I laugh. "Just, only you would respond with 'I'm proud of you' after I told you I stabbed a man to death."

"Is that wrong?"

"God, no. It's one of the things I love about you."

For some reason he goes stiff as a corpse against me. "Thank you." His arms drop from my body, and he steps away with his eyes to the deck.

I've done something wrong again. The compliment. I forgot he hates when I praise him. I'm going to do my damndest to break him of that habit. "You're welcome, Blondie. I mean it."

"Thank you," he says, head still hung. "I'm going to, um ... excuse me."

He turns his back on me and starts back toward the house. I've just been dismissed, haven't I? Yeah, that's not happening. "Must feel good to be home," I say, following behind.

"Yes."

"Your house is beautiful. Adam said you built it yourself."

"Yes."

"See? I was right."

"How?"

"In the car. I guessed you were a master craftsman, and I was right."

"Oh. Thank you," he practically whispers.

We step onto his porch, then through the sliding glass door inside. He picks up the pace into the kitchenette, but I will not be ignored. He's going to have a hard time shaking me this time. No escape. "Would you like me to make you something to eat?" I ask.

"No," he says, pulling out frozen chicken from the freezer.

"Really, if you want I can. I know how to cook a thing or two," I lie. "I've already cleaned your place, one more domestic duty won't kill me. Least I can do after everything you've done for me." I chuckle at the idiocy of that statement. "The *very* least. Feels like I should give you my firstborn or something."

His mouth sets tight as the mask falters, throwing me a glare that'd turn Medusa to stone. "You don't owe me anything, Vivian." His eyes lower but the glower remains. "You never did."

I never knew subtext could pack such a wallop. My stomach actually lurches. Anger blooms from the sharp point of those words. "After all we've been through together, do you still think so little of me?"

"What?" he asks, seeming genuinely confused.

"Do you think so little of me," I say drawing out the words, "that you really believe I only slept with you out of gratitude? To pay off my debt like a prostitute?"

"No! I ... I don't want to talk about that," he says, eyes down again.

"Tough shit, Blondie." I bridge the gap between us, his body visibly stiffening with each of my steps. "You listen to me, Jason Dahl. I've done a lot of low-down shit in my life, but I have never sold my body for anything. Not for a record deal, not for rent, and certainly not because I thought I owed it to someone. I slept with you because you're sexy and adorable and noble. You're the best damn man I've ever met in my life. *That* is why I slept with you. Because I wanted *you*. It *meant* something to me. Don't you dare try and sully what we shared with your guilt or fear or whatever is making you act like an ass. It's beneath you. So stop it. Right now. And just kiss me like we both know you want to. Just ... kiss me. Please."

His ice eyes have slowly advanced up with each declaration until they finally meet mine. I expect to find lust but see nothing but sadness. Pain. Desperation. Frustration. Fear. His hands ball into fists, I think to stop them from grabbing me. He's fighting like hell, the war visible in every contour of his face. In every twitch. In every tense muscle and crease in his forehead. Those hands slowly start inching toward me as the turmoil churns like a windmill in a tornado in those eyes. He touches my bruised cheek, my split lip with a feather light caress. "I ..." he whispers.

Suddenly, his eyes abandon mine as his gaze jerks toward the front door. His hand drops like my face was a hot potato. What the ... ? I hear wheels crunching gravel a second later. Fuck. Jason steps away from me, eyes on the floor again, almost dazed. "You ... you don't belong here," he says. "Excuse me."

Great. Goddamn it.

I follow him a few seconds later out the front door. Of course. Who else would it be? Frank steps out of his SUV with a smile for his son. His daughter, not so much. The moment he sets eyes on me, the smile briefly falters then reappears, just not as glittering. Haven't seen that look since high school when my honor roll boyfriend brought me to his house after my first arrest and his parents realized I was *that girl*. The bad seed sent to corrupt their precious angel. The cracks in those pleasant smiles told all, just like now. On my own father's face. This stings more than I care to admit.

"Hi, Dad," Jason says as he hugs Frank.

"Son," Frank says, gripping tight. They break apart. "I was just coming to check on you."

"Don't worry, I've been taking good care of him," I say with a smirk.

Both men's smiles falter, and Jason's eyes narrow with warning. Frank clears his throat. "Good." He looks at Jason again. "We have a lot to go over. You up for it?"

"Yes, sir."

"Excellent," Frank says, patting his back. The pride on Jason's face could be seen by Stevie Wonder. I compliment him, he pitches a fit. Frank does and it's word from on high. Frank's gaze moves my way. "Vivi, why don't you take my car back to the big house? They're beginning dinner prep. Could always use an extra hand."

"So, I'm dismissed?" I ask with a fake smile. Frank's expression remains neutral, but Jason's is a mix of anger and fear. I do bring those two emotions out of him quite a bit. And, as usual, those bring out the guilt in me. I drop the smile. "Sorry. That was bratty. I'm tired. Um, I'll leave you two alone. You have a lot to catch up on."

"Thank you," says Frank. Jason's eyes remain downcast as Frank and I wander toward one another. Frank hands me the keys with a quick smile. "Just follow the path."

"Think even I can manage that," I say. "Not one of my strengths, though. Following the right path." I arrive at the SUV, and the men to the door. "Hey, Blondie?" I call. Both men pivot around. "Just remember what I said, alright? I meant every word. Every one." I nod to my father. "Frank."

With a wink for both, I climb into the car and start the engine as the men exchange an uncomfortable glance. I leave them in my rearview. That man's going to ruin all my hard-won progress, I guarantee it. Still got some fight in me, though. To the damn bone if necessary. For once in my miserable life, I'm gonna get what I want. *Him.*

No. Matter. What.

TWELVE

Since I'm not in the helping mood, and I could only stand the glances and whispers for all of a minute downstairs, I retreat back to my bedroom. I'm sure they all mean well, but it feels as if I've landed in a hippie commune with all the smiles and togetherness, neither exactly coming naturally to me. Of course not even the bedroom is safe. I find that stringy-haired teenager sitting at the small desk in the corner typing on his laptop. He leaps up in surprise when I step in. "Oh, God! I'm-I'm-I'm sorry. I was just … I needed to get online. This was the only place to—"

"It's okay. Chill."

His bony shoulders lower an inch. "I-I'm Devin."

"Viv."

"I-I know. We-We all know."

"God, been up for two hours and already I'm infamous," I say, walking over to the bed. I lay down. "It is a gift."

"N-No," Devin says, even more skittish than before. "I just, I meant we all know you're Mr. Dahl's daughter and-and you fought like five werewolves and saved Jason's life, and you're a singer, and ... most of us never knew you were alive, and you're awesome. It's ... cool."

I stare at this strange boy, assessing if he's bullshitting me or not. The huge brown eyes that match his hair over a small nose continue twitching slightly. No, this boy isn't capable of tricks. "Really? I thought they all hated me or something."

"Why?"

"I don't know. I almost got Jason killed. I was rude. I'm an interloper. I'm ... me. Pick one."

Once again his eyes grow double in confusion. "You're not an interloper. You're Mr. Dahl's daughter. You killed to defend us. You're pack."

Jesus Christ, they know I killed someone? Of course they do. No secrets within the pack. I grab a pillow to hug. "Right." Devin's quiet for a second, just gawking at me as if he wants me to read his mind and answer some unknown question. "What? Ask."

"How did you do it? How did you ... fight? How did you not freeze?" The boy asks me this with almost desperation, as if my response will save him. God, everyone's so intense here. Must be a werewolf thing.

All I can say is, "I don't know. Didn't have much choice really. All I could think of was how Jason was out there. Alone. How it was one against five. That if I didn't fight, they'd kill him. He was willing to fight for me, I had to be willing to fight just as hard for him, no matter the cost. I was petrified, almost chickened out nine hundred times. I broke a finger, got shot, was beaten to crap, but I had made up my mind to keep going. You just ... summon the strength.

Find the right fuel for any fire and you can run around the planet twice. Nothing can stop you."

The kid's quiet again, even hanging his head. Great, I've said something wrong again. I wonder if they have a muzzle around here before I get myself into more trouble. "I..." he finally works up the courage to say, "my-my dad. They-They s-shot him. In front of me. I just, I couldn't move. I couldn't get out of the car. His-His head..."

"Jesus Christ, kid." I sit up. "I-I'm so sorry."

"But I froze! I didn't chase after them! I could have ... I should have fought. That's what we're supposed to do. He was my dad. He was pack. I—"

"How old are you?" I cut in.

"Eighteen."

"How many were there?"

"T-Two."

"I assume they had guns. And you had ..."

"N-Nothing, but—"

"Then without question you did the right thing. Getting yourself killed too wouldn't have helped a damn thing. It sure as hell wouldn't have brought your dad back. Now you get to live to fight another day, one where you actually can do something other than get dead. You have nothing to feel guilty about, kid. And it doesn't make you less of a man or wolf or whatever. It makes you smart."

A quick smile crosses his face. "Thank you, Miss Dahl."

"I only speak the truth, kid. And it's Viv."

"Viv," he says with another quick smile as if he's honored by this privilege or something. "So, I better, um ..." he gestures to the computer. "Trying to get into that Marshal's computer. It's password protected."

"Try 'evil asshole bastard,'" I say, lying down again.

Another brief smile earned. "I-I'll give it a shot."

I switch on the TV, surfing until I find a mindless action flick as my new buddy taps away on his laptop. This is nice, doing something normal like watching Angelina raiding tombs. I need a week of laying here, veging and—

The bedroom door opens with a sobbing Nicole being carried into the room by the pretty blonde teen. Guess werewolves aren't big on knocking. The teen sets her big gray eyes on me and stops dead three steps in. "Oh, I'm sorry. I—"

"It's fine," I reply over my niece's sobs.

"I just, she fell in the mud and the other bathrooms are occupied, and—"

"Do what you gotta do. The more the merrier."

"Thank you." The teen rushes into the bathroom, not even glancing at Devin who, despite his lowered head, steals glances at her. Someone has a crush.

The water begins running in the bathroom. "Um, Miss Dahl?" the teen calls a minute later.

Shit. So much for my adventure with Angie. With a sigh, I force my aching body out of bed. Nicole's still sniffling in the tub as I walk in. "Yeah?"

"I forgot her new clothes. Can you watch her while—"

"Oh, I don't really think she wants me—"

"Thanks," the teen says, rising and walking past me.

Fuck. Nicole stares up at me, lower lip trembling as she sniffles. "O-kay," I say, stepping toward her. Those dark eyes bug out of her head as I approach and bend down to her level. "Um, is the water okay?" She barely nods in affirmation. "Right." Okay, I have zero experience with kids. I can barely keep plants alive. I'm at a loss as to what to say or do next, especially when the kid in question seems shit scared of me. "So, um, how'd you fall in the mud?"

"Mason pushed me," she says quietly. "He was chasing me, and when he caught me, he pushed me."

Oh, boy troubles. We've reached my wheelhouse. "He probably did it because he likes you. Boys are weird like that."

"Really?"

"Yeah. They chase and chase you, then when they catch you, they don't have a clue what to do with you. They don't get much better as they get older either," I say, making a silly face. The girl smiles. Score. "If he does it again, just cry and tell him how much you hate him. It's the girl equivalent of a punch. He'll feel really bad for days."

"I told Miss Claire. She put him in time-out."

"That works too." I grab a washcloth, soak it, and start cleaning her face of the mud. "I can see why he likes you. You're a very pretty girl. You'll be fighting them off with a stick in ten years, I guarantee it."

"Eww. Boys are icky. Dustin wipes his boogers on me!"

"Yuck. Well, he doesn't count. He's a brother, not a boy. Not all boys are icky."

"Yes, they are," she says with certainty.

"Is your Grandpa icky? Uncle Jason? Your da—" I stop myself on that last one. "They're boys, they aren't icky."

"Uncle Jason pulls the guts out of fish with his hands. Daddy too. They're icky."

I think Linda should start saving for law school with this one. "That is pretty gross. Okay, all boys are icky. Congrats, you've sold me."

The teen, I assume Miss Claire, rushes back in holding another flowered sundress. "Sorry."

"It's okay," I say. "If you want, I can finish up here for you."

"What? Really? Oh, thank you," Claire gushes. "I don't really trust Mac or Troy to watch the others. It sounds like World War III down there."

"Yeah, go. We're bonding over the ickiness of boys."

"I sold her," Nicole says with pride.

"Okay," Claire says with a nervous chuckle. "Thanks, Miss Dahl."

"Viv."

"Viv. Nicki, be good for your aunt, alright? Bye." The harried girl scurries off again. Bet this isn't how she imagined her summer, chasing after werewolf children.

I turn back to my niece with a grin, then grab the shampoo. "Let's wash your hair, huh?"

"I can do it," she says triumphantly.

I hand her the bottle. "Knock yourself out, kiddo." I watch as she expertly performs the task. "You have pretty hair."

"You have hair like Grandpa. It's pretty too."

"Thank you." She dunks her head to rinse out the shampoo. When she surfaces, I wipe the remaining soapy water from around her eyes. "There. Can you do the conditioner too?"

"Yep." I slap it in her hands.

"Thank you, Aunt Vivian."

"You're welcome, Niece Nicole."

She starts working the conditioner into her black hair. I remove the stray goop from her face with the washcloth. "Am I your only niece?"

"My one and only."

"Then why didn't you ever send me a birthday present like my other aunt and uncles?"

Oh, boy. "Because I didn't know I had a one and only niece until a few days ago."

"Oh. Well, will you give me them now?"

"I will. I promise. Now, dunk."

She takes a deep breath and goes underwater again. When she resurfaces, I hand her a face towel. "I want the big Barbie where you put makeup on her and brush her hair and give her jewelry. My birthday was two months ago, but you can buy her for me now."

"We'll see. I'm sort of grounded at the moment. Not much shopping in my future. Are you all clean? Ready to get out?" She nods. I grab a towel from the rack and lift her from the tub. This kid stuff isn't so terrible after all. Kind of fun actually. After I dry her hair, I pick up her dress. "Need help putting your dress on?" She shakes her head no. "Here you go, kiddo. I'll be in the next room if you need me."

"Thank you, Aunt Vivian."

"You're welcome, Niece Nicole," I say, walking away.

Oh, goody. When I return to the bedroom, Devin is still clacking away on the computer, but we've gained another visitor. Dustin has made himself at home on my bed, flipping through the channels. He's even nested, spreading Legos around like a fan. I feel like I'm in Grand Central Station minus the winos. "Uh, hello. You need a bath too?"

"I hate baths," Dustin says. "I want to watch *The Fairly Odd Parents*. I can't find *Nickelodeon*."

"Um…"

"Channel 163," Devin says.

"Thank you," Dustin says, turning to the cartoon.

"Aunt Vivian," Nicole says, walking in fully dressed, "can you brush my hair?"

"Don't be a baby, you can brush your own hair," Dustin chides.

"Don't insult your sister," I warn. "It's not nice."

"Well, Aunt Vivian's gonna buy me a Barbie and she's not gonna buy you anything cause you're mean and icky," Nicole spews back.

"Nu huh! She's gonna buy me a super-soaker and I'm gonna soak you!"

"Both of you stop it or I won't buy you anything," I snap. "Nicole, my brush is in the bathroom. Go get it." I walk to the bed as she obeys. "You. Scoot." Dustin moves to the right so I can sit down again. I pick Legos out from under my butt while Nicole returns. She leaps up and scooches between my legs before handing me the brush. Dustin lies back to watch the TV. When I finish with her hair, a hundred strokes at her insistence, we follow her brother's example. The show's inane but not terrible. Before it's over, Dustin dozes to my right and a few minutes later to my left his sister follows suit. They don't wake as I change the channel back to Lara Croft or when Devin slinks out. I think they missed their naps.

Not even Lara can keep my mind off Jason. As usual guilt and mortification are the predominant emotions as I conjure up his face just before Frank arrived. I mean, I understand he doesn't want Frank to know he banged his daughter, and it'd be hard to hide our trysts now we're here, but he was downright petrified to kiss me as if I'd suck out his soul if our lips touched. I just don't get it. He likes me, the sex was phenomenal, we can be careful, this is do-able. I'll just have to make sure I'm around him as much as possible whether he likes it or not. I literally fought to the death for that man, he isn't getting away from me now. Especially when I know with every one of my cells he doesn't really want to. I'll show him who doesn't belong.

Tomb Raider ends, switching over to *Men in Black*. As Will Smith chases an alien, Dustin whimpers softly and sticks his thumb in his mouth. Bad dreams. Lot of that going around. Poor kid. Poor *kids*, Devin included. I know what it's like, growing up without a father. The twins will be lucky if they have even a few memories of him. They're probably too young to know what death really means. That he'll never tuck them in again. Never kiss them. Maybe that's a blessing. No grown-up should have to deal with all the shit raining down on us let alone a child. Even if the adults are making this seem like summer camp, kids aren't stupid. They know something's not right. They sense it like an animal does a natural disaster. It prickles their skin, but they're powerless to do a damn thing. I know exactly how they feel.

I smooth Dustin's soft black hair. This is too fucking weird. I have a niece and nephew. They are nestled beside me right now. They were comfortable enough to fall asleep beside me. I apparently have to send them presents every year. They expect me to be in their lives, stick around for parties and dispensing life lessons like their Uncle Jason. Boy are they in for disappointment. Ugh, this family shit makes my head hurt. I turn back to the TV. Take me away, Will Smith.

Will's barely been recruited when there's a light knock on the door. The twins' eyes flutter. Crap. A second later, a sweaty Frank steps in. Double crap. He notices the children he just woke and shoots me a sorry smile.

"Hi. Sorry. I didn't…"

"Hi, Grandpa," Dustin says through his yawn.

"Hi, munchkins," he replies. "Have a nice nap?"

"Grandpa, Mason pushed me into the mud," Nicole tattles.

"That wasn't nice of him," Frank says.

"Aunt Vivian said it's because he likes me, but I think he's just mean and icky."

"Actually, I think your aunt's right on this one," Frank says with a smile my way. I don't reciprocate.

"I don't care. He's still icky."

Frank chuckles. "Well, you guys must be hungry. They're serving dinner downstairs. Better go before they run out of food."

"Okay," Dustin says, scooting off the bed. Nicole follows suit, running out of the room.

It's harder for me to move as inactivity has made my body sore again. I wince a little, especially when I put pressure on my broken finger. Frank takes a few steps toward me to help. "I got it," I say.

"You should ask Deandra for more pills if you're still in pain," Frank suggests.

I manage to get to my feet. "Will do. Thanks."

"I hope the twins weren't too much trouble. I've instructed everyone to give you some space, but—"

"I'm not a wilting flower who gets knocked down at the first breeze, Frank."

"So I've heard," he says with a quick, uncomfortable smile. "Still. We can be an overwhelming group to take in all at once. If it gets to be too much, let me know. I'll talk to them. No one will blame you if you need to … separate yourself from us. We'd all understand."

As I stare at him for a few seconds smiling at me with tenderness, the urge to kick him in the balls grows stronger and stronger. I've manipulated enough people through the years to spot a con a mile away. The fact he's using the guise of pretending to give a shit about me just makes it that much more sickening. I'm surprised he doesn't just tie me to the bed and lock the door to keep me from his precious Jason. I force a smile on my face. Never let them know you know. Learned that early too.

"I appreciate that, thank you. I'll keep it in mind."

"Good. I just, I want you as comfortable as possible."

"Of course you do." I grin again. "Well, I'm starving. I'm gonna go grab a plate."

"Okay. I need to shower and change. Be down in about ten minutes."

"I'll let them know." I walk past my father, smile dropping the second my back's to him. Asshole.

It's a freaking zoo in the dining room. I'm surprised there isn't more snapping and growling from the pack. The entire table is covered with food. Trays of smoking steaks, pork chops, and chicken piled high with men carrying in more meat. Women emerge from the swinging kitchen door with containers of cole slaw, macaroni and cheese, potato salad, corn and chips. Children, including Nicole and Dustin, are served by Claire and Devin, who steals glances at her while dropping slaw on the paper plates. Dear God there are a lot of them. More than forty men, women, and children at least, all laughing, joking, helping one another. Men kiss their wive's cheeks as they pass with food. Mothers lift their children to fill their plates. Friends whisper into each other's ears, garnering laughter. I've never seen anything like this before. *You don't belong here …*

"We have to stop meeting like this," a familiar man's voice says behind me. I spin around to find Adam wiping sweat off his face with a bandana.

"Like what?"

"You, looking lost. Me, rescuing you. I'll begin to think the rumors about you are untrue."

"What rumors?"

"That you're a butt-kicking babe who can carry a tune while digging bullets out of werewolves. You do have a reputation to protect, you know." His smile infects me. I sprout one too. "Come on, we don't bite." He nods his head for me to follow him. "Except on the full moon, of course."

I shadow my new best friend into the chaos. The people smile and nod as I walk by, including Linda, who sets down a salad bowl. Like Adam I grab a paper plate and plastic cutlery. When we join the line, a short woman in her late sixties with silver hair in a bun makes a B-line toward us.

"There you are! I haven't seen you all day," she says to Adam.

"You saw me get home this morning, Mom," he says, "Sorry." He kisses the top of her head. "Frank put me right to work."

"I haven't seen Jason either," she says.

"He's fine," I answer. "I spoke to him earlier."

"Vivian, my mother Maureen. Mom, Viv," Adam says.

I shake her hand. "Nice to meet you. Jason told me great things about you."

"He's a sweet boy. Don't let anyone else, including him, tell you otherwise," Maureen says.

"I'm a believer, ma'am."

"Good. Now, excuse me. I need to borrow my son," she says, wrapping her arm through his.

"But—"

"You'll be fine," Adam says before being dragged off.

Great. I just keep my eyes down as I fill my plate with enough carbs to create a colony of cellulite. Even the salad is slathered with Caesar dressing. Most of the other women I notice are dainty eaters as well. Only the men have steaks stacked three high. And, with the exception of Nicole and two others, the smaller children running around are boys. Must be a werewolf thing, having more males than females. Makes—

"Excuse us," a man says. I glance up to find a couple in their early twenties grinning at me. "Hi, we're Mike and Dahlia Chambers. Just wanted to tell you we're so glad you got here safely. We were praying for you and Jason."

"Thank you," I say for lack of something better.

"Your father's an exceptional man," Mike continues. "I'd be dead if he hadn't found me after I was turned. We just wanted to introduce ourselves."

"If you need anything, let us know," Dahlia says.

"Thank you." The couple smiles in unison and moves down the table toward the meat. Okay, that was weird. Nice but weird. I have a feeling that's going to be a theme for the rest of my stay at Hotel

Werewolf. Whatever. I reach across the table for the macaroni spoon, accidently hitting my bad finger against it and wincing.

"Oh, here. Let me," Sam, who stands beside me, says. He ladles the macaroni onto my plate with a grin.

"Thank you."

"Do you need any help with anyth—"

"I got it, thank you." Enough food. I bypass the horde toward the end of the table where the drinks are. If there is any Kool-Aid being served, I am not touching it. As I get a Sprite, Claire sidles up beside me. "Hello."

"I just wanted to thank you for taking care of the twins. I didn't mean to impose, it's just—"

"It's fine. You had your hands full."

"I know, right?" she asks, eyes doubling in size. "I love them all to death, but with all the sugar and boredom they're all going nuts and driving me there in the process. And the guys are no help. They're as bad as the kids!"

"Sorry."

She frowns. "No, I'm sorry. I'm venting. I'm really super-proud Mr. Dahl trusts me enough to put me in charge of them. Please don't tell him I complained, okay? I know we all have to pitch in and stuff."

"I'm sure everyone appreciates all your hard work, especially Frank."

"Really?" she asks, beaming.

"Definitely. Told me so himself," I lie. I do on occasion use my powers for good.

"He did? Oh, wow! Thank you!"

"Welcome. I'm gonna…" I gesture toward the door. "Enjoy dinner."

I make it all of three steps before a huge man in every way with a trucker's cap moves in front of me. "You're Frank's daughter, right?" I nod. "Welcome home, girl." And he walks away without another word. O-kay.

"Aren't we Miss Popularity, princess," Tate says as he passes. I shoot him the evil eye but he chuckles. Dick.

Since Frank is still upstairs, and I don't want to give him the satisfaction of seemingly obeying him, I make my way down the hall to the back patio where I pray there are fewer people. Of course a quarter of the others had the same idea. Damn. There are more tents back here with barbeque grills still smoking. No escape. I spot a friendly face lowering himself onto the grass. I descend the stone steps and sit beside Devin. "Mind if I join you?"

"N-No."

It becomes readily apparent why he chose this spot. Claire prances down the stairs over to a tent where a middle-aged man with thinning hair and a woman with graying hair sit on lawn chairs, enjoying their meals. She kisses her mother's head before plopping down on the grass with her back to us.

"Ah, young love," I say to myself.

"W-What?"

"Nothing. So, did you hack Donovan's computer?" I ask, shoving food in my mouth.

"My encryption system's working on it. Should be a few more hours."

"Any chance you can hack into the fugitive database and erase my warrant?"

225

"Sorry. Their firewalls are mental."

"Too bad. I'm sure I look like shit in my mugshot."

"Can I sit at the cool kid's table too?" Adam asks as he takes the last stone step off the patio. I pat the grass where he sits a second later. "Hey, Dev."

"Hey."

"Sorry about leaving you back there," Adam says.

"I'll forgive you. One day," I say dramatically. "No, it's fine. Everyone was extra super duper helpful and friendly. It freaked me the fuck out."

"You're our Alpha's glamorous, only daughter who survived six hostile werewolves and several days alone with Jason Dahl. They're in awe of you, especially for that last one," Adam explains. "I'm surprised they're not bowing. Just smile and be gracious."

"Like a princess?" I ask. "Yeah, even as a girl I never wanted to be one of those. I was more a Debbie Harry wannabe." I eat a forkful of cole slaw. "Speaking of Jason—"

"We were?" Adam asks with a smirk.

"What'd you mean about them being in awe of me because I was alone with him?"

"Nothing. It was a joke."

"No, tell me. I'm your princess, I order you to tell me."

"You can't order—"

"He's terrifying," Devin chimes in. "We're all scared of him."

"He's not scary. He can be … intimidating," Adam says, staring at Devin. "But that's just because most people don't bother to get to know him."

"He doesn't exactly make it easy," Devin mumbles. Adam shoots him a nasty look. "What? I've known him all my life, and he's said maybe twenty words to me."

"And I guarantee you've only said ten to him," Adam retorts. "He's our Beta. Everyone should show him more respect."

"We respect him. He's just … he's menacing. We all know what he does."

"What he does, he does to keep us safe. He doesn't enjoy doing it, but he still does it. For us. And maybe if you, or anyone else made the effort, you might find out he isn't the big bad wolf everyone seems to think he is."

"I guess," Devin says, properly cowed. He stares down at his plate.

Adam shakes his head. I get the feeling this isn't the first time he's had this conversation. He's Jason's behind-the-scenes PR manager/cheerleader. Wish I had a friend like that. Wish Jason didn't *need* a friend like that. Me, they welcome with open arms just because I share some genes with their fearless leader. Jason's been around for almost two decades, literally risking life and limb for them, and he feels the need to take his meals alone. He'd die for any one of these people, and they probably don't even ask him over for a beer. I know he cares. He pretends not to. They probably take it at face value. Something should be done.

We eat in silence for a while, just watching the happy families and friends enjoying the evening. They act like they haven't a care in the world. Chatting, chowing, teasing their children. Safe. They feel safe. Maybe I should drink the Kool-Aid. Jump in with both feet. Try to live up to my undeserved rep. I am stuck at Casa Howl for a while. I'm already bored with TV. Sitting still was never my forte. Okay, really I just want to piss Frank off. I do owe him seven years of missed teenage rebellion. I'd get another tattoo or crash his car, but I can't leave the house so this'll have to do. Plus, when I did those last two, they weren't really as much fun as I'd anticipated. An evil plan begins percolating, bringing a smirk to my face. You showed your cards, Frank. Time for me to go all in.

The man himself saunters out, freshly showered. Everyone snaps to as if Elvis is in the building. He graces Claire's family first, saying a few words, patting her father's shoulder, then moving to the next group on his goodwill tour. It's the same with them all. A few words and they all glow. Once again the urge to scream rises. The love and respect they have for this man is downright Christlike. The Great White Ginger Hope. Whatever keeps them going, I guess.

When it's our turn on the campaign trail, my two companions turn into glowworms as well. I give him a quick smile just to be civil. "Hey, guys," Frank says.

"Sir," Devin replies.

"Enjoying dinner?"

"Yes, thank you," I say.

"You really should try Pookie's pork chops. Don't tell anyone, but they're my favorite."

"I'm actually a vegetarian, so …"

"Oh. I'm sorry, I didn't know," Frank says.

I shrug. "How could you?"

Frank smiles uncomfortably. "True. Next time they go shopping, I'll be sure to tell them to pick up some tofu or veggie burgers."

"That's okay, don't put yourself out for me. I can make do."

"No, I want you to be as comfortable as possible here. I'm, um, done upstairs if you want to retire. Rest."

I seriously want to slap that gracious smile off his face so bad but instead slap a matching one on mine. "No, I'm good here. Thanks. Don't want everyone to think I'm some stuck-up princess hiding in my tower. Besides I'm making loads of friends. Doing my best to … belong with my new family now the chance has been given to me after all this time. Think I'll be seeing a lot of them from here on in. *All* of them."

The corners of his mouth twitch. "Whatever you think is best."

"Um, er, sir," Devin mutters, "I-I've almost got the computer unlocked. My-my decrypter program's working on it."

"Excellent. Thank you. Keep up the good work. And enjoy your dinner." He briefly meets my eyes, I think in a challenge. "All of you. Excuse me." He walks off to bask in further glory.

I roll my eyes and shovel more food into my mouth. Dick. The animosity I thought I did a good job of hiding apparently did not go unnoticed by my dinner companions. The guys steal glances at me between bites of steak. Guess they're not used to people openly disliking their fearless leader. Whatever. If they ask, I'll answer with the truth. They don't ask, though. Liking them more and more by the minute. "So, Adam, who should I talk to about getting work around here?"

"What do you mean?" Adam asks.

"I mean guard duty or laundry or whatever."

"You don't have to—"

"Yes, I do. Everyone pitches in, right? I shouldn't be an exception."

"Okay. Then, my mother. She's sort of taken over the running of the house."

"And where might she be?" I ask.

"Probably the kitchen."

I rise. "Then that's where I'm off to. See you boys later."

As advertised, I find Maureen dining with two other elderly women at a small table in the corner of the mid-sized kitchen. There are a dozen pots, pans, and dishes scattered around the sink and counter with two women and a man already cleaning them. A well-oiled machine around here. The three women smile as I approach. "Hello, dear," Maureen says.

"Hi. Sorry to bother you."

"It's fine. How may I help you?" Maureen asks.

"Actually, I'm here to help you. I want a job. Put me to work."

"Oh, don't worry about it. You don't have to do anything. You've been through such a trying ordeal and—"

"But I want to. I know Claire needs our assistance with the kids. Poor thing is so overwhelmed. She told me as much. I was a summer camp counselor once," I lie. "I have a lot of experience around children. They love me."

"Helping with the children would be great. You can start tomorrow if you're up to it."

"Tomorrow it is. Thank you. I won't let you down, I promise. Enjoy your meal."

I saunter off with a smug smile, nodding at the washers who grin back. Yes, these people are going to love me come hell or high water. Let the games begin. I'm coming for you, Jason. And Blondie, you don't stand a damn chance.

THIRTEEN

I WASN'T COMPLETELY LYING about my summer camp experience. Mom and Barry shipped me off from ages seven to fourteen. I loved every second of it. The crafts, the swimming, the counselors, especially the talent shows. Me and some of the girls always did a Whitney or Michael number. I can still remember all the moves to "Thriller," and I am a master wallet sewer and beader. They stopped sending *me* to save money, though Jessie got to enjoy many a summer after that.

I heard somewhere, probably Oprah, kids need structure or they get bored and nuts. Much like adults. So I grabbed Claire after dinner for a pow wow. After the squealing and hugging, I calmed her down enough to brainstorm. We came up with several activities from soccer to pajama day. Since most of the kids are boys, the majority of activities will be heavy on the physical, which the teen boys can join in with as well. With that decided, we culled together a list of supplies, including healthy snacks and juice so the kids aren't running around like meth heads after espresso shots. We have a week planned. Any longer and I'll probably want to drown them all.

Maybe sooner. I'm woken at the butt crack of dawn by a knock on my door. Claire, bubbly even at seven in the fucking morning, swans in with a cup of coffee for me. My body still isn't at its prime, but I pull myself out of bed with minimal groaning. Me and my bright ideas. I could have just stayed in bed and had werewolf minions bring me food, but I had to open my big mouth. Prove myself to perfect strangers. I haven't been up at seven on purpose since high school. After chugging the coffee with an Advil chaser, I step into the shower, braid my wet hair, put on my Daisy Duke shorts and purple t-shirt, cover the bruises, and conjure up a smile. If I don't lose or maim one of the children, I will consider this a successful day.

Starts out well. There's no set time to begin so parents drag the kids in a steady stream into the living room where we're setting up. The electronic babysitter does the heavy lifting as the kids wake up. After breakfast, and my third cup of coffee, the day begins in earnest. We move the horde outside for a game of Capture the Flag. My jock assistants, Troy and Mac, jump into this activity with both feet. The parents even stand on the sidelines cheering the kids on, my father included, who gives me a reverent nod. Not gonna lie, that feels pretty damn good.

We break for lunch, then nap time for the youngsters in the parlor, and a movie in the living room for the three older kids and teens. Even Devin stops *World of Warcraft* to enjoy *Harry Potter* and sneaking glances at Claire. I take this brief respite to change into my bikini and re-dress for the next activity. Poor Jason's about to be invaded. I saw him in passing this morning as he and

Omar walked to their car. Omar delivered several bags of the items requested up here during lunch, but Jason was AWOL. If Blondie won't come to the party, I'll bring it to him.

After organizing my new supplies and checking on the kids, I make my way to the dining room for a water bottle. Lunch has been cleared but Adam is slowly picking at a bowl of the pretzels, almost examining them like a quality control officer. That is when his eyes aren't glued to the woman chatting with Frank outside on the patio. I haven't seen her before. Curly, mousy brown hair, a few inches shorter than me and a few years younger, about forty pounds over-weight, dressed in black jeans and floral t-shirt. Not a head turner, but judging from Adam's laser-like focus on her, he'd disagree. He's so busy staring, he doesn't register my existence until I whisper, "Stalking's illegal, you know."

"What? I'm not … shut up."

"Who is she? Ex-girlfriend?"

"No. She's just, she's the High Priestess of the Goodnight Coven."

"I have no idea what that means. Is it impressive?"

"It's the biggest witch's coven in America, so yeah," Adam says, sounding none too thrilled by this. "They have a sort of alliance with the pack. She's here to put up some protection—oh, shit!" He turns his back to the patio doors. O-kay. Frank opens the door for the witch, who holds a wooden box, and they both step in as Adam starts shoveling pretzels in his mouth.

"Hello, Vivi," Frank says.

"Frank."

"Um, Mona McGregor, this is my … this is Vivian."

"Nice to meet you," Mona says with a smile. She's downright pretty when she smiles.

"She's here to—"

"Magical security system," I cut in. I place my hand on Adam's shoulder. "Adam here was filling me in. Thank you for coming. Feel safer already, don't we, Adam?"

He glances at me, eyes widening at me. "Yes. Absolutely."

"Well, I'm sure the pack will return the favor someday," Mona says.

"Let's hope the need never arises," says Frank, "at least for your sake." He smiles at Mona, then turns back to us. "Adam, Mona needs a ladder, hammer, and nails to hang the charms and amulets. Go get them, please," he says with that same fake smirk he gave me last night. An order masquerading as concern. It rankles me as much now as then.

"I can get them," I chime in.

"No, it—it's fine," Adam says with an undercurrent of fear. "I'll go, sir. Excuse me." With his head hung, he scurries into the kitchen.

Frank pretends not to notice. "Vivi, are the children still asleep in the parlor?"

"They are."

"Then can you please show Mona to the living room? She can begin there."

"You're the boss, sir. And they are watching *Harry Potter*. Rather fitting. This way, Miss McGregor." I wait for her to reach me before I begin our trek. "It is Miss, right?"

"Oh, yeah," she chuckles. Score one for Adam. "Terminally."

"So, you're a witch? You're my first."

"Yeah, I didn't think I'd seen you around here before," Mona says.

"Long-lost daughter, werewolves trying to kill me, kidnapping, shoot outs, kind of a boring story."

"Yeah, sounds like it," she chuckles. We stroll into the living room where the kids are still immersed with Mr. Potter's adventures. Mona smirks as Harry waves his wand around. "God bless J. K. Rowling. She'll keep me in business for years to come."

"Is she a real witch too?" I ask.

"If she isn't, she must know one. No Hogwarts though."

"Damn. I was hoping you'd write me a letter of recommendation."

Mona laughs again. Good sense of humor. Beginning to see why Adam's smitten. His paramour sets down her box on the end table to unlatch it. Inside are vials filled with multi-colored liquids, baggies of herbs, crystals, strange amulets, candles, even a knife with a pentagram on the handle. She notices me examining the contents. "You should see my shop."

"I lived in New Orleans. One of my roommates worked in a voodoo emporium for a few months. Most customers were tourists looking for love potions. Never realized it could all be real."

"We work hard at that. I have no desire to be burnt at the stake, thank you very much."

Hearing heavy footsteps, we spin around as Adam walks in with a ladder and the other tools, his eyes never leaving the blue carpet. Didn't take him for shy. "Um, here," he mutters, placing the hammer and nails beside her box.

"Thanks," Mona says.

"Welcome," he mutters.

This will not do. "So, Mona, Adam here is gonna take over hosting duties for me. I have child wrangling to do."

"Okay," Mona says.

"No, I have—" Adam starts.

"Anything you need, great or small, he'll get you," I cut in. "Refreshments, nails," an orgasm, "what have you." I meet his wide blue eyes. "Isn't that right, Adam? Don't be rude to our honored guest."

His eyes grow to insect proportions, but a fake smile forms on his face. He is not pleased at being trapped. He'll thank me at his wedding. His gaze moves over to Mona, and the smile becomes genuine. "Of course."

"Uh, thanks," Mona says skeptically.

"Perfect then. It was lovely meeting you, Mona. I leave you in very *very* wonderful hands. Excuse me." I squeeze Adam's shoulder as I strut out. I love playing cupid. Got two marriages under my belt. One of those ended in divorce, but still. It's the thought that counts. Nothing wrong with being extra-super nice to my prey's best friend.

Claire follows me into the hallway. "We should wake the kids soon," she says. "They still need to change into their swimsuits."

"Okay. You and Dev oversee that, and have Mac and Troy inform the parents in case they want to join us at the shore."

"Yes, ma'am."

"For the millionth time, call me Viv."

"Yes, ma—Viv." She turns back into the living room to rouse the teens. I glance in and smile. Adam holds the ladder for Mona as she climbs up with a hammer, nails, and amulet. She doesn't notice the tiny smile and tranquility on Adam's face, but I do. The face of a man in love, or sure as hell getting there. Only one ma has gazed at me like that, as if just being close to me was akin to touching the clouds, peaceful and perfect. Better than any drug times ten.

I leave the lovebirds, and start down the hall toward the kitchen to grab more supplies as my minions and charges move out of the living room to complete their tasks. Hope Adam takes full advantage of alone time with witchy poo. Since we're between meals, it's not as crazy in the kitchen. Only Maureen and Frank remain, both sitting at the small table with coffee mugs and lists, which they seem to be reviewing. Feeding more than forty people every day cannot be an easy task.

"Hello, dear," Maureen says. Frank pivots around to see who is here, then swivels back with nary an emotion.

"Hi. We're taking the kids for a swim. I want to fill a cooler with granola bars and juice to take with us. We have a cooler, right?"

"Of course," Maureen says, rising from her chair to help.

"Some of the children don't know how to swim," Frank says, back still to me.

"I know. That's why I asked for water wings, and those kids will be paired with an adult at all times. A lot of the parents are coming anyway."

"Sounds like you have things well in hand," Maureen says, opening a cabinet.

"Hope so."

Frank rises and turns with what I think is a fake smile on his face. "Yes, thank you for all your help today."

"Just pulling my weight like everyone else. I am pack, right?" I ask with a matching smile.

"Yes," Frank says, not losing his façade. "Just make sure Adam goes with you. He's excellent with children."

"Oh, I got it covered. He's busy right now anyway. He's helping that witch—"

"He's what?" Maureen asks, downright horrified by this news.

Even Frank's fake mirth vanishes in an instant, replaced with irritation. "Damn it." Frank stalks past me without another word, jaw set so tight he's about to break a tooth. O—kay, what the hell just happened?

Fearing for my new buddy, I move to follow Frank out. "Frank, what … he's not …"

Maureen grabs my arm to stop me. "You best not, dear."

"But he—"

"Leave it be. Help me here. Get the juice boxes from the fridge. Please."

I want to protest, but Maureen is staring me down. "Fine." Need to pick my battles. Body slamming Jason's surrogate mother won't endear me to him, that's for sure.

Just as I'm closing the full cooler, Adam trudges in, head bowed and shoulders slumped like a moping Charlie Brown. I can practically hear that piano dirge that trails Charlie when he's depressed. Jesus, what the hell did Frank do to him? And why do I get the feeling it's all my fault? Hell, lately what isn't?

"You alright, son?" Maureen asks.

"Fine," he replies with a half smile. "I'll just, uh, go get the water toys and chairs from downstairs. Excuse me." He doesn't even glance at me as he passes. Yep, definitely my fault.

"Excuse me," I say to Maureen before rushing out of the kitchen in search of Frank. When I step into the busy hall where the excited kids and their parents scurry up and down, I notice Mona climbing up the ladder by the patio doors while Sam holds it steady. I roll my eyes and continue to my destination. Frank's office. The doors are closed but I'm too pissed to be polite. I barge in, throwing the right one to the side. The bastard himself lays on a cot in the far corner pinching the bridge of his nose with his eyes closed. He's in pain. Good. His weary eyes open. "Vivi, please. Now is—"

I slide the door closed. "What the hell did you say to Adam?"

With a deep sigh, my father slowly rises. "That isn't your concern. He was disobeying a direct order, that's all you need to know."

"He dis—*what*? He was just holding a damn ladder, Frank."

"He isn't supposed to be alone with her. He knew better, and he did it anyway. I just reminded him of that fact. It was for his own good."

"Oh, that's just insane. He likes her. He was helping her."

Frank stands. "He disobeyed his Alpha. He's under strict orders to avoid her."

"Then be mad at *me*. I boxed him in. I gave him no choice, okay? I saw he liked her, I set it up so they'd have some alone time. I don't see the big damn deal."

Frank's nostrils flare as he huffs. "You're right, you don't see what the big deal is because you just run blindly into situations you don't have all the facts about and meddle for your own purposes."

"He likes her!"

"He cannot be with her!" Frank fires back with the same intensity.

"This isn't the Marine Corps, and you're not a General, Frank! You can't control everything and everyone. You don't get to decide who falls in love with whom!"

"And you don't get to come into my pack and toy with my wolves' lives, especially when you don't take time to get the full picture," he practically roars.

I'm momentarily taken aback by his ferocity, even leaning back on instinct. But only for a moment. I eat bullies for breakfast, and I'm fucking famished. I match his grimace. "Why do I get the feeling we're not talking about Adam anymore?" He doesn't respond. I take a step toward him. "Listen to me, asshole. You know nothing about me, and you sure as hell have no right to judge me or my motives. Not you, of all people. You lost that privilege twenty-eight years ago and you aren't going to earn it back now. So go fuck yourself, *Dad*."

I twirl on my heels and stalk out. The hall is still full of happy families, and I stomp past them all to the front door. Outside. The moment I slam the door shut, I take a deep breath and let it out. Then another. I shouldn't care what he thinks about me. I really shouldn't. He hasn't earned that fucking right. Then why the hell do I feel like bursting into tears because deep down he thinks I'm a cold-hearted bitch?

Probably because I believe the same damn thing. Just gonna have to keep trying to prove us both wrong.

———

Even with almost half the pack along for the trip, wrangling the kids proves a feat. It's like herding wolverine/roadrunner hybrids. They've either been sneaking sugar or crack, perhaps both behind my back, I don't know. The hellions sprint down the gravel driveway squealing and laughing in excitement. We haven't even gotten there yet and the activity's already a hit.

Adam takes point, so the majority of wrangling falls to him. We haven't said a word to one another since the Mona incident as the few times I approached him, he rushed off to grab a wayward child. I'll corner him yet.

By the time we reach the beach, we're already drenched in sweat. So much for looking like a fresh yet sexy daisy for Jason. The front of the pack dashes straight into the water, giggling and squealing intensifying so they can be heard all the way to Europe. As I watch them splash around while setting up the snacks and chairs, a smile creeps across my face. The barbarians may be at the gate but they can't touch us or our fun here. At least I've contributed that. I wait until a swim trunk-clad Adam returns from Jason's bungalow with more aquatic equipment before I venture to impose on Blondie's hospitality. Frank's words about meddling sing through my brain, but I flip the volume down as low as it'll go. There isn't an ounce of harm in getting Jason to join the festivities. At least I hope not.

I heard the band saw running when we walked past the bungalow on our way here, so I know he's in there. I let myself in through the patio door, making a beeline to the workshop. This time I knock before stepping in. Jason glances up from the workbench where he's sanding out the edges of the guitar he's been assembling. I wasn't who he was expecting judging from the way his mouth opens and closes but no words come out. God, I love how awkward he always is when he lays eyes on me. The word "adorable" doesn't begin to cover it. I give him a sweet smile as I step in.

"Hi. I've come to recruit you."

"What?"

"We've invaded your beach. I'm claiming you as a POW and putting you to work, handsome. I've got almost a dozen Energizer Bunnies splashing around down there, including our niece and nephew, and not enough adults," I lie.

"I don't—"

"Resistance is futile, Blondie. Don't make me pull out the big guns."

"Big guns?"

"I have two incredibly cute twins on stand-by ready to whine, scream, and cry until their beloved Uncle Jason comes outside to play with them on this beautiful summer day." Theatrically, I raise an eyebrow. "I'll do it. You know I fight dirty." The sides of his mouth momentarily twitch up in a smile. Almost there. I saunter over to him, grin intact. "Seriously, though. It's a gorgeous day, the twins really do want to see you, and I could use another set of eyes. I don't really trust three teenage boys to pay attention to anything but a bikini-clad Claire. Please, Blondie?"

It takes a few seconds, but when he actually smiles back, I know I've got him. "Okay. Fine."

My grin grows. "Thank you, thank you, thank you. You are an absolute prince." I almost kiss his cheek but slam the brakes. Don't want to scare him off. "See you out there."

That was easier than I thought. Of course who could turn down a group of adorable children romping in the sunshine? I step out onto his wooden porch and stare down at the frolicking group. Adults paddle beside their kids, the older ones seem to be having a swim contest, and the few parents on the shore chat with others like we're at a barbeque. Carefree. I'll begin to enjoy it too once I take care of something.

Adam has set himself up as lifeguard sitting on the beach scanning the water. The last line of defense. After helping Mason tie his falling swim trunks, I grab one of the free folding chairs and drag it beside him. I know he clocked me since I started toward him, but he pretends not to notice until I'm right there. "Join you?"

"Sure," he says with a quick smile. I sit and take off my shirt to get some sun. To his credit, Adam doesn't stare at my rack. "He coming down?"

"How'd you …" Damn I'm transparent. I chuckle. "Yeah."

"Good."

"Not gonna lecture me for meddling too?"

"Whatever gets him down here having fun with everyone, I'm okay with. Speaking of …"

He nods toward the path. *Damn.* If I had my way he'd never wear a shirt. Or pants. Or underpants. I'll settle him in blue swim trunks sans shirt, skin and hair literally glowing in the sun and highlighting all the contours of his hard-earned muscles. Once again … *damn.* I'm not the only one who appreciates the view. Claire, Mason's mother Terri, hell every woman takes a moment to drink him in. Of course no one is happier to see him than Dusty, though for an entirely different reason. The boy's mouth drops open and he sprints out of the water right into Jason's arms. It literally warms my heart to see Jason scoop the boy up, pulling him tight into a hug. The love passing between them is almost palpable. And growing thicker. Nicole wades out of the water too. Jason picks her up too as Dusty chatters away, through I'm too far away to hear the words.

"He's great with kids," Adam says. I tear my eyes from this Rockwellesque portrait of family. "Loves them to death. Adults, not so much."

"Yeah, picked that up. Any thoughts on how to fix it?"

"I've tried for years. By all means, take over. You got him down here with them. You're a damn miracle worker."

His words bring another grin to my face. In spite of everything, I think I've smiled more in the past week than the entire month before. "Thank you," I say.

"I only speak the truth," Adam says.

"No, not for—well thank you for that too—but thank you for being nice to me, especially after getting you in hot water with *der Führer*."

"You didn't get me in trouble, I did. I could have left or found an excuse."

"No, this one's on me. Apparently I shouldn't have put you in that position. You just so obviously liked her, and you've been nice to me. I wanted to be nice back. I never in a million years thought I was doing anything wrong or out of bounds. I'm sorry you got chewed out because of me."

"You couldn't have known," Adam says.

"So I've been told." I shake my head with a scoff. "Even when I try to do good, I fuck it up. No wonder I don't do it often."

"You didn't fuck it up," Adam insists. "You just … it's complicated."

"What's so damn complicated? You obviously like her. She's single, you're single. I don't get it. It's none of Frank's business. He's not a dictator. He can't behead you for going on a date. Wait, can he?"

"No, nothing that severe," Adam says with his usual quick smile. I stare at my new friend for a few seconds, my eyes slowly narrowing to add pressure. I want the damn story. When my eyes are mere pinpoints he looks away, shaking his head. Worked on my ex-husband too. "She's a witch, I'm a werewolf. There are ... issues, rules that forbid fraternization. If we ever decided to get married, especially have children, I'd have to go rogue. Leave the pack. My mother, my brother, Jace. I'd be all alone. I just don't think I could do that."

"Jesus, are all you werewolves hopeless romantics?" I chuckle. "Just because you sleep with someone doesn't mean you have to marry them. A tumble in the hay may be enough to get her out of your system. Worked for me a time or two."

Now it's his turn to stare at me. All of a sudden I feel naked, hell like I don't even have skin. He knows. Of course he knows. I'd be shocked if everyone on this beach didn't. I seriously want to take back those words. I have to look away. My gaze stops at Jason, who now has a line of boys waiting to be thrown straight up then down into the water, squealing with joy the whole time. "But not always," I add. I square my jaw before turning back with a smile. "Still worth a try, right?"

"Not in this case."

"Come on. Don't let Frank bully—"

"She's my mate. It wouldn't work," he says with finality.

"So she's your mate. I don't ..." I shake my head. I'm missing something again.

"I keep forgetting you're new here," he chuckles. "Feels like I've known you for years. A mate ..." He clears his throat. "It's like soul mates, I guess. The person you're meant to mate with. We don't know if it's pheromones or a magical psychic link, but when a were-wolf meets his or her mate, they *know* it. And that desire, that knowledge does not go away no matter how much we fight it."

I do a double take. "Why would you? It slashes through all the bullshit. You're meant to be. End of story. And there's no chance you'd tell the love of your life to fuck off like most of us probably do. Probably cuts the divorce rate down too."

"Unless, like me, your mate is someone you can't be with," Adam counters. "There have been others whose mate was already married, a ... close family member, or someone couldn't overlook the werewolf factor and all it entails. If they find them at all. You know what it's like to be in love with someone and not be able to be with them? Not be able to touch them? Wake up next to them every day? To be around them when they barely know you exist? A carrot dangling forever a millimeter out of reach, and even if you grab it, you fall into the abyss below with no guarantee you'll reach the ground safe? Hell. It's pure hell."

"I'm sorry," I say, because what else can I say? "But ... I don't know. If it's important to you, if *she's* important to you, and it's meant to be, you'll find a way. It may require sacrifice, compromise, but hell if true love isn't worth those things, what is?"

Those eyes of his study me for a few seconds. I'm getting sick of people not believing I'm being straight with them. "What if he lived thousands of miles from you? What if you had to leave your entire life, your friends, job, the whole shebang? Would *you* do it?"

"Me, personally?" I chuckle. "I live in a shithole apartment, I have no true friends to speak of, my career is going nowhere, and I have over fifteen grand in credit card debt and all that was before I was a wanted fugitive. Shit, there's nothing to leave behind."

A quick smile passes across Adam's face. "I'm sorry, does my miserable life amuse you?"

"Sorry, it's just … never mind." He nods to the right. "Incoming."

I turn to find Nicole sprinting toward me. "Aunt Vivian, I have to potty."

"Okay," I say, rising. "To be continued." Adam smiles as Nicole slips her hand in mine and we start walking. "You having fun?"

"Uncle Jason threw me up in the air. It was cool. He's strong like Daddy. Mason was scared and wouldn't do it," she says, super-seriously, "and he's a boy."

"Well, I'll let you in on a secret, kiddo," I say, matching her tone. "Boys are always more scared than girls. That's why we have to do everything. We're a lot stronger than you think, and a lot stronger than them."

"Okay," my niece says as if my word is gospel.

When we return from answering nature's call, everything remains well in hand. Claire holds sentinel duty as Adam now officiates the swim race, and Mason and Dusty are sitting on the shore making a sandcastle. Jason stands a few feet away watching the boys as he dries his body. Even Claire is close to slack jawed as he caresses his taught muscles with a towel. Blondie's oblivious as always. Nicole toddles over to her brother and his activity, and I to mine. I retrieve two waters on the way. Being that gorgeous must take it out of a man.

"You look thirsty," I say, handing Jason a bottle.

"Thank you." He downs the water, even dribbling some on his chin. I watch with a raised eyebrow as he wipes his chest and chin with a towel again. Damn, just looking at this man makes my g-spot tingle.

"Remind me to bring drool buckets tomorrow."

"Why?" he asks.

"Because every woman within eyeshot needs one right now," I chuckle.

"Why?" he asks, genuinely confused.

I shake my head. "Never mind. Are you having fun?"

"I am. Thank you."

"Well, the kids adore you, that's for damn sure. Should have recruited you earlier."

"I'm not needed. You have more than enough help," he says, face neutral though he's calling me out on my lie.

I keep my smile plastered on. "Can always use more, that's the God's honest truth."

"I don't like being manipulated or lied to, Vivian," he says, mask cracking a little.

"I wasn't . . ." Damn it, I was. It's jarring having someone see right through me. Normally my tricks dazzle them. Not him. Never him. "You never let me get away with anything, do you?" He doesn't respond. "Okay, all cards on the table then. What I said was true, but I did have ulterior motives." I step toward him, stopping close enough to bask in his inner inferno. "It's come to my attention that you have a reputation around the pack as intimidating, if not downright frightening. They respect you and everything you do for them, but they are afraid to get close to you. You're huge, you kill people, it's understandable. Doesn't help that you're shy. They probably interpret that for snobbery, or that you don't care what they think. But you and I both know that's bullshit.

"These people are your family, every one of them—of course you want them to love you as much as you do them. To be accepted. *Belong.* So if I can help do that for you, I will. I know people, how they think. I just wanted to use that power for good for once. By showing them you're good with children, by eating meals with us, by getting you to smile, we can get them to change that opinion. Is that so wrong of me?"

"And that's the only reason?"

"What other could there possibly be? I'm trying to be a good pack member. That's all."

"I ..." Those eyes of his fill with quiet desperation as they always seem to do when searching to my depths for answers to the question I can't figure out he's asking. It must not be what he was hoping for because the steel trap shuts on his emotions. No. *No.* "You just don't get it, do you? I don't think you ever will. I have to go now. Please leave me alone. *Please.*" With a grimace, he walks past the children, whom he doesn't even acknowledge. Their little brows furrow.

"Jason ..." I call, even taking a step toward him but not another. My throat closes from the tumult of emotions coursing through me. Anger. Betrayal. Misery. My bottom lip begins quivering, and I can feel the tears rising again. *No.* I bite my lip, hard, to stop them falling. I will not cry, not over him. Not again.

"Aunt Vivian, where's Uncle Jason going?" Dustin asks with a pout.

I hug myself. "Away." From me.

"Why?" Dustin asks.

Because he sees right through me and doesn't like the view. He is our father's son.

FOURTEEN

I WATCH MY CURRENT prey from the parlor doorway as she says her good-byes to Frank. God, I hope this works. Have to time this just right. Nothing else matters, not the kids behind me playing a board game or the others in the hall, including Tate, who walks up beside me just to stare where I am. I ignore him. I only have eyes for Mona McGregor. She picks up her wooden case and purse, nods to Frank, and steps toward the door. About damn time.

"What are you up to, prin—" Tate starts smugly.

"Fuck off."

He doesn't warrant a glance as I start moving toward the witch. I keep my eyes down as I pass Frank in the hall. Fairly sure he returns the gesture. No awkwardness there. I stop at the end table with a mirror above, pretending to fix my high ponytail but really keeping my eyes on my father out of the corner of my eye. The moment he vanishes into the dining room, I scoop up the purse that I stashed behind the vase and hustle out the front door before anyone grows suspicious.

The sun is about a half hour from setting, that time when the sky resembles a tranquil Monet, and the temperature's gone down enough to be tolerable. Perfect night for an escape. I've been planning this for an hour, worked every angle I could imagine. Staging a prison break is damn hard, nervous work.

My unwitting accomplice is loading her Acura down on the driveway. "Oh, Mona! Let me help you!"

She's already shutting the trunk by the time I reach her. Damn. "It's okay. I got it."

"Oh. Well … off to the Inn then? I heard Frank was putting you up in town for the night," I say merrily. "That's awfully nice of him."

"Yeah, well it's a long drive back to Goodnight, my sister's at my aunt's, and I never pass up free room service."

"Me neither." I pause. "Actually, I was just on my way to town too. Errand for Frank. He said for me to catch you, that you'd give me a ride. Jason was supposed to take me but …" I shrug. "I've been waiting, and he hasn't been answering his phones. You don't have to bring me back. Sam's already in town, he'll do it."

She raises an eyebrow. "Frank didn't mention this to me."

"It just happened. I caught him just after he spoke to you. But I mean, come on, I'm asking for a lift, not for you to help me rob a bank. I'll even make it worth your while. First two rounds on me." Or Frank since I'm using the cash I found still stashed in the suitcase from the trip.

"I-I guess I—"

"Oh, thank you!" I say, taking off like a shot toward the passenger door. I climb in before she can utter another word. I've used this ploy before. I've discovered once you're inside the car, unless you puke or insult the driver right away, they won't kick you out. Too much work.

I'm fastening on my seat belt when Mona gets in. The uncomfortable glances she fires at me don't stop until we do, right outside the gate so she can punch in the code to open it. Just as it begins to slide, and I'm literally home free, Sam zooms up on his ATV. My first instinct is to duck down, but since Mona's already suspicious, I just keep my serene smile on and stare straight ahead. Maybe he won't notice me with the window up. He must not because he doesn't chase after us as we roll out the gate to freedom.

I breathe a sigh of relief when the compound has faded from the rearview mirror. Thank you, God. Of course the tranquility shatters when Mona's phone begins ringing. Oh shit, he did see me. It's Frank calling to order her back. Fuck. "Can you get that for me?" Mona asks. I can't exactly say no. I reach inside her purse and hand her the phone. I'll beg. Tell her the truth then beg, and—

"Hey, Debs," Mona says with a grin. Oh thank God. They haven't sounded the alarm. Yet.

As Mona chats with Debs, who I think is her daughter from the amount of concerned chiding Mona expresses, I pretend not to listen while watching the scenery go by. Wooded patches end at the river. We pass over the bridge Jason was attacked on, which is still missing part of the metal guardrail where he went over. Jesus, he plummeted at least twenty feet into the slow-moving water. It's a miracle he survived the gunfight, let alone the drop. A trickle of fear snakes down my spine. It's a calculated risk—me leaving the compound, I know this. Hell, that's why I swiped the gun in my purse, but I had to get away from there. Away from Frank, from the kids, from the smiles everyone had for me, from Jason. I just had to get *away* before I had a nervous breakdown. The risk is worth the reward.

"…love you too. You and Collins be good for Auntie Sara. I'll see you tomorrow. Bye."

She ends the call and tosses her cell back into the purse of the floor.

"Was that your daughter?" I ask.

"What? No, well not really. It was my sister. I'm her legal guardian so yes and no I guess. It's complicated."

"Well, if anyone knows about complicated family arrangements, it's me."

"Yeah," she laughs. "I heard."

"Oh God, what are they saying about me?"

"In all my expert eavesdropping today, I didn't hear a word said against you. Quite the opposite."

"That's just because I spent all day watching their children. They don't know me. Not a one. Not even Frank."

We drive in silence for a few seconds before she asks, "Is that why you snuck out? Because you don't think they want you there?"

"I didn't …" My mouth snaps shut. Damn it. "What gave me away?"

"The words just out of your mouth," Mona says. "Same ploy works on my sister all the time. I can spot stubborn rebellion a mile off."

"Well, a little rebellion never killed anyone," I say.

"Um … the French Revolution?" she counters.

"You know what I mean," I say playfully. "I just needed some alone time. With tequila. *Lots* of tequila." I give her a sideways glance, and smirk. "Care to join me, High Priestess McGregor?"

"I *should* turn this car around and drive you right back," she says.

"Where's the fun in that? Besides, I owe you two drinks, and I do my utmost to be a woman of my word, though my track record's been a bit spotty of late, don't want more red on my ledger."

The witch mulls this over. I can practically see the angel and demon on her shoulders duking it out. When a smirk forms on her round face, I know I've corrupted another pure soul. Hope this one thanks me for it later, unlike the last. "One drink. But if Frank asks me …"

"I held you at gunpoint and told you to make a break for Canada, I swear."

"Alright, but don't make me regret this."

"Miss McGregor, after a night out with me, may the only regrets you have be that you made out with the hot busboy, and they haven't invented a cure for a hangover."

———

"… two, three, go!"

Lick, pour, suck. The tequila rolls down my throat like battery acid. The lime cuts the taste, but I still shudder from the after burn. Mona spasms too and sticks out her tongue in disgust. She sucks on the lime but shudders again. "Hell's bells, that is awful!"

"Then why'd you do it again?" I ask with a laugh.

"Because …" She grabs another lime and sucks. "Peer pressure?"

"I accept full responsibility."

"Good. Thank you. Should we do another?" she asks with a glint in her eye. "Bartender! Another shot!"

The fifty-something bartender shakes his bald head with disapproval but does as asked. Kind of judgmental here at the Adolphous Inn. Maybe we should have gone to Ocean's Bar at the edge of town, but Mona insisted we come here with its beige wallpaper, paintings of sailboats on the walls, and wooden stools and booths. At least there's some prime talent here tonight with two handsome devils in a diagonal booth checking us out periodically. Vivian from a week ago would have already grabbed Mona by the collar, dragged her over there to be my wingman, and had my tongue down faux hawk's throat. She could have the Italian stallion. Tonight I do my best to ignore them. Once you've had prime rib, a hamburger just won't suffice.

The bartender finishes pouring and Mona holds up her shot glass. "To my first girls' night out in … um … hell if I remember."

I hold up my glass too. "To booze, boys, and howling at the moon because of both." We clink glasses, salt, lick, pour, suck, and shimmy. "Oh, fuck, that is rank. No more."

Mona tosses down her lime rind with a grin. "I am having so much fun. I never get to do this." I notice she glances over at the men and turns red, not from the hooch this time. Her eyes then avert down to the bar, the grin fading. "Do those guys keep looking at us or am I nuts?"

"Mona, we're the only two drunk women in this place, who also just happen to be smoking hot. Damn straight they're checking us out."

"Maybe you," she says with a scoff. "A man hasn't checked me out since Clinton was in office."

If she only knew. Be it the booze, her sadness under the strong façade, or just my lack of ability to keep my mouth shut, I want *so bad* to tell her about Adam. But my new Popeye-after-spinach-strong self-control instead makes me grab the water and drink to keep my mouth occupied until the urge passes. "Sorry. Tequila makes me thirsty."

"What about you? Got someone special back home?" Mona asks.

"It's complicated. *Very* complicated. He ... the man has two settings, lava hot and deep space cold. He's always searching for something in me, and I can't for the life of me figure out what the hell it is. He wants me, he cares about me, but he's holding back. And it's not like I'm asking him to propose or anything." I shake my head. "I don't know. I don't want to talk about it. I came here to get away from that bullshit." I sip my water again. "Let's talk about you. You really haven't been out on a date this millennia?"

She rolls her eyes. "I've been kind of busy. Raising my teenage sister, caring for my dying grandparents, running my shop and house, not to mention being responsible for over a hundred witches and their education and problems. I barely have time to sleep let alone date."

"Does that bother you? Not having any time for yourself? Being at everyone's beck and call?"

"Sometimes, I guess," she says, drinking her water. "But ... they're family. I love and respect them. I give myself, my time be-cause I know they'd do the same for me if they could. That's what family does. That's what love is—putting someone ahead of yourself. That's the true test. And I was always an excellent test taker," she says with a smirk.

"Well, I've failed more than I passed," I admit.

"But I bet the ones you aced the hell out of were the ones you actually cared about," she counters. She leans in toward me. "When it matters, when it *really* matters, you'll be shocked at the strength you have inside you. I guaran-damn-tee it." She leans back with a smile. "Now, if you'll excuse me, I have to see a horse about a man. Excuse me."

Mona leaps off the stool, only to wobble a little. She uses the bar to steady herself before tottering off in search of a bathroom. I sip my water and sigh. She *is* right. I got straight As in music and P.E. I loved those two classes. Maybe that's my problem, I just don't give a shit about anything. Anyone. It's just so damn hard to rev that motor when it's rusted over from lack of use. I—

"Alone at last, Miss Dahl."

I glance to my right, the way Mona went, and notice a large man strolling toward me with a grin. He's tall, almost as tall as Jason, with the same musclebound physique shown off in a white shirt and tight jeans, but softer face complete with shaved bald head and goatee. Not my type even pre-Jason. Something about him, be it the grin or hard brown eyes staring me down, instantly puts me on edge. The moment he's at my side, so are the other two men from the booth, circling me so I have no way to escape. Despite the familiar heat radiating from them, my blood goes ice cold.

"We haven't been introduced. I'm Seth. Welcome to the family."

Fuck.

My hand shoots toward the purse on the bar, but Seth grabs my hand halfway, squeezing it so hard I clench my teeth. "Wouldn't do that if I was you," Seth whispers into my ear. "Not unless you want me to go upstairs and rip open the witch's throat, that is after Mal here shoots you dead with the gun under his jacket." I glance from faux hawk's jacket to the bartender, eyes pleading. I'm met only with terror in his before he looks down and turns his back on me. Bastard.

"How'd you know I was here?" His buddies came in about ten minutes after we did. "Your rat?"

"I have no idea what you're talking about. Get up." Seth literally pulls the chair out from under me before latching onto my arm to guide me out. "See you later, Simon," Seth calls to the bartender as he maneuvers me out.

Fuck. Fuck.

Whether it's the tequila or near-maddening fear, it's difficult to walk through the hotel's small lobby and outside. "I lost some of my best men because of you," the monster says on the death march.

"Good."

He squeezes my arm harder. My teeth may break, I'm clenching them so tight. "Tough. We'll see just how tough by the end of the night. Why should Jason just get his leg over, huh?"

He thrusts me out the hotel's double doors into the warm night. The Inn is situated in downtown Adolphus, with shops and restaurants lining the brick street, and people filtering in and out. People. Hallelujah. Screw this noise. This isn't happening. Not again. I've already seen what's at the end of this road. I haven't healed from the last ride. "Let me go."

"Now why would I—"

"HELP ME!" I shriek at the top of my lungs. "HELP! RAPE! RAPE!"

The men are so shocked at my disobedience we stop moving, giving me time to turn sideways and knee Seth in the groin. He releases me, and I make it two steps toward the bystanders before Mal with the gun lunges. Five years of cardio kickboxing training takes control. My foot pounds into his stomach with all my force as I roar. He folds in the middle as all the air is knocked from his lungs. The third stooge just gawks for a second at his doubled-over compatriots. They thought I'd make this easy for them. Morons. Unlike the Italian, I don't hesitate, I take off toward the hotel.

"Hey!" one of the people down the sidewalk calls.

I don't get far. The Italian catches up to me not ten feet from the hotel door. The fucker grabs my wrist, and spins me around into a bear hug not even a bear could survive. "Fight and I'll snap your goddamn neck," the Italian stallion snarls.

"Let her go!" the Good Samaritan shouts, "or we're calling the police."

The stallion's brown eyes are alight with fury and indecision. He's not used to making the calls. "Let her go," Seth calls behind us. "We have to get out of here."

Without hesitation, the Italian releases me and I back away, panting now I'm able to breathe again. My eyes jut to a snarling, seething Seth who stares me down with utter contempt. I mimic the gesture. "This isn't over, bitch. Tell your father I'm going to rip his spine out. I'm coming back for what's mine, and I plan to rain hell down on anyone who opposes me. Those already dead will be the lucky ones. You're going to be wishing I'd killed you tonight."

"Come on, we gotta go," faux hawk Mal says to his leader. "And you're first, bitch!"

With one final snarl, Seth turns and sprints down the street with his pals a clip behind. I just watch, still panting like I'd just finished the Tour de France, as the threesome climb into a black van and tear out of the parking spot, then down the near empty street. Away. Jesus Christ. My legs finally buckle, and I collapse onto the sidewalk, staring down that road.

Jesus Christ. Can't a girl just enjoy a drink around here?

———

"Really, I'm okay. Stop mother-henning me. I'm fine."

Mona stares down at me, lips pursed with disapproval, but she does back away. She's been fussing over me since she found me outside trying to convince the Good Samaritans not to phone the police. I am still a fugitive after all. They listened to Mona more than me. Despite three shots of tequila, she took charge like a pro, convincing the couple we'd phone the police from her hotel room before ushering me up here. Without another word, the witch sat me down on the bed, poured black salt along the door, then phoned Frank. She just gave him the broad strokes, where we were, then hung up to check on me. For what just happened, I'm oddly calm. No more shaking or trouble breathing. I just sit calmly on the edge of the bed, sip the water Mona got me, and wait for the cavalry. Think the tequila's doing its job, otherwise I'd probably be a mess.

My new friend sits beside me, pulling up the blanket she insisted I drape around my shoulders. "You're not freezing or—"

"I'm not in shock, no. I swear to you, I'm fine," I assure her. "I didn't have to kill anyone, I didn't have to dig a bullet out of someone's arm, there was no car chase. I've dealt with worse, but I'm sorry I dragged you into this."

"I'm sorry I wasn't around to help. Though it doesn't sound like you needed it."

"I got lucky." I scoff. "First time for everything, right?"

The knock on the door jolts us both an inch off the bed. My hand instinctively reaches for the gun by my side. "Mona?"

Oh, I've never been so happy to hear someone's voice. Mona rises to unlock and open the door. Frank sent the big guns. Jason steps in first, followed by Adam and Tate. All for little old me. I am in so much fucking trouble judging from the brutal scowl on Jason's face. That look is more deadly than an army of werewolves. "Mona," Jason says, not removing his eyes from me, "could you please excuse us for a minute?"

"Yeah, you can help me check in. I'm your bodyguard for the rest of the night," Tate says with a gentle smile.

"Is that necessary?" Mona asks.

"Just a precaution," Tate says, ushering her out.

Adam nods at me before following his brother out. He probably hates me right now for putting the love of his life in danger. I don't blame him. I blame me too. He shuts the door behind himself and I'm alone with the very person I was running away from.

"Are you—"

"3GK245, Maryland plates. The car was a black van, a newer model not more than five years old. Chevy I think, but that was definitely the plate number. The rat must have seen me sneak out because the other two wolves got here very soon after we did. I wasn't paying attention, but it could have been anyone in the hall or in the driveway when I was talking to Mona."

"Vivian—" he begins, the scowl melting into impassivity.

I pull the blanket off my shoulders and manage to rise. "I'm an idiot. I know I'm an idiot. I put myself in danger, I put Mona in danger, *I know*. There is nothing you can say that will make me feel shittier than I already do. I just … I had to get out of that house. I took every precaution, but I fucked up anyway. I'm sorry, okay? I'm sorry, and I will never, *ever* do it again. But at least we have a lead and no one was hurt. I'm just … sorry."

Jason just stares at me, unreadable for a few seconds. The silence around us is palpable, deafening even. "Jason, just fucking say som—"

He takes two strides toward me before enveloping me in his arms and hugging tight. I'm too shocked at first to move, but that's over in a millisecond before I embrace him back. I melt into him, into his scent, into his heat and the rapid rise and fall of his chest. I—

Over too soon. He pulls away, mask back on and eyes down to the blue carpet. "Adam will drive you back to the house. You are not to leave it again. I know you won't. Thank you … for your leads. I'll follow them up." He nods before spinning on his heel and stalking out, not even bothering to close the door.

What the … ? I don't think I'll ever understand that man.

Adam steps into the doorway, usually cheerful face as stony as Jason's. I did almost get his mate killed. "You ready to go?"

"Yeah," I whisper. After I stick the gun back in my purse, I follow Adam out into the hallway. We walk shoulder to shoulder, both staring straight ahead. "I'm sorry."

"Yeah, well... I'm sure you'll make it up to us."

And I will.

FIFTEEN

"... gave proof through the night,
that our flag was still there.
Oh, say does that Star-Spangled Banner
Yet wave. O'er the land of the free,
And the home of the brave?"

OUR AUDIENCE APPLAUDS AS the children take their bows with wide, well-deserved grins on their faces. Whew, pulled that one out of my hat well. A day of practice, most can't read the lyrics I printed out for them, and half couldn't keep still in rehearsal. It took every ounce of my patience, including the little I keep in reserve, not to scream at them every five minutes. Glad I had only decided on the one song. The munchkins didn't let me down. I shouldn't have doubted them.

"Happy Independence Day everyone," I say with smile affixed. I glance at Jason, who is making a rare appearance today for the picnic. He keeps his eyes to the ground as he claps. "Let freedom ring."

Three days. It's been three days since my jailbreak and three days until my birthday. Not a word, not a look. The only time I even laid eyes on him was last night from my bedroom window as he dropped Omar off before driving away again. Scuttlebutt is he's been following leads on Seth acquired from Donovan's computer and my keen observation skills. Of course I know this is crap because Devin told me there was nothing but work files on it, not a single e-mail even, and the van hasn't been found or its owner. Guess Frank had to tell them something. There are further rumors that Jason is investigating missing persons, that Seth's building his ranks with new "recruits" like van owner Malcolm Jaffe. Okay, Adam told me point blank there's been the odd wolf sighting, a missing man near Gettysburg, then more reports of strapping young men disappearing around the area as well. Sounds like Seth's getting desperate. I knew that when I looked in his eyes. Not sure if that's a good or bad thing.

Regardless, the natives, me included, are growing restless. Katie, Mac's mother, even admitted to me that her husband Reid is planning on leaving after the full moon extravaganza tonight. He's a hair's breadth away from getting fired from his project manager's job in D.C. He's not the only one, and if he starts a precedent, there could be a mass exodus. Whatever Jason's up to all day and night out there in the world, he better do it quick.

The good news is that I've been too tired, busy, then tired again to obsess over him too much. Only every other minute as opposed to every single one. I thought working two jobs plus auditions was exhausting. It's got nothing on being responsible for ten children and four teenagers. At least Troy takes the job seriously now. After he lost Mason for hours during the scavenger hunt, I threatened to chop off his balls complete with snipping motion. He shaped up. Me too. All in, me. Penance paid one runny nose wiped or temper tantrum quashed at a time. I've barely had the energy to take an always cold shower, werewolves love hot water, before crashing into bed around ten. But I'm shocked how much I'm enjoying myself. Playing with them, talking to the kids, I haven't had so much fun in years. I'm like the fucking kid whisperer.

"Thank you children," Frank says as he strolls up the stone steps. "Vivian." My mouth twitches into a cordial smile before the children and I join the others on the lawn. Devin, Linda, Claire, Maureen, and the children all greet me with proud smiles, which I return. Adam, who stands in the back with Jason and Tate, gives a reverent nod. He earns a smile too. His best friend keeps his head down. None for him then.

"I just want to say a few words," Frank begins, "before we all enjoy this wonderful feast you all worked to put together." He pauses for effect. "It's been a hard time for us all, without question. We've lost members of our family. We've lost our sense of security. We've lost … our innocence. I know you're afraid. Frustrated. Angry. I know you all could let these feelings overwhelm you. Have you make rash decisions. Take it out on each other. Give up even. But … you haven't. As I look across to all your faces, I see no despair. No hatred. Only strength. Love. What could have broken us apart has brought us closer together."

He is very good at this. Even I'm getting fired up.

"They may try to tear us apart. They may try to beat us until we can't get up. But I believe with my whole heart there is not a one of you who will not rise. Who will not continue fighting until their dying breath, not just for yourself. But for the people beside you. We are pack. We are *family*." He looks square into my eyes and smiles. "And I am so very proud of you all."

I think I blush.

"To the pack!" Tate calls, holding up his red cup.

"To the pack!" we all say.

"Then let's stuff our faces and enjoy this beautiful Fourth of July afternoon!" Frank says.

Shante, Percy or "Pookie's" mate, switches on the stereo. Bruce Springsteen starts playing. Can't go wrong with The Boss. Everyone moves toward the tables setup on the lawn so we can all eat together with two smaller tables off to the side for the kids.

The majority of tents have been taken down for tonight's event. We're gonna have a full house. Anyone not turning furry when the full moon rises has to be inside. Linda and the kids are graciously letting me spend the night in their room as I had to give up mine. They're so excited, Nicki even offered to let me sleep with Mr. Sprinkles, her stuffed Panda. Almost took her up on it. Haven't been sleeping well.

Frank sits smack dab in the middle of the table much like Jesus in The Last Supper. People swarm around him, with Jason and Tate edging out the competition for the coveted seats to his left and right. I get as close to Jason as possible, four down, across from Linda and Reid. I wait to serve myself as I've learned never to get between werewolves and munchies. They're like piranha, only more frenzied and with sharper teeth.

"Pass this down to Vivi," I hear Frank say.

A second later Maureen hands me a paper plate with a veggie burger. "Thank you."

"You did an amazing job with the children and that song," she says. "We're so lucky to have a professional singer in the house."

"So glamorous," Linda adds. "Frank once showed us a video of you singing in this club. You were so good."

"Yes, a smart man once told me I'm downright haunting," I say, glancing at Jason, who even now keeps his head down to avoid people's gazes. He does steal a glance at me, but only for an instant. He's listening.

"We should organize a concert one night," Maureen suggests. "Tate plays the guitar."

"I play piano," Linda adds.

For some reason the thought of singing in front of them awakens my nerves. "I don't—"

"Frank!" Maureen shouts. My father turns from Tate to his mother. "Your daughter's agreed to perform at a concert for us. Isn't that wonderful?"

"It is. I can't wait."

"We'll see," I say. I bite my burger and decide to change the subject. "So, full moon tonight. Should be interesting. Do you all look forward to it or ..."

"Hell no," Reid says, scratching his balding head.

"Do you run around? Hunt deer or something?"

"Pretty much," Reid answers.

"It's great to be pack," Pookie adds. "We're lucky. I'm just glad we ain't gotta be caged tonight."

"I'm not," Katie, Reid's wife says. "There are a million windows and doors downstairs. What's to stop one of you from breaking in?"

"It's never happened before tonight," Maureen answers. "Besides we have magical wards all over the house. Nothing with intent to harm can come in as long as they're up."

"But how do we know they work?" Katie asks.

That is an excellent question, but I don't want to add fuel to the paranoia fire. "From what I understand, the witch who put them up is the most powerful in America." And is outstanding in a crisis, even shitfaced. "She's gotta be good, right? Plus I've seen one work. Mason was chasing Aiden after a fight, Aiden ran inside and Mason couldn't get through the door," I lie. "See? They work. Nothing to worry about."

"Oh," Katie says with an unconvincing smile. "Good."

"And Jason and I have already discussed offensive and defensive strategies," I lie again. "We've got all the angles covered. Isn't that right, Jason?" I shout.

Frank and Jason's gazes whip my way. "What?" Jason asks.

"The plan for tonight. I was just telling everyone how worried you were about all of us alone in the house tonight, so you spent hours thinking up every worst-case scenario and its solution." I turn back to Katie. "He really is a brilliant strategist."

"We'll get into all of that later," Frank says. "It's well in hand."

"We'll just look after one another. We'll be fine," I say with a reassuring smile. Katie and a few eavesdroppers grin back.

When I turn straight ahead, I notice Frank and Jason staring. Frank gives me a reverent nod, and Jason's mouth jolts in a quick smile before his eyes dip down again. Once again, in spite of myself, a swell of pride rises. I am definitely getting addicted to them as well.

Jason lasts longer than I thought he would, almost ten minutes before whispering to Frank and rising from the table. Katie regales me with stories of finding the right tutor for Mac, not easy apparently, as he excuses himself. I wait two minutes before claiming a headache, not a total lie, and following his example. I've been waiting three days for this face-to-face with him. Time's up, Blondie.

Of course he seems to have slipped through my fingers again. A quick sweep of the downstairs proves fruitless. Excedrin before continuing, I think. That and I've sweated off my deodorant. Not good, especially in a white sundress. I'm freshening up in my bathroom when I hear a creak like an old door opening, then heavy footsteps in the bedroom. I step out to investigate, but instead of finding one of my cute little shadows per usual, to my great pleasure I find my prey has come to me, through a secret passage no less. Jason glances from the closing panel in the wall with a rusty metal door behind it. I'm the one who should be surprised, but his mouth drops open when he sets eyes on me.

"Hi," I say with a wide grin. "Didn't mean to scare you."

"You didn't. I just—"

"Didn't know I was inside the house," I finish, leaning against the doorframe. "Needed Excedrin. Is that a real secret passageway?"

"Yes. Dad was going to show it to you after lunch. I was just changing—"

"Well, show it to me now," I say, walking over. "One less thing for him to worry about."

"Um, okay." He takes a step to the left. Away from me. "Press the panel. Hard."

I do. After a click, the wall moves back, then forward a centimeter. I pull it open all the way to reveal the metal door with a keypad beside it. "What's the code?"

"0707, then press pound."

"My birthday," I say as I punch it in.

"I know."

The light flips from red to green as I hear the lock disengage. I open the door, finding a very narrow, dark, stone spiral staircase. I'm not a big person by any means, but I don't think even I could fit in there comfortably. "Where does it go?"

"Follow me."

Crap. This place is a claustrophobic's worst nightmare. I have literally had a nightmare that contained this very scenario except those walls had rows of spikes that slowly closed and skewered me like a kebab. Yeah, I need a Xanax just looking at this. Jason has no such worries. He steps into the tomb, and my throat closes up again. *Show no weakness.* I swallow my fear and follow.

I was right. Jason has to turn sideways and duck to walk down, with me two steps behind. The door above closes automatically, and with only one working light bulb on the wall, I can barely see the steps. After three revolutions on the stairs we reach another door with keypad on this side. "That's Dad's office. I programmed the same code for all." We don't linger. There are more stairs to descend. This tour better be close to over because I have about thirty seconds before I'm hyperventilating. My breath's shallow now and hands are clammy. Damn it, I swear these walls grow narrower by the step. They are. I know it. I dig my fingernails into my palm to concentrate on that.

We end the tour at a dark underground tunnel that resembles a mine shaft made of stone and mortar. Jason switches on the lights, but it doesn't help much as there's only a bulb every thirty feet or so. "The door behind you is to the basement."

"Where's the tunnel, um, go?" I ask, voice quaking a little.

"Past the gate. It was built after Jeremiah Conlon turned and accidently ate his mate after he chased her down on the lawn."

"Lovely."

Jesus Christ, it smells like the musky earth in here, just like … oh, fuck. With a blink, I'm transported back to that basement in Pennsylvania waiting to die in a fucking cage about as big as this tunnel. There isn't a millimeter of me not taught and ready to strike from fear. I bunch my dress up with my sweaty hands.

"Most people know this is here, but I just altered the codes. We'll tell everyone right before the change to avoid the mole leaking it."

"Great. Let's go."

"I need to show you … are you unwell?" he asks, eyes narrowing.

"Fine. Excuse me," I say breathlessly. I twirl from the shaft to the metal door, push in the code with my shaking finger, and rush through the millisecond it opens. No salvation here. I step into a concrete room with several cages like the one that held me with a narrow passage between them. Even the odor's the same: salt, blood, urine, and antiseptic that fails to mask the others. I don't know if it's the stench or the playback of my death match, complete with stinging pain shooting through my still-healing gun wound, but bile rises.

"Vivian?" Jason asks behind me.

His hand touches my bare shoulder, and I jolt. I can't fucking breathe. *I need to get the fuck out of this room.* I race out into the basement hallway with Jason a few paces behind. Even in here with more space, I can't breathe very well. I scan the wood-paneled hallway to get my bearings and find the stairs. They're between the freezer and laundry room, which is …

Jason's hands gently wrap around my forearms. "Come here," he whispers before guiding me to the bench a few feet away. He sits me down before lowering himself beside me. I should be thrilled when he uncurls my fingers and entwines his with mine, but I'm still too damn tense. "Just breathe."

"I am breathing," I snap. Just not well. "I'm fine."

"You should have told me you were claustrophobic. I wouldn't have—"

"I needed to know. It's fine." I squeeze his hand harder and stare down at the hardwood floor. "It just … I was suddenly back in that basement getting the shit kicked out of me again. The darkness, the smells, being trapped …" I shake my head to clear the ghosts. "I'm fine. It's over. I'll be fine." God, I'm embarrassed. Almost falling apart over nothing in front of the big bad wolf killer. Real impressive, Viv. No wonder—

"It happens to me too," he says, drawing me out of my ocean of self-pity. I look up. He's got that damn mask of his on. "The flashbacks. It could be something someone says, a smell, a scene on TV, and I'm right back in the worst moments of my life as if I'd traveled back in time. Talking about it helps. Time too. Dad—"

"No," I say with a grimace. I don't want to talk about this anymore. I pull my hand away. "I'm fine. See? The irrationality has passed."

He doesn't speak for a few seconds, then, "You don't have to do that around me."

"Do what?"

"Act strong when it's left you for the moment," he says matter-of-factly. "Even the strong fall from time to time. We all have our weak moments. If and how we pick ourselves up and handle the aftermath is all that matters. And in that, time and again, you've shown great strength. True strength."

"That's what you don't understand. I'm *not* strong," I blurt out. "I'm a lucky fuck-up. I'm scared all the time, even before all this. I'm not like you, I can't turn lemons into lemonade, and you had a ton more lemons than I ever did. You have no idea how much I respect you for that."

"I had help, though. People who loved me, who kept me going when a weak moment hit, who helped me up. Who knew my strength even when I didn't. They gave me a reason to continue on. I couldn't have done it alone."

"You did that for me, you know? In Pennsylvania. You kept me going. You kept me fighting. I think ... I was more afraid of you dying than me. I had to get to you. Save you. *You* gave me strength."

"You are not giving yourself enough credit. You never do."

"I give credit where it's due." I pause. "You're my hero, Jason Dahl."

"Please stop," he says quietly, once again gazing down at his lap.

I fall back against the wall and narrow my eyes. "Why do you always do that?"

"What?"

"Just completely shut down and pull away from me whenever I try to say or do something nice? Do you think I'm lying? Trying to trick you? Find a weakness and exploit it?"

"No," he says, eyes still deflected.

"Then why? Stop shutting me out. You don't get to say wonderful things about me one second, then run off and reject me the next. I'm getting fucking whiplash."

"I'm sorry. I don't mean to."

"Then stop it."

"You don't ..." He stares at me, his mouth open like he wants to continue, but gazes down again in defeat.

"I don't understand?" I finish for him. "You're right. I haven't understood since you freaked out seconds after we made love. Do you have any idea how much that hurt me? That you were disgusted by me?"

"I wasn't," he assures me. "I was disgusted by *me*."

"Why? Because Frank ordered you not to be with me like Adam and Mona? Because according to paperwork, we're siblings? That's white noise, Jason. This is about you and me. Nothing else matters."

His intense eyes finally leap up to my face. "But it does," he almost hisses. "We don't exist in a vacuum, Vivian. I am pack. I am *loup-garou*. That will never change. And you ... you do not *belong*. There is a reason your father kept you away from this world. We're monsters. Danger surrounds us at all times, and not just from outside these walls."

"Cat's kind of out of the bag on that one, Blondie. I am officially Frank Dahl, super-werewolf's, daughter. And, with maybe one exception, there are no monsters in this group, yourself included."

Jason gazes back down at this hands. He wants to leave. I feel the desire to flee wafting off him in waves. "That's not the real reason, is it?" The muscles in his face tighten. "So, what is?"

I don't get an answer. He opts for option B, standing to flee again. "I don't want to talk about this anymore. I have things to do. Excuse me." Sure enough, he turns and starts toward the laundry room. I really, *really* hate when he does that.

Not this time. I spring up as I call, "Don't you walk away from me, Jason Dahl."

I run right in front of him just as he reaches the stairs, blocking him. "Vivian, please move."

"Not happening. Even if you move me, I will just keep chasing you."

This time he stares me dead in the eyes. "Why?" he asks, voice as blank as those eyes.

"Why what?"

"Why would you continue chasing me when I don't wish you to?"

"What?"

"And why did you volunteer to watch the children?"

"To help out. Why else—"

"And why did you offer to help me the other day on the beach? The real reason?"

"I told you. What is—"

"It had nothing to do with us having to spend time together?"

"That was … a bonus. So what? The children have fun, people realize you're secretly a teddy bear, I am not seeing the problem."

He stares at me with such disappointment I want to run back into that tunnel—even that is preferable to his gaze. "The pack comes first. You give before you get. If someone is starving, you give them as much as you can spare, and you do it because it's the right thing. Not because you get something out of it. The needs of the many come before the needs of you. That is love. That is *pack*."

It takes a second for the words to sink in but it finally dawns on me. He thinks I'm selfish. That I'm incapable of thinking of others unless it serves me. The thing is, he's not wrong. It's one of the few things I've prided myself on, the ability to take care of myself because no one else would. I always did my damnedest not to screw people over if I could help it, but I tried harder to make sure they didn't screw me over.

"Well, I'm sorry I don't live up to your impossible standards of nobility, Sir Lancelot. But unlike you, I didn't have a safety net. No one before you lifted a finger to help me. No one *ever* put me first. I had to be selfish out of necessity. To survive. And after twenty-nine years, it is a damn hard habit to break. But goddamn it, *I'm trying*. Doesn't that count for something? And despite one little slip, nothing I've done has hurt anyone."

"That's where you're wrong, and the fact you can't even see that proves my point. What you do, what you say, impacts others. Sometimes you can even be a damn wrecking ball, Vivian. You leave gaping holes in a person's life. It may not be intentional, you may even believe you're doing the right thing, but the damage still remains when you leave. You, of all people, should know that because you are proof of that aftermath. And there will be an aftermath. You *will* leave. I'm just trying to minimize the damage. So, I'll ask again: please leave me alone," he pleads. "Please."

This time I don't chase him. Wouldn't know what to say or do if I caught him.

Even with the headache gone, I'm in a shit mood. Doesn't help I have to give up my room to the Kahn and Foster families in exchange for a sleeping bag on the floor along with the hyper-twins and my sister-in-law, who I barely know. Sleepover from hell in my future. My present isn't much better. As I walk down the hall, every ten feet a nervous wife or husband needs assurances we'll be safe with almost two dozen werewolves running wild outside tonight. I'd be dammed nervous myself if I had the time. I seem to be somehow responsible for tonight's fortification and all the people inside. Where people sleep, guard duty rotation, a billion different "what-ifs" from various women, they all come to me. Like I have a clue what we'll do if there's a blackout and the security system fails. Die most likely.

Jason doesn't know what the hell he's talking about. A truly selfish person would grab some booze, chips, and a shotgun, lock herself in the master bedroom, and if breached use the escape tunnel and never look back. Okay, I have considered it. Even found some bourbon in Frank's dresser. But instead I'm cleaning and loading guns, helping people move their stuff inside, and directing people to their temporary accommodations. And Jason's not around to see me do it, so I get no brownie points from him for all my hard work. I do it anyway, Blondie.

I mean, I'm a little selfish. So what? There's honor—then there's just plain stupidity. If you give all of yourself to others, then what's left for you? And people have to *earn* that kind of devotion. It just kills me that the first person who ever earned it with me thinks I'm some manipulative, rotten bitch incapable of genuine change and empathy. And how could I take a wrecking ball to his life? I don't even have the power to keep him in a room, let alone destroy him or make him a crumbling mess. Our conversation is nowhere near over.

But that's for tomorrow. Tonight, werewolf shenanigans. As I'm loading another shotgun at the dining table between Omar and Sam, Tate strolls in. "How goes it?"

"Almost done," says Omar.

Tate's not really listening, he's too busy staring at me with a crooked smile. "Know how to work that thing, princess?"

I load the last cartridge and pump it. "I'm a fast learner. Sunshine," I say with a shit-eating grin.

"Forgot. You've already got a murder on your ledger."

"Plenty of room for more," I say, my smile unwavering. See? If I were selfish I'd do what I want and shoot this asshole in the leg. Twice. It'd sure make *me* feel better. Instead, I rise from the table. "Excuse me, gents, millions of things to do. Just make sure no kids come in here."

"My, aren't we thoughtful?" Tate says as I pass him. I glare and his smile stretches farther. "Didn't know you had it in you."

I keep walking down the hall. My face burns red from the mortification. Jesus Christ, Jason told him. By tomorrow tales of my narcissism will be legendary. This place is worse than high school when it comes to gossip. I know Scott can't get it up, Tate's banged three of the married women here, Katie abuses Percocet, and that was just the scuttlebutt from the first day. No one's outright asked what happened between Jason and I, but I have noticed once or twice women ceasing their conversation as I passed. I thank my lucky stars I spend the majority of my time with the kids. Give me a discussion about *Invader Zim* over gossip of my love life any damn day.

"Vivi, got a minute?" Frank calls from his office as I pass.

Oh, hell. Just what I need, a minute alone with dear old deadbeat Dad. Since the Adam then Seth debacles, we've been cordial the few times we've had to be in the same room. Smile, nod, update on the day, and off we went to our neutral corners. Right now I stop, take a deep breath, and plaster another smile on before walking in. Frank sits at his desk clicking away with the mouse on his computer. "Your mother e-mailed me. They're all fine. Enjoying themselves in Jamaica. I copied it to the desktop for you to read."

"Thank you."

He glances up with a quick smile. "Welcome. Can you close the doors?"

Great. Privacy. This can't be good. I roll them shut but don't move in case I need a quick getaway. "Yes?"

"I want to go over details about tonight." He casually leans back in his chair. "How is everyone?"

"Nervous but generally fine."

"Everyone moved in?"

"Mostly."

"What about security measures?"

"They all know not to go downstairs for any reason unless on guard duty. We'll have two shifts of two, one person stationed in here and the other in the parlor to cover both front and back, each armed with a tranq gun and shotgun with silver shot. Right now Shante and Sarah are going through the rooms to make sure the curtains are drawn, and everyone knows to keep the lights off and noise down as much as possible so we don't draw attention to the house."

"And if we get in?" Frank asks.

"The two guards will do their best to keep the wolf at bay as the others retreat into the tunnel."

"Jason already showed it to you? Gave you the code?"

Damn it. Just the mention of his name makes me flush. "Yes. I'll tell everyone else after you all leave."

"Who have you selected for guard duty?"

"Donald, June, Deandra, and me."

"Why them?" Frank asks, I think as a test.

"We're all childless, and both Deandra and I have experience firing at actual people." I jut out my chin in defiance. "So? Did I pass?"

"I'm sorry?"

"This little test. Did I pass?" I ask, blood boiling so much I think my hair grows even redder.

His blue eyes narrow in confusion. "This wasn't a test, Vivian. I'm responsible for this pack. I need to know things are under control. I wouldn't have put you in charge if—"

"You didn't put me in charge, *they* did. You didn't want a meddler like me to have anything to do with them, remember?"

"That was not what I meant, and you know it," he fires back.

"No, I don't know that. How the hell could I? I don't know you. I do know when I'm being played, though. It's a skill I had to learn *very* early on," I spit.

"I wasn't playing you, Vivi," he says, matching my harsh tone. "*I* wasn't the one manipulating people. Despite your motives, you stepped out of line. I was merely alerting you to that fact."

"I am not one of your wolves to boss around, who if you snap your fingers will stand at attention. Who think you hung the damn moon. You are just the asshole who abandoned me. You don't exactly have the moral high ground, at least not with me."

"I did what I thought was best for you at the time."

"Yeah, because growing up thinking your father didn't want you is always for the best. Really boosts a girl's self-esteem. I'm sure every woman working a stripper pole agrees with me."

"I wanted you, Vivi. I—"

"No, you didn't. Not really. If you really, *truly* did, you would have come for me. It wouldn't have mattered what Mom said. You could have snuck around her, snuck around your werewolf pals. You would have found a way. You bend over backwards for every person in this house. Hell, you adopted a violent boy and treated him as your own. All I apparently got was a letter once a year I wasn't even allowed to know about. What? Were you afraid I'd come in and wreck your new, perfect family? Corrupt your precious little boys with my dysfunction?"

"Now you're just saying things to be cruel," Frank says through gritted teeth.

"Am I? Then why did you forbid Jason from being in the same room as me? I know you did. He all but told me so. You don't want me around him, you don't want me around Adam, I'm shocked you haven't locked me in one of those damn cages to keep me from my niece and nephew."

"Listen, I understand you're angry with me, and I do not blame you one iota, I don't. But despite what you may believe, what I did, what I still do, is for the good of the people I love. That includes you. It always has. You were never far from my thoughts. *Never*. Not for a single minute," he says intensely. I almost believe him.

"Gee wiz, Dad, you *thought* about me. Want a medal?" I stalk toward him, every muscle close to locked with indignant fury. "I *needed* you. You have no idea how much I needed you. I was your little girl. I needed you to hold me after I had a nightmare. I needed you to pick me up after school and ask me about my day. Help with my homework. Go to my recitals. Make me feel safe. Secure. Loved. Worthwhile. You didn't save me from the wolves, you left me to them."

"I am sorry, okay? I *am* sorry. If I could go back and change it, I would. I would give up my life to change it. But I can't. I was doing what I thought was best to protect you. I never wanted any of this for you. You were shot. Kidnapped. Had to kill someone because of me. Because you're my child. I'm sorry I made you feel as if I didn't care, that I didn't love you, but I am not sorry for trying to give you the best life possible. And I will continue to do that for you, for everyone I love, until I draw my last breath. So if you need to hate me, if that's what fuels you, then go right ahead. All I ask is that you try to extend the same courtesy to the people in this house who have all embraced you, that they're giving you: respect. Kindness."

"Selflessness?" I ask with a sneer. "Yeah, your *son* already gave me this speech. Well, if I am a selfish bitch, you should be proud. I'm carrying on the family tradition established by both my parents." I shake my head. I'm about ten seconds from either punching him or bursting into tears. I don't want to give him the satisfaction of either. "You can play the big man all you like, but don't pretend you really give a shit about me. Don't pretend you're proud of me when you really wish I'd crawl back into the hole I came from. And really don't pretend you love me. You can't love a stranger. Have a nice night with your family."

I throw open the sliding doors only to find the last person I want to see standing down the hall but close enough to hear every word said. The moment I lay eyes on him, fury vanishes and mortification rears its ugly head. Jason reveals nothing whereas I grimace and rush off in the opposite direction outside onto the front stoop, away from silent judgment.

I should feel relief. Closure. I've wanted to have it out with that man for decades. Didn't go quite as planned but still I released the poison. Got it all out there. The demon should be exorcised. The weight lifted from my soul. Then why the hell do I feel like I've just added two tons?

SIXTEEN

HOWLING. MUST THEY CONTINUE that incessant howling all fucking night long? It's messing with my already fragile nerves. I mean, what do they have to talk about? Don't mark the tree I just did? Stop sniffing my butt? Rabbit, ten o'clock? I'm not going to get even an hour of sleep tonight. But hell, even without the chorus outside I doubt I'd be able to drift off. This floor is not comfortable in the least. The snoring boy curled up against me doesn't help either. He snuck out of his mom's bed with pillow and blanket two hours ago when the howling began. Light sleeper, not like his sister and mom. Dustin wrapped my arm around his tiny body and fell right back to sleep. I was glad to be of comforting assistance for once.

This is my penance for earlier. I kept snapping at everyone, kids included. Need, need, need everywhere I went. Pleading with their words and eyes for me to make it all better. To save them from their imagined terrors. To protect them. Best I could do was stick to the script: remain in your rooms with the curtains drawn and run if the shit hits the fan. Some leader I am.

There was no escape from the need, even in my own room. Linda folded the same batch of clothes twice. Dusty kept bouncing on the bed even after a dozen chidings and warnings. And Nicki kept showing me what she was placing in her emergency backpack for my approval. Then Dusty chimed in even louder than his prattling sister, wanting to show me his flip on the bed, and I screamed at them to shut the hell up. Even I was shocked by this outburst. I apologized, played seven rounds of Go Fish, letting one or the other win every time, and even sang five songs to lull them to sleep. Still feel like shit about it. Guilty conscience, frayed nerves, wolves literally howling at the gate, no wonder I can't drift off. I'll bet most of the house is awake too. At least I have a task to perform.

I mastered the art of extraction without waking my companion for a quick getaway years ago, so Dusty doesn't stir as I peel him off me. Deandra's getting off her shift early. I need something to occupy my mind, might as well be guard duty. At least then staring into dark space has a purpose. And it comes with a fun accessory that fires bullets.

With all the lights off, the house is as creepy and still as a cemetery. Over the howls I hear snoring, crying, muffled talking on TV, and the creaking of an old house. I might as well be in an old Hammer Horror film. Peter Cushing's just around the corner, ready to stake me for being a bride of Satan. The flashlight helps keep the ghosts at bay, among other things.

I check on Donald in the parlor who watches a movie on his computer with the tranq and shotguns resting beside. The floodlights outside are motion sensor operated, our first and only warning system. One lights up, we grab a gun and pray. The twenty-three-year-old jerks when I step in the doorway. I smile, nod, and walk back down the hall. I find Deandra, Omar's mate and former Army medic, peeking out of the curtains in the office.

"Problem?" I whisper as I step in.

Deandra spins around. "Thought I saw something in the tree line. It was nothing."

"You sure?"

"Yeah. With the full moon we have good visibility out there," she whispers.

"Good. I'm here to relieve you. Couldn't sleep."

"Thank God. I've been literally jumping at shadows all night. I've patched up soldiers in Kabul with anti-aircraft fire all around and not been this on edge."

"Over in a few hours." Deandra hands me the tranq gun. "Thanks."

"Someone left you a present on the desk," Deandra whispers.

"Really? Okay, thank you. Sleep well."

She nods, switches on her flashlight, and leaves me alone. At last. First stop is the curtain, which I pull back a little. Deandra was right, I can see the expanse of the field through to the tree line. The glow of the moon makes it all seem so peaceful, pretty. Haunting. I shut the curtain and rest the gun on a nearby chair. At this point I doubt the wolves are planning to attack the house. Probably would have done it already. I click on my flashlight and move over to the desk. Sure enough there's a stack of VHS tapes with "Home Movies" written on them along with a folded note on top.

You're wrong. It is possible to love a perfect stranger. Us being here proves it.

—J

Jason.

Without a moment's hesitation, I grab the tapes, tranq gun, and rush across the hall to the living room. After making sure all the curtains are tightly shut, I switch on the TV and turn the volume down low. "Home Movie 2" first. I pop in the tape and pull up a chair close to the TV. This should be interesting. After static, an image of Frank and a young Matt, I'd guess around age seven, on a street fills the screen. Frank holds the back of his son's bicycle.

"Okay, it's on," a woman, I assume Jenny, says behind the camera.

"Let's show Mommy," says Frank. "Ready? Go."

Frank chases after my baby brother, holding the back of the bike steady, then let's go. Matt zooms down the street, wobbling a little at first as his parents applaud and hoot. Yeah, if this is supposed to make me feel better it ain't working. I didn't learn to ride until a camp counselor agreed to teach me when I was twelve. I begged Barry when he was teaching Jessica, but she learned before me, and then he got busy. I was too proud to let my baby sister take over the instruction. Oh, happy childhood memories.

I fast forward past Jenny cooking in the kitchen, a huge Christmas party in this house then another at Frank's with just the three Dahls, a family vacation at the lake. More fast forwarding of boys jumping off the dock, a backyard barbecue with Frank at the grill,

Jenny sunbathing in a bikini, ugh. Don't know what exactly I'm supposed to be getting from this. Maybe Jason wants to torture me for attacking his precious Alpha. Frank playing poker with some familiar pack members, an excited and smiling Matt and a young Adam sitting on some stairs chatting. The camera swinging toward the front door. The cameraman and boys race outside as a frowning Jenny and grinning Frank climb out of their Buick. Matt stops by the cameraperson, but Adam rushes to the back of the car, as does Frank. I push play.

"… be afraid," Frank says to the passenger in the backseat. "You've been here before."

"He'll come out when he wants to," Jenny says impatiently. "Don't rush him."

"Don't you want to see your new room?" Frank asks. "It has a TV just for you." He holds out his hand. "Come on, son. There's no reason to be afraid. I'm right here."

After a few seconds, Jason climbs out. I'd know those cheekbones anywhere. His blonde hair reaches mid back and with a blanket of it covering half his face, but his scowl is still visible. That, coupled with his ramrod straight back and squared shoulders telegraphs the boy is ready for a fight. Even at eight, one false move or look and there would be blood.

"Welcome home, Jason," the camera person, I think Maureen, says.

"Come on, your room is boss," Adam says. "You got *Star Wars* sheets!"

Jenny picks Matt up as Frank and Adam flank the visibly tense Jason. Damn, he must have been terrified walking into that house. Going from abandoned, living in shit, to thrust into *Leave it to*

Beaver in the space of a few months. I would have run screaming or have had to be carried through the door. He does neither, just calmly walks in, though the glower never wavers as they tour the house.

"And here's your very own bedroom," Frank says as they move in. It's sparsely furnished with just the basics and a "Welcome Home Jason" banner on the wall. "Mattie made you that. It says, 'Welcome Home.'"

"What do we say to Matt?" Maureen asks.

"Thank you," Jason mutters.

Jenny clutches her son tighter as if afraid Jason will try to eat the boy. Bitch. "Do you like it?" she asks, toneless. Jason nods.

"We should leave him alone to get acclimated," Maureen suggests.

"Okay," Frank says, squeezing the boy's shoulder. "We'll be right downstairs, son. There's cake when—" The scene cuts out when Maureen shuts off the camera. That poor boy. I'll bet he didn't leave that room for days.

For the next three hours between occasional perimeter checks, I watch as Jason slowly blooms. Going from huddling alone in a corner at parties, refusing to go trick or treating, not answering questions to in the space of a little over a year judging from the time/date stamps, learning to swim and ride a bike. Learning to read with Frank and Maureen. Wrestling with Tate and Adam. Letting Matt help with his homework. Doing the dishes for Jenny. Actually smiling when he opens his Christmas present, a football. A lesser person would have shut off. Kept the others away. After all he was put through, it wouldn't have been surprising. Not him. He stepped up to the unknown and leapt. Allowed himself to be vulnerable. Open. It paid off with interest. I think deep down, way deep, Jason Dahl is a cock-eyed optimist. Another thing I love about him, his ability to keep that spark of hope alive in spite of all the bullshit. He wouldn't have given me the tapes otherwise.

After a quick coffee break and perimeter check, I return to the tapes. More parties, vacations, holidays, Matt in school pageants, and walking around a hotel wearing a Mickey Mouse hat. Matt was such a sweet boy. Patient even as a child. Friendly. Giving. I see a lot of the twins in him. The same enthusiasm for life, same interest in making people feel good. I really wish I'd met him. I wonder what he would have thought about me. Would he have—

"... right after the intermission," Frank says to Jenny, whose exasperated face fills the screen. This is the norm. She always seems pissed off around her husband. "We'll leave right after. I told you, you didn't have to come."

"I wouldn't hear the end of it otherwise," Jenny snaps.

"Dad, this is boring," Matt, now about twelve, says. "Can't we go back to Disney World?"

"Right after your sister sings. I promise."

Holy shit, I knew I recognized that auditorium. The high arched awnings, the medium-sized stage with thick red curtains. It's my boarding school. My first solo performance at age fourteen. I forgot Jason mentioned they were there. In the third row no less. The camera pans to an expressionless teenage Jason. "Jason's enjoying himself, aren't you Jace?"

"Yes, sir."

"Dad, how come we can't say hi to her after the show? I want to," Matt whines.

"Maybe next time," Jenny says. "We have a long drive back tonight."

The lights dim before Miss Tyson, all 4'9" of her, toddles center stage to applause. I was clutching onto the curtain, unable to breathe, and praying I'd stay in tempo and remember the words. Part of me was glad I had no one in the audience except a few friends. If I fell flat or screwed up, who cared? Jesus, had I known my long-lost father and his new family were there I'd never have stepped onstage.

"...Vivian Dahl!" Miss Tyson says.

The audience claps as the spotlight follows my fourteen-year-old self to center stage. God, I never knew I was ever that young. Fresh faced, freckled, hair on fire in the light, virginal white dress giving me an angelic aura. Not a girl, not yet a woman. I'm visibly nervous, only capable of half a smile for my adoring audience. I was so grateful for that spotlight, that I couldn't see the audience. That way I could pretend I was back in the classroom. Just me and the music. The gallery ceases clapping, and the school orchestra begins the intro. Even now, fifteen years later, I tense when I hear that flute. On the TV, the nervous girl takes a deep breath, opens her mouth and starts, "Someone to Watch Over Me" as if she'd sung it all her life. That was written just for me. I *owned* that song. All downhill from this exact moment. My crowning achievement. And Frank captured it—

"Frank!" Jenny whispers.

At the end of the first verse, the camera pans to his concerned wife who points right. The camera moves in that direction, showing a mesmerized Jason taking a step toward the stage like a sleepwalker. His slack face is transfixed, as if God himself had just revealed His true form. The camera shakes as Frank rises, then lunges toward his son. Frank grabs Jason's shoulder and pulls

Jason back down into his seat as I continue my song in the background. "Jason," Frank whispers harshly. "What the hell are you doing? Stay seated."

I fill the screen again, oblivious to everything but my song. I belt out the chorus and another verse before Jenny hisses, "Frank," and Jason's up again. "Damn it." The camera moves to the floor, jerking as Frank holds it by the handle while walking. It moves toward the stage, stops, spins, then jiggles up the aisle as I assume Frank drags Jason out through the door. On screen there's nothing but a dark parking lot with the campus in the background.

"What the hell are you doing?" Frank asks after I hear a door shut.

"I was going to her," I hear Jason say. Damn it, why didn't he point the camera up?

"Going … what? Why?"

"She's my mate. I am to be with her," he says in confusion. If he's unsettled for himself or from Frank's reaction, I don't know. My mind is whirling with confusion as well.

"What? No, she's your sister," Frank says.

"No, she is my mate," he states as fact. "I'm sure. I must go to her. Tell her. I—"

I hear the door open again. "What the hell is the matter with him now?" Jenny asks off screen.

"Nothing," Frank says. "He's fine."

"*That* was not fine," Jenny snaps. "*That* was mortifying."

"Dad, the camera's still on," Matt says.

"I *have* to go back—" Jason insists.

Static. No, wait. That's it? It cuts to a new scene at a hotel with Matt diving in the pool, Jenny sunbathing, and Jason off alone staring into space. Frank prattles on about Disney to Jenny, but I barely pay attention my brain is too busy processing what came before.

Insane. What came before was insane. There is no way *in hell* that happened. It's... insane. I don't believe in love at first sight. Lust at first sight, hell yes, but love? Only in fairy tales. I know he's a werewolf, and pheromones and magic and all that crap Adam told me about, but honestly I took what he was saying with a grain of salt. He was justifying his longing for forbidden fruit. And even if what I witnessed was love at first sight, it was fifteen fucking years ago. I lived thousands of miles away. We had no contact whatsoever. He would have gotten over it. Forgotten about me. He doesn't still... oh, my God.

All the tumblers to unlock the mystery of Jason Dahl finally align. With that click, I feel like I've been socked in the gut. I even hunch over in my chair. He does. Of course he does. He's loyal to a fault. Once you're in his heart, you're in for life. Fifteen damn years he loved me and kept his distance. For me. Like Frank, to protect me. To keep me from all this... death. Then, when the shit hit the fan, he kept me safe again. Was shot for me. Would have walked inside that farmhouse alone to save me, of that I have no doubt. And there I was. The forbidden fruit, the woman he loved, shooting at him. Teasing him. Flaunting myself. God, what a disappointment I must have been. He fell in love with the angel on stage only to find out she was the coked up Whore of Babylon.

And yet...

He loves me. A wonderful, kind, caring, strong, honorable man loves *me*. Still. I know it as sure as I know any damn thing. I saw it in his eyes. I feel it penetrating my skin whenever I'm near him. That sadness, that pain only unrequited love and longing can unleash. He doesn't deserve that. He doesn't deserve a moment of pain, especially not from me.

"Come on, Jace," Frank says on the TV. "We're in the happiest place on earth. Smile!"

Seventeen-year-old Jason peers at the camera as Frank zooms in on his remote face, but those icy eyes betray him. It's as if he's right in the room, staring at me. Miserable. Haunted. I've taken his twinkle, that *joie de vivre* he fought so hard to find in previous scenes. That hope that maybe, just maybe, happiness is achievable in this godforsaken world. He looks away from the camera.

Real-time growling closer than before echoes from the field outside, startling me out of my revelations. Crap. Immediately, I leap up and grab the tranq gun from the floor. As I hustle to the curtains, there are more angry snarls followed by snapping and whining. A fight. I peek out, scanning the field as the noises of combat continue. Snarl. Growl. Nothing. Empty. Louder than before, there's one final growl and whimper before complete silence save for the laughter on the TV. I glance over as Frank pulls a morose Jason to his side and kisses the teen's forehead. "Love you, son."

Oh, shit. When I glance back outside, my throat closes. Right at the tree line, a wolf limps away as best it can with a hurt front leg. It vanishes back into the trees a moment later. I'm still not alone though. I sense something gazing at me from where the wolf first emerged. I stare back into the dark forest for a few seconds, willing it out. It obeys. One step. Two. I flick the gun's safety off. Another step until the glow of the moon spotlights him. Though his snout is drenched in blood and eyes have laser-like focus on me, I have no fear. In fact, I smile and lower the gun.

He's been out there all night, circling the perimeter to keep the others at bay should they come too close. Willing to fight to the death to keep us safe. Even as a wolf he's a better human being than most. And he loves me. *Me.* I meet those intense eyes and fresh tears threaten to escape mine. The clarity of what I have to do sends another painful blow to my soul. But I do it. I turn my back on him and disappear behind the curtain. The long, mournful howl calling for my return is overshadowed by the static on the TV. It's over.

End of tape.

———

I move through the house a veritable ghost. Insubstantial. It's almost as if the others know not to distract me from my mission, that even the slightest word or disturbance will knock me off course. It wouldn't take much, but my resolve and faith strengthen with each step his way. When I'm halfway on my trek down the gravel road to his house, that calm I get when something abominable happens washes over me. I cease noticing the mosquitoes and sweltering heat and humidity that remains between the rain showers. It was coming down hard when I woke from my fitful sleep but stopped just as I began the long walk, as if God himself cleared my path. I even saw Adam and Tate in the big house, so I know he's alone right now. If I believed in signs, or a just God for that matter, I'd take it to mean He thought I was doing the right thing. Not that I need Him to think that. I *know* I am.

Jason's house comes into view, and my hand clenches tighter around the video tapes. Just because I'm doing the right thing doesn't mean I'm enjoying it. In fact, it fucking sucks more often than not. You end up impaling men with rods, getting shot, baby-sitting a dozen kids and breaking your own heart.

Sure enough the moment I reach the door, rain begins pattering down again. Without hesitation, I knock. Good thing I didn't put on makeup or fancy clothes. White shorts, black t-shirt, flip flops, hair in a ponytail, now sweaty and frizzy. He's seen me worse, but he'll never see me better.

I hear his heavy footsteps coming my way until only the door separates us, but that vanishes as well. The sight of him fresh-faced from sleep, judging by his mussed hair and pajama bottoms sans shirt, takes my breath away. Not because he looks like a sun god with almost gleaming skin, hair, chiseled chest. Not because I've never felt such a strong urge to kiss a man and screw us both into oblivion, though those contribute. No, it's because this is the moment I decide I'm *really* going to do this. It's the fork in the road, the point of no return, and for once I'm going the right way. Just not the right way for me.

"May I come in?"

His eyes dart down to the tapes then up. I keep my face an impenetrable mask just like his is now as he studies it. "Sure. Come in."

"Sorry if I woke you," I say, stepping in, "I just—"

"You didn't," he cuts in behind me. "I was resting."

I spin around. He hasn't moved from the door, probably in case he needs a quick getaway. "How are you feeling today? Everyone at the house was shuffling around like the walking dead."

"The change takes a lot out of you."

"I can imagine."

He nods. "I'm just glad there were no incidents last night."

"Well, we have you to thank for that, I think," I chuckle nervously. "I hope there were no hard feelings this morning."

"No. They know I was just … doing my job," he says, eyes finding the floor.

"Right. Always on, aren't you? 24/7."

"Yes. I am."

"Don't you ever get tired of it? Giving and giving and getting precious little in return? I mean, you can't buy love. People shouldn't love you for what you do for them. It's just a smoke screen in the end. You have to let them *see* the person inside."

Those ice eyes dart up to apprize me. "And you're an expert on love?"

I can't help but chuckle. "Yeah, no. Hell no. But I am an expert on selfishness, right?"

His upper lip twitches. "I was … harsh yesterday."

"No, you weren't. You were honest. I am selfish. Never had a reason not to be. You have to be when you're completely alone. Just comes down to survival in the end."

"That's a sad way to live."

"Yes, it is. Of course your way isn't much better, is it? Living only for other people? Not going after what you want for fear that people might think less of you or just simply don't agree?"

"But sometimes those people are correct. Sometimes you do have to make sacrifices. Sometimes, for better or worse, that is love."

My turn to gaze down. Shame weighs heavy. "Yeah. Getting that now. Some mate you got yourself, huh? The fates must have been drunk off their asses when they cast our lots together. I literally can't imagine how disappointed you must be with me. Or relieved. Makes it easier, huh?"

"You didn't disappoint me. In fact … I admire your tenacity. Your ability to think on your feet. Your charm. Your ability to do what's necessary. Your fighting spirit. The way you smell. Your freckles. The way you lift me up when you sing. Your strength. The way you accept people. The way you see through to their soul."

"Then why didn't you tell me before?" I ask desperately.

"What good would it have done? What would have changed? You'd still be Frank's daughter. You'd still be human. You'd still live thousands of miles away. You'd still not *belong* here. You'd still … not love me. Because you don't, do you?"

I want to lie. It's my first instinct. But I owe him this. It's why I'm here. More important, it's the right thing to do. "The truth? I don't think I've ever loved anybody. Not really. Hell, I don't know if I can, if I even have it in me. Never had much practical experience around it. If I ever was capable of it, I think I locked that part of me away ages ago and threw away the damn key. Just hurt too much. But … if I ever could love anyone, it's you. Without question. You are the *best* man I have ever met, hands down. Everything you said I have, you've got in spades, Blondie," I say, voice cracking with emotion. *Just finish. Just don't cry. Just finish this.* "You are so kind, so strong, so noble. Hell, I didn't know people like you existed. And you—you … I have been scared all my life. Lost. But when I'm with you, I don't feel that way. Around you … I *feel* like that person you described. And you make me want to work harder to be that person." I take a step toward him. "So … I'm gonna start really being that girl. Because even at my best, I'm sure as hell not worthy of you. Because you deserve someone who isn't selfish. Who isn't broken. Who brings such joy to your life your soul sings every time you're in her presence. I want that for you *more than anything*. So ... I'm gonna do the only thing I can do for you. What I promised myself I'd do. I'm gonna listen to you. I'm gonna leave you the hell alone. No more plots, no more plans. I swear on our niece's and nephew's lives, I won't bother you again. I'll give you as much peace as I possibly can," I say, meaning it from the bottom of my soul. I bridge the gap between us and once again meet his eyes. "Or at least until I'm that girl you deserve." Slowly, I lean in and kiss his cheek, savoring his smell. His heat. "Bye, Blondie." And I rush out before I completely crumble.

The warm rain drenches me instantly, but I barely notice. I manage to stumble out of sight of his house before my breath starts shaking and the sobs can't be contained a moment longer. I almost double over on the gravel path as the first wail escapes me and do as the second wracks my body. This is horrible. Why do I feel so horrible? Because I lost him. Because I'm alone again. Because I'm lost and alone in the forest again with no rescue coming this time. Because that's what I deserve. He ... oh, God.

I hear the crackling of tires on gravel as Frank's SUV drives up the road. I attempt to quell my tears, try to stand up straight, but I can't. I'm broken.

The car comes to a skidding stop. "Vivi?" Frank calls as he jumps out. His voice is like a shot in the arm. I can't ... I leap up and take a few steps toward the trees to flee but the wracking sobs slow me down. "Vivi? Doll face? You're scaring me, baby. What happened?" he asks, touching my shoulder. "What—"

I swat his hand away. "Don't touch me! Just leave me alone! Please ..." I take another step to escape, but Frank grabs me, attempting to pull me into his arms. "Don't touch me. Let me go ..." I sob. He wraps those arms around me, and no matter how much I push he doesn't release me. "Let me go. Let me …" But I have no fight left in me. I used the last of it to win the battle with myself. I let my father hug me, and within seconds find myself even hugging him back as I cry on his shoulder.

"It's okay, doll face, it's okay," he whispers as he smoothes my wet hair. "I'm right here. I'm not going anywhere. I'm right here."

And my father holds me, smoothes my hair, and whispers everything will be alright until I actually believe him.

———

"At least now I know where I get my drinking gene from," I say, chugging the bourbon.

I am getting plastered with my father. It does not suck. It's actually pretty fucking great.

He's been great. Without a word, my father ushered me into his SUV, drove us home, then escorted me up to the master bedroom. As we dried off, he put on an Ella vinyl, pulled out a bottle hidden in his closet and off we went. The alcohol is helping reassemble my pieces, drying the glue holding my heart together. And I've learned my father is about one step away from being a lush just like his little girl. This kind of makes me like him more. Turned into kind of a bonding experience, this scene.

Frank swipes the bottle from me. "Actually, you have alcoholics on both sides. Your grandfathers."

"I knew about granddad Cliff. When Mom and I lived with him after you left, he was always waking me at night to tell me stories about the Korean War. He'd cry when he talked about his dead buddies. He was a nice guy, though."

"My father was a mean drunk," Frank says, swigging the hooch. "Beat the crap out of my mom, me, my sister Paula. Fucking bastard. He stopped when I got old enough to fight back, but by then Paula ran off to join an ashram, and we only got the odd letter from her here and there. Mama wouldn't kick him out even when he put her in the hospital. I couldn't stand it in that house so when Vietnam started, Pop signed the papers to let me join up. I was sixteen. I only saw him about twice after that when I visited Mama. He died of cirrhosis about two years after I was turned." He shrugs. "Didn't even go to the funeral. Went to hers a couple years after though." He drinks again. "Thought I'd see you there."

"I didn't know her," I say. "Didn't even know she died until I asked Mom about her years later. She sent me a birthday card every year, I know that."

"You were named after her." He hands me the bottle. "Your mom wanted to name you Cher."

"Oh, I am so glad you won that one," I say with a chuckle.

"Yeah, I thought fighting gooks was hard. They had nothing on Michelle when she had her mind set on something. Tunnel vision, that woman. I respected her for it, but it could be such a pain in the ass."

"Did you love her?"

"Oh hell yeah. She was the whole package. Fun, beautiful, driven, knew her own mind even as a teenager. When her spotlight was on you, it made you feel like a king."

I pass the almost empty bottle back. "Then why'd you cheat on her with Jenny? Was she your mate?"

"No," he says with a swig. "That's Michelle. Without question," he says rigidly. "The second I saw her when I returned, it was as if I was hit by a 2x4, like I usually felt around her but times a thousand. Just pure damn love. But your mom was never one to be alone for long. There was a man there. I smelled him on her. Found him in our bed, and I … fucking lost it. Beat the guy to a pulp. Still hadn't mastered the whole werewolf strength thing. Or my new animal emotions. Got a whiff of his blood, and the wolf literally bared its fangs. Hair, snout, ears, all started sprouting, and there wasn't a damn thing I could do to stop it. Your mom had to smack me with a frying pan. Knocked me out." He finishes the bottle. "When I came to a minute later, she told me I had to leave, that the police were coming. So I ran until I hit the park and let the wolf howl. Came back two days later, met her in a restaurant, and she told me in no uncertain terms I was not allowed to be around either of you. That I was too volatile, too dangerous, that if I did come around she'd convince the man I put in the hospital to press charges for attempted murder. She wanted nothing to do with werewolves, with moving to Maryland, with me. She didn't want you growing up around monsters. She wasn't wrong. The things I've seen, hell the things I've done, no one should be exposed to that, let alone my baby girl."

"Is that why you forbade Jason from coming near me all these years?"

He rises from his chair, and saunters over to his dresser. "Hell, yes. I knew from personal experience that with time and distance, you can start to forget her. Can even love someone else." He pulls out another bottle and sits back down in the chair beside me. "Maybe not as much, but it's still possible. But that boy …" Frank shakes his head and takes a swig. "I should have known better. I have never, *ever* met a person with such a deep well of love inside them.

Never. I saw that the moment I looked into his eyes. He'd been beaten, starved, tortured, but that spark, that *love* was still in there. I knew I could save him. That if I didn't, that miraculous well could turn to poison."

"You did a good job. He's fucking amazing, Frank."

"The only times we ever fought, that he ever disobeyed me, was about you. When you were living in New York he must have driven up to hear you sing a half dozen times before I caught on and put a stop to it. It wasn't good for either of you."

"With all due respect Frank," I say, pushing myself up in my lounge chair, "who were you to decide that? I get your heart was in the right place, I do, but it was really fucking unfair. To all of us, yourself included. You should have given us a damn option. You should have come to me when I was old enough to understand, laid everything out, and let me choose if I thought the risk was warranted. You should have let Jason be free to love whoever he wanted to with no guilt attached. That man thinks you hung the moon, and you tore him in two. How could you do that to him?"

Frank studies my face, mouth gaping open a little, before he grins. "You're in love with him, aren't you?"

"I don't know," I say, grabbing the bottle. "Not sure I'd recognize the emotion if I came upon it." I take a generous chug. "I want to be around him all the time. I think about him a million times a day." I pause to smile as his image springs to mind. "I like who I am around him. I like making him smile. I want him to be happy ... even if it's not with me, I think." Another swig. "I do know I don't want to cause him any pain, and it feels like that's all I do."

"Sounds like love to me."

"It's fucking horrible," I say after another sip.

He snatches the bottle back. "How do you think I feel? My son and daughter are in love with each other. I'm in a damn Greek tragedy." He takes another swig. "You don't care he kills people?"

"*I* killed people. Person," I correct. Yep, so getting drunk. "He protects us. And I know he doesn't do it lightly or malic—crap, meanly. I feel safe around him."

"He'll never leave this pack," Frank states emphatically. "Never. And God forbid, he could be Alpha one day. They're family. They're part of the package."

"I know."

He chugs the bourbon again. "Luckily, everyone loves you."

"They do?"

"Hell, I think they like you even more than me." He chugs again. "I'm failing them, Vivi. I should have found Seth by now. Hell, I should have seen this coming. It never should have happened in the first place." He swigs. "I saw the warning signs, just didn't know how to stop it. Still don't. I don't know what the hell I'm doing, Vivi," he says almost afraid and eyes bugging out. "I never wanted this damn job, but someone had to step up. Tate wanted it but couldn't defeat Seth in combat. Me or Jason, only options and I sure as hell wasn't gonna put that on my son." He grimaces. "Maybe I should have. *He* wanted me to kill Seth there and then, but I opted for mercy. First of many bad decisions, and they keep fucking coming. The people I love pay the price. Mattie. Jenny. You. Jason. Some days I wish he'd just kill me. I go out there every day, making myself a target, but he just won't pull the trigger."

"He's afraid of you. That's why he wasn't at the farmhouse. That's why he didn't come after me and Jason himself. I even saw it in his eyes. He's a fucking coward. You beat him once, odds are you'll do it again. All he has is the element of surprise. And the mole. The fucker."

"I've been going out, Jason's been going out with the potential suspects, nothing. One of them should have tried to kill us. We were alone. Vulnerable. But nothing. I don't know what else to do. We can't stay here forever. I know people are a hair's breadth from leaving. Maybe that's his plan, wait us out. If it is, it's damn sure working. I'm so tired of being on the defense. Of not being able to keep my people safe. Of making bad call after bad call."

"Well," I say, "you made at least one brilliant decision. You sent Jason to look after me. You saved my life."

"I did it for you both," he admits. "To get him out of the danger zone. Now I send him out into it every day. Besides," he says, pushing himself up, "I couldn't keep that boy from running after you then even if I'd locked him in a damn cage. He was halfway out the door already when I gave him permission to go. I wish you two hadn't gotten so … close," he says with a grimace, "but I am *so* glad you're here. I'm glad I get to see what a strong, caring, loving woman you've become." He smiles sadly. "And I am so proud of you. *So proud.*"

"But I'm not any of those things," I whisper. "Not really."

He brushes a wet strand of hair from my face. "I don't think you give yourself enough credit, doll face."

I can't help but smile. "Probably get that from your side of the fam—"

A woman's shriek downstairs stops me mid-sentence, but the rapid fire of gunshots instantly sober me. Frank too. He leaps up, head whipping first toward the door as more people scream and holler then the opposite way. *What the hell?* As I find my feet, my father launches himself toward the bathroom. I don't realize the secret panel inside the room is open a fraction and growing until Frank throws his body against it. "Run!" he shouts.

For an instant, I can't move. There's too much going on to focus on one event. Screams, gunshots, howls from outside, but really, I don't want to leave him. They're here. The clock's run down to doomsday. Death is coming through that door. I have no weapon. They're stronger than me. Frank slides down the panel just as three shots cut through the wood where he stood a moment ago. "Baby, run!" he pleads, voice cracking like kindling.

Shit. My body overrides my brain. I take off toward the hallway. Just as I throw the door open, the panel spreads wide enough for the barrel of a rifle to poke through, pointed right at me. The bullets hit the frame just as I pass it into the hallway. Into the mouth of madness. Chaos. Screaming. Crying children. Devin clutching Mason as he dashes into a bedroom. Katie shrieking as Dahlia shoves her into another bedroom. Panicked pack members running up the stairs, down the stairs, toward me, all as frightened and bewildered as I am. Then I realize they're moving toward the tunnel. Toward the gunfire behind me. *Not safe.* I hold out my arms to act as a barrier. "No! Hide!"

Those women sprinting my way quickly change course, diverting into nearby bedrooms. The idea to join them in hiding barely crosses my mind. Frank. Frank needs help. Weapon. Need a gun. Sam races from the stairs, holding a pistol. "Sam, help Frank! Tunnel!" I point behind myself. Like all of us, the man is aching for direction, order in the anarchy. He immediately sprints my way, then past me toward the master bedroom. *Need a weapon.*

I reach the staircase and come to a skidded stop. The gates of hell have opened downstairs. Omar lies at the foot of the steps, chest nothing but viscera and bones with another man, I can't tell who because his face is gone, laying nearby with blood and brain splattered on the wall. Cries of intense pain from both men and women ring out even over the automatic and single-fire gunshots. Like upstairs, pack members and men I don't recognize holding giant guns, run to and fro. A huge black wolf darts after Scott, and I freeze in place. Downstairs, not an option. I don't know what to do. I—

"Viv!"

I turn right and almost break down from relief. Him too. Jason stands down the hall holding not only a pistol but the twins with their faces buried in his neck. He starts running toward me, toward the carnage downstairs and behind me, and all the fog burns away by that now familiar calm. "No!" I shout as I begin moving toward them. I grab Jason's arm and spin him the way he came. "They're using the tunnel."

He nods and changes course with me a step behind, leading us into Linda's bedroom two doors down. I shut the door as Jason continues toward the closet. He sets the children down and they immediately attach themselves to me as Jason shoves suitcases and clothes on the floor aside, revealing a tiny door inside the closet. A crawlspace.

"Jason?" I ask.

He grabs Nicki. "Get in there, Nic." Without a sound, she climbs into the dark hole. "You too buddy." He helps Dusty in too.

"Jason—"

He rises like a shot and grabs my face, eyes burrowing into mine. "Keep them safe, get them out. If I am not back in an hour, leave without me." He presses the gun into my hands. "Kill anyone who gets in your way."

I shove the gun back. "No, you need this more than I do. Frank's at the tunnel and—"

He squeezes my face harder, eyes going Antarctica cold. "Keep them safe, get them out by any means necessary," he says through gritted teeth. "I will be fine."

"You fucking better be," I say, voice quaking.

He pulls my face toward him, kissing me as deeply as I do him. "I love you. Keep our family safe."

"You too." He kisses me again before shoving me down. I get on all fours and crawl into the dark, tiny space. If my fear meter hadn't already reached the top by the siege, being stuck in this dark, cramped room would bust the damn machine. But I don't have the luxury of fear. The children immediately grab me for solace. I wrap an arm around each and tug them into my sides as much for my comfort as theirs.

"No noise," Jason says as he closes the door. "I love you all."

"We love you too," Nicki says.

And we're plunged into almost total darkness, the only light emanating from the outline of the door. Soon even that dims as Jason replaces the suitcases and clothes then shuts the closet door. I hear his footsteps fade into nothingness. A minute. I think only a minute's passed since this began. Less. I clutch the twins tighter and tighter as the screams, the gunshots, the horror of the people I care about continues all around us like Satan's symphony. Ten seconds later another instrument of terror joins the others. I hear the door open again. Quick footsteps toward us. I stop breathing, the kids too. More footfalls. Shit. I point the gun right at the door, willing my hand not to tremble. The intruder scurries around the room before the closet door slides open. My finger finds the trigger. *By any means necessary.* They're not touching these kids.

The light shifts as the intruder moves, searching the closet I think. Then, as quickly as they came, the footsteps run the opposite direction. Gone. He's gone. I let out my breath in ragged spurts in time to my shaking body. I wait ten seconds before allowing my gun arm to lower.

"Aunt Viv," Dusty whispers, "are we gonna die like Daddy?"

"No, baby," I whisper back. I kiss his hair and his sister's. "They are."

By any means necessary.

SEVENTEEN

FIVE MINUTES. IT TAKES approximately five minutes to storm a castle and seize control. I'm guessing on the time because when you're stuck in the dark crawlspace, it's hard to check your watch. It feels like five minutes as the gunshots and shouts begin to space out before stopping all together. Five minutes. I think we lost.

The silence is almost as bad as what came before. Every creak, every voice in the hall keeps me on a razor fine edge, but it's nothing to the random woman's scream or plea for mercy from a nearby bedroom. I cover the children's ears, then say a silent prayer that they don't know what those sounds signify. They're terrified enough as it is. I'd do something—*God, do I want to do something*—but the children are my priorities. If I can help I will, but first I have to figure out how to get these kids the hell out of the house. Nothing else matters. No one is laying finger one on my niece and nephew. They try and I'll bite the damn finger off.

Our best bet is still the tunnel. It served its purpose to the invaders, they shouldn't be guarding it too heavily. Just have to get to it, that is if Jason doesn't return. But he'll come back. *He will.* Just covering all the angles. I start calculating the frequency of the footsteps in the hall by counting the seconds between them, like gauging the distance of a storm from the thunder and lightning. About every two or three minutes someone walks past our door, but who knows how many more are in the bedrooms? Fuck. Too many unknown variables. *Jason, please hurry.*

When the hour passes, and still no Jason, I come close to breaking down. It builds with each passing minute, and I stretch those minutes, but when I can no longer deny an hour has passed, I'm bent to the point of snapping. Like hysterical crying, fetal position, catatonic snapping. Something's happened to him. There is no way in hell that man would leave us unless it is absolutely necessary or if he …

I've never had a panic attack, but I feel one creeping up, poisoning my brain and what little bravery I still possess. Maybe we should just stay in here. They haven't found us yet. No reason they will now. Just give him a little more time. Because the alternative, yeah not ready for it yet.

I concentrate on the children's breathing, their steady feel against me. They may be asleep. Adrenaline crash. I almost gave in to sweet oblivion thirty minutes ago and had to dig my fingernails into my palms to keep sleep at bay. At least in Pennsylvania I had an activity to keep me occupied. Regardless, the twins trust me enough to fall asleep. They have faith I can keep them safe. Jason too. As God as my witness, I will not let them down. I'll die first.

About ten more minutes pass, each more grueling than the seventy before. I'm so thankful I cried all my tears out earlier. I have to go, don't I? He's not coming. They've … Okay, I guess I have a few more tears left. I shut my eyes tight like a prison cell and wipe the few escapees away. *Keep it together, Viv.* Fight now, cry later. My shifting stirs Nicki, who moans a little. Intuitively, I place my hand over her mouth and nose. Nicki quiets, and I remove my hand.

It's time.

I rub Dusty's arm to wake him. He wiggles against me so I assume he's conscious. "You guys okay?" I whisper so softly I can barely hear myself.

"Where's Mommy?" Dusty whispers back.

"I don't know."

"Is Uncle Jason here to get us?" Nicki asks.

"No, doll face."

"Are Mommy and Uncle Jason dead?" Dusty asks.

I am momentarily at a loss for words. "I-I don't know." I kiss the top of his head. "But it's time to go. We can't stay here anymore." I kiss Nicki's head too. "I need to find a way out, okay? But I have to leave you here."

"No, no," both whisper desperately.

"I have to, I'm sorry. I will come right back, I promise."

"That's what Uncle Jason said," Nicki counters.

She's got me there. "This is just how is has to be. I have to make sure it's safe for you, and I need you both to be strong and brave for me, okay? I will come right back for you, I swear. But … if I don't, you both stay here as long as you can. Take care of each other. And if a bad wolf comes, you fight. You kick, scratch, punch, do whatever you have to, to get away from him." I peck them again. "Just stick together, alright?"

The kids hug me tighter. "I love you, Aunt Viv," Nicki says.

Those words bring fresh tears. "I love you both too." *Just go, Viv, before you really lose your nerve.* "Stay quiet. Be right back."

My everything has grown numb from sitting Indian style for over an hour. I release the kids from my embrace to help move my legs so my knees point up. The pins and needles intensify as I press my foot against the door. It's difficult, but I manage to get on all fours and crawl out. I peek my head out first. The closet door is open, so I can see the bedroom. Clear.

I quickly crawl out, close the door, and reposition the stack. They'll be safe there. Please God let them be safe in there. As quickly as I can, I creep across the bedroom, gun steady in my hand and stop by the side of the door. My heart is pumping so fast I feel it in my ear drums. I glance into the hall but can only see diagonally across to an open bedroom. Damn it. *Just get on with it.* I click the safety off the gun, raise it, and stick my head out the door to get a snapshot. Body on the floor, I think Claire's father Chris from the plaid shorts, four doors down. All but three doors open. One guard with his back to me but holding a shotgun as he walks the way I need to go. *Go.*

I move to the next room and immediately hide behind the half open door. Guess that's the plan: go room to room when his back is turned. Six rooms. I can do it. *Go.* I move out the door, but just as I reach the next room the guard begins to turn around. I leap into the bedroom.

"Hello?" the guard calls.

Shit. Shit, shit, shit! This door is almost against the wall and if I move it, he'll notice. No concealment there. I drop to the floor and suppress a gasp when I see a bloody Adam hiding under the bed. The shock doesn't stop me from rolling in next to him. He's

316

still warm. Breathing but unconscious. He lays on his stomach, and judging from the pinpoints of blood up and down his back, along with the gaping hole in his left shoulder, he was hit by a shotgun. Fuck. I hear footsteps thudding closer and hold my breath. The guard must be checking all the rooms because there are steps, a second of silence, then more steps. I can't see his feet, but know when he's checking this one from the noise. A door creaks open down the hall, saving us from further inspection. The guard moves on.

"What's up, dude?" a man asks.

"I, uh, thought I heard something," the guard says. "Think I'm just edgy."

"Yeah, been a hell of a day," the other man says.

Adam shifts beside me and when I turn my head, his eyelids flutter. I cover his mouth and nose to stifle any noise.

"Hey," the second man says, "you want a turn? Might loosen you up. If you don't like the cheerleader type, Mal's got an Asian around here. Or you can choose one from the cages."

Oh, Jesus Christ. Adam rips my hand from his face and grimaces in pain.

"Uh, I'm good," the guard says.

"Dude, to the victors go the spoils. This is a guilt-free zone. War has its upsides. You're not gonna pussy out now are you?"

"It's just, it's mostly women and kids, man. This isn't cool. I—"

I'm not sure, but I think I hear a slap. "Man up and stop being a little bitch. They are not people, they are the enemy. They killed ours, we kill theirs. This is payback. Enjoy it." The asshole pauses, probably to smile. "Good. Now, I'm gonna get something to eat. Worked up an appetite. Bring you back an apple or something."

"Thank you. Sir."

There are more footsteps moving away as I think the second man walks down the stairs. The guard's steps move away too. I can breathe again. Adam too, though his breathing is far too shallow for comfort. "How bad is it?" I ask as quietly as possible.

Stupid question. He's the color of a wedding dress and as sweaty as her shotgun wedding groom. "Still bleeding. Need to change."

Fuck. I can't just leave him here. He's Jason's best friend, *my* friend. He could die. I can't save them all. The only thing I have going for me is nobody knows I'm here. I can't save Claire or Linda or anyone else in those bedrooms because they'll notice they're missing. But him. I can save him. I *have* to save him.

I squeeze his hand again before pulling off my hoodie, not easy with maybe an inch of space above, bunch it up, and press hard on his left shoulder. He winces in pain but suffers silently. I remove my hand and he uses the good one to keep pressure on. "I'll be back for you as soon as I can."

With gun in hand, I abandon my hiding spot and pad toward the door, once again putting my back to the wall before glancing out. The guard is almost at the other end of the hall with his back to me. As fast as I can, I move the opposite way, pausing only to gaze down the stairs to see if the coast is clear. Almost there. I make it to the master bedroom and one step in, stop dead.

Oh God.

Sam, sweet Sam who I sent to this room, lies face up with four bullet holes visible on his white shirt and one in his forehead. His brown eyes stare up at me with no trace of life left in them. I'm sad to admit poor Sam barely gets a glance before my eyes find the second body lying on its side, one remaining blue eye on me. The wind's knocked out of me. I want to fall on my knees, cry out to the heavens but the same thing keeping me going keeps me upright. The back of my father's head has exploded out from the three bullets he took: one to the forehead, the eye, and cheek, along with a shotgun blast to the gut. Overkill. They were afraid of him. Cold comfort.

In a daze, I slowly stumble over to the men, kneeling beside them but gaping at my father. Hesitantly, with my shaking hand, I touch his cold neck. No pulse. He's dead. No question. My daddy's dead.

The clarity and calm that's kept me alive so far blows away like dust on the wind. The tears don't even give me a chance to stop them. My heart hurts, it actually physically hurts. It wretches inside my chest. It's unfair. It's so unfair. I was just getting to know him. I actually … I actually liked him. He was proud of me. He saved my life. He died saving my life, giving me a chance to run away. He loved me. He was a good man. Flawed like the rest of us, but his heart was always in the right place. He loved me. And he's dead. They killed him over a job he never wanted but took to keep this family safe. There was so much more I wanted to know, to ask. I just got him back. "I'm sorry," I whisper. "I'm so sorry."

I just gaze at my father, tears streaming, then up over to the door. The tunnel. It's right there. I could just go through. Run and never look back. I'd make it too. I'd survive. I don't have to go back out there. I can just … *go*. But when I return my gaze to Frank, and know I'll never be able to do that. I hate myself for even considering it. I have to get his grandchildren out. I have to find Jason. I have to keep them all safe like he would. They will not get away with this. They won't. They will not take this house, they will not take any more of our lives. As long as there is a spark of life in me, *they will not win.*

More footsteps wallop me back to the present. The guard. I swipe my tears before rising and sprinting toward the bathroom to hide. I sit on the toilet and close my eyes to listen better. Footsteps come, footsteps go. I stay still, alone with my rage. I grab a face towel from the rack and wrap it around the gun. If I have to fire, it'll muffle the sound. A large part of me prays, *prays* I'll have to use it. Once those kids are safe, all bets are off.

I don't glance at Frank or Sam as I move back to the bedroom door. After waiting for the guard to pass the stairs, I bound to the next open room two down. Then another. Hot footing it, I continue all the way back to the children just as he reaches the end maybe seven feet away. I've made it, halfway at least. Of course now comes the hard part. There's a reason I've gone through life as unencumbered as possible. It's damn easier. With two small kids and an injured man in tow, it will be a damn miracle if we make it down that hall again. The guard trots past once more as I hide behind the door, then wait ten seconds before returning to the closet. "It's me," I whisper before uncovering the crawlspace.

My charges are huddled in the hole, clutching onto one another before both leap out into my arms. They really thought I wouldn't be back. "It's okay, I'm here," I whisper. I pull them off a second later. There isn't time. "Listen, we're going to Grandpa's room. Stay close to me and don't make a sound. If anything happens to me, stay together, run, and hide."

"I don't want to go," Nicki whispers.

"Hey," I say, petting her hair, "you're a Dahl. You are strong and you are brave just like your daddy and his daddy before him.

And I will be right beside you the whole way. Can you do this for me? Please?"

They nod in affirmation.

Dear God, please help me get them out safely. The guard is almost done completing his trip again as we rush to Adam's room, the children behind me in case the bullets start flying. They don't. I stick the kids in the closet out of sight before retrieving Adam. My sweatshirt is close to saturated with blood, but his eyes slowly open regardless. Still got some fight left in him. I glance around the room for something to hold the makeshift bandage—it's better than nothing and can't have him leaving a blood drip path to us—and locate a belt. After gently pulling him out of hiding, propping him against the nightstand, I put on my nurse hat once more and get to work, keeping my head down so I can't be seen over the bed.

"Will you be able to walk?" I whisper.

He nods yes, then winces as I tighten the belt under his armpit. I mouth, "Sorry." We wait for those footsteps to pass before I help him stand. As I re-wrap the gun with the towel, Adam takes a step and wobbles. Shit. I leap up to steady him. He leans against me as his eyes flutter, almost dead weight. "Leave me," he whispers. "Just leave me."

"Yeah, not happening. And I very much doubt Mona McGregor goes for quitters. Want to see her again? Then move your ass, Adam Blue."

Oh, the power of true love. I think the mention of her name ignites his engine. He still needs assistance, but the man puts one foot in front of the other. The kids come out when I nod them over. I hold up two fingers so they know we're going two doors down. After checking the hall, I nod for the little ones to go first.

They sprint down to our rendezvous, making it safely. The guard doesn't turn. Though we're slower, Adam and I reach it too. Then again. We stop diagonally to our destination, so Adam can take a rest. Me too. I'm worried my heavy breathing will be detected. Five seconds only, and this time the adults go first. I want to be in the room to stop any screams when they see Frank. The guard's almost at the other end of the hall when Adam and I complete the run. The children hurry across a second later.

"Hey!"

I hear hurried footsteps down the hall. Shit. I quickly lead Adam to the wall panel, he'll have to open it, as I point the gun at the door. The twins stare at Frank, lips quivering, but I can't worry about that now. Adam pushes in the code just as I spot the muzzle of a shotgun round the corner. I don't have a clear shot as he uses the doorframe for cover and shotgun trumps pistol regardless. He's got us dead to rights. Without hesitation, I step forward to put my body between them and his gun, not realizing I'm doing it until it's done. But the guard doesn't fire. He peeks around the corner, only half his eye visible, not enough for a clear shot.

"Dude, now what?" the second man says down the hall.

The muzzle vanishes along with the eye. I move toward the children and shove them down the tunnel. "Nothing, I'm just paranoid," the guard says. "Thought I saw one of them take a breath in there."

"Go check."

"Yes, sir."

Just as I help Adam inside the passageway, the guard enters. Jesus he can't be more than eighteen with a baby face and wide brown eyes. I can sense his terror from here, yet he keeps the shotgun down. I don't raise my pistol. Immediately, he nods for me to follow the others, and I don't wait for him to change his mind. "No, he's dead!"

I don't look back. The door closes on the tiny staircase. The twins are three steps ahead with Adam only one from them. He winces quietly with each step but endures, gagging all noise when we pass the office access door. Men laugh on the other side, probably toasting their victory. We continue down without stopping. It's quieter on the bottom. Could be my imagination, but I think I hear women sobbing behind the door. Later.

"You two stay behind us," I whisper to the kids before hitching Adam to my side again. "Tell me when you need a rest," I say to my friend.

As quick as possible towing an invalid and small children, we begin down the tunnel to freedom. I can't believe we made it. I could kiss that guard and his conscience. I'd like him more if he freed the women in those rooms and shot that douche-bag rapist—

"Wait," Adam whispers to me a few seconds later. We cease walking as he cocks his head down the tunnel. I don't hear anything but water dropping from the ceiling. "Someone's down here."

"One of ours?"

"Maybe. But if we can hear him, he can hear us."

Crap. "We have to keep going." I spin around to the children. "If I point to the ground, I want you to lay flat on your tummies and cover your ears." They nod.

We continue down the dark hole and soon I begin to hear the footsteps too. After today I'm taking no chances. I point to the children, and they follow orders. I take a second to strategize. Surprise has worked so far. "Think you can shoot?" I whisper. Adam nods in affirmation. "I'll distract, you fire." I hand him the gun, which he tucks down the front of his jeans before covering it with his shirt. I grab hold of him again, and we continue on. The children will be safer back here. We pick up the pace, as does the person. "Hello?" I call out. "Who's there? It's Viv. Hello? We need help!"

Sooner than I'd like, a stranger walks into view under one of the lights, holding what I think is an Uzi. Of course. He couldn't just have a water pistol or foul language. But I can see the finishing line and this bastard is the only thing in my way to crossing it. He's going down. "Stop," the man orders. I release Adam, who topples to the ground, and hold up my hands in surrender.

"Oh, God, please, please don't shoot," I whine still walking slowly toward him. "I just want out of here. Please, sir. I want to go home. Please let me go home."

"I said stop," says the man, advancing with the gun on me.

I obey. "Please. I just want to leave. I want to go home. Please don't hurt me," I plead desperately.

"Calm down, lady."

"No, you're gonna kill me, and I don't want to die, and they shot my friends and—"

He moves the Uzi to the right. "Seriously lady, I'm—"

The moment he's close enough, I kick the man square in the gut like I've done hundreds of times in cardio kickboxing. Shayla would be so proud. The man doubles over and I move aside just as Adam slips out the gun and shoots the fucker right in the fore-head. I'm getting way too used to this crap because I feel no hor-ror as the back of his head explodes out. Not sure if it kills him, but it sure as hell knocks him down. Without hesitation, I grab the Uzi and point it at the fallen man. He stares up at me with dead brown eyes, a trickle of blood rolling down from the hole.

"Shoot him again," I think Adam says but I can barely hear over the ringing in my ears.

I close my eyes, point the Uzi, and pull the trigger. I don't know how many bullets hit home, the gun's kickback makes it hard to handle, so I think some ricochet. I can't look at the man when I open my eyes. I don't need to see. Instead, I glance to Adam who half smiles and reverently nods. No time for pride. I run past Adam back to the kids. They're both sobbing with their fingers in their ears. I scoop them up and hug them as tight as possible.

"Is the bad man dead?" Dusty asks.

"Yeah." I set them down. Not safe yet. "Come on. Almost there."

They cling to my shirt as I rush back to Adam, help him up, and hustle us the fuck out of this tunnel. I'm first up the ladder with the Uzi, punching in the code and lifting the metal trapdoor. The fresh summer air whooshes in. Only remnants of the sun remain, lighting up the thick woods. Dusk. Gorgeous. Even better, there's no one around. I climb out, pull the kids and Adam up, and slam shut the door. I have no idea exactly where I am, but it's the most beautiful place I've ever seen.

"I think I hear something," Adam says.

Me too. Crackling twigs. We both raise our guns and swing that way.

"Don't shoot!"

I breathe a literal sigh of relief as I spot Devin sprinting toward us through the trees. "Oh, my God, you guys," he says as we lower our guns. "You made it." He wraps his twig arms around me, hugging tight. "You made it."

I glance at Adam, bloody and wan, then at the children, eyes bloodshot from still-falling tears and clutching onto each other's hands. Untouched and alive. I did it. I saved them.

It's a damn good start.

———

"You are out of your fucking mind, lady."

I'm sitting in Reid's RV a half mile from the house off an access road, attempting to convince the eleven lucky ones who managed to escape the house of horror to return inside. No great surprise, it isn't going well.

"We all barely made it out by the skin of our teeth," Reid continues. Reid, who at the first sign of cars and werewolves charging through the open gate, put his RV into gear and ran the other way. He did claim to run over a wolf, but if it happened it was an accident. I can see why his wife Katie cheated with Tate. Spinelessness is never attractive.

"Your wife is still in there. Or did you forget about her?" I ask.

"They're not going to kill the women and children," he counters.

"I'm sorry, am I the only one who's ever watched the History Channel?" I ask the group of terrified people. Four children, three women, two teenagers, and three men, one injured. My army. "What do invading forces always do? Slaughter all the men, rape and enslave the women, and unless they're useful, kill all the children."

"This isn't medieval Europe," Mac, Reid's son, says. "This is America. They'll let them go. Eventually."

"Maybe. After a few gang rapes. You may get a new brother out of this," I say snidely.

"Shut up," Reid snaps.

"Don't talk to her that way," Adam warns through his wince. Deandra's doing her best to pick out the buckshot as he lies on the tiny kitchen table. "She's your Alpha's daughter. Show some damn respect."

"My Alpha's dead. They killed him. Probably Jason too. They won. Tate, your mom, they're all dead. And going on a suicide mission won't change that."

"I told you before, Jason isn't dead," Devin insists. "I saw him."

The air's knocked from my lungs. "What?"

"When I was waiting to catch more stragglers, I saw him. He's in wolf form. He was being chased by two wolves and a man with a gun, but it was him."

Don't you dare start crying now, Viv. No weakness. Show no weakness or you'll lose these people. I square my shoulders and straighten my back. "Then we're in better shape than I thought."

"We don't know how many of them are here. We have no weapons—"

"What about the cache of guns in the basement?" Shante asks.

"All the ammo was gone. Like someone stole it," Mac says.

"Probably the same person who took down the witch's wards, gave those assholes the tunnel code, and opened the fucking gate," Pookie says. We've all pooled stories of the attack and escape to get a better picture of what occurred. The men in the tunnel were the first wave, and when the first shots rang out, it signaled the three trucks, each with two men and a werewolf in a cage to ride in through the open gate to invade the house. Our rat rolled out the red carpet.

"So we have no guns, we're outnumbered, our Alpha's dead, and you want us to charge in and kill them using what? Our bare hands?" Reid asks.

"I want you to stop being such a selfish asshole and start being pack," I say. "That is your family in there. The people you've laughed with. Spent holidays with. Ran with, cried with, loved and who love you in return. They are scared. In pain. And they *need* us. Can you really, *really* live with yourselves knowing you turned your backs on them? Literally fed them to the wolves? Because if you can … shame on you. You don't deserve to be pack. Hell, you don't deserve to breathe." I rise from the bench, scanning the faces of my people with a scowl affixed that'd put Jason's to shame. "We are smart. We are pissed. And they will not be expecting us. We can do this. But we can only do it together. I don't know about you, but I'd rather die fighting for the people I love than having a lifetime of misery knowing I didn't step up for them when they needed me. *They need you now*. They love you. *Earn* that damn love. So, who's with me?"

I meet Reid's eyes, Mac's, Shante's, but they all glance down in shame. Shit, I—

"I'm with you."

All eyes jut to Devin, who rises from the floor. "They killed my dad. They killed Frank. Claire's still in there. Maureen. The children. I'm with you."

"Me too," Adam says.

"And me," Deandra adds behind Adam. "For Omar."

"And me," Mac says.

"Son—"

"Mom's in there. Troy too. If I can do something, Dad…"

"Guess we're in too," Pookie says, taking Shante's hand.

Which only leaves…

We turn our gazes to the holdout. Reid squirms in his chair. "Shit." He sighs. "You better have a hell of a plan, lady."

"Well … I am my father's daughter."

EIGHTEEN

GOING BACK INTO THE wolf's den. Voluntarily. I have lost my damn mind. No question. No sane person would walk into almost certain death for people I haven't even known a week. God, being a good person really sucks. I don't know how Jason does this all the time. If we survive this, I'm signing up for more lessons. Until then, I'll have to fake it until I make it. Please help me make it.

Deandra, wonderful Deandra who is handling the death of her husband, Omar, with useful, spiteful vengeance, waits in the tunnel with me. She agreed to sneak into the house with me. And since she was in the army, I am more than glad to have her.

"You sure about this?" she whispers.

"Hell, no." I give her a half smile. "No matter what happens to me, stick with the plan. Get them out."

"Just get that gate open."

I nod. Let's get this over with. Don't want the pre-show jitters to paralyze me.

As quiet as mice, we creep up to the top floor, and I punch in the code. Deandra flips the safety off the Uzi. For the first time ever, I'm putting my faith in the basic decency of a human being. And if it doesn't work, then I'll just shoot him. I slink out of the staircase into the master bedroom, stopping at the door to peek out into the hall. My new friend is still walking the line. I step into the hall, and the guard's mouth drops open. I wave him over before returning inside and positioning myself beside my father. The guard walks in, brown eyes bugging out.

"What are you doing back here?" the man whispers. "You need to go!"

"What's your name, kid?" I ask with a smile.

He does a double take. "R-Rory."

"Hi, Rory, I'm Vivian. Vivian Dahl. How old are you, Rory?"

"T-Twenty. Why?"

"I'm twenty-nine, Rory. I'll be thirty in two days, can you believe that? Two days. Happy fucking birthday, right? And you see that man at our feet? The dead one? Well, that's my father. I just met him about a week ago. He walked out on me when I was a baby. You know why, Rory? You know why my father, who loved me more than life itself, did that? To protect me. From you. From this exact situation. That man walked away from me, then walked in front of bullets for me, all because of you and that fuckhead boss of yours downstairs. The same one who, in a matter of minutes, will tell you to take that gun you're holding, go down to the basement, and begin shooting small children because he has no use for them. We've both met the man. We both know he will.

"Now, I don't know how you got involved in all this, or why you thought you had to come into this house and *slaughter* innocent

331

women and children, but considering I'm not being raped like those women in those rooms, and my five-year-old niece and nephew are safe, I'm going to assume somewhere inside you, you know how wrong this is. I'm also going to assume you are a good person. Are you a good person, Rory? Do you believe what you're doing is right? Really? Truly?"

His mouth opens and closes without sound before he says, "No, ma'am. I don't. I-I-he attacked me. Three days ago. My cousin called me up, said he wanted to take me out for drinks. I ended up bitten by a damn wolf. Been in hell since."

Got him. "Then let's pull your ass out of there, huh? How many of you are there?"

"We came with eighteen, don't know how many are left. I know for a fact you got four of us, maybe more. Some of those who came as wolves are missing too."

"How many guarding the cages in the basement?"

"Two."

"Anyone in with the teenage girl now? Claire?"

"Yeah. Another new one like me. Think his name's Benny. Guys are in with the other two as well."

"Do you have a knife or gun with a silencer?"

"Wh- hy?"

"Because I need to free Claire so she can change. Heal. I figure if we can kill one, we can kill all three, but only if we do it quiet."

"I-I don't—"

"Rory, this is war. I understand you got drafted, pulled into this against your will—believe me, I more than sympathize—but we're in this now. And you can either be on the side of the child murdering, women-raping assholes who turned you into a monster in every way conceivable, or you can help me strike back at these fuckers. Save women and children. Maybe even get some damn payback for ruining your life. What do you say? Want to join the good guys?"

The boy's mouth continues to flop open and closed with indecision. I understand. We are the losing side. "W-What would I have to do?"

Oh, I could hug this guy. If he didn't say yes, option B, I was to kill him. Instead, I grin. "Just three little things, then you get your soul back. Not a bad bargain, huh? Step One: Claire. But first..." I lightly knock on the panel, and Deandra opens it. "He'll bring Claire to you. Tell her what to do. Then wait for the cue. Two in the basement."

"Scream if you need me," says Deandra before she rushes into the bathroom to wait.

I turn to Rory. "Our main objective is to get the front gate open. I have people waiting out there. That'll be your job. The button's by the intercom next to the front door. Just make sure no one sees you. But first..." I hold my hands behind my back as if handcuffed but with easy access to the hidden pistol riding up my spine. "Congratulations, you just captured me. Now take me to Claire's room."

Holding onto my hands, Rory escorts me down the hall as if it were the Green Mile. Could very well be if everything doesn't run like clockwork. He lightly knocks on the door. When no one answers, he knocks harder. We wait a few more seconds before I hear footsteps. A man with long, grayish hair wearing only pants opens the door. "What?"

"I was told to switch them," Rory says.

Benny, the rapist fucker, eyes me up and down. "Haven't had a redhead in years. Bring her in."

333

Dear God. My throat closes when I spot the seventeen-year-old girl tied to the bed by silver chains. She stares up at the ceiling but probably doesn't see it. She's gone far, far away. "You bastards."

Rory positions me with my hands against the wall. "Do you have the keys?" Rory asks, moving toward Claire.

Benny gestures toward the dresser. As Rory unshackles the catatonic girl, who doesn't even blink, Benny all but licks his chops at the sight of me. In his mind I'm already spread-eagled like Claire just was. Rory wraps her in the bloody sheet then carries her like a bride out of here, hopefully hustling to Deandra. I just need to buy him twenty seconds.

"So, what'd he promise you? Your Alpha?" I ask.

"Looking at it. Pussy, nice house, hanging with the boys. Someone even brought cold beers. What more could I want?"

"Humanity? A soul?"

"Overrated." Benny saunters toward me like the cock of the walk, eyes zoomed in on my breasts. "You gonna fight me?"

My hands lift up the back of my shirt, and I grasp my gun. "Hell yes."

He steps in front of me, hand immediately snaking up the front of my shirt to grasp my breast. "Good. I like it—"

I bring my knee square into his groin. Twice. The rapist bastard doubles over with a groan, stumbles a step back, and I kick him in the stomach. He falls on the bloodstained bed as I swing the gun around, training it on him. I know what I have to do, it's my plan after all, and staring down that waste of space amid the stains of torture, I really do feel nothing when I pull the trigger. Again. And again, literally blowing his brains out. Jason was right, it does get easier each time.

Running footsteps move closer out in the hall. A second later Rory opens the door. His mouth drops open. "What was that?" another man asks behind him.

Rory steps in and points his shotgun at me. "Drop your weapon," he orders.

I obey and hold up my hands in surrender. Another man, then a third, the Italian stallion from the Inn, rushes into the room. "My name is Vivian Dahl, Alpha Frank Dahl's daughter and mate to Jason Dahl. Take me to see Seth Conlon. He's been looking for me."

"Then too bad he's dead," one of the men says.

My throat closes up so I can barely squeak out, "What?"

"Took a shotgun to the head from one of your people," Italian snarls.

Okay, not anticipating that. Not sure how to proceed. Once again Rory saves my bacon, stepping forward and grabbing my arm. "The new boss'll probably want to see her anyway. She might be useful. Come on." He yanks me toward the door. I pretend to struggle, but he shoves the shotgun barrel into my side. The others watch as he drags me into the hall toward the stairs.

"So, who's your new Hitler?" I whisper.

"Never met him. This is the first I'm hearing this too," he whispers as we descend the gore-covered staircase.

"Doesn't matter. Just remember: open the gate, then the front door, then hide. I don't want you getting caught in the crossfire. The cue is when I start singing."

"Singing?" We pass two men lifting Troy's body from the hallway floor as we walk toward my father's office. A tall man holding an M-16 stands in front of the door. "This is Frank Dahl's daughter."

"Let them in," a familiar voice says on the other side.

Of course. I am never wrong about a person.

Not a single part of me is surprised when we walk in and I come face to face with the mole, sitting at my father's desk as if it's always belonged to him. "Moved right in, I see."

"It is technically my birthright now," Tate says as he rises. He glances at Rory. "What happened, son?"

"I don't know. She must have been hiding somewhere. Benny must have caught her, and she shot him."

"Well, good job, son. I won't forget this."

"Thank you. Sir."

"You may go," Tate says, bowing his head reverently to his minion. Rory glances at me before releasing my arm and stepping out. I'm left with evil incarnate, who just grins. "Surprised?"

"Nope. I had you clocked as an asshole the moment you opened your mouth. Just didn't realize how big a one. Killing your own mother, brother, friends for a house and money?"

"For power, princess. For my *birthright.* I am now the eldest living male heir of Bobby Conlon."

"I assume it was you who killed Seth tonight. Shot him, blamed one of us because you couldn't beat him in a fair fight?"

"There can be only one. Brains before brawn, right? Besides, he outlived his usefulness. Don't need a front man now I've captured the castle."

"Was it you from the beginning?" I ask with a sneer.

"More the middle. Seth got the ball rolling months before, rounding up rogues, making his own army, but the guy always was a fucking moron. He wanted to start an entirely new pack in this territory, rub Frank's nose in it. What he forgot was many tried and all failed through the centuries. The Eastern Pack always put them down. He probably would have thought of a hostile takeover eventually but was shit scared of Frank. No fear is a top requirement of a true Alpha. That's why Seth'd never make a good one."

"That and you have to give a shit about people," I say snidely.

"You obviously never met my grandfather," he says with a scoff. "There was a reason he lasted until a ripe old age. First sign of trouble, say like him discovering his wife was carrying on for years with her cousin, he would have gone biblical on both their asses. Twice. Not like your daddy dearest."

My eyes narrow. "You and Jenny?"

"On and off since we were kids. Only reason she seduced your father was to get back at me during an off period when I wouldn't run away with her. Go rogue. Ended up with more than she bargained for, huh? Stuck with a man not her mate, who loved someone else too? The pack and its stupid rules. First cousins can't breed, then there's my idiot brother and that fat witch. I plan to make changes, that's for sure," he chuckles. The mirth drains from his face. "God, I loved that woman. Didn't realize how much until we killed her."

"You killed her?"

"It wasn't part of the plan. In fact, it completely fucked up the plan. We were going to wait another month, shore up more recruits, but fucking Seth showed up at my house unannounced when she was there, and Jenny lost her shit. I tried to explain. There was no love lost between her and Frank, even told her I'd spare Matt, but maybe she did love old Frank because she threatened to rat. Seth whacked her with a fireplace poker, and there was no going back."

"Why Matt and the others?"

"Clear a path for Seth, or that's what he thought. I just hated the little shit. And Matt was a little shit, no question. Whiny, Weak. But he was the heir apparent, and everyone loved the little bitch. We tried to take out anyone who could challenge Seth and in turn me."

"And me? Why drag me into this?"

"*We* didn't. Jason, the imbecile, did. I wasn't paying attention for a second, and the next thing I knew he was off to Los Angeles on his white horse. Out of everyone, he was the one person we truly had to neutralize. So when I found out where he was going, I knew it was right to you. No secrets in the pack, right? Frank worked so hard to keep you a secret but Jason couldn't shut up about you, at least to me. So Seth sent Donovan and Cooper to intersect you because if we got you, we'd get him. Love, right? Nothing makes us more reckless and stupid."

"So, now what? Kill us all? Your mother, brother, the children?"

"I'm not that cruel. No, this show of force should keep the survivors in line. If there's even a hint of rebellion, they all know what I'm capable of now. Those who don't toe the line will be put down. There *are* more of us than them. Just one more loose end to tie up, and look what God delivered to me," he says, holding up his hands at me.

"He's one of your best friends."

"He's in my way. Why the hell should I ever bow to him? Or Frank? They're not pack. They're not family, not really. Your father was just the asshole who knocked up my mate, who stood by as she made a cuckold of him for decades. And Jason? Just a rabid mongrel your father forced on us. They aren't fit to lead an orchestra, let alone the greatest pack in America. The fact I was able to pull all this off under their noses proves that. *I* will bring this pack back to its former glory. Make us a force to be reckoned with. It's a new dawn, princess."

"You're insane," I say with a hard edge.

He gets right in my face so our noses touch and presses his pistol against my temple. I don't flinch. "Maybe. But at least I'm gonna see a new day. Unlike some."

Inside I'm about to pee my pants, but outside I just scowl. "You're not gonna kill me."

"I'm not? Do tell."

"You're not because you and I are gonna strike a little bargain. I give you what you want, Jason, and then you give me what I want, freedom. I want the fuck out of this house, this state, and for you to forget I ever existed. In return, I hand you the last piece of your megalomaniacal puzzle, who is, as I speak, probably eating one of your lackeys. You're gonna look pretty shitty if he's gone through half your men by your new dawn. We both know he's capable of it, as we both know I'm probably the one person he'd throw caution to the wind to save."

"And you'd set him up like that?"

I scoff. "Have you met me? Hell, I already warned him I would. He was a good fuck, but not that good. All this shit has nothing to do with me. It never did. I just want to go home. Live. Survive. If it's come down to him or me ... me. Plus, if I'm lying, you can always kill me. At least this way I have a chance that you won't. You don't need me after I deliver him. Let me go, one less body to explain away. You're a smart guy. You know I'm right."

"Or I could torture you until he comes," Tate says with a cruel grin.

"My way saves time. Less clean up too. Win-win."

He studies my face with narrowed eyes. I keep it a mask. Learned from the master after all. He holds all the cards here, and we both know it. I have to at least attempt this tactic to save myself from unneeded torture if possible. And it is possible. Tate lowers his gun. "What exactly do you have in mind?"

"Only one thing I know that sooths both savage beast and man alike: music. Get your men in position along the back windows with guns. I'll handle the rest."

"Vinnie!" Tate hollers, still not removing his gaze from me nor I him. The door opens and out of the corner of my eye I see the Italian step in. "Our five best shooters. In here and the living room with guns aimed at the backyard. Lights out too."

"Yes, sir." Vinnie departs with nary a glance for either of us.

"One false move, princess, and I blow your pretty head off."

"Dictator less than an hour and already paranoid. Doesn't bode well," I say with a smile. "You need to cut me. He'll smell the blood and follow it." Right to you, asshole.

"Great minds think alike," he says with a matching expression.

"There's nothing great about either of us. We're scum."

"But *living* scum. Only the good die young, princess."

Two men and Vinnie return a second later, all three holding huge guns, one with a scope. This could be a massive clusterfuck if everyone doesn't act as I anticipated. "Lloyd, your knife," Tate orders. The man with the scope pulls a Bowie out of its holster and hands it to Tate. "What do you think?" He caresses the blade across my cheek. "Your pretty face?" He traces the edge down my chin, my neck, to my chest. "Carve my name into you as a rem—"

With one quick move, I grab his hand with the knife, raise my free one, and cut across my palm. It stings like a bitch but the blood starts flowing. "Or we can stop playing games and get on with this." I pat his bicep with my bleeding hand, leaving a stain on his shirt, before stepping away to the corner. I watch, bleeding into a tissue as the men prepare: shutting off lights, opening or breaking windows not already shattered to get into position. *Oh God, please let this work.*

"Get outside, princess," Tate orders me. "Let him smell you."

As I pass him, I flick more blood onto his shirt. "*Sieg heil.*"

There are three men in the living room preparing the same way. They don't notice as I run my bleeding hand along the wall from office to the back patio door. I'm all out of breadcrumbs. It's a muggy night, but all the adrenaline pumping through my veins chills me. My life in others' hands. My wolves at the gate, the women in the cars, Rory, Deandra, Jason. I give myself a 5 percent chance of survival. Those men will either shoot me or a werewolf will rip my throat out by mistake. Yet, as I walk to the middle of the clearing to take center stage, I'm not as frightened as I imagined I would be. At least my death will mean something. I'll be remembered. Revered. The story of this night, of my heroism, will be passed down through the pack for generations. I made a mark, a good mark on people's lives. At last.

I stop in the middle of the clearing, making sure I'm downwind, and scan the tree line. He's out there somewhere. I sense him. Watching. Waiting for the right moment to strike back. I hold open my bleeding hand and clear my throat. Time to bring him home. My turn to watch over him.

I open my mouth and begin our song with my whole soul behind it. The performance of a lifetime. The song I was always meant to sing. My voice echoes through the trees, haunting its emptiness until the crackling in the trees to my right begins accompanying me. I sing harder, louder as if he were right in front of me. The only man I think of with regret. The one who carries the key to my heart. And just as I reach the end of my song, there he is. The shepherd for this lost lamb takes one step out of the wilderness. The one to watch over me.

A man's scream in the house stops my song dead. They were fast. Right now Adam, Mac, Reid, Devin, Pookie, and Claire—I hope—are all charging inside like wolf cruise missiles while Shante barrels behind in the RV to crush any assholes who flee outside. Too bad their best men are back here, huh? The gunshots begin almost immediately, some of which I hope come from Deandra springing out of the tunnel with the Uzi and mowing down the guards to free everyone from the cages. I drop to the ground to avoid any stray bullets.

Jason and another wolf with a limp and bloody neck sprint toward me. Jason reaches me first, stopping by my side for a moment with a whine. There are claw marks and bites all over his huge body, but *he's* worried about *me*. "I'm fine." I pet his bloody head with my good hand. "It was Tate. He did this. Now go take our pack back from the bastard."

My mate growls, baring his teeth before starting toward our house with his ally limping in tow. He has to finish this. For Frank, for me, for Adam and Matt and everyone else. I've played my part, uniting the army with their leader. I watch with a tiny smile as he charges inside without a moment's hesitation. Men's wails of pain, gunshots, and snarling echo through the otherwise tranquil night. If I had a weapon I'd go in, fight alongside them, but I'm needed elsewhere. He's got this. I pick myself up and dash to meet the others at the tunnel exit, all the while listening to the sweet music of retribution as my family reclaims our home, our pride, and our indivisibility. Live together or die alone. Know which one I've chosen.

NINETEEN

Burning my father's corpse on the back lawn was not how I envisioned spending my thirtieth birthday. Getting drunk, possibly high, then hitting more bars with Cyr to get drunker and higher was the plan. Instead I'm sitting behind his desk, watching as pack members carry shrouded bodies from the freezer to the massive pyre a story tall we've been assembling since last night. Sam, Omar, Lee, Pookie, Scott, Maureen, Troy, Donald, and Frank will all be placed around the pyre and cremated together in accordance with pack tradition. Tate and the others were thrown into a mass grave Jason insisted on digging all by himself. Anything to be alone these past two days. Having your father die, learning one of your best friends is responsible, and inheriting a pack of traumatized werewolves requires time to process. I can handle everything else for him.

"So, they'll be considered missing persons?" I ask Dr. George Black, Ph.D. and head of the F.R.E.A.K.S.

344

The impossibly tall and thin man sits across from me in his pressed black suit. When the calm settled, and I had over two dozen dead bodies on my hands, I contacted the F.R.E.A.K.S. because hell, I didn't know what else to do. Dr. Black listened as I unraveled the story, then proceeded to lay out his displeasure in the nicest way possible. I don't think the man's voice is capable of rising.

"Yes, and all their cases will be run through my squad," Dr. Black says, sipping his water. The heat sneaks through the plastic covering the broken windows. Dead bodies first, home improvement second. "We'll also issue death certificates signed off by our own ME, your father's included."

"What about my fugitive status? Jason's?"

"Already erased. You can leave here whenever you like, a free woman."

"Thank you," I say with a smile. "And I know I've said it a million times but thank you for everything you've done, flying out here, cleaning up our mess like this."

"Well, your father *should* have contacted me the moment he learned civilians were being attacked," Dr. Black chides. "I've put forth a request to enact a new law that if a wolf commits any felony that we have to be immediately informed, and we have the oversight to investigate or not. This cannot happen again."

"I'm sure that will go over well with the other pack leaders," I say sarcastically. "Regardless, I appreciate all you've done for us and for being here. I know it would have meant a lot to my father."

"He was a good man. A good leader. A friend even."

"Thank you." There's a knock on the door and a moment later Rory pokes his head in. I insisted he stick around, make himself useful with the million odds and ends, so everyone can get used to him. We inherited him and the wolf Darius, whom Jason fought into submission. They earned their place too. Understandably people have been chilly and downright hostile toward them, but we'll make pack out of them yet.

"Um, they're almost done moving the bodies," Rory says.

"Has anyone seen Jason?"

"No, ma'am."

"Okay," I say, rising and smoothing my black sundress. "I'll go find him and then we'll begin. Thank you, Rory." The boy nods and leaves us. "You, Jason, and I can continue this after the ceremony, if that's alright?"

Dr. Black stands too. "Of course."

I round the desk and walk out with him. "There's food in the dining room. Feel free to help yourself."

Dr. Black smiles and moves toward the dining room. Now to locate our wayward Alpha. I do a sweep of the house. A bruised and battered Linda rests on the couch, clutching her children as the other munchkins watch *Monsters Inc.* Rory got her and Sarah out during the confusion of the siege. Neither woman has really spoken since they returned from the hospital with Deandra. Claire either. Devin's been sitting by her side reading books aloud in her tent all day. She's strong, they all are, and with time and attention it will get better. We just need to be there for them anyway we can.

As I pass the dining room, I spy Mona McGregor greeting Dr. Black by the chip bowl. Across the table Agent Price listens as the Central Pack Alpha Tim Merrill, a man as old as Dr. Black, speaks. Jefferson Monroe, Western Pack, and Desmond Preaker, Eastern

Canada Pack leaders, were unable to attend but sent flowers. Nice of them.

I find Adam in the parlor as I have many a time in the past two days, engaged in intensive home repair. Right now it's plastering over another bullet hole in the wall. Repairing the damage his brother wrought. I can't even conceive of the conflicting emotions cycling inside him. He won't talk about it, at least not to me. Keeping busy is working for now.

"Have you seen Jason? We need to begin the ceremony," I say.

"Check his house."

"Thank you." I'm about to step away but stop myself. "Oh, Alpha Merrill was asking to see Jason earlier. He seems old school, wouldn't talk to me. Maybe he'll speak to Jason's Beta. He's in the dining room. Can you…"

"Sure." He sets down his spackler. And if in his hour of need a certain witch comforts him, more's the better. The man deserves some damn happiness, and I'll do everything in my power to make sure he gets it. I squeeze his hand as he passes.

I climb into Frank's SUV and drive down the gravel path. For the first time in days, I'm nervous. I haven't said but thirty words to Jason, all of those on pack business since the attack. He's been keeping himself isolated with really only Adam to keep him company. I don't even know if he'll come to the funeral. People are beginning to talk. They need their leader strong. There. *I* need him there. He's never let us down before, he won't today.

"Jason?" I call as I step inside his bungalow. I hear sanding from the workshop. Of course. Jason has his back to me when I open the door. He's still working on that guitar, hand sanding out the rough edges from the frame. "Jason?"

"I thought you were going to leave me alone," he says, still sanding.

"Well, I'm not here for me. I'm here for them. For you."

Neither of us says a word. He just sands. After thirty seconds, he breaks the silence. "I was making this for Tate," he says without turning around. "For his birthday. I ... want to finish it for some reason."

"He was your friend longer than he wasn't," I say, slowly walking over. "It's gonna take more than two days to reconcile the man he became to the one you grew up with. Who taught you to shoot a gun and fight. Who was like a brother to you. It's impossible to just flick a switch and turn off that love." I stand by his side and touch the guitar's neck. "Besides, it's beautiful. It deserves to be finished. Maybe you can give it to Dusty or Nicole."

"Or you," Jason offers, glancing up at me. "Birthday present."

"I'd be honored."

He bows his head, a bit of wood sprinkling in the light like glitter. "Is it time?"

"Yes. We're just waiting on you."

"I'm sorry. It's just been ..."

"I know. And you more than deserve some time alone. I can pick up the slack for you." Hesitantly, I place my hand on his shoulder. "But right now, they need you there. They need you there *strong*. They need you to help them say good-bye to those they loved. Who died fighting for us all. You need it too."

"I ..." His head lowers even more. "I'm scared. I'm scared I'll say or do the wrong thing. I'm scared I can't lead these people. That I'll let them down."

"You passed the first test. You saved them, Jason. Now … you just have to pass the next million, starting with the one waiting at the house. You need to step up, step out, and say good-bye to our father, our friends, and let those people who remain know you will be there for them no matter what. You need to show them you are the man Frank knew you were. A leader." I lift up his chin to meet his tear-rimmed eyes. "A good man who loves and would die for each and every one of them. Like his dad." I smile. "And I will be here, as long as you'll have me. Picking you up when you fall. Making you smile when you need one. Being the woman who is always in your corner, who'll always sing you home. The woman who will do her damnedest to be the mate you deserve. Watching over you as you have me. Because we're stronger together than apart. So … I'm here as long as you need me. *If* you need me, I'm yours." I kiss his forehead. "See you down there, Blondie. We'll be waiting."

I wipe his tears away, give him one last sweet smile, and walk away. I make it through the door before he calls, "Vivian?" I barely spin all the way around before he's in front of me, staring down at me as if I were the only woman in the universe. He grabs me around the waist, pulls me in, and kisses me like the world's about to end if he doesn't. And with this kiss any and all doubts leave me.

This. This is where I belong. In this man's arms. No more being lost. Or frightened. And if this isn't love, I'll never know what is. He pulls away, searching my eyes once more for the same thing he always has. When a smile stretches across that adorable face, and I can all but hear his soul sing, I think he's found it at last. Me too. "I'm ready. Let's go join our family."

He slides his hand into mine and leads me out into the sunshine where the birds fly high and the breeze drifts on by. And damned if I'm not feeling good.

THE END

ACKNOWLEDGMENTS

I have to thank the usual suspects.

First, my agent Sandy Lu. This one's for you.

Thanks to the Beta Bunch: Jill Kardell, Susan Dowis, Ginny Dowis, Theresa Friedrich for their suggestions. I love you all.

Thanks to Terri Bischoff for agreeing to allow me to go down the road less traveled with this series. Also thanks to Connie Hill and everyone else at Midnight Ink for your continued support.

To the Prince William Public Library System and the Fairfax County Library Systems for giving me a place to work. I would never leave my house without you.

To all the bloggers who hosted me through the years. I hope you continue to let me grace your sites so I can hawk my books. May I never bore you or your readers.

Finally, to my father, who is nothing like the fathers in any of my books except that, without question, he would die for me. Thank you for sticking around, supporting me in every way possible, and building my self-confidence up. You may sometimes regret the last one, but it was all you and Mom. I love you both more than words can cover.

© Bill Fitz-Patrick

ABOUT THE AUTHOR

Jennifer Harlow (Manassas, VA) earned a BA from the University of Virginia in Psychology. Her eclectic work experience ranges from government investigator to radio DJ to lab assistant. Visit her website www.jenniferharlowbooks.com to read her blog, *Tales From the Darkside*; listen to the soundtrack to this book; and more.